THE IBERIAN
FLAME

JULIAN STOCKWIN

THE IBERIAN FLAME

HODDER

First published in Great Britain in 2018 by Hodder & Stoughton
An Hachette UK company

This paperback edition published in 2018

1

A CIP catalogue record for this title is available from the British Library

Paperback ISBN 978 1 473 64103 7
eBook ISBN 978 1 473 64254 6

Typeset in Garamond MT by Palimpsest Book Production Ltd,
Falkirk, Stirlingshire

Printed and bound in Great Britain by Clays Ltd, Elcograf S.p.A.

Hodder & Stoughton policy is to use papers that are natural, renewable
and recyclable products and made from wood grown in sustainable forests.
The logging and manufacturing processes are expected to conform to
the environmental regulations of the country of origin.

Hodder & Stoughton Ltd
Carmelite House
50 Victoria Embankment
London EC4Y 0DZ

www.hodder.co.uk

THE IBERIAN FLAME

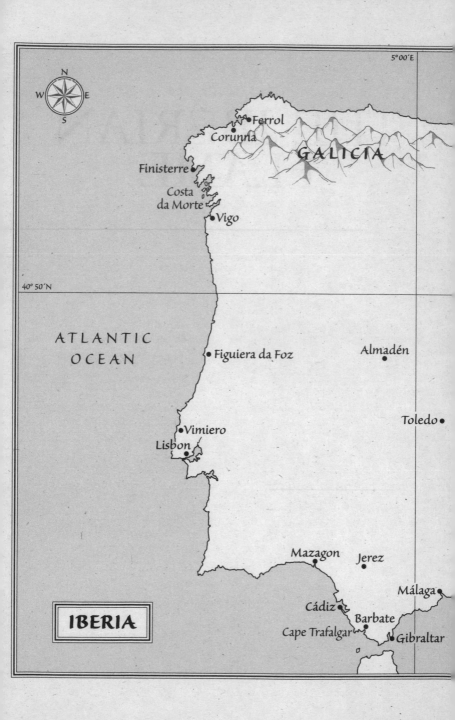

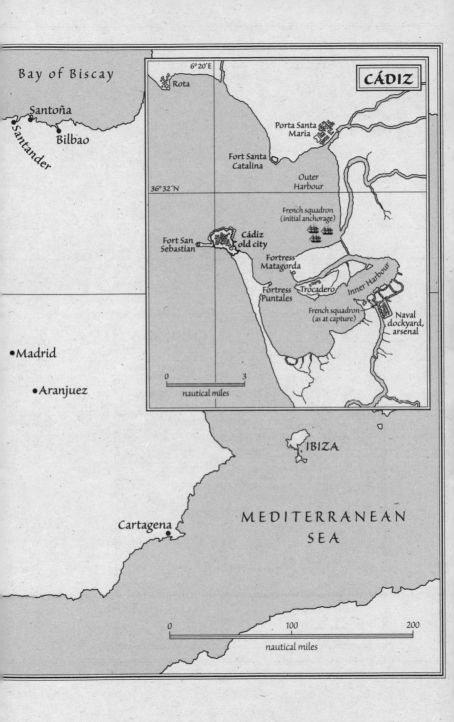

Bay of Biscay

Santoña
Santander
Bilbao

•Madrid

•Aranjuez

CÁDIZ

6° 20′E

Rota

Porta Santa
Maria

Fort Santa
Catalina

Outer
Harbour

36° 32′N

French squadron
(initial anchorage)

Fort San
Sebastian

**Cádiz
Old city**

Fortress
Matagorda

Fortress
Puntales

Trocadero

Inner Harbour

French squadron
(as at capture)

Naval
dockyard,
arsenal

0   3

nautical miles

IBIZA

Cartagena

MEDITERRANEAN
SEA

0   100   200

nautical miles

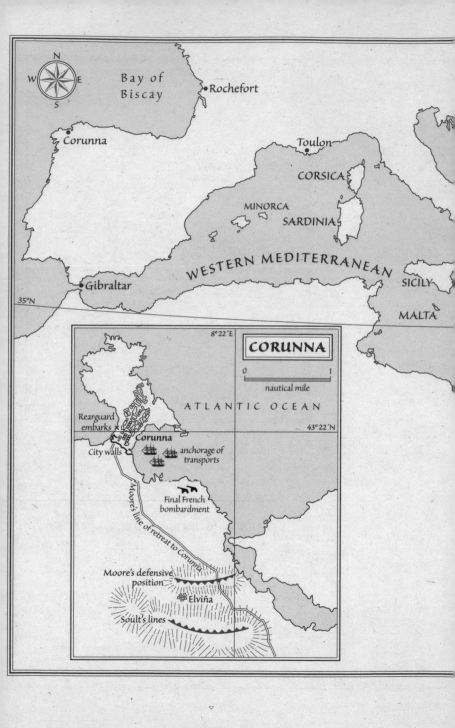

Dramatis Personae

*Sir Thomas Kydd, captain of HMS *Tyger*
*Nicholas Renzi, Earl of Farndon, friend and former confidential secretary

Tyger, ship's company

*Bowden	second lieutenant
*Bray	first lieutenant
*Brice	third lieutenant
*Clinton	captain, Royal Marines
*Darby	gunner
*Dillon	Kydd's confidential secretary
*Dodd	sergeant, Royal Marines
*Doud	quartermaster's mate
*Gilpin	midshipman
*Halgren	coxswain
*Joyce	sailing master
*Maynard	master's mate
*Pinto	petty officer

*Rowan	midshipman
*Stirk	gunner's mate
*Tysoe	Kydd's valet

Others

Allemand	French rear admiral in command Rochefort fleet
*Appleby, Mrs	housekeeper of Knowle Manor
Beresford	British general under Moore
Bonaparte	French Emperor
Brightman	captain, *Concord*
Broadwood	captain, *Lynx*
Burrard	commander of British Forces, Iberia
*Campbell	flag-captain to Rowley
Canning	British foreign secretary
Carlos IV	King of Spain
Castlereagh	British secretary of state for war
Collingwood	commander-in-chief, Mediterranean fleet
Dalrymple	lieutenant general
De Courcy	admiral, *Tonnant*
*Dolores de Vargas	Spanish patriot
Dom Antonio de Castro	bishop and leader of Oporto junta
Dupont	French Imperial Army flying column commander
Espartero	aide to Montijo
Ezquerra	Spanish scholar and jurist
Fernando	Prince of Asturias, son of Carlos IV
*Fray Mendoza	Spanish cleric
Ganteaume	French vice admiral in command Brest fleet
Godoy	first minister to Carlos IV
*Grieves	lieutenant, 38th of foot

*Rowley	rear admiral, *Conqueror*
Solano	royal governor of Cádiz
Soult	Marshal of France and pursuer of Moore
Strachan	vice admiral, Rochefort squadron
Thornbrough	vice admiral, *Royal Sovereign*
*Tovey	blacksmith, Ivybridge
*Uribe	guerrilla commander
Wellesley	general, future Duke of Wellington
*Wishart	lieutenant, liaison officer to the Spanish Crown

'I am the successor, not of Louis XVI, but of Charlemagne!'
Napoleon Bonaparte

Prologue

Spring 1808

Not forty miles from Paris, the Château de Fontainebleau lay in pompous repose. Before the Revolution its richly ornamented rooms had echoed to the pampered and carefree gaiety of the court of King Louis XVI. Now, a solemn and purposeful mood prevailed under its new occupant, Emperor Napoleon Bonaparte.

The palace was ancient and vast, set among magnificent gardens and fountains. A pale stone edifice, it was filled to breath-taking resplendence with loot seized from every conquered nation. A matchless display of pomp and imperial might, it also served as a receiving place for the procession of defeated kings, wavering allies and helpless suppliants, who made their way to the centre of power of the civilised world.

Sitting stiffly in the gilded and sculpted Salon de Réception, Eugenio Izquierdo was not immune to its overpowering effect. An envoy of the King of Spain, His Catholic Majesty Carlos IV, he was a loyal and valuable ally who could count on respect and honour. Yet he quaked to think that in a short while he would be called into the Grand Council Chamber to stand before the Emperor himself.

He knew that Bonaparte usually worked alone in a modest study from dawn until long into the night, no detail too slight for his attention. He was served by a corps of devoted and ambitious marshals and functionaries. When the military genius appeared in the council chamber there would be no time for prevarication, pretence or airs: it would be down to the essentials, which had to be flawless in detail and, above all, have at their core the overriding interests of the Emperor.

Izquierdo had been trusted by Spain to lay before Bonaparte a proposal that would bring the two nations closer than ever before: a daring plan to seize a crown and nation for their common devouring. It should be an irresistible lure to the great man now at the height of his powers and chafing at the irritations arising from the impudence of the last nation in Europe to defy him, Great Britain. He hoped for a good hearing – but what if he were out-foxed by the wily victor of Tilsit? Known for his unpredictable cunning, Bonaparte might well take the plan and, ignoring Spain, move alone to secure the prize.

But his master, Manuel Godoy y Álvarez de Faria, first minister to Carlos IV, had foreseen this possibility. The relationship was not to be a loose understanding open to interpretation. Izquierdo had to see to it that he secured a formal treaty between sovereign powers that spelled out not just the distribution of spoils but the duties and obligations of both, such that there could be no going back on the word of a principal.

Izquierdo knew it would take every nerve in his being to stand before the conqueror of the world to demand such a condition.

He heard voices and the scrape of chairs in the next room. Heart in his mouth, he waited. The doors swept open and Marshal of the Palace Géraud Duroc appeared in all his magnificence. 'His Imperial Majesty is now in audience,' he announced coldly.

Five days later, weak with exhaustion but buoyed with exhilaration, Izquierdo sat at his desk and began to write.

For Godoy, it had been a wearisome and nerve-racking wait. His hold over the amiable and ageing King was undiminished, but this shaking of the foundations of the proud traditions and long history of Spain by an outsider threatened the old order – and who knew when it would settle to the familiar ways once more? This daring proposal to Bonaparte must succeed.

The unwelcome war between Napoleon's France and her ancient rival England had caused untold ruin to the economy, not the least being the severing of ties with their South American colonies by the marauding Royal Navy, with the flow of silver and produce virtually cut off. Spanish troops had been taken up by Bonaparte to far parts of the world to aid in his conquests and a subsidy of millions in silver *reales* had been demanded.

He'd had to play off factions, keep grandees satisfied with tawdry honours and, by a network of spies and informants, watch for unrest and discontent in the sprawling, rugged and individualistic land that was Spain. Godoy, known as the 'Prince of the Peace', was the most hated of the king's advisers. Ironically, his enemies included those who stood to lose most if he failed – the ancient lineage, the haughty aristocracy who hankered after the days of Spain standing astride the world, a handful of conquistadors carving out vast empires in a new continent to the glory of God and the Spanish Crown.

Yet as long as he retained the unquestioning trust of the

King he was safe, and this he ensured by interpreting the buzz and confusion of the outside world to him in a soothing and glib fashion, every so often uncovering some plot or intrigue to demonstrate his loyalty and devotion. He had early taken the precaution of becoming the Queen's lover, the sottish woman insatiable, a trying burden now she was in her fifties, with nothing to do but plot.

'Excellency.'

It was a messenger – and he bore a missive. Swallowing his apprehension Godoy held out his hand then waved the man away and retired to his desk, almost afraid of what he would read.

A quick scan reassured him and, in rising excitement, he took in the hurried phrases.

He'd been right to entrust Izquierdo with the business: Napoleon Bonaparte had taken the bait.

In his eagerness he'd been willing to make a binding agreement, the Treaty of Fontainebleau, and in it was detailed the formal dismembering of the corpse of Portugal, now bereft of its sovereign, who had fled to Brazil.

Portentously, the Emperor had pronounced that: 'The name of Portugal is to be removed from the list of nations', the land divided in thirds between them. Oporto and the north would become the kingdom of Northern Lusitania and go to the young King of Etruria. The centre, including Lisbon, was to be administered by France until the conclusion of a general peace. But gloriously, wonderfully, all of southern Portugal, including Alentejo, was to be made an independent principality . . . under the rule of one Don Manuel Godoy, to be styled Prince of the Algarves.

In lesser paragraphs there was detail on how it was to be accomplished. With the gracious permission of King Carlos, French columns would enter Spain, and thereby be made quite safe from the predacious Royal Navy, enabled to march overland to join in a descent on helpless Portugal from both north and south. It was expected that the whole affair could be concluded in no more than small months.

At last – no more waiting. In a paroxysm of impatience Godoy got to his feet. There was no point in delay: he would get the business under way immediately.

'Chancellor Godoy, Majesty.'

'Oh. Come in, *mi primo*,' King Carlos grunted genially, holding his arms high as his slim-fitting leather hunting surcoat was eased on. 'You have something for me?'

Godoy had timed it well. Affairs of state were a tiresome intrusion when the hunting field beckoned, as it so often did. It shouldn't take long. 'Good news, sire, much to be welcomed in these parlous times. An initiative I've caused to be raised before the French Emperor has been received with a pleasing degree of acclamation.'

'Really. Then well done, Godoy. Er, what's it all about?'

'Bonaparte is restless, seeing Portugal without a ruler yet flouting his offers of friendship – and, worse, seeking to plot with the British to our common distress. There is a solution I have humbly offered, which he has seen fit to accede to. It is, sire, the answer to centuries of Spanish humiliation – no less than the final unifying of the Iberian peninsula under our banner.'

'What can you mean by this, Godoy? How can—'

'In return for a fair division of the proceeds of the dissolution of the Portuguese nation into a Spanish province, he will provide sufficient troops to join with us in our reordering of the progress of history. For this he undertakes to enact a grand treaty between our two nations, to remain secret until we are ready to march.'

The King paused, his face comically pulled out of shape by the tight surcoat inching its way on. 'That's all he wants?'

'That, and permission to march to Portugal through Spain, thereby defying the English fleet.' He allowed his voice to acquire a more reverential tone and went on, 'He does aver that such will be the resulting great accession of territory to the Spanish Crown that it may be necessary henceforth to refer to the King of Spain as emperor – his suggestion is "Emperor of the Two Americas", sire.'

The coat finally settled in place while the King blinked happily. 'A fine and statesmanlike resolving of an ancient problem,' he pronounced at length. 'What should I do?'

'Merely the ratifying of the treaty will answer, sire. I've given the clauses my personal care and attention so you may be sure there will be no difficulties.'

'Yes, yes, I shall. You've done very well, *mi primo*, and let the world know how grateful I am for your ministry. Is there aught else?'

Godoy's face fell, his features carefully sorrowful. This final move would set the seal on a brilliant stroke, serving to rid himself of his deadliest and until now untouchable adversary.

'Sire, why is it that the gods raise us up with one hand only to cast us down with the other?'

King Carlos frowned. 'There is an impediment to the treaty?'

'No, sire,' he hastened to say, 'rather it is a matter of personal sadness that I feel obliged to divulge to you.'

'You can tell me, old friend.'

'My man in Fontainebleau, while in the process of negotiation, discovered a grave and sinister design, no less than your deposing and replacing by another more pliable to the foreign cause.'

'Have you the details?'

'As of last evening, unhappily, I have, sire.'

'The wretch shall be made to pay for his villainy!'

'It is in truth naught but an attempt to bind Spain for ever to France through an unequal and demeaning marriage.'

'Deposing – what in Heaven's name is this damnable roguery?'

'Majesty, it is the act of one who has agreed – in writing – to take whomsoever the French Emperor chooses as pledge of loyalty and obedience.'

'He shall die, of course. Who is he – do I know the treasonous Judas?' he spluttered.

'Sire, it grieves me to say it but we have the evidence that it is the foolish intriguing of none other than . . . the Prince of Asturias.' The King's son Fernando. Impatient heir and implacable foe of Godoy in whatever he did.

'No!'

'I fear it be so, sire. Acting on information received, I made search of the royal apartments and found certain letters that shall be laid before you that are unanswerable proof of his perfidy. Shall I . . .?'

'Seize him and take him to El Escorial,' King Carlos said heavily. 'He shall be dealt with.'

Luxuriating in the satin caress of the big four-poster bed, Godoy smiled indulgently at his mistress. 'As it was a coup rarely seen, Pepita. In one afternoon I have vanquished that toad Fernando but much more than that – to be made a prince of Spain with a demesne of my own to rule as I please!'

'Prince of the Algarves,' murmured Pepita, sleepily. 'I like that. Does your wife still have to be with us?'

'As crowned head I shall put her from me, *mi pichóncita*,' Godoy said airily. 'Besides which, you plainly haven't deduced what all this will lead to.'

She wriggled round to see him more clearly. 'To more? Tell me.'

'You really want to know?' he teased.

'If it touches on you and me, of course.' She pouted prettily.

'Then I shall tell you, *cariño*. After so much hard striving, the biggest prize of all is within my reach.'

'Yes, yes, go on.'

'With the heir to throne now disgraced, and as the only Prince of Spain not in the royal line of that old imbecile, there are many advantages to my acceding . . . to the throne myself.'

'You!' she squealed.

'I.'

'But . . .'

'I will not weary you with details, Pepita, but there's one that stands above and beyond all others.'

'Tell me!'

'Consider this. I am not a Bourbon. The French exerted themselves to extraordinary lengths to rid themselves of that decrepit bloodline, and Emperor Napoleon would like nothing better than to ally himself to one not tainted by such. As prince, I will be in the line of succession. He will undoubtedly bring much pressure to bear on the Cortes that will, in the end, see me King of Spain!'

Chapter 1

The Hamoaze moorings, Plymouth, England

'Very good. You may stand down sea watches, Mr Bray,' Captain Sir Thomas Kydd told his first lieutenant.

He took a deep breath and looked around in satisfaction. After her far voyaging, *Tyger* had picked up moorings in the broad stretch of water fed by the river Tamar between Devon and Cornwall that went on into Plymouth Sound. On its eastern bank was the well-equipped King's Dockyard. While the ship's small hurts were attended to, all would have time for leave and liberty.

And not far inland, over the soft green rolling hills, his heart had its home: Knowle Manor, nestling in the Devonshire countryside, now the seat of Sir Thomas and Lady Kydd.

Persephone would not be expecting him – the hastily mounted Northern Expedition into the Baltic that had called him away had had all the signs of a savage and protracted confrontation. As it happened, it was now over, leaving Admiral Saumarez and his Baltic Fleet predominant at sea.

Some ships had been released to return to their original

duties. For *Tyger* this meant rejoining Admiral Collingwood's Mediterranean Fleet and its eternal blockade of Toulon and the western seaboard of Europe – but that would come later. First, liberty!

For her ship's company it would be the delights of an English shore where they could raise the wind a-rollicking in a sailors' town to drown memories of gales and iron-bound coasts, a shipmate lost to the sea or the rage of battle. And with prize money to spend they would make it a famous time.

And for her captain, a release of shipboard cares. With his valet Tysoe at pillion, he took coach to the pretty village of Ivybridge, then a hired trap from the London Inn, his heart thudding with anticipation. The road followed the crystal waters of the river Erme, then veered off into the wooded foothills below the moors before the quaint loveliness appeared of Combe Tavy, with its pond and goose green.

Without stopping, they trotted up the little country road . . . that left-hand bend . . . the enfolding woods and then . . . the ancient wall and the gatehouse, its arch bearing the precious legend, Knowle Manor.

Tysoe brought the horse to a walk as the trap ground grittily along the driveway to the entrance – but Kydd had seen a female figure at the roses by the creeper-clad walls look up in surprise. In a single mad movement he vaulted from the seat and raced forward, crushing her to him.

'My darling – my love! Seph, I've so missed you!'

'My dearest . . . you're home! My sweet, my—' Her voice broke with emotion.

They kissed, long and passionately.

'Oh dear,' she said shakily, brushing the dark earth from her gardening apron, 'and I'm not fit to be seen.'

'Seph, you'd look as comely in a pedlar's rags, my love,

never doubt it,' he said tenderly, kissing her again and taking her arm.

A beaming Mrs Appleby, the housekeeper, held open the door, then made much of primping the cushions on the two comfortable armchairs by the fire. 'Aye, but you an'' the captain'll have much to talk on, so I'll leave ye be.'

Kydd dragged his chair closer and they sat, hand in hand, lost in the moment.

'There, my dear. My very own kitchen garden.' Persephone beamed.

The morning sun was warm and picked out the neat rows of plants. They meant nothing to Kydd, but he smiled winningly and expressed his admiration. To his rescue came a distant memory of Quashee, a mess-cook whose flourishing of his 'conweniences' had been a legend in the flying *Artemis* on their round-the-world adventure.

'You've planted an adequacy of calaminthy, of course,' he said, in a lordly tone. 'A sovereign physic in any situation.'

'Calaminthy? I don't think I have.' She frowned uncertainly, in the process managing to wring his heart with her loveliness.

'Oh, er, the common sort would know it as the basil, m' dear.'

'Basil?' She shook her head. 'But the rosemary is growing splendidly, and tonight you'll taste it in Mrs Appleby's venison ragout.'

The improvements she'd made were impressive. The garden was now tamed, the front of the manor with its red Tudor brick freed of the overgrown ivy, but with enough left to frame the darkened oak doors. The weathercock atop its tower was now proud and square and the lawn had been meticulously mown.

Kydd made acquaintance with Persephone's new horse Bo'sun, the noble brown face, dark ears flicking, looking at him curiously. He knew his wife was an excellent rider and judge of horses but this beast was exceptionally handsome. A full chestnut of some fifteen hands and gleaming with condition, its lithe musculature spoke of effortless speed and endurance.

'We'll lease a mount for you while you're home, Thomas,' she made haste to assure him. A horse was an expensive article and another could not be justified when he was away at sea for so much of the time.

He beamed, looking forward to riding with her on the moors. 'Yes, Seph. We'll see to it directly.'

Workmen were still busy on the small buildings at the back: a charming summer house and a discreet garden shed where Mr Appleby was preparing his pot plants.

'I want to talk to you about a pavilion, Thomas dear,' she murmured, as they roamed arm-in-arm along the wilder southern fringes of their property. She pointed out a fine place for a small private shelter with a picnic view into the steep, wandering valley of the Tavy.

Back inside the house, a shy maid stood aside as Persephone asked him anxiously if he approved her choice of dinner service – a Spode setting of exquisite artistry and, to Kydd's eyes, perfectly attuned to the bucolic placidity of Knowle Manor. Not the pompous gold-lined ornateness of Town but joyous limned English flowers and butterflies on delicately formed ivory porcelain. The selection of cutlery had been put aside until they could consult together on a trip to London.

Combe Tavy folk soon knew that the squire was back from his sea wanderings, and in the Pig and Whistle the one-eyed innkeeper, Jenkins, grinned from ear to ear as he served the alarming number of villagers who had found it convenient to rest from their labours.

Kydd heard from the soft-spoken old sheep-farmer, Davies, of the loss by braxy over the winter of three of his flock, which a long-winded account put down to their consuming grass while still frost-speckled. The beady-eyed thatcher, Jermyn, came in with a harrowing tale of a roof fire in the remote hamlet of Horrabridge that had had him trudging over the moors in wind and sleet of an unpleasantness that a gentleman like Kydd could never conceive.

After politely asking after him, others listened as he contributed a morsel concerning the perils of horse-riding on the hard sea-ice of Finland and the grievous conditions for reindeer looking for forage under snow that had lain undisturbed for four months. It left them bemused as they quaffed their moorland ale.

The days passed in a sweet warmth that Kydd could feel imperceptibly rooting him to the place. Curling up together in front of the fire, he and Persephone made comfortable decisions about their hearth and home, such as where the grand portrait of Knowle Manor she had painted should be hung.

But Kydd's attempts to win over the sleek tabby, Rufus, who held sway over this *his* kingdom were forlorn.

'One night during an awful storm he suddenly appeared as though it were his long-lost home,' Persephone told him fondly, picking the cat up. 'Licked himself all over for an hour in front of the fire and settled in. I hadn't the heart to turn away the rascal.' The creature accepted a twiggle of his ears, while continuing to stare at Kydd with striking lambent eyes. 'He'll be used to you by and by.'

Persephone didn't press him for details of his adventuring

but Kydd suspected that she was guessing at what he didn't say so strove to round out the details. Coming from a naval family, she knew the sea cant and did not require tedious explanation. He found himself recounting a dramatic clawing off a lee-shore with the familiarity of a seasoned mariner and saw by her expression she understood perfectly.

'I'm blessed beyond my deserving,' he murmured to her, not for the first time.

Chapter 2

The morning was clear and warm when Kydd and Persephone set out for Tavistock across the moors, a score of miles distant. They took it at a brisk canter, spelling their horses at the Goodameavy stables, where Kydd had once despaired of her feelings for him.

It was Thursday, the pannier market was in full swing and Kydd let the bustle of the town envelop them. Tavistock was inland, between Bodmin Moor and Dartmoor. Surprisingly, the town's most famous sons were all mariners. The chief was Sir Francis Drake, whose seat of Buckland Abbey was close by. Sir Humphrey Gilbert, the colonist and explorer lost at sea, would have had his last memories of home as Kydd was seeing it, and Grenville of *Revenge* was suzerain of Buckland at the time of his famous last fight. His cousin Sir Walter Raleigh had grown up nearby, and many more had found their calling upon the sea from the towns and villages on the road to Plymouth.

Sir Thomas and Lady Kydd wandered together among the stalls and booths, the produce and crafts of Devonshire on exuberant show, the hoarse cries of the stallholders mingling with the babble of market-goers, jostling good-naturedly and enjoying the delights of the day. Folk were of all stations in life: smock-clad farm workers, beefy merchants, gentlemen and their ladies.

The thick, pleasing odours of country life eddied about them, and Kydd mused that he couldn't be further from the stern reality of the war at sea. With a beautiful woman on his arm and the day theirs, he would be pressed to bring to mind a heaving deck, taut lines from aloft, the menacing dark blue-grey of an enemy coast on the bow . . . This was another place, another world.

'Oh, how quaint!' Persephone exclaimed, admiring a pinafore extravagantly interwoven with lacework of a previous age, unusual on such a garment. She fingered it reverently, the seller, a man, watching her silently.

Kydd's gaze wandered. There were many more attractions and they could easily—

Standing motionless not more than a dozen yards away, a gentleman in plain but well-cut attire was regarding him gravely.

Kydd didn't know the man . . . or did he? The distinguished greying hair, the direct, unflinching hard gaze, the stern, upright bearing . . . Like the master of a ship . . .

It couldn't be, but it was: the defeated captain who had met him on the deck of the last of the three frigates *Tyger* had overcome in her epic combat in the southern Baltic the previous year. *Preussen*, yes – a French-manned Prussian and commanded by one Marceau.

After a moment of shock at the sudden clash of worlds, Kydd gave a polite bow of recognition, which was solemnly returned. Clearly the man was not on the run and neither was he closely escorted.

He walked amiably up to Kydd and spoke in French. '*Capitaine de vaisseau* Jean-Yves Marceau,' he offered, the eyes as Kydd remembered, cool and appraising. 'Guest of *sa majesté* as a consequence of—'

'Captain Sir Thomas Kydd, and the circumstances I do remember with the deepest of respect, sir,' Kydd answered in French. So Marceau was a prisoner of war, and as an officer had no doubt given his parole to allow him this freedom. But an educated and polished gentleman of France in Tavistock?

Persephone regarded them curiously. 'Oh, this is Lady Kydd, my wife. My dear, this is Captain Marceau whom I last met on the field of honour.'

The French captain lifted her gloved fingers to his lips. '*Enchanté*, m' lady.'

'A singular place to meet you again, M'sieur le capitaine, if I might remark it,' Kydd continued.

Marceau gave a small smile. 'Having duly lodged my parole with your esteemed Transport Board I was assigned this town to reside, always within its boundaries, in something approaching comfort and refinement, here to wait out the present unpleasantness until it be over.'

'A civilised arrangement, I'm persuaded,' Kydd responded. Did captured English naval officers in France have the same privilege? But then a surge of compassion overtook him. This was a first rank sea officer, transported to captivity in the countryside of his enemy. Robbed of the graces and enlightenments of his patrimony, he was eking out his existence, probably of slender means and seldom to hear the language of his birth.

The man bowed, a glimmer of feeling briefly showing.

'Yet a hard enough thing for an active gentleman,' Kydd continued. 'May you travel, sir, visit others at all?'

'Should I stray further than the one-mile stone on any road away from Tavistock then I shall be made to exchange my present existence for that of the hulks,' he replied evenly.

It was an imprisonment but of another kind, and Kydd impulsively warmed to the man – wryly recalling that it was his actions that had placed Marceau here.

An absurd thought surfaced and he found himself saying, 'Then my invitation to your good self of a dinner evening at my manor must therefore be refused?'

Persephone looked at him sharply but he affected not to notice.

Marceau stiffened, then bowed deeply. 'Your most gallant and obliging politeness to me is deeply appreciated, Sir Thomas, but in the circumstances I should look to be denied.'

'I regret to hear this, sir.'

The Frenchman paused, looking at him directly. 'Yet if I trespass further upon your good nature there is perhaps a means to that end.'

'Say on, sir!'

'The parole agent of this town may be approached and, for a particular occasion, has the power to grant licence, I'm told.'

Mr Nott was at first astonished, then gratified to make acquaintance of the famed frigate captain.

'As your request is not unknown, Sir Thomas,' he allowed, pulling down a well-thumbed book from the shelf above his desk, 'but seldom granted, I fear.'

'Why so, sir? I would have thought it a humane enough thing.'

'Ah. Then you are not aware of the parlous state of affairs in the matter of the confining of prisoners of war in this kingdom.'

It cost Kydd nearly an hour's listening to the man but it was a sobering and enlightening experience.

The arcane eighteenth-century practice of making such prisoners the responsibility of the Sick and Hurt Board of the Admiralty had been superseded by the equally obscure assigning of them to the Transport Board, known more to Kydd as the procurer of shipping for army expeditions. Captured enemy officers were offered parole or made to suffer incarceration in one of a number of prisons in Britain. Foremast hands had to endure the hulks or prison without the possibility of parole.

Kydd had shuddered at his first sight of the distant lines of hulks in the Hamoaze, and he remembered the Millbay prison louring across the bay from his previous lodging at Stonehouse.

Nott's duties were to muster his charges regularly, to issue them weekly with the sum of one shilling and sixpence per diem in subsistence, and to handle private remittances, with all correspondence to go through him for censoring before it reached the post office. For their part the French found modest lodgings, which they undertook to return to by curfew, generally eight at night, and to refrain from activity that could be deemed in any way seditious.

He received little enough thanks, Nott complained, and there were increasing numbers absconding, breaking parole, and presumably finding their way back to their home country. It was a growing scandal, especially, as Kydd knew, it was a matter of a gentleman's honour. The France of Napoleon was a different nation from that of earlier days.

'Captain Marceau is still here,' Kydd said pointedly.

'How do you mean, sir?'

'If he'd wanted to break his parole he's had a year or more to do it. I fancy an evening entertainment will not see him inclined to run on its account.'

It cost Kydd a ten-guinea bond but Knowle Manor would know no less a personage than a French frigate captain as a guest to dinner.

Chapter 3

The evening was accounted a success from Marceau's arrival and extravagant admiration of the oil painting in the hallway, portraying the sublimity of Iceland by an artist unknown to him, to the exquisite manners he displayed at table when good Devon mutton made its appearance, accompanied by a sauce whose piquancy had him exclaiming.

Afterwards, when the cloth was drawn and a very acceptable La Rochefoucauld cognac was produced, the atmosphere warmed further. A dry smile followed Marceau's complimenting Kydd's taste in brandy, both leaving unsaid that no doubt it had been a prize of war from a British cruiser on blockade of the region's big seaports of Rochefort and La Rochelle.

'Do you hail from those parts, sir?' Kydd asked, refilling his guest's glass.

'Ah, no. Far from the sea. In Auvergne, the Haute-Loire, which is possibly further from the sea than any other quarter of France. Far famed for its divine cheeses – the Saint-Nectaire is of a particular fragrance.'

'Then, sir, would it be impertinent of me to enquire as to how you heard the sea a-calling?'

'Like your nation, Sir Thomas, we French are a maritime race at heart. In my youth the sagas of the Pacific explorers stirred my soul — Surville, Jean-François de Galaup, whom you will more probably know as the Comte de Lapérouse. These do still inspire. And yourself, pray?'

'Oh, a small Surrey town, Guildford. And likewise, far from the sea's siren call.'

'And so . . .?'

'Taken up as a common seaman and finding myself beguiled, sir.'

'To reach this eminence? I confess to being lost in admiration at your achieving, sir.'

Kydd coloured. 'A bitter thing it is that we must war against each other to find our true selves.'

'As is my feeling too, sir,' the Frenchman responded in a soft voice, lowering his eyes.

'I — I do trust you are not overborne in your spirits, as we might say,' Kydd said. 'Your situation is not one deserving of a distinguished mariner, to pass his days on shore in idleness and despair.'

'I bear my lot in patience, sir,' Marceau said heavily. 'Yet . . .'

'Yes?'

'Yet it bears upon my soul that I can do nothing for the men I had the honour to command, my ship's company, who now lie miserably in prison for the monstrous crime of loyally following my orders.'

Kydd's heart wrung with pity. This was an honourable captain, one who cared for his men yet could do nothing for them. He could hardly conceive of the pain it would cause him if he were in his place to know that, after a ferocious but losing battle, only a prison cell was the reward for each of *Tyger*'s company who had fought for him — Stirk, Doud, the cheery captain of the foretop, the sturdy afterguard, the long-service fo'c'slemen – all left to rot their lives away, like any wretched criminal.

'If only it were in my power to reach to them, say words of solace, to manifest to them that I care of their fate, they are not forgotten by me . . .'

'I understand you, M'sieur le capitaine,' Kydd muttered. 'If it were me . . .' But there was no conceivable way that this could be made possible.

Marceau looked away suddenly, his face a mask of grief.

When he turned back his gaze was directly at Kydd. 'Sir Thomas, you are a sea-captain like me. I have a small request that you have every right to refuse and I expect you will. Nevertheless, my humanity drives me on to ask it.'

'Sir, do allow that we are not foes at this time. Ask it if you will.'

'Then . . . can you find it in your heart to perform a small service that would nevertheless mean a great deal to me?' He hesitated, his face rigid. 'Sir, in your next visiting to Plymouth town it would infinitely oblige should you call upon such of my men as you can find and distribute to them a small basket of *bonnes bouches* with my tenderest regards for their condition. Sir Thomas, this gesture from one so lately a triumphant enemy would be deeply valued and respected by them.'

Kydd was touched. A simple thing, a commander contriving to let his company know that they were not forgotten in their endless enduring – and with Kydd to say the words there would be no rousing call to glory, no chance of inflaming passions. Why not?

'I think it not impossible,' Kydd said cautiously. '*Bonnes bouches*?'

'Comestibles of the homeland not found in England – *les macarons, la confiture* . . .'

'Where . . .?'

'There is a small but close community of French officers in Tavistock. We seek amusement in our various ways, offering language classes, dancing instruction, the contriving of intricate *objets de bizarrerie* – your lady will recollect the lace pinafore. This is our Gaston Dominique, third of the *Preussen*, seeking a little recognition and grateful pelf.' He gave an almost shy smile and finished, 'And others do conjure culinary delights precious to the memory of *la belle* France. These only do I long to share with my *matelots braves*.'

Persephone touched his arm. 'Darling, is it so much to ask? Those poor sailors locked up for ever, a little enough thing.'

'Very well. I cannot promise when next I shall be in Plymouth but I will do as you ask – if permitted by the authorities, of course.'

Chapter 4

It was even worse than Kydd had been prepared for. The high, blank walls and grim barrack blocks enclosed a vast dusty exercise ground where ragged prisoners ambled dully, endlessly, equally indifferent to the sky above and the dead earth beneath. Bored and blank-faced guards in tawdry red uniforms moved slowly among them, muskets shouldered. And lying over everything, the sickening reek of confinement.

At the gatehouse Kydd's reasons had been met with raised eyebrows but brought no objection, his hamper of sweetmeats searched and allowed. It was not uncommon for do-gooders and others to come to gawp at the spectacle and some even to bring gifts.

He learned that the guards were functionaries of the Commissioners for Conducting His Majesty's Transport Service and for the Care and Custody of Prisoners of War. They took no orders from the navy or other military, and Kydd guessed that any 'pickings' from sharp practice would be jealously defended.

They did, however, obligingly turn out the mess-hall so Kydd could address the French prisoners in question and he took position at the front of the fifty or so Preussens. A proud ship's company they were no longer. Many of the men who faced him had a hangdog listlessness, others a snarling aggression, with clothing that ranged from a thin but cared-for remnant of uniform to the shabby dreariness of issued prison garb to tattered rags. But he'd heard that in defiance of the Revolution they still called their navy 'La Royale'.

They gazed up at him with varying expressions: curiosity, hostility, emptiness. Some threw looks of undisguised contempt but, in the main, they seemed prepared to accept this interruption to their interminable day. Kydd thought he could pick out the ship's characters – the hard-faced boatswain's mate, the sagging whipcord muscles of a topman, the broad chest of a gunner, the far gaze of the deep-water seaman, now condemned to the sight of nothing but four grimed walls.

'My name is Kydd,' he began simply, his French not equal to the rich slang of their lower deck, as venerable as his own. 'I'm a captain in His Majesty's Navy.' It brought puzzled looks, wariness.

'And I'm here to bring greetings and notice from my friend.' He had their reluctant attention now and went on quietly, 'Yes, my friend, who is Capitaine de vaisseau Marceau.'

As it sank in, there were disbelieving gasps and a snort of derision from a heavily built individual to the left. 'Ha! What *merde* do you cast at us, *mon putain de capitaine anglais?*'

Kydd winced but replied, 'If he were not my friend, I should not be here. Your captain desires only to be remembered to you, to let you know that he cherishes your loyalty in times past and hopes that it will go some way to sustain you in these hard days.'

He let it hang then added, 'And, as a captain myself, this is what I would feel for my own company. He's a prisoner, too, so he's unable to stand before you but in token of his regard he sends a gift, a basket of *bonnes bouches* in memory of France, to share between you all.'

The wary looks had now changed to stares of disbelief but the big man spat stubbornly. 'How's *le patron* going to get the stuff from Brittany at all?'

Kydd was being tested. 'Capitaine Marceau comes from Auvergne, the Haute-Loire, as well you know. And he's caused them to be made by those in captivity with him who do pine after the *friandises* of the homeland.'

He brought forward the hamper. 'Who's in charge?'

Eyes turned to the big man who, with an acknowledging grunt, stepped up, his large hands unconsciously curled into the characteristic 'rope-hooky' of a deep-sea sailor.

'I give you this from your captain. It's a small enough thing but comes with his sincere regard.'

In the astonished silence Kydd turned and left.

At the gatehouse the sergeant was cynical. 'A fine thing ye does, Captain, but I'd not let ye think ye've changed anythin' for 'em. Ye must know for gamblin' they can't be beat. Wagers off their clothes, t'baccy, even their next day's rations. Them things won't be ate, they'll be stakes in somethin' until they falls to bits. Nothing else for 'em to do, see.'

Kydd ignored his contemptuous smirk. He'd done for Marceau what he'd seen as right and honourable.

'Oi, Sarge!' A guard bustled in. 'There's a Frog outside wi' something, as wants t' see the captain.'

It was the big French prisoner, carrying a substantial object covered with a cloth. When Kydd emerged, his stony features softened and he carefully drew back the cloth to reveal a ship model, beautifully worked, rigged and fashioned in the tell-tale ivory of carefully-put-by beef bones. An exquisite production that must have taken untold hours to bring to perfection, it bore the pennant of La Royale pugnaciously to the fore.

'Cap'n. I'd be much obliged should you present this'n to the *capitaine* with our humble duty and respects, as he did remember us.'

The man's eyes pleaded and Kydd melted. 'O' course I shall, *mon brave*. From you – the very next time I see him.'

He threw a look at the sergeant as he left, but the man was staring glassily past his shoulder, refusing to take notice.

Kydd had seen it through. And with the Preussens together in Millbay there was thankfully no need to make visit out to the prison hulks and their burden of misery.

They were moored in a line well up the Hamoaze away from any settlement, kept to the centre of the river, leaving on either side a quarter-mile of swampy shore to trap even the most determined fugitive. Mostly captured French ships no longer fit for the open sea and reduced to bare lower masts, they were a bleak and heart-rending sight.

Shaking off his creeping depression Kydd returned to the land of the free, duty done.

Chapter 5

The London Inn at Ivybridge was more than a common posting house. As a horse-changing stage on the highway to London, it was a centre for rumours and gossip, a place for the sighting of important people on the way to and from the capital. It was also where the mail coach made its call.

Kydd had got into the habit of taking a ride there with Persephone, a very pleasant forty minutes, in time to see the London stage jingle and crash into the cobbled courtyard with the day's newspapers aboard. While she visited the shops, he could take in the stories of the hour in the taphouse over a fine west-country ale, considerately leaving his paper for others to read in the gleaming brass and sawdust warmth.

On this day he saw that, with the Baltic now a highway for British trade, Boney in Europe was the subject of speculation again. At one end of the continent he would have little opportunity to press on to new lands as his conquests lapped up against his ally Russia. At the other end, as he was now occupying Portugal, he'd reached the far extent of the land world. *The Times* leader asked what the ruthless Emperor would do next, disbelieving that he'd be satisfied with what he had.

Kydd wondered too. *Tyger*'s addition to Collingwood's fleet had to be a measure of the anxiety this was causing.

Further into the paper there was the court circular, then a tedious dissection of what had passed in the House during the week and, at the back, columns of commercial intelligence.

He sighed and turned to hear the local moorland news. As lord of the manor, if only as a figurehead, he was expected to keep up with the concerns and vexations of his tenantry but, in truth, he didn't know if congratulation or consolation was due to the farmer whose ewe had brought forth a lamb with two heads.

'Good morning t' ye, Cap'n,' a breezy voice broke in. It was the corn factor, whose quaint Elizabethan mill downstream still creaked on in the middle of the village.

'Good day to you, Mr Glanville,' Kydd replied genially.

'Exeter stage be in.'

Kydd nodded. He'd heard it arrive.

'Wi' strangers,' Glanville added, with relish.

'Oh?'

'Good 'uns an' all,' he went on, in his soft Devon burr. 'One on 'em says they's all from Sweden, b' glory!'

Kydd emptied his glass, his interest aroused. He had a certain regard for these Scandinavians after coming to know Jens Strömsson, the Swedish captain who'd escaped from Sveaborg with him. What they were doing in this part of the world was baffling when their country was in such agitation, but he felt they'd be appreciative to hear a few words from someone who'd been so recently in that far place and he'd picked up a little Swedish.

He strode out to the courtyard. It was easy to find them: four individuals, in outlandish dress in a tight group away from the others, stretching their legs and talking in low mumbles.

Going up to them, he smiled and hailed, '*Hej, hur mår du?*' They stiffened.

'I not understand your words,' one replied, in a strangely stilted French, edging slightly in front of the others.

Kydd bowed. 'I'm sorry if my Swedish is so execrable.'

Persephone appeared at his side, elegant and commanding in smart riding attire. 'Darling, who are these people?'

'Oh, they're Swedish gentlemen,' he replied to her, in French for the sake of the group, 'from the Exeter stage, whose acquaintance I'm desirous of making to let them know something of their motherland as I'm so recently returned.'

There was a tension about the group, all unspeaking, watchful and still.

In English she murmured, 'They don't look much like Swedes.'

Kydd remembered she'd made a visit there on a painting expedition the previous year. It was true: the restrained cut of the Nordic dress was not much in evidence – if anything, these men gave the impression of wearing a more modish attire held in check. It was odd.

'*All aboooard*! Exeter stage, *all aboard*!' The driver, with his many-layered topcoat, puffed his way up into his seat and importantly accepted the whip passed to him, while ostlers held the horses and impatient passengers clambered in.

The four strangers quickly followed but, damn it, there was something that . . .

He had it! Kydd snapped to attention and roared, '*Vive l'empereur!*'

Inside, faces turned his way and a muffled shout responded instinctively.

'They're French officers on the run!' Kydd blurted, to a

startled Persephone, and rushed forward. 'Stop the coach! In the name of the King, stop, I say!'

But the big four-wheeler was on its way with a sudden grinding and jingling, swaying out of the yard and up the road in a dusty cloud, a vigorous cracking of the whip a caution that the driver would not delay the Exeter stage simply for one forgetful passenger.

In dismay Kydd saw it disappear around the corner, then realised there was still a chance.

'I'm going after them,' he said. Even his workaday hired sorrel would be more than equal to the trotting stage-coach.

'Thomas – there's four of them,' Persephone said urgently. 'What do you do after you stop the coach?'

He grimaced. Four desperate, possibly armed men against just himself . . . but there was another way.

'My horse! Saddle up this instant, d' you hear?' Kydd barked. He told Persephone, 'I'm to ride to Buckfastleigh – there's a militia barracks near there. I'll go up on the moors, more direct, get there first and turn out the redcoats.'

'Yes, dear,' she said, adding, 'and I'm coming with you.'

It was pointless to argue and in minutes they had taken the winding road up to the Western Beacons, high above Ivybridge, where the windswept moor lay before them, bare and mysterious.

'Go!' cried Kydd, exultantly, and spurred his mount forward. It thrust out, the endless landscape of tussocks and folds under a vast open sky seeming to galvanise the beast into a willing gallop, thundering over the featureless heath.

He snatched a glance at Persephone to his left. She was low over Bo'sun's mane, perfectly attuned to his fluid motion, her eyes shining, her chestnut hair free. Catching his mood, she laughed in delight as they spurred on together in a synchrony of purpose.

It quickly became evident that Kydd was out-classed. Bo'sun was a thoroughbred and Persephone was natural-born to the saddle. She gave her horse his head, and despite Kydd's best efforts, she quickly pulled ahead. He yelled at her to wait for him but all he got was a delighted cry and a wave as she sped out in the lead and was soon lost to sight.

As Kydd clattered down the stony path into the barracks he took in the sight of the South Hams Volunteers in martial array, with fixed bayonets penning the four Frenchmen. Persephone stood nearby, an impish smile on her face. She whispered, 'I told the officer on parade that if he didn't get his men to stop the coach Sir Thomas would have him keel-hauled!'

Kydd went up to the lieutenant in charge, who glared at him imperiously and said, 'Have a care, sir. These are dangerous men – French!'

Kydd held back a grin. This were probably the first and possibly only encounter that the man would have with the enemy. 'Have they been searched?' he asked.

'Yes.'

'And?'

All that had been found was the respectable sum of fifty guineas in banknotes and a single piece of paper with cryptic directions – but it was enough to indicate that this was no impulsive act. It had been organised.

Later Nott, the parole agent, called into Combe Tavy to thank Kydd. 'You'll be pleased to know you're entitled to a reward of half-a-crown a nob, Sir Thomas. Small enough recompense for putting a stopper to those runners. As to your organising, you're in the right of it but how do I get to the bottom of it, pray? The banknotes are forgeries, I'd wager, and nothing to be gained from the paper.' He sniffed dismissively. 'A parole-breaker need only get to London to find a snug berth out in a neutral ship, or quicker still, buy passage out with a smuggler, the vermin.'

'For both it needs organising.'

'Aye. But there's always those who'll make their way smooth for a rub of silver.'

The four had lost their bid because they had had the misfortune to come upon the only man in the Devon countryside able to penetrate their masquerade. It was galling, but there was nothing more Kydd could do about the flight of any other French officers.

Chapter 6

There was little enough time before *Tyger* must sail and Kydd was determined to make the most of it. He and his wife spent an agreeable musical evening laced with memories of times past in Plymouth, meeting Persephone's friends and Kydd singing some of his favourite pieces, lovingly accompanied by her. Then they attended a warm assembly at Bramblebye, the mansion of the gregarious Percival Luscombe, his nearest neighbour to the north, and hosted another dinner for Capitaine Marceau, who listened gravely to Kydd's account of his arrest of the parole-breakers. He said little, clearly mortified by the dishonourable behaviour of his countrymen.

One morning Kydd took a barn-door hinge to the Ivybridge blacksmith to be mended.

The genial Tovey filled the smithy with sparks as he hammered energetically at some sort of agricultural implement, his ancient workplace a-flare with the ruddy glare of his forge. Kydd waited for the piece to be returned to the fire.

'An' what can I do for ye, Sir Thomas?' Tovey said, wiping the beads of sweat from his reddened face.

'This bracket is all,' he replied, handing over the old, creakily worn hinge.

The blacksmith took one look and shook his head. 'Be takin' your cobbs for nothing should I do it. Y' needs a new 'un, no mistake.'

'So be it,' Kydd agreed, and became aware that there was another in the smithy behind Tovey. The man was silent, watching him carefully. In a fisherman's jersey and sea-boots, there was no mistaking his calling, but what he held caught Kydd's attention.

Those far-off days in *Teazer* when he'd waged war against the smugglers down the coast – it all came flooding back at the sight. With its dull black finish, cavernous interior, the removable lid and, above all, the long nozzle, it could be nothing else but a smuggler's spout lantern, a device that could funnel the light out to sea and not be seen from the shore.

At Kydd's gaze, Tovey defensively tried to move the object out of sight.

'Er, what's that you're holding, pray?' Kydd asked innocently.

Tovey eased into a tight smile. 'Why, bless ye, Squire. That there's a waterin' can as we use hereabouts on our plots o' greens. Gives extra reach as saves us a row or two o' walking.'

'Oh, I didn't know. A lot of new things I'm learning in Devon.'

The blacksmith and the other man visibly loosened.

'Well, I'll leave you to it, Mr Tovey. A good day to you both.'

Kydd went to the side door, closed it noisily, then tiptoed back behind the rack of tools that divided the workspace.

'Thursday. Must have it b' Thursday.' The man's tone was gruff and commanding.

'Oh, aye. Λ run then, is it? As will see me with a right true rummer in m' fist b' midnight?'

'Not this time, cully. Froggies only, it is. Thursday, I said?'

'Ye'll have it.'

Kydd withdrew quietly. He'd stumbled on an escape arrangement for French parole-breakers.

There was plenty of time to warn Nott. But what could a single man do – especially against an armed and dangerous smuggling gang? He'd have to alert the Revenue.

His note to the Salcombe Watch, the nearest, was curtly returned with an accompanying message that they'd be obliged should he allow that they knew their district better than he, and without intelligence of their own to corroborate, they would need considerably more evidence to move on it, short-handed as they were.

Kydd was damned if he'd let it go. He knew what he had seen.

In his mind he went over the old smuggling haunts along the coast between the Great Mewstone at the entrance to Plymouth Sound to the Bolt Head before its turn into the fleet anchorage of Torbay.

There were sandy beaches, some snugly concealed with good communication inland but, while they were fine for landing goods from boats and getting them away fast inland, what was needed was a well-sheltered hidden arm of the sea extending inland that could be approached stealthily, which would cloak the actual taking up of the men, and was far from meddlesome settlements.

In this rugged stretch of coast he could think of one that stood out from the others, which he knew well – the place he'd landed all those years ago with the young Lieutenant Binney, who'd then travelled overland to Plymouth to discover the truth about the great fleet mutiny.

The lieutenant was native to these parts and, taking a ship's boat, they had landed unseen, not far from Ivybridge, up from the mouth of the Erme.

It made a great deal of sense: the other two possibilities, Bigbury and the Yealm estuary, were overlooked by villages.

But if the Revenue didn't want to be involved, who was he to take action? If he were aboard *Tyger* it would be quite another matter. Could he call out the military? There was an army post at Wembury, he recalled, but files of redcoats, floundering about in the dark, was not the answer.

Just beyond Yealm Head, though, there was a small company of Sea Fencibles. A form of naval militia, they'd been originally created to stand against the waves of Bonaparte's invasion barges and still remained at their posts, for the threat had not gone away. Consisting of fishermen and others with sea experience, they trained weekly and, for their pains, were protected from impressment.

Chapter 7

The day before the planned run Kydd reconnoitred the area. It all came back: the meandering path through thick woodland to the water's edge where the rickety landing stage still existed; the Erme river, some hundreds of yards of placid water, with its right-hand bend leading a full two miles further to a bar before the open sea.

Kydd saw how the escapees could be brought down the path and assembled by the landing stage while the man with the spout lantern would stand at its end to sight and bring in the smuggler's boat.

The next day, as dusk drew in, Kydd had his men in place, well back from the path, out of sight in the undergrowth and armed with cutlass and pistol. The Sea Fencibles lieutenant stood with him. It was a cool evening, still and quiet. The moon would not rise for an hour – at this moment the smuggler would be ghosting inshore to lie off clear of the bar, then getting his boat in the water for the pull up the Erme shallows.

If he was right in his reasoning.

A far-off animal cry startled him but almost immediately

his senses came to a full alert. There was movement. He could not hear a thing but he knew in his bowels that somebody was abroad.

His eyes tried to penetrate the gloom: a luminous shimmer was beginning to assert itself, the prelude to moonrise. It would not be long now.

Kydd was just beginning to make out the sky as a loftier glow above the blackness of the earth when a sinister shadow passed noiselessly across his vision, followed by another and then another.

Down at the river there was low murmuring, whispers. He couldn't make his move just yet – he wanted to take the smugglers as well, and a false move might cause them to scatter and get away.

It was lightening by degrees as the moon began to lift, tingeing leaves with silver, a dancing glitter on the water, and down at the landing stage shadowy figures stood silently. If any of the Fencibles coughed or fidgeted, their quarry would melt into the night.

One of the figures moved out onto the landing stage. He reached the end and lifted the unmistakable spout lantern, carefully aiming it out into the blackness. Kydd tried to follow the direction and, before long, saw a dark blotch intrude on the moon-path. The boat.

Tense, he remained still as it drew nearer, then angled in, direct to the shadowy group. Fingering his boatswain's call, he waited until a line was thrown ashore when all eyes would be on the boat, then raised it to his lips and gave a fearsome single blast.

After a split second, the scene dissolved into chaos, shouts of rage mingling with whoops of satisfaction, vague shapes barrelling into the undergrowth. To Kydd's gratification, a hoarse bellow came that he recognised instantly, Tovey the blacksmith roaring into the night that they'd been betrayed and to run for their lives.

In the darkness it was impossible to make out how many they'd succeeded in apprehending. 'Round 'em up and secure them well,' he told the lieutenant. 'I'll be back.'

Kydd made his way to the Ivybridge smithy, slipped into the workshop and waited. Nearly an hour passed before he heard cautious steps approaching. There was the tap of steel on flint and a lantern threw out a fitful glow, revealing the dishevelled figure of Tovey, who set down the light with a sigh of relief.

'A shabby night's work,' Kydd said, stepping out of the shadows.

Tovey wheeled round, staring at him.

'Not to say paltry, as you're all taken up and must suffer at the assizes.'

There was no fear in the man's eyes, only a calculated wariness.

Kydd was ready for him. Before the big hands closed over a hammer shaft, he brandished a heavy hand mandrel. 'I've downed Frenchies twice your size,' he said, in measured tones.

'There's only the one o' yez.'

'For a reason.'

Tovey paused, his eyes narrowing. 'Oh?'

'You're headed for chokey, so your wife and little ones will go on the parish. You're not a bad 'un and I'd wish it were the other. And I've a mind to make it so.'

'What do ye mean?'

'I'll swear that no Frenchy ever stepped into that boat. In the eyes o' the law it was floating about in the river just at the same time you were taking the evening air. No one can prove you were doing anything else – what the Frenchmen were up to is their business.'

'Why are doing this'n?' Tovey said carefully, his voice low. 'Nothin' I can do back.'

'Yes, there is. You'll swear to me that you're done with this business for ever and all.'

The blacksmith remained silent.

'And tell me who's giving you your orders,' Kydd added.

Tovey looked away, still saying nothing.

'Else you bear all the punishment and he gets away with everything. Who says one has to take all the risks and the other none?'

The eyes dropped.

'Besides which, you tell me and none's to find who said it, for no one knows you spoke to me, do they?'

Chapter 8

The lieutenant of the Sea Fencibles was exultant. 'A splendid haul, Sir Thomas. All but one, who got away. We have five absconding French officers and the smugglers – you were right to station the launch and carronade behind Beacon Point. Took the lugger and then—'

'So you're now taking your haul in irons to the Wembury garrison?'

'Aye aye, sir.'

'Then please to lend me a few men, there's unfinished business.'

With a petty officer and three others close behind, he hurried through a sleeping, silent Ivybridge until he reached a house at the end of Fore Street, set back from the road. There were lights ablaze inside and Kydd sent a pair of men to the rear.

When they were in position he went to the door and gave a thunderous knock. 'Open! Open in the name of the King!'

Voices rose in protest and died. He hammered again and the door opened.

'Mr Morton?' he said, before the little man could speak.

'I'm taking you in charge. Aiding and abetting the King's enemies, a capital felony, sir.' Kydd was not certain this was true but he needed to bring pressure to bear.

Morton fell back in dismay. 'Y-you've no right to——'

Kydd gave a cynical smile. 'As squire of Knowle Manor and justice of the peace, I've every right. My men will now search your residence. Stand aside, please.'

'No! You can't——'

'Sir, I nabbed this 'un taking a run out the back.' The petty officer held a sullen-faced man secure, like a press-gang catch.

'Well, well. I think we'd better have a talk, sir. Inside?'

The furnishing of the drawing room was quite out of keeping with the prospects of a village merchant, and Kydd had no compunction in setting out the man's probable fate.

'Sir, you face the full rigour of the law. I cannot hold out hope for you in any wise.'

At the door a woman shrieked and fell senseless to the floor.

Chalk-faced Morton asked, 'How did you . . .?'

'You were informed upon, sir. I have many to swear in court to your complicity in these treasonous acts.' He let his gaze rest on the unfortunate man in weighty silence.

'Sir, I beg you, is there something I might do that . . . that . . .'

'Um. Attempting to bribe an officer of the law? This will not help you, sir.'

'Then?'

'A special plea in the higher court may answer.'

'Yes?'

'As will reduce your sentence to transportation to Botany Bay – for life.' Kydd felt a stab of guilt. The man was only a pawn in the hands of whoever was organising the escapes, but he had to get through to the principal by some means.

'There is, of course . . .'

'Yes?'

'You may wish to consider an alternative that may see you respited – even restored to liberty.'

'H-how?'

'By entering King's evidence, Mr Morton. If now you are open with me, uncover the workings of the arrangements, provide names, details, as shall put a stop to this iniquitous trade, then I'm sanguine you'll have nothing further to fear.'

When it came out, it was a wondrous tale.

Morton was one of a number of agents whose task was to find and cultivate a string of inns, coach drivers and others to pass along the absconders. The parole-breakers would be made to pay for their freedom and the agent, after seeing those involved were well rewarded, would pocket the remainder.

It was well organised. Instructions would come to him from the parole towns as French officers came forward to the organiser to buy themselves liberty, a line of escape then needing to be activated. This would come by secret means – in the case of Morton, he was to place a case of Flete Abbey tonic wine on the Tavistock stage once a week for the fraternity of French officers. It was in the empty bottles on return that his instructions would be concealed.

Kydd could see that much thought had gone into this: one on the inside, close to the Frenchmen who would generate the bids, and those on the outside making the vital local arrangements, each depending on the other.

The last question was the most important.

'Who then is your master, your principal?'

Morton said mechanically, 'French gent, Marceau. Navy officer.'

It hit Kydd like a blow from a fist – but who better to

draw in from the circle of French officers than those about him he knew could afford to abscond, and possibly even those who couldn't? And Nott had mentioned Marceau handled private remittances for his brother prisoners. His high talk about standing true by his word of parole: was that nothing more than keeping himself in post as organiser, and adding to an increasing fortune?

But it didn't ring true, given what he'd seen of the man. It was more likely that he was undertaking it like a military operation, setting up and carrying through actions that would result in valuable officers restored to French service, an object that he had reasoned transcended old-fashioned ideas of honour among gentlemen.

Or it could be that Morton was saying whatever came into his head – but he would gain nothing by it.

Kydd had to get proof, and there was one sure way of finding it.

It wasn't difficult. A cart came, stopping at the London Inn for the empty tonic wine bottles, and while the carter was refreshing himself, Kydd went to the row he'd been told about. Neatly spiralled in a thick brown bottle was a message. He took it, felt about and found four more.

Each was headed with the name of a bird: kingfisher, shrike, swallow, others, clearly a code for the right recipient. In the body was further writing – numbers, times, references to 'hedgehog' and 'stoat', no doubt referring to others down the line. It didn't matter: he had proof.

Nott was impressed, as much by Kydd's reasoning as the unmasking of the conspiracy. 'I'm to arrest the villain this instant. Shall you come, sir?'

'I will.'

But Kydd found he was strangely reluctant to be witness

to the final step. This distinguished and intelligent naval officer was destined for the misery of the prison hulks as a direct result of Kydd's acts – and it had been his original actions that had made him a prisoner in the first place.

'He's not at home,' the prim landlady of Marceau's lodging said, with heat. 'As he went out before ever it was morning and he leaving his rooms all ahoo.'

It was plain there'd been a hasty departure: scattered clothing and oddments spoke of a hurried selection of articles. With a pang Kydd saw on top of the dresser the bone ship.

Could he have been played for a fool? It would not be beyond Marceau's organising genius to have devised a communication method to keep him in contact with his ship's company, written it down as he had the bottle messages and concealed it in the sweetmeats. The ship model would be their way of relaying back to him that the channel was understood and open. And in both cases Kydd had been the unwitting courier.

'Our bird has flown,' Nott said sorrowfully, standing down the two constables. 'I'll send descriptions but I fear he's now gone.'

For a moment Kydd was glad he'd vanished.

No doubt Marceau, like himself, was willing to take chances for a larger goal. And if he was as true to his ship's company as Kydd was to *Tyger*'s, it raised some interesting questions. Would he callously leave them to their fate while he took advantage of his own escape arrangement? He doubted it.

Then did this mean he would do something about it? His pulse quickened.

In his place what would he do?

The Preussens were securely in the Millbay prison. It had been built to house American captives, and its location had been chosen to make it a short and easily guarded march from the docks up and through the massive gate. If he were contemplating any kind of escape or break-out there couldn't be a better place: the gates thrown open by some means, then a storming run down to the wharf, crowding aboard a waiting ship and putting to sea before anybody thought to move.

This was far-fetched, but quite in keeping with Marceau's intelligence and his undoubted bravery.

The thought wouldn't go away.

Then a more serious one began to take shape. If Marceau was going to take his men with him when he made his break, it had to be soon, before he was recognised and arrested.

Kydd's imagination filled in the rest. An urgent notification to the prisoners and another to the ship to come alongside and he would be at this very moment flying down to Plymouth to join them. It might be highly improbable but Kydd couldn't take the chance – he had to go and see for himself.

Chapter 9

Plymouth was in its usual crowded bustle and Millbay was no exception, boats a-swim, the docks working, cargo and carts of all description hurrying in every direction. Along the waterfront the sailors' taverns were alive with jollity.

A short distance up the hill was the grim face of the prison. It was all too easy to conjure the sight of those big double gates bursting open and a flood of men racing down the short distance to the ships.

He had to do something. Go to the authorities? With what? A carefully planned uprising in the prison would have to be kept concealed at all costs. If he went to them with his hypothetical tale of mass escape he'd be taken for a madman.

Kydd's mind raced. If he was right, a ship nearby would be prepared for the break – and almost certainly Marceau would be getting himself aboard in readiness.

He had to find that vessel. In dismay, Kydd looked around at the vast body of shipping. It would be impossible for him to search every one. He needed help.

At a run he made for the nearest tavern, the Mermaid. Still in his comfortable country breeches and gaiters he threw open the door and bawled, 'A Tyger! Any Tyger, ahoy – I need a Tyger!'

The noise fell away in astonishment then Brewster, a fore-topman, pot in hand, called from the rear, 'Aye, Cap'n – what can we do for ye?'

'Where's gunner's mate Stirk take his noggin?'

'Why, the China Gate, just along, sir.' There was growing incredulity as it spread about who was asking. Several sailors got to their feet to see better as Kydd waved an acknowledgement and left hurriedly. Some spilled out into the street in curiosity.

The China Gate was an old but well-favoured establishment. It was no stranger to King's men wanting to be away from the usual haunts in dock.

He found Stirk in the snug with Doud and Pinto. They looked up in bewilderment at seeing their captain before them. 'Toby, can ye bear a fist?' Kydd said breathlessly, unconsciously falling back into seaman's lingo.

It took him just minutes to set out the situation and then, with a whoop, they hurried outside, quickly joined by others.

'A ship o' size, high in the water – no freighting but outward bound.' Kydd was guessing but it was a reasonable assumption. 'Probably a neutral.'

With a dozen or more men spreading out it wasn't long before there was a brisk hail from Pinto, pointing at a barque, *Marie Cristobal* of Bremen. With no sign of handling cargo, not only was she sea-ready with sail bent onto the yards, but significantly her lines ashore had been singled up, boats in the water ready for hauling off.

And a lack of crew was telling: just one figure on her poop looking down in dismay. She could easily be crewed by the fleeing captives.

It fitted.

Kydd ran up the brow, Stirk close behind. 'In the King's name!' he roared at the quaking ship-keeper, who rapidly stepped aside. 'Get below, see if you can rouse up the Frenchy,' he told Stirk.

'The glory hole, begob!'

Kydd grinned. This was the hideaway most merchant ships possessed for valuable men they wanted hidden from the press. 'Go to it, Toby.'

In minutes he'd returned with a struggling Marceau. 'Scragged the bugger! An' there's a couple more we've caught with him as can wait.'

Marceau gave a sorrowful shrug but said nothing.

Kydd had his proof. He could give warning and be believed – but in his surge of satisfaction, an iron coolness intervened.

Millbay opened out directly into Plymouth Sound and the open sea. The obvious time to set sail was at the top of the tide, catching the full flow of the ebb. And that would be in a very short while, at a little after three – in less than fifteen minutes.

There would have to be a meticulously prepared form of revolt of all the Preussens at the same instant, timed to happen at the turn of the tide. Therefore what better signal to rise up than the prison clock striking the hour nearest this?

It had to be.

Kydd snatched out his fob watch – bare minutes to go.

It would be no good warning the prison – that would tip off the plotters and trigger the uprising. The nearest military were the Royal Marines in Stonehouse barracks, a good half an hour away. To get to them, turn out a fair-sized detachment and march them back would take more than an hour, far too late. The Citadel, the main garrison fort? But that was on the other side of Plymouth Hoe, even further.

Only one thing could stop the break and Kydd didn't hold

back. 'Toby, we put blockade on the chokey until we get help. Rouse out every hand from the taphouses to muster at the prison gate. Those who come I'll square up with a good fist o' stingo afterwards.'

With roars of good humour the taverns began clearing of seamen, who converged on the prison gate carrying improvised weapons – lumps of wood, chair legs, fire pokers.

At the massive black gates they stopped, spreading out as more and more arrived, fifty, a hundred, two hundred.

Above, in the walkway of the clock tower, a sentry gaped down at the throng. As he did so the clock struck three – and almost immediately he was snatched out of sight.

'Stand by!' Kydd hissed.

From inside there were scuffles, shouts and a single shot.

The gates swung wide and a flood of prisoners raced out impatiently.

They were met with a vast roar from the King's men, who fell on them with a will. Swinging their weapons gleefully in an unholy scrimmage, they were soon driving them back inside.

'Hold the gate!' Kydd bellowed.

They'd won – and a little later came the sound of marching feet as the Royal Marines swung into view, responding to a hasty note Kydd had sent when he'd apprehended Marceau.

Chapter 10

The Bay of Biscay

Kydd squinted up into the shrieking rigging, clinging to a shroud as *Tyger* laboured in the heavy weather, her deck heaving and falling as the seas on her quarter added a vicious twist to her motions.

Just days after the prisoner escape attempt had been foiled, Kydd had sailed to join Admiral Collingwood's fleet in its traditional station off Cádiz. Now he was facing a North Atlantic blow of unseasonal vileness.

Long known as a 'foul-weather jack', Kydd took grave pleasure in Nature's sensual assault of wind and seas, a tactile reminder that a prudent mariner never defied Neptune but was always ready to concede, conform, then turn to account the wild ride to follow.

'We'll take a double reef in those topsails,' he ordered. The big driving courses had long since been furled and, in deference to the wind's direction relative to their track, most head-sails had been taken in as well.

The hard conditions were unrelenting, but on their way

around Ushant from Plymouth, they'd distantly sighted the Brest blockade squadron, hardly recognisable in the flying white murk, in line ahead, contemptuously leaving close to leeward the frightful chain of rocks out from Pointe du Toulinguet.

Those ships had endured for months in this hard weather and would faithfully stay where they were into the indefinite future, locking the door on the great French fleet that lay within Brest. How could *Tyger* complain when her orders were sending her on through this to the sub-tropical balminess of Cádiz?

It had been sobering to learn from the Plymouth port admiral in his instructions on sailing that Bonaparte was far from resigned to the stalemate that saw him victorious but impotent on land while England roamed the seas without rival. Since Trafalgar, he'd acquired through conquest and a massive shipbuilding effort at least eighty line-of-battle ships, more than replacing his losses, with another twenty on order. And all the time the invasion fleet of barges in the French Channel ports remained at the ready, their numbers ever-increasing.

The only reason they hadn't been unleashed in an all-conquering storm on the shores of Britain was the watchfulness of the blockade squadrons lying relentlessly athwart the big naval ports of France, preventing their combining together in an irresistible armada.

Stretched to their limits, the Channel Fleet kept the seas off Cherbourg, Brest, Rochefort and many minor ports. Other squadrons clamped their hold on the Spanish at Ferrol, Corunna and Cádiz, while the Mediterranean Fleet kept a tight grip on Toulon. Absence or failure in their task would be calamitous; in fair weather or foul the heavy battleships were on station within rapid striking distance of the enemy harbours, while frigates and a host of smaller craft daily sailed within sight of the berths and anchorages in daring reconnaissance.

Kydd glanced forward as the fore-topsail was laid for reefing. It took judgement to brace it around to the right angle to take the strain off the canvas and allow the men out on the yard. He liked to see the sail just lifting rather than the fretful movements of 'splitting the wind'. This was being done, and he was pleased to see Brice on deck, standing back to let Midshipman Rowan make the call. The young lad, who'd initially disarmed him with eyes so like Persephone's, was showing promise.

The weather braces rounded in and reef tackles hauled out, the topmen passed the second reef, pinning the first to the big spar lowered just enough. It was a lively, well-orchestrated show performed simultaneously on all three masts, a feat that would have entranced a circus audience.

Tyger responded with a will, her roll lessening, the thump of her bow working into the seas less violent. As he always did, Kydd warmed to her bluff and hearty ways. This was a ship he could take into any peril, knowing she would not fail him.

The wind in his teeth and the taste of salt spray was such a contrast to the rural tranquillity of Knowle Manor, now just a warm memory. He and Persephone had parted lovingly, she now in possession of a detailed ship's chart of the Iberian coast and he with a lock of her hair in a silver box, while *Tyger*'s cabin spaces now boasted a fine show of rural Devon miniatures around the bulkhead. Blockade could be long and tedious but he would not want for reminders of home.

Dillon had procured stocks of books in anticipation, his fascination with languages apparently limitless. The gunroom had laid in various defences against ennui and Kydd knew the long-service seamen had, besides their scrimshaw and needlework, any number of games of chance, from the venerable and illegal Crown and Anchor to cards and dice.

'Glass dropping, sir,' remarked the sailing master, Joyce. 'As I recollects once in 'eighty-five after the American war. *Raisonnable* frigate, we was, or was it 'eighty-six? Anyways . . .'

Kydd let the man chatter: a yarn-spinner was a marked asset on watch in dirty weather. Each of the officers had a fund of experiences and memories they could draw upon, and at every telling, a yarn would grow taller. A man of years with the navy could be relied on to pull out a story to suit any occasion and need never fear to be scorned.

'A black line squall out o' the north, that's what did for us . . .'

Joyce had seen more than most: ships long gone, men lost to history but not to their shipmates – even Nelson, as a junior lieutenant. This translated to a compendious and sweeping acquaintance with the sea world that was priceless in a tight situation. He had a wife in Sheerness and never failed to bring fascinating curios to her in an attempt to ward off her nagging that it was time for him to retire to the land. But Kydd knew that the only way Joyce would quit *Tyger* was with 'DD' next to his name in the muster roll – 'Discharged Dead'. Would he himself at some point leave the sea for good? He knew Persephone would never press him to do so, and while Bonaparte continued to threaten England he had his duty. Yet who could foretell the future?

Scud was beginning to drive across the sky in ragged streamers below an ugly grey background of cloud. It would get blashier before it got better, and the watch hunkered down below the bulwarks.

'We've a current with this blow, Mr Joyce. Shall we ease to loo'ard, do you think? We've offing enough, I believe.'

As always, the master paused, sniffing the wind fastidiously as though seeking an answer from its origins, then allowed that he thought it possible.

Tyger fell away a little, the coast of France under her lee still a good dozen leagues distant. Their change of tack across the north of Spain would take care of the additional easting but now the frigate was more in tune with the wave motion and gratifyingly more comfortable.

Kydd went below to take his noon meal with the thought that, by forty degrees latitude, they would probably clear this roil of thick weather, a matter of a couple of days at most. They were fully stored and watered and could look to immediate employment in Collingwood's scouts or cruisers. A storm-worn and fatigued frigate would in turn be released to its well-earned rest.

He'd hardly started on his soup when his ears pricked. Against the solid roar of the wind he'd heard a faint hail from the tops. A lookout had seen something: mindful of the wear and tear on her gear a merchant ship would not be making the crossing of Biscay in this weather. Only a warship would be keeping the seas.

At this latitude it was probably one of the Rochefort blockaders, even if she was quite a distance out and therefore off-station. There would be no need to close with her.

Kydd continued with his soup, in a half-filled bowl and on a neat doily wetted to prevent it sliding into his lap.

There were more hails. The entire squadron this far seaward? He frowned but stayed with his soup – it was good.

Bray knocked on the door. 'Sir – sail to the east'd and signals us.'

This could not be by flag: nothing could be seen at that distance. It had to be a throwing a-fly of the fore-topsail or other contrivance to attract attention.

'Very well. I'll be on deck directly. Bear away for him, if you please.' There was still time to finish the soup.

When Kydd made the quarterdeck, not only was the vessel in sight but others had been spotted beyond. 'Interesting,' he muttered. 'This is certainly the Rochefort squadron – that's Sir Richard Strachan's command, o' course. And those are his sail-o'-the-line. Bear up for *Cæsar*, his flag – that big eighty-gun fellow in the middle.'

The fleet was in extended order of sailing over miles of sea but it was hardly making way.

Tyger came up with the flagship and hove to, gratefully in the lee of the two-decker.

'*Cæsar*, ahoy! *Tyger* frigate bound for Cádiz station as per orders.'

A figure in the waist hailed back, but the roaring wind snatched away the words.

'Cannot . . . hear . . . you!' Kydd bellowed, gesticulating unmistakably.

The figure threw down his speaking-trumpet in vexation, then, in exaggerated movements, indicated a launch alongside, pitching and heaving. The largest boat aboard, it had been put in the water as *Tyger* approached.

Its crew tumbled in, double-banking the oars, then pushed off into the narrow sheltered area between the two ships. This gave Kydd time to don oilskins and sea boots, and when it thumped alongside, he grasped a man-rope and dropped into the wildly bucking boat. He was helped into *Cæsar* and led aft to the half-deck under the poop, where a ruddy-faced officer waited.

'My thanks for coming aboard in this, sir,' he opened gruffly. 'As you may believe, it is of a dire necessity.' Under a worn cloak Kydd caught the gleam of an admiral's lace.

'Sir Thomas Kydd, captain, *Tyger* 32—'

'What's your state?' Strachan wanted to know how fit his ship was for sea.

'Just out of dockyard, water and stored, orders to join Admiral Collingwood off Cádiz and—'

'Sent from heaven above, by God! You're now taken under orders, Kydd.'

'Sir? I can't—'

'You can and will,' the admiral snapped. 'For one very good reason. The French are out, damn it, and I'm at a frightful stand. Until you came along, that is.'

'May I know—'

'Why they came out and why aren't I after them? It's simple. This dirty weather stopped the victuallers attending on the fleet. We're down to our last piece o' hard tack, no more beef or pork, and in distress for water. I came out to see if I could find what's holding 'em and Allemand took the chance to put to sea with six o'-the-line, which includes a brute 120-gun first rate. It's obvious to anyone I can't go after 'em, no endurance.'

It was the very thing to be feared above all others. If this force joined with one more it would need another Trafalgar to put it down.

'Then—'

'As of this moment you are to go after them and stay with 'em wherever they go. Mark my words, sir – you lose them at your peril!'

Kydd knew this meant doggedly keeping them in sight and sending word back as and when he could. Pursuing battle fleets would thus be spared useless casting this way and that in a futile search of an empty ocean or, worse, the splitting of forces to look into every possible bolt-hole.

It was a frigate's job, and *Tyger* was eminently fitted for the task.

'Aye aye, sir. Um, your orders, sir?'

'You'll have them directly.' Written orders, albeit brief, would be needed to justify to the Admiralty the withdrawing of a valuable frigate from the order of battle, however important the object.

Tyger got under way without delay while Kydd wrestled with his conundrum – sail north or south, or even west across the Atlantic? Strachan had seen the French once only, heading out into the murk just hours before, but had no indication of their eventual course.

If north it could only be Brest – where Allemand would meet the traditionally largest blockade fleet. It would be well matched to his own in any confrontation with no assurance of being able to push past to a combining. Not really a choice for the French.

If south, then the possibilities were many more.

Along the north coast of Spain, in Ferrol and Vigo, there were concentrations of naval strength. These were sufficient for the Admiralty to mount a squadron of deterrence but not enough to attract as a strategic destination for Allemand's break-out.

Further on was Lisbon, newly taken by Bonaparte and a major port. Still with no French naval presence to speak of, it was an obvious objective. Kydd could make straight for the north-west corner of Spain, trusting he'd pass Allemand and his squadron sailing at the speed of the slowest and be in place to intercept them before they made their southing to Lisbon.

The fresh gale increased, its spiteful blast sending painful stinging spray across the deck but Kydd relished it. The lighter-built French ships would be at a disadvantage in these conditions and could not carry on sailing like *Tyger*, built for ranging the oceans of the globe.

Once he sighted them, all uncertainty would vanish: he'd clamp a hold on them like a bulldog for as long as it took to bring up the British battle fleets – *if* he was right in his reasoning about Lisbon.

Their new course meant the north-westerly was coming in from directly abeam, hard and savage, driving surging rollers mercilessly at *Tyger's* sides in an unending series of white-capped combers. However, Kydd kept bar-taut high canvas aloft that took the wind's force in a constant stream and held the masts a-slant, while the fierce waves coming in merely lifted and settled the ship as they passed under her keel.

The high, craggy coastline of Galicia appeared ahead as the day broke, bare mountains, dark and bleak, above a band of white mist thrown up by the Atlantic in its age-old battering of the land.

Kydd had now firmed his plans. Whatever their final desti-nation, Allemand's squadron must round this corner. A little further was Ferrol but they had to pass him first to make it.

Here they would stand off and on for three days, and if the enemy was not sighted in that time he would have to accept that he was wrong and must think again.

For the rest of the day there was no sign of them as the gale blew itself out. At night they were granted a gibbous moon that would throw a passing fleet into stark shadows – but none came.

Chapter 11

The next day opened on a dreary waste of tumbling waters, but as the light strengthened a cry came from the masthead. Sail had been sighted further out to sea, not one but several – many.

In huge relief, Kydd set *Tyger* to close and quickly had his glass up.

It was a grand and fearsome sight. The great four-decked battleship was Allemand's 120-gun behemoth. Accompanying it, in a loose gaggle, were four 74s and an escorting frigate on either beam. With them was a cloud of sloops and victuallers. This was a full-fledged sortie out for trouble – and Kydd had been proved right in his thinking.

Possibly they thought that *Tyger* had chanced on them, part of the watch and guard squadron off Ferrol or further to the south. Whether this or any other conclusion, the reaction would be the same – they'd expect the frigate to close with them to get a measure of their force, then spread all possible sail in a hurried dash to warn the British fleet commander, unavoidably giving away its position.

This was not how it would be, though: *Tyger* was a scout

with an independent command and would not be quitting her place. It would be a challenge to get a warning off but Strachan had made its final destination their overriding goal.

Easing her helm, *Tyger* fell away, letting the squadron pass well out to sea, a succession of men-o'-war in baleful and arrogant progress, who took no interest in breaking formation to go after a single frigate. Kydd kept his ship sidling around their rear for he wanted to make observations and to end in position to windward. For once, the stormy winds were with them: brisk and hard from the north-west they were unchanging and therefore reliable. *Tyger* slipped into place downwind of the enemy and began her relentless shadowing.

'Take this down, Mr Dillon,' Kydd said, bracing his telescope.

One by one he detailed what he saw, other officers contributing their count until a fair picture of what faced them emerged – in strength equal to any the English could bring against them and, if combined with those lurking in port, an irresistible force. An uneasy quiet reigned about *Tyger*'s deck as men stared across the tumbling seas, none in any doubt of the deadly significance.

As the day wore on the squadron's track revealed itself – past the dark crags and precipices of the extreme north of Spain southward to the Costa da Morte, the Coast of Death.

Ferrol was within thirty or forty miles, then Corunna. If neither of these was their destination, it would be around the stark headland of Finisterre for the plunge directly south past Vigo to Lisbon. A day's sail.

They left Ferrol and Corunna out of sight well to leeward, as Kydd had expected, but then everything changed.

In the fading light of dusk the bleak ruggedness of Finisterre passed astern, but the course they'd taken to round the corner of Spain was held – at south-west, diagonally out to sea instead of the drop south.

Then both French frigates fell away from the line and, wearing about purposefully, made for *Tyger*.

It was a move to be rid of their stubborn pursuer: Kydd had not made off inshore to alert the nearest squadron, which implied he was an independent, bent on staying with them and their eventual purpose.

Kydd immediately gave his orders. As if in dismay, *Tyger* sheered away, heading inshore. The two followed, barrelling along in the stiff winds, drawing apart to make sure of intercepting.

A wan twilight was all that was left of the day.

Suddenly *Tyger* hauled her wind and, in a dizzying curve, took up as close to the breeze as she could, then headed back out to sea. Too late, the two frigates realised they'd been deceived, swinging about in an ungainly rush. But Kydd had won through and was making his offing.

In the fading light the squadron's sails were still in sight but Kydd didn't care if they disappeared. His move had ensured he held a trump card: he could keep up this manoeuvring as long as they wished it, but in the end, inevitably, they had to break off to resume escort on their commander and his squadron. In so doing they indicated its whereabouts, like a pointing finger.

Kydd's duty was to keep from engaging or undertaking any risky act that could result in a reduction in capability. The stakes were too high.

And his plan depended on his ship having the speed to get away and close as needed. However, the Royal Navy had an unbeatable edge. It kept the seas in all weathers, honing ships and men to perfection, while the French were bottled up in harbour for months at a time with little opportunity to shape raw crews to the same degree of skill. All other things equal, the Royal Navy could out-manoeuvre and out-sail their opponents.

In these fresh winds *Tyger* was comfortable and secure and, recently docked, had a clean bottom; Kydd would have no qualms about clapping on sail. If, however, the weather turned light and placid the finer-lined French craft – as his old *L'Aurore* – would relish the conditions and it would be a different story.

He put it out of his mind. There was quite sufficient to worry about for now.

Chapter 12

The two frigates made their move. First one, then the other vessel broke off, presumably to rejoin Allemand. Intelligently, they took contrasting courses: which was the feint away from the squadron?

But it didn't matter. In the end both hapless captains had to head for their squadron and as long as Kydd stayed with one the result would be the same.

In the gathering gloom there were betraying flashes of white wake but they faded as night drew in and Kydd brought *Tyger* closer, letting the dark shape of the frigate loom unmistakably out on their bow. This was the hardest part. So close, any sudden move of the enemy could catch *Tyger* unaware and bring about an engagement he must avoid, and in the shadows they could be up to anything. He doubled the lookouts and had the watch-on-deck take position by the sheets and braces in readiness.

Night became absolute.

At a glass past nine, before the betraying moonrise, simultaneous shouts rang out along *Tyger*'s deck. The chase had suddenly altered course to take the wind more on her quarter and was heading away quickly.

Kydd's orders came crisply and *Tyger* swung about to follow, well before the frigate was swallowed in the darkness. Almost certainly this was now the intersecting course for the squadron.

Crossing to the binnacle, he looked down at the dim compass card. Uneasy, he glanced up to meet the master's steady gaze. 'Makes not a lot of sense,' Joyce said, in a low voice. 'Sou'-sou'-west is fair for the trades, not much else. Where's the villain off to?'

The north-easterly trade winds were what impelled ships past Iberia to Africa and beyond. This course would take them ridiculously far out to sea from Lisbon, if that was ever their goal.

'We stay with him,' Kydd ordered.

Hour by hour they stretched out into the Atlantic. The moon lifted above the horizon, gilding fretful clouds and spreading a hard glitter on the dark seas, throwing the frigate into sharp relief. They could not lose it now.

But it was unreadable: if this was a true course to meet up with the squadron it could be bound anywhere – across the Atlantic to the Caribbean, around Africa to the Indian Ocean, as the French Admiral Linois had done earlier, or even south to round the Horn . . .

The chase continued through the night and into the grey day following.

Then, with no warning, an hour or so after midday, the frigate threw her helm over and, directly before the wind, charged down on *Tyger*.

Kydd's rapid orders had his ship conforming at once and sheering off out of its way – but the Frenchman didn't vary his course, plunging on without deviation, past *Tyger* and away.

And suddenly Kydd understood. Quick work with a Gunter's scale on the Iberian chart confirmed his reasoning.

'Allemand's made a dogleg to seaward to get around Cádiz without being seen by Collingwood's scouts. If we extend the second leg back we get a point of intersection as near as damn it to thirty-six and twenty degrees to Gibraltar's thirty-six and eight. The beggar's headed into the Med!'

Kydd had relied on falling in with one of the many cruisers and sloops that were part of the Iberian blockade to tell the news of Allemand's breakout. As he'd been unable to do so, the intelligence was still not known this far south. The prospect of a powerful force entering the vitally strategic waters of the Mediterranean had to be passed on.

But Allemand was no fool. He'd transit the Strait of Gibraltar under cover of darkness. If Kydd left the pursuit to go in to warn them, it was at the risk of being trapped in the notorious currents and failing in his primary task, which was never to let them out of his sight.

The frigate was joined by the other at six degrees west longitude, and later in the day the massed sails of Allemand's squadron lifted above the horizon. Kydd had been right, but his hands were tied. Frigates on scouting duties were usually sent in pairs or with fast cutters in company for just this situation; by no fault of Strachan's, he hadn't been able to detach one to get the intelligence to where it was most needed.

And Kydd found he was correct on another matter: under easy sail the squadron idled the afternoon away, then headed out from the dying sun into the strait, just a dozen or so miles across.

He closed up gun crews. With Gibraltar's lights twinkling faintly to larboard, the stealthy passage of the squadron in the night was rudely interrupted by the flash and blast of a full-blooded eighteen-pounder, then another, and another, like a minute gun in fog. Kydd was hoping to signal the presence of ships and that Gibraltar would send out a vessel to see what the fuss was about.

No doubt Allemand would be beside himself with rage at the impudence, but if he sent any of his force against *Tyger*, their guns would add to his and the whole world would be awakened to the deed. But no sail was sent out to investigate, and well before dawn the French squadron, with wind and current urging them on, had slipped through.

This was now a grave state of affairs. As far as Kydd was aware, he was the only one with the knowledge of what was happening and now they'd passed into an entirely hostile sea. The nearest British were the storm-tossed blockaders off Toulon, some thousand miles onwards, and a friendly port was even further – in Sicily, halfway through the Mediterranean.

As for Allemand's final goal, this was exactly the same position Nelson had faced before the Nile when he'd had to criss-cross the great sea for months, looking for his quarry, before finally running it down. It couldn't be allowed to happen again.

Grimly, Kydd set *Tyger* to her task.

The privateer lair and Spanish frigate refuge of Málaga was left well to larboard and they sailed deeper into the Mediterranean, the weather easing.

Off Cartagena, course was set up the coast, and when Ibiza was sighted, a low grey-blue against a morning mist – and to starboard – Kydd's suspicions sharpened. Some two or three days' sailing directly ahead was the biggest naval base in the Mediterranean: Toulon. If he was right, Allemand's plan was to combine with Ganteaume's fleet under blockade there. Together they would be unbeatable over anything the British had in the western Mediterranean.

He toyed with the idea of breaking off and flying back to

Gibraltar to raise the alarm. Urgency hammered at him but he took the decision to stay with them as they made steady progress north-east, a Toulon destination very probable.

Yet there was one comfort. There, he would come up with friends, the blockading squadron beating offshore, and he could hand over his burden, then water and victual.

They sailed on until ahead lay the frowning mountains surrounding the port – and before it a frigate Kydd recognised as *Phoenix*, Captain Mudge, his senior. There was nothing that the two frigates could do to interfere with the squadron's passage and they drew apart to see it proceed inside to its rest.

The two ships lay together in the slight swell as Kydd hailed to pass his news.

Mudge cut him short: 'I'm on my own here. *Active* is down the coast. Admiral Collingwood at present lies in Syracuse, and we have other sail-o'-the-line in Palermo. You've done your duty, sir, now allow me to do mine, to let 'em know how it is. Do remain on station, if you please, until relieved.'

It was galling but *Tyger* was an outsider, *Phoenix* one of them. The frigate lost no time in spreading canvas and was soon out of sight, leaving *Tyger* to continue on watch.

Morning broke on a dreary sea. The few fishermen abroad witnessed *Tyger* make the usual foray inshore to take a peek down the length of the harbour. But what Kydd saw chilled him: the inner harbour was alive with shipping under way for the open sea.

Singly and in gaggles the French fleet was issuing out, in numbers that could only mean Allemand had combined with Ganteaume. That the sortie had happened the day after Allemand's arrival implied that the lengthy and hazardous breakout had been carefully planned. No lean battle-fleet, it included a nucleus of transports – store-ships, troopers, horse-carriers, powder hoys, a military enterprise on the move.

One thing was frighteningly clear: a mighty force was now on its way to make challenge for Neptune's trident, and *Tyger* was the only one to know it.

Should he go to find *Active*, said to be somewhere down the coast, or race after *Phoenix* to add his shocking news? Even as he pondered, Kydd knew there was only one answer: as before, stay with them, never let them leave his sight until the end objective was known.

Chapter 13

The armada, with the same north-westerly now on their quarter, made best speed to the south. Twice frigates tried to circle and close on *Tyger* but the elements were not on their side; any diversion from this swift advance required that time be made up beating back and this they evidently didn't have.

Where were they headed? With Corsica and Sardinia somewhere out to larboard and the Spanish coast five hundred miles to starboard, it could be anywhere. But when they reached the latitude of Sicily there had to be a decision. With North Africa ahead, it was either left or right – the eastern or western Mediterranean: Gibraltar and the open Atlantic, or Egypt and the Middle East, the wind fair for either.

At thirty-eight degrees the choice was made.

'The Levant – eastern Mediterranean,' Kydd said, half in relief, half in bafflement.

'Turkey!' declared Bray.

'Greece, as they'll want to bargain with the Turks,' Bowden, the second lieutenant, said immediately.

'Mr Brice?'

'In course, Syria as will give 'em the other side of the strait,' the third lieutenant replied.

Kydd didn't argue. This was now more than a mere matter of opinion. He had to get the intelligence to Collingwood without losing touch before they disappeared in the far reaches of the distant eastern sea. And *Tyger* herself was far from in the best shape to press on with the wild chase. There'd been no opportunity to recover from the hard wearing of rigging in the stormy weather off Iberia, and in the lighter breezes now it was essential to have all taut and trim. Not to mention finding water to replenish their casks.

Especially galling was the knowledge that, while they made a broad reach on to the south of Sicily, Collingwood and his Mediterranean Fleet, according to Mudge, were in the north, at Palermo. *Tyger* was helpless to tell them that, on just the opposite side of Sicily, they would find the French armada they'd been yearning to meet at sea for many years.

But as the ragged shoreline of the ancient island firmed out of the haze, Kydd came up with a plan. He'd set one of the ship's boats afloat in the open sea, to round the island, proceeding along the north coast to find Collingwood and alert him to the awesome threat to his south. The launch, under sail with volunteers, would be commanded by Brice, a first-class seaman.

An open-boat voyage was no mean exploit, as well he knew. Bad weather springing up out at sea could overwhelm the little craft well before it reached safety, and it was prey to even the smallest enemy vessel. But it must carry the priceless intelligence of Ganteaume's breakout to Collingwood or perish in the attempt.

As darkness stole in, *Tyger* sent the boat on its way, low calls of encouragement and wishes for good luck following it into the night.

Taking up again, the lone frigate closed with the darkened shapes and resumed her vigil.

Through the next day and the next, the ships sailed on, leaving Cape Passaro and the last of Sicily astern and entering the eastern Mediterranean.

And their destination was at last revealed.

'This battle-fleet and invading transports – only for Corfu?' Bray rumbled.

'The Ionians,' Dillon said quietly. 'As Bonaparte was at pains to demand of the Russians at Tilsit. The keys to the Adriatic. Now he controls both sides of the entrance – if he can sustain and defend them.'

'So you're saying this is naught but a reinforcing?'

'If you were a French commander, would you think anything less than a cloud of battleships as cover for your venture, knowing the dread Admiral Collingwood lurks somewhere in the offing?'

'I do believe you may be in the right of it, Mr Dillon,' Kydd agreed. 'We'll soon see.'

In hours after the sighting of Zante, the first of the Ionians, the fleet broke up. Each division, closely escorted by an unassailable ship-of-the-line, made for one of the seven islands and began discharging. Kydd's long chase was over, the mystery solved.

There was little he could do to stop them. The French had planned well: an escort of invulnerable dimensions to take the transports safely to their destination, and as well to ensure their delivery to each individual garrison. It was not a battle-fleet Kydd had been following but a simple convoy with an outsize safeguard.

He'd done right to alert Collingwood, but now the

commander-in-chief would be at sea on his way to meet the threat he'd warned of. He must complete his report with the true situation.

Leaving the scene, Kydd reversed course and laid his bowsprit westward. Within a day he had intercepted his commander-in-chief.

Ocean was flagship of a powerful fleet that included every ship-of-the-line that could be brought together, but at *Tyger*'s appearing with urgent signals, the order to heave to was given and Kydd took boat to report.

'Sir, it's Corfu – the Ionians.'

Quickly he detailed what he'd seen and his reasoning that led to his quitting the chase.

Clearly relieved, the weary admiral broke into a smile. 'You may rest content, sir. You have done your duty nobly – as did the officer of your ship's boat that set me to sea. As to Ganteaume, his claim to triumph for his fleet is naught but the filling of the bellies of a lonely garrison, a paltry enough pretence, I believe.'

'Yet he's at sea at this moment, sir. A battle-fleet of size that's at large and—'

'Which at this point I fancy he'll desire to preserve at all costs – and now has no use beyond trying conclusions with myself, which I greatly doubt. No, sir, if he's not this very hour scuttling back to Toulon, you have my express leave to call me a Dutchman.'

Kydd returned his smile. 'Then, sir, I report *Tyger* as joining your fleet as per Admiralty orders, wanting only victuals and water to return to active service.'

'Captain, you shall please me no greater should you do so, then fall back on Cádiz to await me there. This alarum is now concluded and I look to joining you for a modicum more restful existence.'

Chapter 14

The Escorial Palace, San Lorenzo, Spain

'It's blundering lunacy, makes no sense – none at all!' Chancellor Godoy spluttered, throwing the sheaf of ill-written dispatches to the floor and pacing nervously to and fro.

His grand secretary Enrique Herrera picked them up, his stooped frame creaking under the effort. When he rose it was with heavy patience and mute resentment – Godoy was the King's principal minister and held all power, but he was blind to what was happening, most of it the direct result of his own inept ambition.

'Look at it! The idiots are turning our soldiers out of their own castles and moving in as if they were their private estates!'

Herrera held his tongue. The French were arrogant, over-bearing and difficult, to be expected of the liege men of Napoleon Bonaparte, the master of all Europe. And now, while the secret Treaty of Fontainebleau allowed their divisions to cross Spain and fall jointly on Portugal, they were taking their time about it, advancing into Spain as though into an enemy country, insisting on securing strong-points and leaving garrisons in their wake.

The treaty made explicit provision for how it was to be done: a long column moving forward on each side of the country to unite at the Portuguese border. Yet there seemed to be no pattern in what they were doing, taking whichever road they fancied in alarming numbers.

'Confound it, as if we've not enough to worry on, they're upsetting the rabble by their antics. God's bones, but it's a trial!'

'*Principe*, the people do not know of the secret treaty. All they see is Frenchmen marching into Spain. Can you blame them for being restless?'

'Bonaparte should heed what I say,' Godoy burst out. 'The stakes are clear and he risks losing all for want of a little patience.'

Their room was high up in the austere palace that was the administrative centre of the Spanish Empire, but faint noises could be heard from below – crowds pressed up against the railings, demanding the King show himself and reassure them that this was no French plot. Well, they were going to be disappointed, mused Godoy, bitterly. King Carlos had departed for his usual sojourn in Aranjuez, his summer palace thirty miles away.

The reply he'd received from the Emperor of France to his offer of a marriage alliance between the Crown Prince of Spain, the Prince of Asturias, Fernando, and a Bonaparte princess was quite out of all understanding. The haughty Marshal Duroc in Paris had replied on behalf of his master that the proposal was tainted, given that the prince had so recently been arrested and condemned by his own father.

Godoy asked himself time and time again: why had he

turned it down? By this simple dynastic act he could have secured an unparalleled position of influence and bound the two nations as close as he desired without the need of complex diplomatic or even military manoeuvring.

Voices sounded outside and the Conde de Montijo strode in, the quick-tempered court functionary whose family had been grandees of Spain before the time of the virtuous King Felipe II and who never ceased to provoke Godoy as he plotted and schemed against him.

'Ha! What are you doing here, Godoy, when the French are marching on us? Hey?'

'Calm yourself, Montijo. You know of the treaty and—'

'You've not heard the news,' the man said, with fat satisfaction. 'They're not telling you, are they?'

'What are you prating about?'

'Your French friends are overreaching themselves, Godoy. Now that toad Murat is himself on the march – to Madrid!'

Godoy went cold. There could be little mistaking the significance of the act. His entire understanding with Bonaparte had degenerated into a one-sided disdainful keeping-at-a-distance. 'There are military reasons for this, or do you not perceive them?' he said icily.

'I perceive that the people and the Cortes want explanation of why the French are here at all. Can you give 'em one?'

'Yes, of course,' Godoy said venomously. 'Now be so good as to leave us. I've much to do.'

With a dark chuckle, the man departed.

Godoy tried to make sense of the situation. Murat, chosen by Bonaparte to be the head of all French forces in Iberia, was unscrupulous, aggressive and vain. To be openly marching on the capital in defiance of the provisions of the treaty would need the complicity of his emperor, even the personal connivance. What did it mean?

Herrera gazed at him accusingly, then said, in a low voice charged with emotion, 'He wants the throne for himself.'

'Impossible!' But as soon as he said it, Godoy could see how it might well be. In a replay of what had happened to so many crowned heads across Europe, it was going to happen here.

He'd been deceived, tricked. The Treaty of Fontainebleau had been nothing but an elaborate charade to enable Bonaparte to flood Spain with his troops to support his coup.

Heedless and impetuous, Godoy had allowed talk of Prince of the Algarves to go to his head – he, the son of a poor scion of Badajoz to be set on a throne. Now, in a cruel reversal, it was plain he was to be sacrificed cynically to the mob, who would blame him for allying with the invading French.

Furious thoughts roared through his brain. As long as he had the King's ear he could do something. But what?

Then he had it. Stuffing papers into a valise, he shouted to Herrera to ready himself to travel to Aranjuez.

The man obeyed, and in bare minutes they were in a coach that took them through streets alive with sullen, unpredictable crowds, who shouted and screamed at their noble conveyance. Was this a taste of what would take place if the revolutionary poison came to do its work?

Godoy sneered at the idea: Napoleon Bonaparte wanted a crown and subject people, not an ungovernable horde.

Some time later the carriage swerved into the vast winged courtyard of Aranjuez and stopped at the imposing red and cream edifice. Palace soldiery stood on the steps, splendid in their accoutrements – more than the usual number, Godoy noticed uneasily.

He was shortly granted audience.

'Oh, Godoy, *mi primo*, I've waited for your attendance on me,' King Carlos greeted him, cheeks a-quiver. 'And our queen, she cannot feel safe without you are by our side.'

'Majesty, it has been hard for me in these fevered days.'

'Yes, yes, I quite understand. Now what is going on out there? Tell me! Tell me!'

'Sire, it is grave news. I do not know how I might explain other than to say that we have been betrayed.'

'B-b-betrayed?'

'I fear, sire, that the French have not kept the terms of our treaty concerning Portugal. It was a ruse to enter Spain with their armies to achieve their goal – to seize the Crown of Spain.'

'The Crown! B-but—'

'Just so, Majesty. As did happen to so many other kingdoms before the weight of the Emperor's power.'

Grey with worry, the King asked, 'What can we do? Nothing can stand against him.'

'There is a course we must consider.' One that even a Bonaparte could not prevent.

'Oh?'

'Sire, you must do as the Portuguese did with such success. You will transport your crown and government to your loyal colonies in America and from there rule as King of Spain still.'

'I cannot!'

'Why not?' Impatience made him sound sharper than he'd intended. With Carlos out of reach of Bonaparte and his battalions, he himself would still retain influence and power in an exiled court and he had to see it through.

'The Royal Navy, our sworn enemy of the ages,' the King said more strongly. 'I will be taken on the high seas and paraded through the streets, like a common captive. What will the world think of us then?'

Godoy cursed under his breath. 'Majesty, you will travel from here to Seville, then rest in your royal chambers while we summon your loyal vessels. From Cádiz, Málaga, Cartagena – your fleet then sails for the New World, knocking aside the unprepared foe and sailing on to safety in your realms beyond the seas.'

God's blood! There was so little time to do what was needed – dire threats to the Spanish commanders if they did not put to sea, a secret approach to the British admiral parlaying a safe passage for a fat slice of cargo from the Manila treasure galleon, forged orders to the French men-o'-war in Spanish ports . . .

'We must consider this carefully, Godoy, *mi primo*,' the King said shakily. 'I will seek guidance in prayer.'

'Yes, sire,' Godoy said coldly, inwardly furious. 'I await your decision in my home here.' Bowing stiffly, he withdrew. Things were spiralling out of control; if he couldn't move within hours he would lose the race – and probably his head.

Montijo was waiting, arms folded, in front of a detachment of royal guards. 'Why, Godoy – in a hurry?'

'Out of my way, fool,' he snarled, in no mood to be taunted by his rival.

'You've been upsetting His Majesty, haven't you, little worm?'

'King Carlos leaves for his American colonies for his own safety in a very short while and is—'

'He's going nowhere. You've lost the game, Godoy!'

'You think so? Then—'

'The royal guard. We're the real guardians of the Crown, not you. Now the people are speaking – you hear them?'

Outside there were confused shouts, angry exchanges.

'I've told them it's you who invited in the French, with that miserable treaty, you interfering with the royal will – they're after your blood, vermin.'

Godoy paused, but only for a moment, then pushed by Montijo, who allowed him to pass, a sardonic smile playing on his lips.

'Go on!' jeered Montijo. 'They'll want to spit on the traitorous pig who's taking their king away from them!'

Seeing the gathering mob, Godoy knew it was past time that he could influence matters. He wheeled about and ran into the palace, went through to the back, to the mews, and threw himself into his carriage, scrabbling to hide as it picked up speed for the race to his mansion.

The crowd had found their way into the palace gardens and forecourt and swarmed over flowerbeds, trampling ornamental hedges and raising a fear-driven howl of protest. From the window the terrified King goggled at the surging throng, completely at a loss, his queen wringing her hands and wailing piteously behind him. There was only the thin line of royal guards between them and the seething mob. Soon there would be scenes last witnessed when the French king had met his end.

'Montijo, what should I do?' King Carlos called out in terror.

The man sheathed his rapier and darted up the stairs. His face betrayed cruel exultation when he reached the King. 'Majesty, only one thing will steady them.'

'Yes, yes!'

'Release the Prince of Asturias. Bring him out. Show him to the crowd, proving that he still lives.'

'Y-yes. Do it now, if you please.'

Summoned from the Escorial, the King's son stalked into the room, his glance contemptuous, his thin lips curling in triumph. 'So, Father, you have need of me? A villainous felon who—'

'That is over, my son. A mistake.'

'Which you greatly regret, of course.'

'Whatever you say, dear *infante*. Fernando, it would be of great comfort to me if you'd speak to that vile assembly below. Do calm them, will you? Say something or we're like to be murdered, like poor King Louis!'

'And I'm then fully restored.'

'You are now, my son.'

Montijo threw open the window and bellowed down for silence. '*Su alteza real, el Principe de Asturias!*'

Fernando strode over to the window and held up his hands. It brought a happy roar from the concourse. 'People of Spain! My people!' With Montijo at his side he launched into a passionate diatribe, sympathising with their travails, the wanton trampling of the French over their lands and heritage. 'But this day I bring you release! The author of your misfortunes, the villainous and accursed First Minister Godoy, is now dismissed from his post and from the royal presence entirely.'

The tumult grew and swelled into a thunder of ecstasy. In his hiding place in the attic of his nearby mansion Godoy quivered and trembled.

The crowd in the streets lessened but it was still there the next morning when it was joined by many more who'd come from Madrid, eager to be present at the incredible scenes.

In the palace the King and Queen hid in terror. A number broke into Godoy's mansion, wrecking and looting in a murderous spree. He was discovered, but before the crowd could tear him to pieces, the royal guard found him and dragged him to the palace to display beside the distraught King.

The crowd roared but soon a shout went up. '*El Deseado!* *El Deseado!*' The wanted one – Fernando the Hopeful, the young, the desired!

'Then, Father, it seems it is I they call upon.' His features bore an oddly serene expression, as the baying outside went on and on.

'W-what shall I d-do?' King Carlos gobbled, sunk in fear.

'Why, that should be obvious, Father. You will yield your throne to me. Abdicate. Here, paper and pen. Write – I shall tell you the words.'

Kneeling in subjection on the floor, Godoy looked up slowly, a twisted smile on his face. Whatever lay in the future for him, this was not what Napoleon Bonaparte had bribed Montijo to do. Montijo had allowed a Spanish king to take the throne through public acclamation, not the Emperor's appointing.

Chapter 15

At anchor, off Cádiz

Kydd reflected for a moment. This city, as his particular friend and former shipmate Nicholas Renzi, now Lord Farndon, would have reminded him, was a name that sprang from the pages of history, with the Phoenicians, the Romans, the Moors and Christopher Columbus. Here it was that Sir Francis Drake had singed the King of Spain's beard, and the treasure ships of the Americas had poured out their golden cargoes. And where, over the centuries, so many officers of the Royal Navy had seen through their professional careers against the traditional maritime foe.

Cádiz lay now under *Tyger*'s lee, the long, low coast, with its distant jumble of white and terracotta buildings under the warm sun, set in a glittering turquoise sea, as unchanging as Kydd remembered from his first experience there many years before. And now he was joining the band of brothers who alone were halting Napoleon's hunger for conquests at the very water's edge.

Around him were the veterans of the southern blockade

from the tense and dramatic days before Trafalgar, sail-o'-the-line that had seen admirals come and go, battles fought and won and now, after years of punishing service, ready for more. In recognition of their mastery of the seas there they were, lying peacefully at anchor across the enemy's harbour mouth.

And the longest-serving of them all was 'Old Cuddy', Admiral Collingwood, in *Ocean*. At the height of the battle he'd taken the reins of command from the mortally wounded Nelson and since that time had never once been relieved or spared a homecoming to his beloved Sarah. It was said that no one of stature could be found to replace him in this, the most crucial diplomatic and strategic station, and therefore, bowing to duty, he remained aboard ship, his health slowly ebbing. Collingwood was fair, and just to a fault, and Kydd could not have asked for a more nobler commander-in-chief. He was gladdened when the signal was made for the traditional dinner, the fleet assembled as one.

It was a time for gossip, for newcomers to learn the eccentricities of a blockade squadron, old friends to meet again, fresh faces to take on character. And for all to make measure of each other.

Admiral Collingwood took his chair in the centre, with his subordinate admirals at either end of the cunningly extended table. 'A right good welcome to you all, thou gentlemen of England,' he said pleasantly. 'As our little alarum is now concluded.'

The calm features and courteous manner were as Kydd recalled, but the face was exhausted, deeply lined, the eye sockets sagging at the corners. His sea-worn uniform seemed too big for him – a shrunken figure. This was a man who had tasted nothing but fatigue and tension for years beyond counting.

His words were met with a murmur of polite comment. Nothing had been lost as a consequence but it had been no occasion for congratulation: a powerful enemy battle-fleet had been at large for weeks on end in the politically charged Mediterranean.

'Now, before we show appreciation of our dinner, for those who have not had the pleasure of making the acquaintance of my squadron commanders, allow me to introduce one and all.'

In the etiquette of the Royal Navy, it was never the prerogative of the junior to speak to a senior before he was addressed.

'To my larboard is Vice Admiral Thornbrough, who in *Royal Sovereign* will be attending to Toulon. To my starboard is one who deserves general notice, for he's my new-appointed commander of the Inshore Squadron, one whose flag in *Conqueror* is as equally new-hoisted. This is Rear Admiral Rowley, late of the Channel Squadron.'

Kydd had started in surprise when he'd first seen the man. Rowley was no stranger – he'd known him from his time on the lower deck when he himself had been shipped out to the Caribbean to avoid damning testimony being given against him. Later, as a lieutenant under his command in a ship-of-the-line off Toulon, Kydd had been cast out of his ship for trivial reasons. That it had been the means of his receiving his first ship as captain had been no thanks to Rowley.

There was the same hauteur, the patrician disdain – even if the cheeks were now flabby and the body rotund. And still the faultlessly cut uniform, the peep of lace at the cuff, the thinning but elaborately coiffed hair dyed to an improbable black.

As he nodded a greeting around the table there was no trace of recognition, and for that Kydd was thankful. He had no wish to acknowledge their earlier association. Far too much had passed for him to feel anything but contempt for the man.

'I say, Sir T, weren't you third of *Tenacious* in the last war?' It was a fresh-faced, willowy officer to his right. 'As did something right clever when we took Minorca?'

Kydd brightened. 'A signalling scheme only, atop Mount Toro, but nothing as will stand against Captain Popham's patent system, I'm persuaded.'

'Not as I heard – oh, Hayward, fourth of *Leviathan*, as was there on the quarterdeck when your intelligence was sending Gen'ral Stuart into an apoplexy.'

'And now?'

'Owner of *Vigilant* frigate, on station these last eight months. Something of a bore. But then again I heard that our new Flags is out to make his mark, his service to this date being a mite south of conspicuous,' he added, in an odd tone.

Kydd kept his silence. Rowley had no doubt used his influence to find himself a sea command as admiral when so many better men were languishing at a lesser elevation. And unless he was, God forbid, a fleet-attached frigate with all the tedium that that implied, he would be with the Inshore Squadron and under him.

'Some years since I was on this station. Quiet, at all?' he asked lightly.

'Not as who should say. Now, with Boney taking Lisbon and all Portugal, we have the whole coast in arms against us. Makes it easier, o' course – near every sail an enemy, as it were.' He grinned, then in sudden respect added, 'But nothing as could offer diversion to one of your talents, Sir T.'

That Collingwood was keeping the seas off Cádiz instead of Toulon or Sicily was a measure of how the commander-in-chief saw the importance of the largest port the Spanish possessed.

The dinner passed agreeably for Kydd, shadowed only by Rowley's presence and that of Mason of *Riposte* – by his graceless manner their recent antagonism off Börnholt clearly not forgotten. Still, of the twenty or thirty present, there were just those two he didn't warm to.

The cloth drawn, amiable groups formed for brandy and cigars and Kydd joined in the easy banter of those who knew each other from long acquaintance and whose yarns were received with as much acclamation as his own. But despite the camaraderie of the gathering one particular thought was unspoken. Who knew whether they would find themselves on blockade for many more years to come?

Chapter 16

It was odd that Rowley, as squadron admiral, did not send for Kydd in the usual way to make face-to-face familiarity, ease the formality of remote command and set a tone, as had been the case with every other fleet commander Kydd had served under. Was he deliberately shunning Kydd? Peeved that a reminder of his past had again crossed his path?

Instead, the signal 'send a lieutenant' was thrown out and Brice returned with a signed-for order book containing the squadron's new Fighting Instructions and signal variants that would govern the conduct of the Inshore Squadron under Admiral Rowley.

There were few surprises: it was little more than a repetition of Collingwood's sparing prose and additions of detail that, no doubt, were intended to add a degree of individuality. Kydd passed it to Brice for the signals, commended it to his other officers and waited for some form of activity to be signalled.

Not until the third day was there movement, and that turned out to be the issuing of an order pack. Kydd allowed that Rowley and Collingwood had probably been in deep colloquy over operations and opened the oilskin package with anticipation, expecting an initial order of battle, a deploying against the tasks and challenges, but instead he saw that Admiral Rowley was taking the squadron to sea – for exercises. Flag in *Conqueror*, with his only other sail-of-the-line, *Thunder* and *Spartiate*, with his nine frigates. Sloops and unrated to remain on station.

Unbelieving, Kydd leafed through the orders.

The Inshore Squadron largely comprised lighter, shallower draught vessels, speedy and capable of deep reconnaissance – frigates, with captains of daring, initiative and individual reliability, who could be left to their own resources to achieve their objectives. Never to act together as a fleet!

Yet it was Kydd's duty to obey. As an admiral, Rowley had every latitude to handle his fleet in whatever way he wished and if this was to take it to sea to detect strengths and weaknesses or for any other reason then Kydd and *Tyger* must do their part.

On the day following, the squadron stood out for the Atlantic, in order of sailing as specified, the three sail-o'-the-line in the centre, three frigates in the van, four in the rear and repeating frigates, one each to leeward and windward.

It looked an imposing show but to what purpose? Frigates would never be placed in the line of battle.

'Sir. Our pennant and "Assume the van".'

Accordingly *Tyger* fell out of the line to leeward and began the long process of overhauling, from her station in the rear element, the entire line of ships ahead to reach the foremost, a senseless manoeuvre in Kydd's eyes.

The line stood on close-hauled, speed undiminished, as *Tyger* spread as much canvas as she could to obey the order, but as she came into the wind-shadow of each vessel she sagged away more and more to leeward until she was half a mile downwind before she picked up a steady breeze.

It took over an hour to get up with the first and Kydd to begin the evolution of taking the lead, but before he could do so there was another signal.

'Sir – our pennant, negative and "Assume the van".'

What the devil? Presumably this was countermanding the first and, if this was so, he had to find his old place in the line and ease back in, a dangerous procedure at the best of times. Fuming, he gave the order to spill wind and slacken speed but close with the line again. Was this an attempt to show him up before the others?

Out of the corner of his eye he saw the repeating frigate busy again and saw that another ship was being ordered to assume the van, the light frigate *Jason*, also from the rear element. He could only imagine the conversation taking place on her quarterdeck at the foolishness.

The line made whole again it was the old but taxing order of tack into line.

This required the line-ahead formation to go about onto the other tack all together to assume a new heading. It was a woundingly difficult manoeuvre for ships-of-the-line, each taking their time from the next ahead when every ship had different sailing characteristics from the others.

With frigates included in the mix, it was a sailing master's nightmare. How to slow the reactions of a fast frigate to keep with the ponderous turns of a battleship? It was near impossible, and the inevitable happened: kept in irons to wait for the bigger ships to come around, they gathered a stern-board and swung in reverse of the last helm order, others missed stays altogether and fell away in confusion and still more paid off to leeward to avoid a collision.

Thunder and *Spartiate* wisely kept time on the flagship and the three ships-of-the-line were able to take up on the new heading, leaving the frigates in sad disarray.

A tumble of flags appeared at *Conqueror*'s mizzen halliards, with another hoist. At the same time a gun cracked out, peevishly drawing attention to them.

'Sir, "squadron heave to" and "all captains",' Maynard said heavily.

Admiral Rowley stood in his great cabin before his captains, all sitting with varying expressions of truculence or sullen resentment.

'A shameful and disgusting exhibition, which I will not tolerate in any fleet that His Majesty sees fit to give me to command.' He took a lace kerchief from his sleeve and sniffed delicately, the arrogant eyes roving among them as if seeking out fault. 'For the rest of this day you will exercise agreeable to my orders, and if there is not a marked improvement, the squadron will repeat the manoeuvres tomorrow.'

Kydd took in the pompous, self-important manner, the lift of chin to stare down his inferiors. This was nothing more than a posing fop playing at admiral, enjoying the power and circumstance with none of the intelligence and insights necessary for the job.

Rowley's gaze flicked to Kydd and, despite himself, he tensed.

'It's clear to the basest fool where the fault lies. Not the sail-of-the-line – but the frigates. My order to *Tyger* was simple and direct, but what did I see? Sir Thomas Kydd of popular fame floundering in an attempt to obey, thereby imperilling the whole squadron.'

Kydd burned but did not give the satisfaction of an objection.

'Likewise *Jason*, which at one time I suspected was falling asleep.'

There was no amusement on the assembled faces.

'The less said concerning the staying about into line the better – a monstrosity that can only lead the unprejudiced observer to believe my frigates are inept and ill-conducted to a surprising degree.'

This time there were low growls of protest about the table.

'I send you back to your ships with my warmest recommendation for improvement. Carry on, please.'

On *Conqueror*'s quarterdeck, while waiting for their boats, the captains stood stiffly, barely able to contain their resentment but not daring a critical comment while in the flagship.

Chapter 17

'Be damned to the strutting peacock!' Kydd ground out, as Dillon hovered solicitously. 'God help us if this is what he thinks we should be about.'

It was back to manoeuvres in the afternoon: column to line, line ahead at differing lengths apart, wearing in succession. And not even a whisper of gun drill, let alone live firing. The talk of staying out for further exercise the next day was nonsense: Collingwood would never allow the inshore blockade of Cádiz to weaken for that time, and dusk saw them cast anchor opposite the twinkling lights of the old town at the end of the outer peninsula.

Unlike the Brest blockade, the station was an unrelentingly active post, engagements with the enemy not uncommon, with the prospect of a French break-out to the north and subsequent reinforcement of the dozen or so ships-of-the-line that lay in safety in the inner harbour always possible.

This should be the time when the Inshore Squadron got to work, a roster of frigates continually at sea up and down the coast, intercepting enemy communications, sea-borne supplies and reinforcements and generally making life hard for the enemy. Every day a pair of frigates should have looked into the inner harbour, at great risk from gunboats and frigates, to warn of sea preparations among the enemy anchored there while another sailed south to Tarifa to spy around the spiny rock guardian at the nest of privateers concealed within. But under Rowley none of this was happening.

Unexpectedly there was a call: frigates for a special purpose. Rowley summoned three – Hayward of *Vigilant*, Mason of *Riposte*, and Kydd of *Tyger*.

'I desire we take the war to the enemy by any means,' he said, with a theatrical frown, 'as will awake them to the presence of my squadron.'

Kydd held his silence. This could be anything – Collingwood ordering him to get on with his duty, a wish to be seen as an active admiral or simply more strutting.

'Lisbon. The French under Junot have taken possession of our best port in these parts and I don't propose to allow them enjoyment of it. I want to see a night attack by boats upon the vessels they've got in there such that they'll not contemplate adding to their numbers in the near future.'

'A cutting out?' Hayward asked.

A destructive foray – in and out – was one thing. A cold-blooded attack on shipping, with a view to snatching prizes, was quite another. Were prizes Rowley's hidden motive?

As if reading Kydd's mind, Rowley went on, 'Not prizes, no. Merely a descent on their ships.'

Kydd heard real regret in the tone. Almost certainly this was a direction from above, a stirring to action from Collingwood or even the Admiralty.

'Do you have intelligence of what lies in Lisbon, sir?' Kydd asked.

'Of course I do, man! Why else would I trouble to mount an assault?'

Hayward lifted an eyebrow in unspoken sympathy, then asked mildly, 'Who shall lead the venture, sir?'

'Who then is the senior?' Rowley said, looking pointedly between them.

'I believe it to be me,' Mason answered immediately.

'Then it shall be you, Mr Mason,' Rowley said as quickly, with a beaming smile. It had been too prompt – the two had been talking beforehand.

Hayward flashed a wry look at Kydd.

'My intelligence is that there are worthwhile targets at Doca de Belém – a species of East Indiaman alongside, with a light frigate ahead of her, and quantities of barges on all sides, enough for one evening, I'd suggest.'

No Portuguese-flag ship was to be harmed – these would be at moorings off the waterfront; the French were in the superior berths alongside and convenient to the warehouses, as was their frigate.

'The Doca – this is well past the entrance and before Lisbon,' Kydd said quietly, 'Three to five miles in from the Tagus bar. A hard stretch in without wakening the Frenchies, and even harder to come out when they are aroused.'

'You seem well informed, Kydd,' Rowley said sourly.

'As I served ashore here at the evacuation of the royal family.' There was no point in going into details.

'We know all this, sir,' Mason threw out impatiently. 'Can't we get on with it?'

Kydd held his tongue. Rowley had his pick of nine frigates and he'd chosen these three: himself to provide the fire and initiative, Mason to keep him in check and Hayward a relative nonentity. Not a well-thought unit. If Rowley really wanted to reap success from the backs of others, it would have been far better to give Kydd the lead and responsibility, then add ardent followers. As it was, the warlike talents of *Tyger*'s captain would be smothered by a mediocre Mason, leaving Hayward to follow the line of least resistance.

Kydd had a fleeting vision of Mason privately begging for command, getting even for the time at Börnholt when Kydd had humbled him. If this was what it was about, placing the satisfactions of petty boot-licking above the success of the expedition, his respect for Rowley diminished even further.

Well, let Mason make his moves. If they were reasoned, he would follow them to the success of all. If not?

It was a pretty dilemma. In terms of professional competence and skill at arms, he knew himself to be rarely gifted – this not in a boastful way but as a cold matter of fact. Some quirk of mind had fitted him for sea warfare above the usual run of men, and this he had to accept.

At the same time, as a consequence, there would be those set above him whose prowess was less than his. If they issued an order that Kydd saw was poor, did he object or did he obey without question as duty demanded? Even if it meant that men must go to their deaths? It was a moral quandary that would make for interesting debate with Renzi but, of course, his friend was not there.

Mason cleared his throat. 'Boats. Not so many as can be seen, but each well loaded with seamen and marines.'

Kydd began to speak but thought better of it.

'What is it, Kydd? You have an objection already?' Rowley snapped.

'Keep the marines separate. They can then independently lay down a fire from their boat to cover the others on a boarding or such. And more boats – with casualties you'll be—'

'Opinion noted,' Mason said sharply, 'And my orders stand.'

There was more but Kydd let it go. He could think of so many ways in which things might snarl up for them – night, boats, the accompanying frigates stopped at the bar and unable to assist, the lack of knowledge of where the French garrison troops wcrc, no local pilots.

'To clarify, sir, our objectives are the destruction of the Indiaman and the frigate and none else.'

A gratified flash of satisfaction betrayed that the 'sir' was not wasted on Mason.

'To carry both to be prizes would be—'

'Captain Mason, the object of this operation is the bringing down of confusion and dread on the enemy in a harbour he thought safe,' Rowley said testily. Surprised at his comment, Kydd could only nod in agreement.

'That is to say,' Mason continued smoothly, barely hiding his cupidity, 'where the primary objective is met, the additional advantage of flaunting ships of value to the enemy as seized by us is not to be scorned.'

'Timing therefore being of the essence.'

Mason frowned. 'In what sense, sir? The moon will not be up before—'

'If we go in with the tide on the flood, the ships we have, er, seized must be out over the bar before the ebb traps them inside.'

'Well, of course, man! Captain Kydd, I do desire you will wait until you have my full written orders before you make free with your objections. Shall I go on?'

The operation was set for three days' time.

Chapter 18

The orders specified that a division of seamen and marines in three boats be provided by each frigate, which would lie off the bar in company to recover the craft.

The assault would go in at eleven that night, being dictated by the flood tide an hour earlier and the moon, rising at one thirty. Speed and surprise were emphasised, the boats throwing their men ashore at each end of the vessel to be stormed, battling their way onto the deck where the sail handlers would race aloft while fighting was still going on.

The Indiaman was prey for *Riposte*'s division, the frigate *Tyger* and *Vigilant*'s. If there was trouble, in view of the tide state and the bar, any talk of rescue by British frigates was off the table, whatever the peril. The entire engagement was expected to take just three hours from departure to return.

In an attachment, there were complicated signals, involving false fires and rockets concerned with recall and abandoning the mission – quite useless, for once discovered there was only one course, to fight free, and unquestionably it was up to the commander on the spot to act as he saw fit.

Kydd called his first lieutenant. 'Mr Bray. You shall be

leading the Tygers.' It brought a deep grin of satisfaction. 'And as such you will make preparations as will conform to our orders.'

By evening the lieutenant had them ready. The launch would be commanded by himself, with a boat carronade mounted forward and containing the first wave of seamen boarders, the blue cutter with the second wave under Mr Bowden, and the red cutter, carrying marines, to stand off and maintain fire with Mr Midshipman Rowan.

The boats would have spare oars becketed up under the thwarts, a boat's bag with plugs for shot-holes, and copper tingles that could be nailed over as a patch on larger breaches. Each man would be equipped with a brace of pistols and a fresh-sharpened cutlass, some with rigging-slashing toma-hawks, and all in their loose clothing able to swarm into the tops fully armed.

Kydd wandered down the deck as the work proceeded, reaching for the right words to say to men who would be going into mortal conflict at his order. He knew they were watching him, drawing strength from whatever they saw in his bearing and manner when dealing with matters as they came up.

Rowan, looking absurdly young, stood among a line of well-built seamen at the armourer's grindstone. He smiled uncertainly at his captain, his face pale and serious. For a fleeting moment Kydd nearly gave in to the temptation of finding some excuse to stand the man-child down but knew he must not. He comforted himself with the thought that in charge of a boat standing off he would not be in actual hand-to-hand struggle with the enemy.

As the time for the expedition approached, Kydd weighed up the odds.

Lisbon was by no means easy meat. This was a world-class

harbour with forts each side of the entrance and along the river shore garrison citadels at unknown intervals. It was all of four or five miles to the docks and, unless they were lucky, they could be under fire all the way.

On the other hand it was the last thing the French would be expecting and, with their objectives limited to specifics, there was every reason to be done with the job and get out.

At ten the three frigates closed with the entrance to the Tagus and took position, anchoring, the bows quickly swinging seawards with the incoming tide.

All was in utter blackness, except the glow on the horizon upriver that was Lisbon docks. They could be properly made out only with a glass in the tops, so Kydd climbed up and carefully trained the telescope, the image leaping into focus upside-down as it was a night lens.

He studied the scene. River traffic seemed to be settling down, boats and lighters still at work around the vessels moored out, some in numbers that needed them to be rafted together, useful cover.

Shifting the glass along, he scanned the wharf slowly, the Indiaman clearly visible by its size, and closer to seaward the frigate, looking improbably small. The length of working quay from its beginning at the quaint Tower of Belém onwards was straight, gratifyingly well lit for handling cargo, and therefore suitable for close action.

After another quick look round, he returned to the deck. 'Well, Mr Bray, it seems quiet enough. I see nothing to dismay us.'

Riposte was close by, difficult to make out in the darkness. A dim lanthorn flickered into life on her quarterdeck: it was raised, lowered, raised.

'Board your boats!'

Men thumped down into their places with a mutter, a feeble

joke. Kydd's eyes sought out and found the slight figure of Rowan, correctly waiting for his cutter to fill before he went down over the side, his blackened face glancing back just once to the quarterdeck. May God preserve the youngster, he thought.

The pinprick of lanthorn light turned blue as a filter was passed across it.

They were off – there was nothing now that Kydd could do for any of them.

In the blackness of the outer limits they were soon invisible, but he knew where they were going: not directly into the broad entrance of the Tagus with its forts but away to the south, across the wide Bugio sandbar and behind the squat Forte de São Laurenço whose cannon were expecting ships to attack through the mile-wide entry into Lisbon. The sandbar was treacherous and shallow, but for boats on a flowing tide it gave a chance to reach deep within the harbour.

As long as the weather held and they were not seen.

It seemed an age before there was any change in the night scene. Then, in a silent display, there was unreadable confusion – too far away to hear firing but within sight in the tops, a vivid criss-cross of gun-flash centred about the two ships. The assault was on.

In a fever of frustration Kydd tried to make out what was happening, but from near five miles distance, it was too chaotic to disentangle. He could just see fighting on the wharf close to them and firing from boats in the water, which shortly petered out.

He held his breath – but there was nothing further.

By now there should be activity in the Indiaman if they'd taken it by boarding from the cargo quay but he could see nothing. Neither was anything happening close by the frigate

– a slackening and faltering in the action was not to be expected where Bray was involved.

It was galling to be a helpless spectator, not knowing or even able to guess what was going on. Still the unnatural quiet. As if they'd been swallowed by some sepulchral power.

A sudden *whoosh* sounded in the darkness – a flaring red rocket sent up from the deck of *Riposte*. This was the recall signal. Yet there was no apparent response from the scene, no replying firework . . . nothing.

Another rocket ascended, and on the frigate's fore yardarm three lights appeared – break off the action.

But no answer or acknowledgement.

Kydd felt something was deeply wrong. Over there, far in among the enemy, Bray and the others were in trouble.

'Away my barge,' he ordered.

A distant voice answered his hail at *Riposte*'s deck-line. 'What is it, Kydd?' Mason's voice was tense.

'The expedition appears to be in trouble, sir.'

'So what do you expect me to do about it? They know what—'

'I propose to take a boat and lay off and, if I can, see what's troubling them.'

'And then what will you do about it?'

'Why, come back and report, of course!' It was unanswerable: if Mason refused, any unfortunate consequences would be to his account. If he let Kydd proceed and he failed, it would be his own fault.

'Be quick about it, then!'

The barge's sails soared up, catching the night breeze handily.

'Where's the boat compass?' Kydd demanded, then set a course direct for the docks, unavoidably taking him at a raking angle across the main channel. He would be spotted, but in the darkness a lone boat under its odd spritsails would hopefully not be seen as a threat.

They made good time but the boat had no carronades, not even a swivel gun, and all aboard were unarmed – himself, coxswain Poulden, bowman Pinto and two other seamen. What were they thinking, seeing the black mass of Portugal slide past as they moved deeper into hostile territory?

As they neared the dock area Kydd eased their speed, trying to assess the situation.

The two ships still lay alongside and, as far as he could tell, were untouched. Other ships moored further out were doing their best to be gone from the area; with no crew on board to speak of while waiting a berth they were drifting away, helpless. Others had simply taken to the boats and were heading away in all directions. So where the devil was their expedition?

Closer still there was noise, shouting, cries of fear and panic. Kydd brought his barge in cautiously. Then, above the confusion and uproar, he heard a thin cry, a hail out of the night.

'Brail up!' Kydd ordered. Sail off the boat, it glided on and came to a stop.

Again the hail – down further, past the Indiaman.

A naval cutter was heading for them. It was Rowan, with the marines crouched down among the thwarts.

'Sir. They're in trouble. I – I don't know what to do.'

It didn't take him long to tell Kydd what had happened. The assault had gone in without difficulty, the men had landed and the Ripostes had boarded the Indiaman with little opposition.

For the Tygers and Vigilants, it had been a different story. By the worst of chances an army barracks was situated on the hill behind and soldiers had come swarming down, catching them from the rear as they attempted the frigate. Their luck fell away even further when the frigate's guns had opened up – completely unexpected, as guns were normally left unloaded to be safe while in harbour.

Caught between two fires, the assault party had taken to the closest warehouse where they were now sheltering. Yet they were dogged by further ill-fortune: the Indiaman was not only nearly discharged of valuable cargo but her sails had been sent ashore, rendering her useless even to take off the beaten raiders. Aboard her the Ripostes were in possession but were keeping their heads down, unable to do a thing.

It was stalemate. If those in the warehouse tried to take the frigate they would be slaughtered by its guns sweeping over the quayside. If they went for their boats the soldiers would close in and fire down into them as they tried to get aboard.

And it couldn't last. Reinforcements would arrive before long, and then it would be the end.

Lying out of range, Kydd studied the frigate with his night lens. As the shadows resolved he saw that it was not a light frigate but what the French called a corvette, the size of a large brig-sloop but full-rigged like a frigate. About her decks there were men but not so many – did this mean most were in the taverns ashore? It made no difference: while an entire broadside of guns was trained on the wharf not a soul could move.

The moon was rising and, remembering his timings, he knew that the tide had turned and was now on the ebb. In an hour or so the bar would be impassable.

He snatched up the lens and held it tightly, concentrating on one spot.

There! They had a chance if he could get word to Bray and the Ripostes in the Indiaman.

He looked at the black, cold waters, then at the shadowed

mass of the big ship and beyond to the tall, anonymous frontage of the warehouses. It could be done if . . .

'Mr Rowan.'

'Sir?' The voice was so young, so frightened. Was it right to continue?

'Your schoolmaster told me that he once gave you a dozen on the breech. What was that for, pray?'

The lad goggled at him, them steadied and answered in a wondering voice, 'For skulking lessons and swimming in the river with my schoolmates, sir.'

'Are you good at it?'

'Er, my friends say so,' he admitted, with a pathetic touch of pride.

'Then do you think you could swim over to that Indiaman at all?'

Rowan held still for a moment, then replied calmly, 'What is it I shall say to them, sir?'

He slipped into the water on the dark side of the boat and began a steady stroke out to the stern-quarters of the ship, where he used a painting stage to reach up and tap on a window. After a moment it opened and he was pulled in.

Kydd watched patiently, and a little later a small figure darted from the ship's side and across to the warehouse, taking the besiegers off guard.

'What do we do now, sir?' Poulden asked, in a low voice.

'We wait, is all,' Kydd said quietly.

It was out of his hands – Bray would give the word and set the plan in motion.

Shortly, with a fearsome bull roar, Bray broke from the warehouse with his men and sprinted across to the corvette, directly in the path of her broadside – but there was no gunfire. Imperceptibly the tide had ebbed enough that its line of guns had settled below the edge of the wharf.

Hearing the cry, the Ripostes erupted out of the Indiaman and joined in the frantic rush to board.

It was over quickly, the corvette's reduced crew overwhelmed, throwing themselves over the side in their haste to get away, while the two boats of marines stood off to blaze furiously at any soldier who showed himself.

Bray's stentorian voice lashed the men into a fury of exertion, making ready to carry the vessel to sea, and in minutes lines were thrown off and the corvette caught the current, beginning to drift out on the ebb and into the night.

Chapter 19

London

No other prospect could be more enchanting, thought Nicholas Renzi, as he strolled along the canal in St James's Park in the late spring sunshine. At the very centre of one of the biggest cities in the world, it was nevertheless a charming island of dappled verdancy and blossoms in a world at war, and it worked on his soul.

He threw some bread to the pelicans that waddled fearlessly up to him until it was clear he had no more then shamelessly abandoned him for the water.

Children shouted at their play, adoring couples sauntered by without a glance, completely oblivious that they were passing one who had burdens of the world beyond their conceiving. But with the felicity of his personal situation safeguarded by those like Captain Sir Thomas Kydd, his closest friend, whose selfless striving against the enemy was England's bulwark, how could he ignore what was being asked of him?

Whitehall had played it well: the call from Congalton of

the Foreign Office had been in the nature of desiring a favour, his reception that befitting a respected nobleman, the sixth Earl Farndon, as he now was.

Spain, the traditional foe, proud and stubborn and with a long history, was now being buffeted by the titanic struggle between Bonaparte and Britain and suffering cruelly.

Word was that there had been a palace coup. The swaggering Godoy had lost his post and the King had been made to abdicate in favour of his son Fernando. In the system of interlocking factions and obligations there was now a realignment with unknown effects, the only constant being the all-pervading French presence as they sought to swell their influence. There were now many more troops in the country on their way to dismember Portugal in accordance with a treaty that could no longer be termed secret.

There was unrest, of course: King Carlos had been a known quantity, a figurehead for those who yearned for the ancient ways, a bulwark against those who wanted change. What would the new King bring?

The fervent mix of allegiances and ancient hatreds held with Iberian passion made every piece of Spanish intelligence questionable. It was Renzi's mission to uncover the truth at the highest level he could reach – and by its light seek out what he might of opportunities for himself or others to subvert the French alliance.

He'd been given a free hand in how he wished to proceed.

Spies and the like had their methods but they were not his. His success depended on his identity and status being openly known: someone of consequence whose word could therefore demonstrably be taken at sight.

It had sufficed on other occasions – at the court of King Christian in Denmark, the Turkish sultanate of Selim III – but this was different. It was an enemy country.

On the canal a smart model yacht heeled to the wind – close hauled on the larboard tack, he noted. A child was following it along the bank and stopped, looking up at him uncertainly. He straightened and took off his hat solemnly to the little craft. Delighted, the boy skipped on.

How the devil could he, as an Englishman, enter the kingdom of Spain without being taken up as an alien, or worse?

It had to be open and above suspicion, allowing him to retain his name and rank, his presence in Spain being for an unimpeachable reason.

A quite impossible demand, of course.

And then he had it.

Congalton looked up from his desk with polite interest. 'My lord?'

'A possibility.' Renzi took the visitor's armchair, drawing his thoughts together. 'My much-loved cousin, of papist persuasion and roguish reputation, lies mortally ill and is not expected to live. He repents of his erring and was sent a vision: if he makes pilgrimage to the same shrine as his mother once did in faith and performs obeisance to her memory he will be forgiven his sins.'

Congalton gave a tiny smile. 'This shrine to be in Spain, naturally.'

'Quite. In view of his condition I shall travel there in his place to undertake the offertory – if this be allowable.'

'Certainly. A not uncommon request and generally met by an appropriate passport and travel under cartel.'

'Excellent. This, then, is my play. I'm trusting that as a well-placed grandee of England, as it were, there will be those who believe me privy to the attitudes and intentions of our rulers to the changes taking place and will seek to learn these by some means.'

'Friendly or otherwise.'

'We may accept they will be of the party having the most to lose.'

'That of the new King – who has legitimacy but not power.'

'Most likely, yes. From their fears I might deduce directly their weaknesses and its origin – discovering perhaps names, a cabal.'

'Which you will then privily approach with the same object.'

'Just so.'

'A workable conceit, I believe, my lord. To quiz a notable of the English ruling class face to face is a temptation indeed. I shall, of course, provide you with a crib of answers of value to His Majesty's government.'

'And, ahem, the furnishing of the name of a place of pilgrimage suited to my purpose would oblige.'

'Certainly. Might I remark, my lord, that matters in Spain are proceeding at a startling pace and your early appreciations would be most gratifying?'

Chapter 20

Spain

The scorching, dusty central plains stretched out as far as the eye could see, an endless ochre-tinted earth sparsely populated with bushes, and then, at last, the rock-strewn passes leading to his goal, Toledo, with a history of richness and antiquity of centuries beyond counting. Squarely within it was the magnificence of Santa María de Toledo, the greatest of the high Gothic cathedrals of Spain.

The long journey from the cartel port of Cartagena had been a trial but the Spanish had been faultless in their attentions to the English nobleman, providing carriage, four-man escort and a tonsured cleric, Fray Mendoza, an impeccably mannered translator and guide, who gravely answered Renzi's interested questions without reservation. Renzi had thought it prudent to keep his facility with the language from them. He'd won it in quite a different circumstance in the insurrection and invasion of Buenos Aires years before.

Despite himself, his pulse quickened. This was his first visit to the Spain of Castile and León, El Cid and the Reconquista from the Moors; this arid country they passed through held so many relics of the past but there was no time to linger. He knew that it was the domain of the enemy, but how could the ragged, picturesque peasantry he saw at labour in the parched fields be rightly termed foe?

Jago, his dark-jowled under-steward and man of affairs, rode behind in a less well-appointed conveyance, with two servants. What must he be thinking as they ground on ever deeper into this land? Renzi would never know: the man was gratifyingly close-mouthed, and if he suspected his master to be more than he seemed, he kept it to himself.

The road steepened; the horses slowed as the carriage crested at a tight curve – and there was the muddy green Tagus river, which, in perhaps half a thousand miles, would finally reach the Atlantic, at Lisbon. Nestled atop a mountainous bend in the river was the fabled city of Toledo, dominated by the massive tower and nave of the great cathedral.

Renzi's mood of wonder and admiration fell away as they arrived, and he contemplated the scale of his undertaking. In itself it was not perilous – he'd been briefed on how he should behave at the shrine and this was all that the Spanish expected of him. If nothing happened he would return to England. It was what would follow, if an approach was made as he desired, that held the dangers; there was much to be gained but only if much was risked.

They jostled along the antiquated thoroughfare, the stench making him grateful for the pomander that Mendoza had thoughtfully provided, the sound of their horses near drowned in the cacophony of the street. Quarters had been prepared at a secluded monastery, and Renzi thankfully bathed and allowed himself to be garbed in a penitent's robe, the better to contemplate the morrow's events.

* * *

In his grey vestment, barefoot and carrying a missal, Renzi set out very early in company with Fray Mendoza. The cathedral was truly impressive and he made much of his approbation and awe, performing his devotions slowly and reverently – the object being to touch through discreet iron bars the very stone upon which the Queen of Heaven had once trod. A blue-lettered mosaic tile set by its side was translated in a whisper by Mendoza, Renzi's offering accepted and taken away.

Some hours of endless tedium at a service followed – and then he was suffered to go.

Mendoza politely offered to show him other churchly inspirations of Toledo but Renzi pleaded a headache and took to his room, readying himself for the approach – if it came.

In the morning, lying on the plain bed in his cell, the scent of the monastery's orange grove stealing in with the wafting warmth of the early breeze, he considered his position. As far as he could detect, King Fernando had assumed the throne without overmuch disturbance, and certainly there was nothing so far that might allow for intervention or suborning. As for the French, it was said they were well into Spain on their way to the Portuguese frontier, but he hadn't seen any. Unless there was some form of overture, his report would be thin.

Fray Mendoza arrived a little before midday, his features compassionate.

'Excelentísimo, how do you fare this morning, pray?'

'A marked improvement, the Lord be praised,' Renzi said politely. 'As I was yesterday overcome by the splendour and magnificence I saw, an experience I will never forget.'

'Which is not an uncommon thing in many who make pilgrimage to the glory of Spain.'

Renzi acknowledged it with a small bow, and Mendoza went on, 'And it allows me to inform you that your noble presence here in Toledo is noted by the royal court, who desire to extend to you in small measure the hospitality due to your station.'

'That is most kind in you, sir.'

'In the most informal way, of course, as our countries are unhappily not at present in a state of amity.'

'I understand.'

'*Su majestad el rey* is not in a position to give audience but the first minister would be delighted to take *la comida* – how you say? – the midday meal, with you privily.'

It was happening! And discreetly. Safely in private, the minister could be quizzed and, whether unforthcoming or of value, could be discarded, or otherwise, with no one the wiser.

Chapter 21

Madrid was but forty miles along the fine royal road, but before they arrived at their destination, the Escorial, they were met by a strong escort, which formed up on the discreetly illustrious carriage, and proceeded at a smart clip, scattering peasants and traders alike. Twice Renzi saw sullen groups pulling back with angry shouts and snarls, and once the cavalcade stopped for consultation before setting off for the palace in a different direction.

It didn't take much to deduce that in the capital there was a much different, volatile mood. If the masses had been driven onto the streets in the face of royal repression, was he seeing the first stirrings of revolution?

The tranquil calm of the palace was at odds with its lavish ostentation. Where England's palaces had their crystal and marble, they could never compete against the flow of gold and silver from the New World that encrusted the vast chambers.

Renzi was ushered into one of the smaller rooms with a dining table at the end. A thick-set, extravagantly decorated officer rose to meet him, a major-domo by his side. An older individual, with a spade beard and an intelligent bearing, stood apart.

'M' lord Farndon,' said the major-domo, in thickly accented English. 'This is the Conde de Montijo, *ministro de estado* under the King, and I am his aide, Don Manuel Espartero.' The older man made no attempt to approach.

After the flurry of bowing subsided, Renzi was invited to sit and an exquisite array of dishes was brought.

Montijo's cruel face adopted a polite smile as he enquired after Renzi's health and the progress of his pilgrimage. Renzi answered that he'd been most touched by the beauty and grace of the cathedral.

The Spaniard seemed to shrug it off as unimportant, then leaned forward, his words deferentially translated by Espartero. 'Your good king Jorge. How does he?'

'His Majesty flourishes, I'm happy to tell you, sir.'

Eyes flashed between Montijo and the older man. 'Even in these fevered times monarchs must retain their majesty, their respect. Does he by chance convey by you any expression of brotherly regard to our recently enthroned gracious sovereign, King Fernando?'

In an instant Renzi understood. They were opening an avenue for any informal approach with which the British authorities might have primed him. An utterly unexpected and priceless opportunity – but one for which he was unprepared.

'Er, His Majesty desires only the early restoring of peace between our nations,' he declared carefully, adding, 'and the preserving of the person of King Fernando in these so troublous times.'

Again the flashed glances. He was conscious that tension had been released – disappointment, or the conclusion that he was no more than he appeared to be?

Montijo continued silkily, 'Quite. Our country is at this

time racked by a trouble-making rabble bent on bringing it down to a base ignobility by their actions. I do hope you have not been inconvenienced, sir.'

The meal concluded, Renzi was ushered to an apartment in the rear of the palace, a suite with an airy balcony.

Whatever impression he might have drawn, there was no mistaking the character of those in power. He'd seen too many courts and chancelleries to be fooled: those were the King's men and derived their dominance and command from him, to rise and fall with the monarch.

If Fernando fell in with the French, so would Spain. How could there be a chance for any British exploitation of the situation?

Renzi brooded on the impossibility of it all.

It left only the other side, the instigators of the unrest. Did they have plans for an uprising? If so, what was England's position in relation to them?

He gave a wry smile. Did it matter? What he'd seen of the disturbances was minor and scattered, no basis for a full-scale revolt. And in any case, how could he find out who the opposition was, how to contact them?

A tentative knock at the door intruded into his thoughts.

He got up to see who it was, but it was only a maid, who bobbed shyly and asked in accented English, 'Your service, El Marqués?'

She slipped in, closing the door quietly.

'Er, there is nothing I require at this time, señorita. Please to—'

She did not listen, crossing rapidly to the balcony to check outside before returning to confront him, the dark eyes wide and troubled. 'Sir, I must trust you,' she said urgently, her voice low. 'There is a great matter I 'ave to ask of you. There is no time to satisfy who am I. Will you hear me, sir?'

Renzi's senses came to full alert. If this was . . . 'Go on.'

She gave a fleeting smile. 'Thank you, Excelentísimo. I tell you somethin' now in fear of my life.'

'It will be safe with me.'

Her look of gratitude was quickly replaced by a frown of concentration. 'The party of the King – we call them the Fernandinos – is in power, but they little understand that the people secretly hate them. Many, many do pray for their downfall.' She gazed at him, pleading. 'Sir, they are ready to rise up to overthrow them, cast out their false friends the French – and create a new world where men are truly equal!'

Renzi tensed. If the woman was to be believed she was in touch with a revolutionary underground that might just have the scale to set against the Napoleonic battalions. 'How many are there of you?' he asked.

'Above a hundred thousand. In Madrid and nearby,' she said immediately. 'Wanting arms in their 'ands only.'

This was astonishing but credible. Too long the Spanish people had been tyrannised by the old, stifling ways, a degenerate and selfish aristocracy – it was a wonder it hadn't happened before. 'Who is your leader?'

'He is . . .' She glanced at the door fearfully, pulling him away and over to the balcony. 'The name is of no consequence if he has vowed to die for the cause. Sir, what is of greater importance is your answer to my question.'

'Oh?' With a sense of inevitability Renzi knew what she was going to ask.

'Excelentísimo, will you help us? Can you speak with your king, beseech him to send us muskets, soldiers, big guns to join us in our glorious revolution? We cannot do it alone, we need your help.'

Renzi paused, his mind racing. It was far past his remit to commit the British government to military involvement on such a scale but there were other considerations. If he refused to answer, even gave the impression of not wanting to commit to an expression of support, then the British would be held to be no friends of theirs and an alignment would almost certainly be with France. This could not be allowed to happen.

These were a simple people, consumed by hatred, and would not see subtleties. They needed strong words of sympathy and pledges now, not after months of parliamentary deliberation.

'You will have it,' he told her. This was no false promise: Canning would seize the opportunity to intervene with both hands.

Her eyes widened. 'You will help us with guns and soldiers?' she said breathlessly. 'Say you will!'

'In the name of justice for the people, we shall.'

Unexpectedly she fell back from him, her features unreadable.

Renzi caught his breath: something was wrong.

'*Agarra, todos ustedes,*' she called loudly.

From the balcony where they'd been concealed three palace guards thrust into the room and pinioned him to the wall.

A sick anger washed through Renzi. To be taken in so easily . . .

'You shall stay here until we decide what to do with you,' she said, almost sadly.

'Why?'

'We had to know what position England takes in our time of unrest under our new king. You have made it very plain, Excelentísimo.'

'We?'

'Los Fernandinos, of course. Who look to His Majesty for protection and stability in these bad times.'

She went to the door. 'Remain quietly in your apartment.

You will be well guarded. Know that if you forget yourself so much as to attempt to leave, these quarters will be exchanged for a prison cell.' She made to leave, but hesitated and said gently, 'I'm sorry, please forgive.'

Then she was gone.

Renzi was released, the guards pointedly taking up position outside, and he was left to his own company.

After the first rage of chagrin, he took stock. It was vital that he got word out of what had happened, if only to let the Spanish realise that his confining, a noble of the English aristocracy, was known to the wider world. After that, who knew? He was now an enemy of the state in breach of his cartel conditions by communicating with rebels.

He sat and awaited his fate.

Chapter 22

The night wore on endlessly and Renzi was left to his bitter thoughts. Not until the soft light of dawn shone through the balcony did he feel inclined to face his predicament, but there was little he could do.

Congalton would suspect he'd fallen foul of the Spaniards in some way but at the same time know that nothing could be done for him. There were spies and agents, true, but necessarily he'd kept clear of them – and even if he could get word out it would take weeks for communications to set up anything. Essentially he was on his own and he'd lost the race.

Later in the morning shrill shouts eddied up from the road below. Renzi looked out and saw a figure in the centre of a small crowd gesticulating and pointing towards the palace. The crowd grew and the shouting intensified, until royal guards trotted up to disperse them.

It didn't deter others. Before long the crowd had reached some size, angry yells and hoots bringing more soldiers, who hung back to allow a small detachment of cavalry to arrive at the gallop, the glitter of their sabres ominous in the sunlight.

The crowd broke and ran.

Renzi wondered what it had been about – the angry gestures towards the palace were unmistakable. Were they baying for the King's blood?

He caught sight of several more gatherings, seeming to converge on the palace. Something was afoot and it was growing ugly.

With a sudden crash, the door was flung open by the 'maid', looking distraught and breathing heavily. 'Come – we must leave!' she commanded, handing him a cloak.

Taken aback Renzi could only splutter, 'Señorita, what does this mean?'

'We've been betrayed! There's no time to argue, Excelentísimo,' she added firmly.

'The guards?' he said weakly.

'They've left, run away from here. Now come!'

She scuttled down a staircase and he followed, pulling the cloak about him.

At the bottom there was a door. It led out to the forecourt, with gardens, statues and shrubs. She ran across it to an ornamental wall with a small iron gate at the end.

Carefully she looked out then said tightly, 'Listen to me. We're brother and sister who walk together. Take my arm.'

They stepped out side by side, Renzi aware that Doña Dolores de Vargas was a beautiful woman, darkly handsome with an appealing vitality.

She told him what had happened. In a hasty and shocking move, King Fernando and the old monarch had set out for the frontier. Then, in an act that had stupefied and angered equally, they had crossed into France to Bayonne where they were to meet the Emperor for reasons unknown.

To abandon his people at this time was nothing less than

a betrayal – unless this was a kidnapping by the ruthless Bonaparte, as had happened before to the ill-fated Duc d'Enghien, executed by firing squad. Either way the hope that had been raised so high with Fernando's accession was now extinguished, the future desolate.

Dolores had taken it badly. In her eyes the King she had looked to was now a contemptible creature who had run away cravenly from his responsibilities and was not worthy of his subjects. She had deserted his cause and was about to pledge to another.

She had returned to Renzi because she thought he might be able to speak to his king to ask for help to bring order and peace and rid the kingdom of the French.

So where were they going? She knew of one Mariano Vicente de Lis, a much-respected scholar, who'd often written against the injustices and wrongs of the ruling caste. He would have the wisdom to advise her on how an English lord could contribute to the cause of freedom.

They hurried down a side-street, leafy but for some reason forbidding. In the distance there were scattered musket shots and the visceral rumble of an angry crowd. After his experiences in Constantinople, Renzi felt an icy foreboding.

At another crossroads they turned into a wider avenue, at its end an animated mob surrounding something in a turbulent show of temper. Dolores tugged Renzi to the other side to pass it but, with a sick realisation, he knew what was taking place.

On the ground three forms were pinioned by men who knelt on them, urged on by the mob. A fourth, with a bloodied face, was held upright as he struggled to get away. It was a French grenadier, who thrashed wildly as a rope was brought and looped round his neck. The crowd screamed in ecstasy as he was propelled to the nearest tree, the lower part of his uniform dark-stained as the young man had lost control of his bladder.

'Come, Dolores, this is no sight for a woman,' Renzi said thickly, but she held back, looking at him curiously.

'He's only a French pig,' she said without emotion.

The screams climaxed as they moved by, but he knew that a point had been passed. The marching columns under Murat would never forgive this.

Chapter 23

It was several minutes before the door was answered by a frightened housekeeper, who hastily pulled them inside.

'*El señor*, is he at home?' Dolores asked respectfully.

'I am here!' said a gentle voice at an inner door. It belonged to a strong-faced man with a meticulous moustache and in a garb that made him appear as if he'd stepped out of the pages of history. 'Doña Vargas, you have come to make your apology for doubting me?'

His quick glance took in Renzi.

'*El Erudito*, I have abandoned my trust in and allegiance to the King, and desire to be set on a course that is more worthy for the land of my birth.'

'I understand, the news of Bayonne grating upon the soul as it does, demanding an answer. Who is this gentleman?'

'A noble lord from England who does pilgrimage to Our Lady of Toledo and has unhappily been taken up in our troubles. Sir, we saw bloody things on our way. What is their meaning?'

A passing burst of shouting outside made him wince. 'The people are angry – do you doubt it?'

She held up her hand and frowned, listening intently. The noise grew, passionate cries piercing the clamour, the underlying roar stronger. It began moving off and she said, 'Something has changed. I go to see.'

In a very few minutes she was back, her face white. 'I cannot believe it, but the one I spoke with swears it is true.'

'Señorita, what is it?' Mariano Vicente de Lis asked.

'King Fernando has been deposed. Spain has no king.'

'No king? This is—'

'Bonaparte declares that King Carlos was feloniously deposed by his own son and thus Fernando cannot be the lawful ruler.'

'Therefore King Carlos reigns!'

'Not so! He abdicated of his own free will and without objection. What has been done cannot be undone, Bonaparte says.'

Mariano sat down abruptly, his face tight. 'That a Frenchman tells a Spaniard who shall sit on the throne of Spain is monstrous,' he breathed.

'There is worse. As a boon to the Spanish nation, he is willing to provide a more virtuous sovereign, one with power to pacify the unrest we are suffering.'

'Who is this?'

She gave a twisted smile. 'Why, his own elder brother, Prince Joseph, the King of Naples, who comes with eighty thousand bayonets at his personal command.'

With a bitter stab, Renzi understood. It had finally come about – the kingdom of Spain had slipped into the hands of Napoleon Bonaparte as, no doubt, he had planned from the beginning. The Spanish had been out-manoeuvred and now he had the pick of Spain's treasures, its colonies, even its soldiery to deploy as he pleased.

Only one thing could stop him. 'Sir. What of the revolution, the people's rising?' Renzi asked. 'Will your leader step forth and—'

'I know nothing of these, sir.'

'A confection of mine to keep him warm,' muttered Dolores. Then, more passionately, 'There will be one and I must know of him!'

Outside, the sullen roar was shot through with hoarse, angry bawling as the crowd swelled. Mariano went to the window and drew aside the curtains, revealing a stream of people surging past, one or two with muskets, others with makeshift weapons – poles with scythes crudely fixed to them, sharpened stakes, bludgeons.

'I pity any Frenchman on the streets today,' he said, then turned and went back to his chair, his head in his hands.

'What must we do now?' Dolores growled. 'Sit about like old men and women while others throw the French out, like the curs they are?'

Mariano looked up wearily. 'Señorita, calm yourself. You see out there the commonality, the beating heart of Spain – but they are like sheep to the slaughter. They have no leaders, no plan, no weapons. How then can this be a revolution?'

'A leader will arise and—'

'Who is this to be? He who supports a restoring of the old ways of the conquistadors or one who execrates the regime and desires the people to reign? One who will march with the French, or another who sees the devil incarnate in Napoleon Bonaparte? Who will listen to whom? What does your spirit tell you is right?'

Renzi knew he was hearing the still small voice of reason and his heart went out to the humble scholar.

'Ha!' spat Dolores, and rounded on Renzi. 'Then here is an Englishman. How say you, Excelentísimo? Will you help us as you promised?'

To be their leader? Renzi smiled without humour. 'Señorita, you may have forgotten that I am the enemy of your people.'

'With soldiers, guns!'

Mariano put his hand on her arm. 'No, señorita. Do not ask it of him. This is Spain's trial. We must save ourselves by our own sacrifice.'

'To cave in to the French?' she snapped.

Mildly he answered, 'If necessary, yes. Would you rather the flower of our youth lie heaped in death on the battlefield or live to create a new Spain?'

'To fight for honour!'

Renzi thought of the cruelly ambitious and ruthless Murat, by now camped outside the capital. Were his troops already on a forced march into the city, and in strength, with nothing to hold them back? The excited crowds he'd seen would have no chance at all.

He went over to the window and looked out. The crowd had swelled, now including ragged children with their mothers, the whites of their eyes showing wildly in the gathering dusk.

Mariano came to stand beside him, his sensitive features drawn and stricken.

'I go to them!' Dolores cried. Before they could stop her, she'd thrown open the front door and, pausing only to blaze forth a passionate declaration of support, which was met by an answering roar, was lost in the seething mob.

Mariano tore himself away from the window and, like a broken man, went to his chair and stared into an unknowable future.

The crowd surged away on some mindless impulse, and in the relative quiet a different sound lay on the air: sinister, ominous. Renzi recognised it.

Musketry. Not the ceaseless random firing of pot-shots but the disciplined volleys of troops from positions on the periphery as they advanced into the city. Murat had begun his retaliation.

How many troops did he have? Forty, fifty thousand? It didn't matter. With a dozen columns converging on the centre of Madrid they could clear the streets as they marched in with no fear of opposition. Now he heard the sharp crack of horse artillery with them − grape shot that would tear a crowd to bloody shreds and send others fleeing in terror.

What deeds of useless heroism were being acted out at this moment? He'd seen much of war and his imagination supplied him with the details, but this was not war: it was punishment inflicted on the common people by a tyrant emperor who wanted nothing less than domination of the world.

He gulped with a surge of feeling. Dolores was somewhere out there in the carnage − or was her torn body to be left cold and lonely in some street, the scene of despair and vanquishing.

The sounds drew nearer, harsher, and suddenly the street was filled with the thunder of massed hoofs as a troop of cavalry swept past the door. Mamelukes? Some nameless division having no attachment or respect to the ancient kingdom? It left the street deserted, strewn with debris and one or two bodies.

Half an hour later the tramping of soldiers intruded into the quiet. A column of infantry swung into the street, in the darkness eerily menacing, the reality that Spain now lay under their feet as they marched on. Faceless numbers, the steel of bayonets glinting.

It went on and on, then faded.

Renzi had feared that Madrid would be given over to sack and plunder, as was the age-old way of invading armies, but he realised now that this would not be so. These were not conquering heroes: they were enforcing the will of the new sovereign of Spain, Prince Joseph, against those who would object to his rule. The kingdom's chattels would remain inviolate – but the people would suffer.

The servants had long since fled so he went to the scullery to find something to eat for them both, returning with a little ham and wine. Mariano was still sunk in a stupor of melancholy but thanked him graciously, eating mechanically and silently. At one point there was a harsh screaming quite close until it was broken off in a chorus of vengeful shouts.

The night wore on. By degrees the occasional shrieks and wails fell away and Renzi drifted off in his chair.

It was still dark when he was jolted awake. Another crowd had gathered, quite different from the earlier one. This had a purposeful tread and, in place of the passionate shouts, there was an ugly growl, the menace chilling.

He went to the window and saw a sizeable group, at its centre a squad of soldiers with muskets. A wider line stood beyond them with bayonets fixed, facing outwards at the crowd. A sergeant in a high plumed shako had a sheaf of papers and halted his men, then stepped forward importantly, the crowd falling back.

Renzi strained to hear – the gist was clear.

It was an order-of-the-day from Marshal Murat to the effect that any person found under arms, making public speeches or otherwise opposing the authority of the state, would suffer the maximum penalty.

Then, in the flickering torchlight, he noticed a tightly guarded small group; men, women and children, weeping, cowering, praying, begging for life. It was a barbarous scene of horror for Renzi knew what must happen.

A pair of soldiers were sent off at the trot. Their musket butts made short work of the door opposite and from it was dragged an old man, a cripple. He was thrown forcefully in with the others.

Then the soldiers came straight for the house in which Renzi stood. They smashed the door into a splintered ruin and thrust inside.

'The traitor Mariano Vicente de Lis!' snarled one, his eyes flicking dangerously from Mariano to Renzi. 'Quick! Who is it?'

Mariano rose slowly. 'There are no traitors in this room, but I am he.'

Renzi was left, stricken with pity and helplessness, as Mariano was taken out.

He went back to the window to see the rest of the cruel drama play out.

Harsh orders were bellowed and the pitiful group was thrust before a wall. The children were wrenched from their mother's despairing reach, then made to kneel and face their end. Soldiers formed in a line at near point-blank range. The shrieks and beseeching, moaning and weeping tore at Renzi, and in the centre he saw Mariano standing nobly, his arms aloft as he called for forgiveness. Then came the hoarse command and the crash and smoke of the muskets.

And when it cleared, bodies, bleeding and obscene. And very still.

The soldiers formed up and marched away without a backward glance.

Trembling, Renzi lurched back, fell into a chair and wept helplessly.

In the cold dawn he forced his mind to an icy calm. Alone and in circumstances that could not have been more hostile, he had to get away, every instinct tearing at him to flee, away from the madness, the insanity.

Outside was the stillness of horror, of spreading desolation. To go out into it was lunacy. He'd stay where he was until things had settled somewhat and then . . .

When evening came he went upstairs, found a bed and fell onto it, knowing that he had to endure many more hours before light returned.

Then his mind came to an abrupt focus. He'd heard something from below, a scrape, a moving of the wreckage of the door.

There was an intruder.

Without a weapon he froze. Then a small voice called. 'Señor Mariano?'

Dolores!

'Señorita!' he called back breathlessly, and hurried down the stairs.

'Excelentísimo!' she gasped, and hesitantly threw her arms around him in a Continental hug. 'You're safe – but where's *El Erudito*?'

Renzi paused, letting his expression of grief reach out to her. 'They came for him,' he said simply.

Tears started. She bit her lip to stop them. 'Where is he now?'

'He still lies with the others. The death cart has not yet come.'

It took some time before they could talk, plan.

'He was right,' she sobbed. 'So right. The French, they're everywhere, Spain lies a corpse under their feet. There's been no revolution, no great leader. Everything's quiet – we're finished, conquered, slain.'

There was no comforting her. Without a focus, a figurehead, there was no opposition that could be supported in a struggle for liberation, however much Britain might desire it. Spain must now be left to its fate.

'Señorita,' he said gently, 'I fear to ask it, but will you help me leave Spain?'

She dried her eyes and looked up with a small smile. 'Yes, Excelentísimo,' she answered, at once.

'I rather think Cádiz.' The thought of stepping aboard one of the blockading cruisers in all its timeless naval order and tradition was intoxicating beyond belief.

Chapter 24

At anchor, Cádiz

One by one the captains of the Inshore Squadron filed uneasily into *Conqueror*'s great cabin. Each had been abruptly summoned from his station up and down the coast by dispatch cutter and held in his own ship until all had arrived, all, that is, except one. They'd then been called to a meeting with Admiral Rowley – not the usual 'all captains' but an individually written order requiring their presence on board the flagship at this hour.

Even more disquieting was the absence of both officers and men from the after end of the big ship: no midshipmen at work in the coach, no seamen at their various tasks on the poop deck, no one coming and going into the cabin spaces about their business. A marine sentry at sharp-eyed attention stood at each door.

The captains sat in their usual places, murmuring guarded greetings to each other and avoiding any comment on such strange goings-on.

As soon as they were assembled the admiral swept in, taking

his place in the centre. His complexion was flushed with an air of barely suppressed excitement and his fists oddly clenched.

He called for his steward. 'A snifter for all these gentlemen – the Amontillado, mind – then get out.'

In a tense silence Rowley's eyes darted from one to another as he waited impatiently for the refreshments to be served.

'Cap'n Mason,' he barked. 'Be s' good as to see if we're quite alone.'

The officer got up, mystified, but went to the door and looked out. 'We are, sir, bar the sentry.'

'Dismiss him, please.' Rowley gave a tight smile. 'My apologies for all this mystery, but it's for a reason. A damned important – no, a vital one!'

Taking in the expressions of bafflement on his captains' faces, he went on, 'As sets fair to pull up Boney by a round turn, by which I mean it will be a stroke as will bring his haughty ally Spain to its knees.'

A rustle of relief went around the gathering. 'Secret intelligence, what?' Layton of *Jason* puffed. 'The only thing it could be, I thought to m'self.'

'Just so,' Rowley purred. 'An approach to me as reigning admiral from what I can say is a well-placed Spanish merchant cove, bearing on their most well-guarded secret of state, and I mean to act upon it.'

'Has the commander-in-chief been informed of this, sir?' Hayward of *Vigilant* wanted to know. Unspoken was the question that, if it was so vital, why hadn't Collingwood assumed the initiative?

'He's still on passage,' Rowley snapped. 'In this instance, because time presses, I've taken it upon myself to move it forward without waiting to consult.' He shuffled his papers meaningfully, his eyes challenging Layton's.

'Ah, of course, sir.'

'Shall we go on? This secrecy is in force to preserve the unexpected, which is crucial to our success.'

He had their complete attention. If it was going to lead to a fleet confrontation and battle in the near future, that would certainly explain the admiral's animation. Like Duckworth at San Domingo, even a mediocre commander, if lucky, could find fame and renown in a surprise descent on the enemy.

Rowley continued, 'This operation will require precision and rapid obedience in all, not to say diligence.'

Several of the captains looked at each other in puzzlement. They were seasoned and tested in battle: such qualities were surely understood. And if it were a fleet action a frigate's duties were secondary to the role of those lying in the line of battle – and there was none of that class of ship represented.

'And self-restraint.'

Not courage, endurance, heroism? Just self-control?

'Er, I don't follow you, sir,' Hayward said carefully.

Rowley gave a beatific smile. 'That is because you don't know what we're going after, Hayward.'

'Sir?'

'Gentlemen. I've been given the sailing time and place of the *flota de los galeones*, which, for those of you without the Spanish, I should explain is the means by which the Dons ship across to their mine-workings in America the mercury without which they can't swill out their ore to get at the silver.'

'A mercury ship!' breathed Mason, leaning back in admiration. Rare and legendary beasts, the mercury they carried was so much more valuable than the silver or even gold of the treasure fleets.

'The loss of such will be a catastrophic blow to the Spanish. They are desperate to restore their fortunes in the Americas, for which they'll need their quicksilver.'

'And—'

'And of course I cannot deny that in the process we ourselves shall be rewarded in full measure.' Rowley's eyes gleamed. 'In fact,' he said, his voice lowering, 'my calculations are that each of you before me shall be the richer by not less than two hundred and forty years' pay for that one day's work.'

They looked at one another in wondering disbelief.

'Yes, gentlemen, in a very short while you shall be wealthier than you could ever dream of.'

'So . . . this is why the secrecy,' Mason said in a whisper. 'Don't want to scare off the Dons.'

'Er, just how good is your intelligence, may we know?' rumbled Layton, with a grimace. 'All seems too good t' be true, if you ask me.'

'I vouch for it personally,' Rowley said loftily, 'as the gentleman in question is both at an eminence in court and stands to share in our good fortune, as it were.'

'Then . . .'

'*Yes*, Mr Hayward?' Rowley drawled.

The captain reddened. 'Nothing, sir, do stand on.' This was not the time to bring up that it would appear Rowley had kept the intelligence so secret to restrict the prize distribution to himself only and the captains under his direction. This would ensure that there would be no others on the scene to claim a share, the usual rule being that those in sight at the time were included in the proceeds.

'Good. Then I shall be brief.'

Mercury, it seemed, came from a very few places in the world, by far the largest being the mines of Almadén in the centre of

Spain, known since Roman times. It was prepared for shipping and sent down to Seville, then to Cádiz, where it made its way across the Atlantic.

'The last *flota* was three years ago, and they're in serious straits for want of it, our blockade being so active. Now they're trying another way – bringing it by mule to a lonely part of the coast and taking it aboard a transport there. My information gives this as Mazagón, in two days' time.'

'Ah. That's . . .'

'Some fifty miles north of Cádiz, inside a sandspit at the mouth of some heathen river. I've no knowledge as to how many transports, the escort and so forth, which is why I'm making sure of it by bringing you all in.'

This was met with thoughtful expressions: he would need to be very sure of success to justify removing the inshore blockade even overnight.

'A straightforward enough operation, I would have thought,' Rowley continued smugly. 'Two offshore north and south, the remainder to seaward, with one bearing my flag in the offing. A matter of lying in wait for them to come out to us. The flag vessel will take care of the transport,' he said smoothly. 'In the event there are two, *Riposte* will take the other,' he added, smiling indulgently at Mason.

'Orders?' said Hayward, pointedly. He was asking for written orders, which in themselves would point to Rowley's neat appropriation of the operation and its proceeds.

'No time, no time,' Rowley boomed, collecting up his papers. 'We sail tomorrow noon. Now, are we all clear about our part?'

Layton shifted in his chair. 'Just one thing, sir,' he said awkwardly. 'Don't you think it a hard thing that Captain Kydd is not here, to take his portion with us all?'

'Kydd is away to the south and can't be reached,' the admiral said quickly. 'A sad pity, but I rather think that this must be accounted a party to which he's not been invited.'

The Inshore Squadron sailed the next day, standing well out to sea until the land was sunk, then shaping a course north. Watchers on shore would no doubt conclude that these were fleet exercises again, but aboard every ship there was tension – confined to just one man: the captain. Their mission could not be compromised by excited talk so their true purpose was unknown to all others, officers and seamen.

The trap was simple but effective: an impenetrable semi-circle about the departing port, Mazagón, with every ship just below the horizon. When the mercury convoy sailed it would find itself facing the seaward frigates but by then it would be too late. Others to the north and south would have closed in behind to complete the circle and it would be over very quickly.

The one thing that could bring it all to a ruin was a frigate sighted from shore. Aboard each, therefore, the sailing master found himself under the harshest direction as to the ship's position, and a mystified crew kept at the first readiness for . . . what?

As if in sympathy the Atlantic winds moderated to a useful south-westerly breeze and in perfect weather the frigates took up their positions, hours only from wealth immeasurable.

Chapter 25

Aboard HMS Tyger

From her deck Cape Trafalgar, abeam to larboard, was unimpressive, simply a low bluff on a sandy tongue of land with a stumpy lighthouse atop. It had not only witnessed the greatest sea battle in history but was one of the major seamarks between Cádiz and Tarifa, the privateers' nest sixty miles on at the entrance to the Mediterranean.

Even the lowliest midshipman knew it well, sighting it for exercise in running fixes, and aware of the numberless offshore sandbanks and rip-currents that made it notorious to every sailor. Most often it was given a generous offing and course laid direct for Tarifa across the bay.

This day, however, the wind being fair, Kydd ordered the helm put over to follow the bay around. There was nothing of significance within before it came out again at the seamark of Cape Caramiñal, past the little fishing village of Barbate on its river, but it varied the scenery.

In a mile or two they raised the nondescript scrubby heights that led along the coast, and after another few miles, set back from the monotonous flat sand dunes, reached Barbate. It was time to ease south-east.

A sudden piercing hail from the masthead brought the deck to an alert. '*Saaail!* Sail two points t' larboard agin the land. A frigate!'

Kydd was rudely jolted out of his reverie. A frigate – this was no English vessel, *Tyger* was southernmost of the blockade cruisers, and in any case, what was it doing so close in?

He crossed to the leeward side and raised his glass. It was full-rigged, certainly no merchantman with that single gun-deck and low, war-like lines. It could only be enemy.

'Quarters, Mr Bray,' he ordered crisply. A chance encounter, an opponent of equal size, guns ablaze in the forenoon. Precisely what *Tyger* was built for.

In the commotion of readying he studied the situation. It was almost as if the frigate had recently put to sea from Barbate, the near parallel river mouth delivering the ship in a wide curve to seaward. But why in Hades was a ship of consequence visiting the humble village?

The frigate seemed untroubled by what it must have seen and, under all plain sail, continued out to sea towards *Tyger*.

Uneasily, Kydd kept his glass on it. Something about the confident standing on, the gun-ports still closed, so many men about her decks . . .

Almost lazily it went about and headed out to sea, royals appearing above its topgallants as if spreading its wings for an ocean passage.

Astonished, Kydd followed its track. It would intersect with theirs about a mile ahead. 'Close with the beggar,' he ordered. 'And keep our gun-ports shut as well.' It meant hauling in each gun and dropping the lids but if the other was determined on a peaceful aspect so was he, until he learned otherwise.

The frigate picked up speed but *Tyger* was in place to intercept in time – and all became clear.

'He's a Yankee,' he said, the colours now no longer end on. But this brought with it a new mystery: what was an American doing this side of the Atlantic, given that Congress, with its Embargo Act, had recently made it near impossible for their merchantmen to trade and therefore need protection?

'I'll speak with him, I believe. Lay me a pistol shot to wind'd, if you please.'

There was no sign of fear or trepidation as *Tyger* eased up on the American. Neither was there any show of respect, but that was to be expected. Kydd had served with their young navy some years before and knew them to be a proud race, not inclined to bow and scrape to any.

The two frigates surged along side by side in the pleasant breeze, giving Kydd time to inspect the American.

He knew that the US Navy had six frigates at least, big ones and well able of handling all in their class, but this was more like a Royal Navy vessel, a mid-range eighteen-pounder and to all appearances as capable.

Scores of curious faces looked back at them from the deck-line as Kydd stepped up to hail. 'The American frigate, ahoy! What ship?'

A plainly dressed officer on its quarterdeck raised a speaking trumpet. 'United States Ship *Concord*, Sam Brightman commanding,' he replied, in a broad nasal twang. 'Out o' Boston. You?'

'His Majesty's Ship *Tyger*, Sir Thomas Kydd commanding, of the Cádiz blockade.' He hid a smile to hear the colonial accent he'd been introduced to those years ago.

'What do ye want then, Mr Kydd?'

The curt reply did not invite a conversation but, then, since his time in the USS *Constellation* things had changed. In an ill-advised show of superior might off the New England coast, HMS *Leopard* had fired into USS *Chesapeake* when she'd refused a boarding to search for deserters. It had nearly brought about a war, and relations between the two navies were now delicate.

But did this explain why the crew opposite to a man were silent, tense, watchful – it would be much more in character for them to jeer and hurl insults, good-natured or otherwise.

The two ships seethed along together, the swash and hiss making it hard to discern the words.

'Just wondering what brings a Connecticut Yankee this side of the ocean, is all.'

A pause before the answer showed that his recognition of the accent had been a surprise, but it brought no warmth in the reply. 'That's my own darned business, sir, not yours!'

Kydd's intuition pricked. Something was not square with his memory of the new navy but he couldn't put his finger on it.

'And I'll thank ye to get out o' my wind,' Brightman added venomously.

'Take us to loo'ard,' Kydd ordered, racking his brain for an answer.

Tyger spilled wind and eased back, then manoeuvred around the other's stern, coming up on its leeward side. If he was not careful, this could lead to an incident of international proportions. Should he simply let it go, see it on its way, or . . .?

If this was a merchant ship it would be easy. Stop and board, let its papers tell the story. But this was a warship and there was no question of a boarding and therefore no way of establishing its legitimacy. He would have to let it go.

Then a glimmer of something began to firm.

It was midday, time for the noon meal, and so close, down-wind, snatches of the fragrance of their cooking came on the light breeze. 'Get Petty Officer Pinto here,' he rapped. 'Quickly!'

The thick-set seaman padded up, clearly mystified as to why, with the ship closed up at quarters, Kydd had summoned him.

'Pinto,' Kydd said, 'the barky over there is going to dinner shortly. I want you to take a breath and smell, then tell me what they're having.'

Around him officers and men recoiled in amazement but they did not dare to make comment.

Taken aback the Iberian-born sailor nevertheless did as he was bade. 'Why, an' it's a right good serve o' *bacalhau* to be sure,' he said mildly, scratching his head. 'Wi' garlic and—'

Kydd couldn't help flashing a grin of triumph at the others. 'Thank you. Carry on, please.'

It was no American, that frigate. He knew it because his unconscious had told him its smell had not been right. But should he go into action only because of its reek? If he did and the frigate *was* from the US Navy, it could be a prelude to war and his disgrace. He had to find more.

A sarcastic bawl came from *Concord*'s quarterdeck. 'You planning on gabbin' some more, or do we get about our business?'

He had seconds only to . . . There! He had it! The frigate's proud colours aloft – thirteen stars for the thirteen colonies that had rebelled.

With rising elation he remembered that in *Constellation* they'd been at pains to show him the new flag authorised only two years before – and it had fifteen stars. Whatever this ship pretended to be, it most certainly was no proud member of the US Navy.

'Run out the guns!' he ordered crisply, then bawled, '*Concord* frigate – heave to! I mean to board you!'

There was hesitation and Kydd thought he hadn't been heard.

Then the American colours were snatched down and the familiar red and yellow of the Spanish took their place. At the same time a savage chorus of squeals sounded as gun-ports opened, and down its length the black snouts of guns appeared.

Kydd acted instantly. 'Helm hard up!' he roared and *Tyger* swung immediately downwind – but towards *Concord*, her bowsprit slewing in an arc until it aimed like a spear into the enemy's bowels. Taken utterly by surprise, the frigate hesitated – fatally.

One or two of her guns fired, the shot going wide, but its captain had seen the trap: if he did likewise his stern-quarters would rotate obligingly past *Tyger*'s broadside and he would be disembowelled. Flinching from *Tyger*'s coming fire, he went the other way and inevitably caught the wind aback, slowing in a cloud of flat and angrily flapping canvas.

Tyger completed her turn and, under the impetus of the breeze, gathered way and passed by the high stern of the helpless ship, her guns steadily crashing out one by one, the mullioned windows dissolving into flying shards leaving smoking black cavities and trailing wreckage.

Just as soon as she was past, *Tyger* wore about in a wide circle.

It gave *Concord* the slenderest margin to recover, to throw out jibs and staysails a-weather to fall back on her original tack, but by then *Tyger* was fast coming up – with her opposite broadside.

There was chaos on the enemy decks as they bore down, Kydd saw grimly, but it was no time for pity. Once again she passed the battered stern and her guns began their execution.

Afterwards, with perfect discipline, *Tyger* prepared to go round again but there was no need: colours jerked down wildly and *Tyger* came to a graceful stop, the enemy lying to under her guns.

'Mr Bray, do take possession, if you will.'

The kill had been rapid, efficient and bloodless, as far as his own ship was concerned. It was clear evidence that this Spanish captain had little combat experience and he felt a twinge of sympathy for the man that he'd come up against a veteran like *Tyger*.

Bray needed no urging. Blaring for a boat's crew and marines, he was off promptly, the rowers bending to it with a will. Not only was there head money, gun money and the rest, but there was every prospect the fine-looking frigate would be bought into the Royal Navy to the satisfaction of their purses.

For Kydd it was the more serious business of securing the vessel.

A prize crew would have to be made up – led by Bray, for this was a significant possession to bring in. But there were more than a few problems to face. A crew of several hundred would need strong guarding, and a full-rigged ship of a size with their own meant providing a full watch of the hands just to handle the ship. Others would be needed to attend to any damage threatening its soundness. All in all, he was looking at sending away near half of *Tyger*'s company.

This would require him to abandon his cruise to escort the prize back – and where to? Gibraltar or the Cádiz anchorage?

The latter: it was his working base and he'd be able to return to his cruise quickly. As well—

'Trouble, sir,' Bowden muttered, his gaze on the boat returning. It had only one passenger. Midshipman Gilpin and the men at the oars were at sixes and sevens, catching crabs and floundering as if driven by great fear or superstition.

Kydd went cold. A fever ship? Some terrifying, ghastly object discovered in the hold? All the half-remembered fables and dread lore of the sea that he'd absorbed as a young seaman began surfacing as the boat neared.

It hooked on and Gilpin stared up, his face working. 'Sir Thomas, Mr Bray desires as you shall join him wi'out delay. There's a matter he can't . . . that is, he doesn't know how to deal with.'

The boat's crew were acting in the strangest way, glancing back at the prize and refusing to answer any questions thrown at them by anxious shipmates.

Kydd called for Dillon to join him.

Moments later they were beside the frigate. 'What is it, Mr Bray?' he asked nervously, as he went aboard the Spaniard. There was the usual pitiable scatter of battle wreckage and bloodstains but nothing he could see out of the ordinary that would set his lion-like first lieutenant to this agitated and keyed-up state. The Spanish stood in a sullen group, their expressions murderous.

'Down in the hold, sir, if y' please,' Bray said hoarsely, thrusting ahead. 'It was one of the carpenter's crew found it. I've had to put him under restraint.'

It was hot and claustrophobic in the lower hold, smaller than English practice, dark and noisome.

'Light!' Bray called thickly. A lanthorn on a pole was handed down to them and they stumbled forward over casks and stores. Beyond was a cleared section in which three Tygers, with their own lanthorn, stared back at them, the whites of their eyes startling in the blackness.

Heart in his mouth Kydd reached them. Wordlessly, one pointed to his feet. He was standing on a line of crates. Each had a plaque attached to it: the Royal Arms of Spain.

One had been ripped apart. Inside stood a series of barrels, each not much larger than a country kilderkin. Each held, tightly packed, three leather containers, laced at the top. One had been opened. Dillon dropped to his knees to peer at it.

'S-sir, it's . . . it's . . .' he breathed. He held up a stout glass bottle and in it was the unmistakable gleam of mercury.

No wonder Bray and all who'd seen it were thrown into a moil. Holding up the lanthorn Kydd saw lines of crates leading away in neat parallel rows near a hundred feet forward, and who knew how many layers deep? An immense fortune.

This was a near mythical mercury ship, and as of this moment every man jack aboard *Tyger* had become insanely rich, for there had been no others in sight to claim a share – this was entirely theirs.

'Um, a guard, then, Mr Bray.' Even the best-tempered crew could become unpredictable in the presence of such wealth.

Kydd returned on deck, his mind still on the serried ranks of quicksilver below. His share would allow him to present a castle to Persephone, an estate of boundless extent, a matchless inheritance for their children.

And for his seamen – some would carouse until their bounty ran out, others buy a sailors' tavern, naming it Tyger and Spanish Silver and regaling their customers endlessly with the story of this day.

He pulled himself together. Nothing had changed, merely the value of their capture. An effective prize crew had to be found and the ship secured in the usual way.

They returned to an expectant *Tyger* where the news was met with a roar of excitement. Kydd, however, spoke firmly to his distracted first lieutenant. 'Mr Bray, you'll take the prize to Cádiz. I'll give you a full watch of hands and all the marines. You've no need to fear a rising. I'll be sailing in company within hail at all times. If you need to, don't hesitate to shackle the prisoners. Clear?'

'Um, yes, sir.'

'Then we'll—'

A startled cry from *Tyger*'s masthead came down to them: '*Sail hoooo!* I see one, no, two tops'ls to weather, four points!'

It would be too late for any coming on the scene now, Kydd thought smugly.

'Deck ho – now five, seven – it's a fleet o' sorts standing to the nor'ard!'

Instantly the situation had shifted.

Out of sight below the horizon on deck he had to see who they were and leaped for the shrouds.

Panting, he arrived in the top and the lookout gestured. Along the rim of the horizon were the regular-spaced pale rectangles of a progression of ships, proof that this was a disciplined squadron or fleet, not the blocked-in huddle of a convoy.

He fumbled for his pocket glass, wedged himself against the topmast and saw more. These were big, some of them at least two-decker ships-of-the-line. Far off as they were, if *Tyger* and the frigate were sighted, it would be to end well and truly boxed in against the land in this bay. *If* they were the enemy.

Feverishly he ran over the dispositions of their own forces and realised that these were not regular cruisers or even a detachment. Fleet movements on this scale were not a trivial happening and were notified well in advance. He'd never heard one mentioned.

They were all in sight now and he counted them. And again, slowly.

Five ships-of-the-line, two frigates, and, after a decent interval, a swarm of sloops and brigs, resolutely under sail for the north. Exactly the number expected if Allemand was returning from Toulon to join the Rochefort squadron in Basque Roads, north of Spain.

They were well abeam by now and Kydd knew that the focus of attention of lookouts was generally in the forward-looking sector. If they hadn't been spotted by now, their sails doused and against the land, they'd probably got away with it and were safe.

As a cruising frigate, his response should be to drop everything and attach himself to the menace to see where it was headed, as he had with Allemand on his outward sortie.

But if he did that, what about the prize?

Let Bray take it on to Cádiz while he went in pursuit? But there would be problems if he did so. The first and insuperable one was that he couldn't let Bray have half of *Tyger*'s complement. He'd need a near-full crew himself to maintain a day-and-night chase and perform daring sail manoeuvres as Allemand tried to shake off their dogged pursuer. As well, there was no knowing where the fleet was headed, for if the French admiral was performing the same seaward dogleg to avoid the ships clustered around the blockade ports, and if *Tyger* wasn't there to follow, he'd be crucified by an angry Admiralty.

In dawning horror, the inevitable was forcing itself upon him. He must abandon his prize to go after them.

His mind at first refused to accept the conclusion – a siren persuasion rushed in that no one would know if he let them go on their way, quietly lying out of sight until they'd gone past, then seeing his prize safely home.

He crushed the thought. Everything that he'd stood for, fought for, striven for over his years of service would not allow it.

Was there another way? Leave a smaller force on board? It would be asking far too much of them to guard the hundreds of prisoners and work the ship. They would be slaughtered in mutiny long before they made port.

Then perhaps take off his men but first render the ship

disabled by cutting every line that went aloft – shrouds, halliards, braces, tacks and sheets – then returning later. It wouldn't work: even with such a crippling it was not outside the resources of two hundred men to contrive a workable sail plan to make a nearby port, and who knew how long *Tyger* would be away?

Transfer the mercury? The substance was heavy, each bottle a hundredweight of fragile glass, which must be left in its crates to be swayed up by yardarm or stay tackle. It would take far too long – it could be that this was the latitude that Allemand put out to sea on his dogleg, and by the time the transfer was complete, the fleet would long be out of sight before they could follow. That couldn't be risked.

He pounded on the fighting top grating in frustration, the lookout shying in bafflement at his behaviour.

Taking one last glance at the stately line of pale blobs disappearing over the horizon, he swung out into the shrouds. He'd give himself until he reached the deck to come up with something or accept the inescapable conclusion.

Anxious upturned faces greeted him as he landed on deck.

'Cruel luck,' he said heavily. 'We have to go after them.'

A babble of voices rose until Kydd cut in: 'No arguments! We've a duty to follow.'

'The prize?' Bray demanded. 'We can't leave it here!'

'We can, and we will,' Kydd answered curtly. 'Recover all our people from it and prepare to set all sail conformable to the weather.'

The voices grew charged, fretful.

'Silence on deck!' Kydd roared. 'I don't like this any more than you, but we have our duty, I'll remind you!'

Seamen came running up, disbelieving the news.

'Mr Bray! Any man who isn't at his post will taste the cat and that's my promise!'

From out of sight below, cries of outrage were soon joined by more. Accusing looks darted his way, unvoiced but venomous.

'Find out who those mutinous dogs are and bring them before me!'

Bray stomped forward and stood before Kydd, his eyes dangerous. 'There's time to save our prize and—'

'No, there isn't, Mr Bray, and you know it. Give me a plan that lets us also get after the Crapauds right now and I'll listen, else we sail.'

Lieutenant Bowden remained silent, his features unreadable, and Brice had taken to pacing the far end of the quarterdeck.

'Nothing? Then we get under way this hour.' Turning away he realised that, caught up in the confrontation, he was forgetting something. 'The gunner to report to me,' he snapped.

Darby finally appeared, touching his hat with a set expression. 'Sir?'

'Take a party and lay a charge to *Concord*'s main magazine.'

Kydd turned and found Dillon. 'Go with 'em and tell the crew to be off their ship immediately. Boats, rafts, anything. Barbate is close so they'll be picked up quickly.'

The Spanish had tried hard to get through by a well-thought-out plan that would have succeeded with the usual run of naval officer but it had been their ill fortune to come across one who had experience with the United States Navy and had uncovered their trick.

When it came, the detonation was a dull crump and brief flare – this was no real frigate on a war-like cruise and wasn't stored for any protracted fight with tons of powder. Nevertheless the ship took the blow in its vitals and bowed in agony before disappearing beneath the waves.

Kydd turned on his heel and went below.

Chapter 26

At anchor, Cádiz

It was near deserted when *Tyger* sailed in on the balmy zephyr that was promising sultry conditions before night. Apart from *Conqueror* and a gaggle of victuallers, there were no others and she had no difficulty in finding a berth.

The mystery fleet *Tyger* had seen had turned out to be Admiral Strachan's unannounced return from Toulon to his station off Rochefort, with a coincidental same number of vessels as the French commander, and while the preventive sinking of a prize was unfortunate, it was by no means unusual.

In full dress Kydd took boat for the flagship to make his report, but on boarding he stepped into a graveyard-like gloom.

Not a smile, careless remark, or light-hearted leap for the shrouds – it was a disturbing feeling.

The flag-lieutenant who met him had all the appearance of a whipped dog, and when Kydd asked if something was amiss he mumbled inaudibly and led the way below to the admiral's day cabin. Outside he paused, as if about to say something, then seemed to think better of it and announced Kydd, then retreated rapidly.

Rowley was behind his desk and looked up as Kydd entered. There was an ugly set to his expression and his eyes narrowed. Was this where the ship's bad feeling had its origin?

'Well?' he barked.

'My cruise report, as is required by you on its conclusion, sir,' Kydd said mildly.

'So?'

Kydd placed a single folded sheet in front of the admiral. The sooner this was over the better.

'I've no time to read that! What does it say?'

'The coast south is largely quiet, no hostile activity to speak of. In the last week, I fell in with an enemy frigate close inshore and, despite a stratagem to deceive, I succeeded in raking him twice in succession at which he struck.'

'Then where is your prize, damn it all?' Rowley stood to gain a one-eighth share as presiding admiral and was taking a rapacious interest now.

'At that moment there was sighted well to seaward a large amount of sail, in number the same as Allemand's squadron. I judged it more important to go after the fleet than secure the prize, which I destroyed by touching off its main magazine.'

'You did what?' Rowley spluttered. 'Caused a perfectly good prize to be put down when . . . when . . .'

'Are you saying I was in error to put the unknown sail under chase?' Kydd said tightly, noting Rowley's complete disinterest in the fleet and where it was at this moment.

'Damn right I am! Any naval officer with half his wits would have left a prize crew and—'

'Not possible . . . sir.' Kydd bit off. 'Two hundred prisoners, a full-rigged ship needing sail handling, and *Tyger* facing a close-run voyage with half her crew? I don't think so . . . sir.'

Rowley glowered. 'There's always a way for those with a mort of seamanlike backbone. The trouble with you is—'

Kydd smouldered, then looked directly in Rowley's face. 'It had a lading of mercury,' he said icily.

Recoiling as though slapped in the face, Rowley goggled. 'Mercury? You mean . . . the Spanish Atlantic shipment? In a frigate?'

'Disguised as a United States Navy frigate. Far smarter than using a transport.'

Rowley exploded. 'Do you realise what you've done?' His voice was a rising squeal of outrage. 'We'd be as rich as Croesus, every one! I stripped the whole coast of every frigate and lay off Mazagón as where the intelligence said it was – and nothing! Then you're lucky enough to trip over it and you think to throw the whole stinking lot away! What kind of gooney fool are you, Kydd? Hey? Hey?'

Kydd felt a slow burn rise up as it struck him. Stripped the Inshore Squadron of all frigates? Then why hadn't he been called, too? He'd been deliberately excluded from the tawdry affair in order to miss the share-out.

His face went red. 'You wanted me out of it, didn't you? You didn't need a frigate in the south. You knew it was peaceful. You deliberately decided not to bring me in.'

Rowley glared dangerously but Kydd went on recklessly, 'So, now you're hoist by your own petard. If I'd had company the mercury would be under hatches now, but you took 'em all to go off on your fool errand. False intelligence – and you fell for it!'

Breathing deeply, Rowley ground out, 'As soon as you came before me I knew you'd be trouble, Kydd. You're a foremast jack who's clawed his way up and wants to be mistaken for a gentleman. Oh, yes, I've heard about your dandy prat rollicking in Town but, let me tell you, I know where you came from and you're not getting away with it in my command. You're under me and, by God, you'll dance to my tune when I tell you. What do you think of that, hey?'

'What do I think? I'll tell you. When I first clapped eyes on you, I knew what *you* were. Yes, I was a common jack tar in *Artemis* but I knew your kind. Got your place by arse-licking at the highest and never deep-water seamanship or standing with the guns. Because of you I spent years in the Caribbean, nearly lost my life, all to save you from—'

'Shut your mouth, sir!' Rowley shouted. 'I've heard enough! Know that I'm going to see to it you pay for your words, Kydd. Pay dearly for them, you hear? Now get out! *Get out!*'

It was in the open. The balance of power had shifted. Rowley was admiral with all dominion and authority, but Kydd could, if he wanted, bring him ruin and disgrace on his own station.

In the famed frigate *Artemis*, Kydd had been quartermaster at the conn when Rowley, as lieutenant officer-of-the-watch, had allowed the ship, through a foolish helm order, to become embayed, then wrecked on the wicked reefs of the Azores. At the subsequent court of inquiry Kydd had refused to withdraw his damning evidence and been shipped, through Rowley's bare-faced exercise of influence, to the fever islands of the West Indies before a court-martial could be convened.

At the time he'd burned with the injustice, but at his lowly level there was nothing he could do and he'd let it go, with the resilience of youth, moving on to greater things and even, in the fullness of time, to the quarterdeck. It was all part of a different world, a different time and place, and he'd put it aside in the face of more momentous events.

Until now, when the man's arrogance and greed had brought

back all the emotional revulsion.

Should he do it? Let the world know what kind of poltroon occupied the admiral's cabin in the flagship? After all these years to take sweet revenge for the hurt Rowley had done Kydd and those sailors whose bones still lay with *Artemis*? But did he want to become known as the officer who destroyed an admiral for his own gratification? And would his respect for the naval code of an officer's duty to a superior hold him in check?

Chapter 27

On the road to Cádiz

The last miles from Jerez to Cádiz were a slow, grinding torment. Renzi was crammed next to a dust-smothered Dolores on the seat of a cart, Jago and the two servants packed in the rear with three others, part of the stream of refugees fleeing Madrid for the outer provinces.

Fortunately the encircling French had not troubled them but the carriage they'd taken to Toledo to recover Jago had been seized, and all they could find in the chaos was a country farm vehicle, now threading through the hostile mob. Ahead was the last range of hills above their destination.

Easing his aching limbs Renzi took in the passing countryside. The sight of Cádiz from the interior had been given to no one he knew and he tried to take an interest but there was nothing except olive groves, orange orchards and abandoned, crumbling farmsteads in the dry, ochre scrub.

He recollected hazily that Medina Sedonia must not be far from here, where the eponymous duke had retired after bringing the remnants of the Grand Armada straggling back, following their disastrous invasion attempt on Elizabeth's England. The peace and loveliness must have been in his thoughts through the storm and bloodshed he'd endured, an impossibly remote dream that had finally firmed into a real presence.

Then Renzi's eyes were caught by the scene opening up below, a long peninsula parallel with the coast, a close-packed city at its end enfolding a complex of inner harbours and settlements.

He breathed it in. Cádiz was of extraordinary antiquity – a thriving Phoenician trader a thousand years old in the time of Julius Caesar.

A fragment of Avienus came to mind:

Hic Gadir urbs est, dicta Tartessus prius;
Hic sunt columnæ pertinacis Herculis, Abila atque Calpe
The city Cádiz was formerly called Tartessus, here are the columns of Hercules, Abila and Calpe . . .

Mythical columns leading out to the vast unknown, and there below him, the ancient frontier of the known world – and was this not the Tarshish of the Old Testament? Both notions were the worry-bones of academics ancient and modern, but he absorbed the reality before him.

Several miles later, after grinding across reedy marshland, they were on to a broad foreland, the Trocadero, which aimed at the middle of the peninsula and divided the spacious Cádiz harbour in two – left and right, the inner and outer harbours.

He spied a dense cluster of ships-of-the-line in the outer harbour, and as they drew nearer, he noted their French ensigns. It was a sight that Collingwood and his squadron had never seen for all their years on blockade.

Now he was in an excellent position to describe what, at

great peril, British frigates braved forts and tides to discover. Did they know that at this moment sail was bent on the yards, countless boats criss-crossing to the anchored ships, sure signs that they were putting to sea, in days at most?

He counted them: five, with frigates. A powerful force, which could conjure havoc instantly, should it get to sea unhindered.

And in the inner harbour, several miles distant at its furthest point in, there was a more scattered grouping with bare yards but too far off for him to make out any colours. Almost certainly he was seeing the Spanish Navy at their arsenal, their near impregnable base.

Unexpectedly the cart rounded to a humble hamlet on the foreshore under the frowning eminence of a medieval fort. As far as he could see it was in full working order, with another opposite, able to throw impassable fire to any attempting the inner harbour.

Groaning with aches and pains, Renzi helped Dolores down. 'Over there,' she said wistfully. 'Cádiz.'

A bare mile across the water he had a view of the whole length of the peninsula, along its tip the thrilling mix of towers and miradors of every antiquity. While they waited for the ferry he savoured the moment, aware that the future for any one of them — Spaniard, French or British — was quite without knowing in a world of war and betrayal.

'We stay with my friend, Benita. She's in the old city in La Viña — we grew up together,' Dolores added shyly. 'Do not pay mind to her *marido*, her man. He is rough but kind to her so I like him.'

The door, with its cast-iron grille, was a long time being answered. Eventually a nervous maidservant made much of wanting to know who they were, disturbing her mistress in the hour of siesta. Renzi, a blank-faced Jago and the others waited in the street, a narrow, cobbled passageway, Corralón de Los Carros, atmospheric with its mustard yellow and dusky red stone dwellings.

When Benita appeared she dissolved into delighted squeals. 'My dear, and I was so worried for you in Madrid! We've heard such dreadful tales and all these strangers running, hiding! Do come in . . . Oh, these are your friends?' she said, in sudden suspicion.

'*Mi querido amiga*, I've much to tell you. But, Benita, this is an English lord here to do pilgrimage, and is caught up in our disgraceful happenings. Do let us in!'

'Of course. *Entra, caballeros* – oh, they don't understand Castilian. Tell them they're welcome, Dolores, please!'

She glanced at Renzi, in whom any sign of competence in the Spanish language would suggest a spy, and said coyly in English, 'Miss Benita invites you in, m' lord.'

There was much discussion, resulting in Renzi being awarded the topmost bedroom while Jago and the servants would sleep on the kitchen floor.

The cold bath that followed was welcome, but what Renzi most appreciated was the view. From his window, a floor higher than the houses about them and not so far from the entrance of the outer harbour, he could look out to sea – and, wonderfully, make out the regular shapes of ships at anchor. There was the Inshore Squadron of Collingwood's fleet under some admiral he couldn't know but who was the direct inheritor of Lord Nelson's mantle when he'd been the courageous leader of that squadron before Trafalgar.

He counted four ships-of-the-line and only one frigate.

Kydd had told him he was being attached to Collingwood's fleet and, with his record, he would certainly find himself part of it. Was that *Tyger*? A pang of longing touched him: it was approaching the first dog-watch and the men would be looking to their well-earned issue of grog. They'd be gossiping about the day's events, which on blockade would not be gripping or blood-curdling but in the warmth and fellowship would go far to make up for its tedium.

He returned to the present: the French had won. They'd turned the Fontainebleau treaty into a means of plucking the second largest country in Europe and now, with the Bourbon kings in their grasp, it was all over. The uprisings in Madrid had been leaderless, easily and savagely put down, and there was no opposition left worthy of the name.

He went downstairs. The women, it seemed, had much to talk about. Cádiz was far from Madrid and had yet to taste the bitterness of French occupation and control, certainly not the brutality of retribution, and Benita listened wide-eyed to what Dolores told her of the scenes in the capital.

'Benita, *mi alma. Hola!*' A deep masculine roar came from the entrance.

'Oh! Pedro – I'm coming,' she called.

She returned beside a powerfully built Spaniard, with deep-set, suspicious eyes. He started in surprise when he saw Renzi, but before he could move Benita purred, '*Mi amado*, where are your manners? I have a surprise for you. This is an English milord, *excelentísimo señor*, Conde de Farndón.'

Pedro gave a jerky bow, then suddenly exploded, 'English? In my house? What are you doing, you stupid woman?' His hand fell to his rapier.

She smiled. 'No, not the enemy, this one. He docs pilgrimage to Our Lady of Toledo under special protection, and was caught in all our trouble.' Turning to Dolores, she said quickly, 'Do tell your lord that my husband means no harm.'

Dolores curtsied prettily to Renzi and said in English, 'You are enchanted to meet Pedro, are you not, sir?'

Renzi took his cue and answered politely with a bow.

It seemed to suffice and he went to his room to leave them to their talk – and find time to think.

There was no point staying any longer in Spain. He'd be telling Congalton that French occupation was spreading fast in the absence of a focus for resistance and therefore the British had no part to play in encouraging any kind of revolt. Under Bonaparte's able generals, the subjugation of Spain would not take long.

But how to make his departure? He'd have to leave as soon as he could for, without doubt, the French would be bringing their garrisons here in the near future.

He went down to the evening meal, in the Spanish fashion held well into the night.

Pedro was the host and Renzi was made to know it, but was given a place at his right hand, resigned to an unspeaking role while happy chatter swirled around.

Unsuspected, he listened to it all, the gossip, what the day had brought, the rumours.

And then he heard something that brought him to full alert. Pedro, it seemed, was a fiery member of the town council, his opinions decided and acute. And this day the business was entirely dominated by what they were hearing of the atrocities in Madrid. It was believed that Cádiz, the ancient and second greatest city of Spain, would not fall prostrate before the tyrant, and no less a personage than Don Tomás de Morla, general of the army of Andalucía, had sworn in front of the entire assembly that, before God, with its position and defences it would stand.

Renzi saw there was a fleeting chance to bring about a common front. He wouldn't trouble with the town council:

they were representative of the feeling of the people, certainly, but at his eminence he could command the attention of the royal governor.

'Dolores,' he asked, at a break in the animated conversation, 'my stay in Spain has been . . . eventful, yet it would be my pleasure and obligation to express the sensibility of my gratitude at its indulgence of my presence. To the governor in person would be my desire. Does Don Pedro think this at all possible?'

He had the measure of the man. It seemed it could be arranged for a town councillor to make introduction of English nobility at the highest regal level.

Chapter 28

The next morning, arrayed as befitted an audience with Don Francisco Solano, Marqués del Socorro, royal governor of Cádiz, they waited on the august being.

Solano made an impressive figure, his uniform elaborate and extravagant, but his features were austere, unsmiling, and his elaborately pointed beard spoke of a Spain of glorious centuries past. He was polite but firm to Renzi. 'Excelentísimo, I'm honoured beyond measure, but find it most irregular.'

Dolores translated faithfully, her hands together and head bowed in respect to them both. Don Pedro had been neatly ushered outside after the initial introductions.

'Sir, I wished only to pay my respects in person to the Spanish Crown, which I hold in the highest regard.'

'Nevertheless, is it not strange that a noble at your station finds it necessary to make pilgrimage at this precise time?' Solano asked quietly. The level gaze was too calm and intelligent to be comfortable.

'Alas, sir, I return to one who lies mortally ill, he who entrusted me with the charge. I pray I'm in time to tell of its accomplishing.'

'This is an age of tumult and rivalry. Nations struggle and contend. I wish you well for the future, Conde.'

Renzi took a breath. He was being dismissed – it was now or never.

'Thank you. I return to an England equally pressed by a disorderly world. But as a grandee of that country I find myself with command of the ear of the highest. If there is something you feel might be accomplished by my intercession, then do be open with me, sir.'

'You will wish to talk of a conjoined front against the French.'

Renzi fought down his elation. 'I'm sanguine this is not impossible,' he allowed neutrally.

Solano made a dismissive gesture.

'Sir?'

'The French are here, you are in your island fortress. Who then shall we offend?' There was no faulting the logic.

'But—'

'Besides which, as you will grant, this requires a cessation in the state of war that exists between us.'

Renzi bowed without comment.

'And a declaration of hostilities by Spain against the French, both of which are unthinkable.'

'Sir, I cannot see—'

'For the simple reason that it is His Majesty alone who can set seal to such. And he is at the moment in Bayonne, guest of Emperor Napoleon Bonaparte, not free to act as he chooses.'

A gate had just slammed resoundingly shut.

The man, whatever his convictions, was moderate and reasonable. Yet his hands were securely tied and there was nothing he could do except carry out the orders of his royal master, who, very shortly, would be Joseph, the brother of Bonaparte.

Renzi felt a deep sympathy for what this honourable and rational man was facing. 'I understand, sir. And wish you well for your own future.'

Solano saw him to the door.

The evening was drawing in. As the warm breeze died, the streets and passageways started to fill with noisy, shouting streams of humanity, some jostling rudely, others with bottles in their hands.

Pedro pushed to the front and drew his rapier. 'Out of my way, you pox-faced villains!' he bellowed, challenging to left and right.

The crowd drew back but its mood darkened and ugly shouts pierced the hubbub.

Pedro scornfully stood his ground. 'Any who wants to be skewered on my fine Toledo steel, come to me, *mi pequeño cordero!*'

Renzi noted, with more than a little alarm, that not only were they massing in numbers but many carried weapons – bludgeons, kitchen knives, rusty swords.

'Who's your French friend, then?' a fat, sly-looking shop-keeper cat-called.

Pedro wheeled on him. 'Watch your tongue, oaf, or I'll cut it out and feed it to the dogs!'

The cry was taken up, '*Francés, francés, francés!*'

One closer yelled, 'Let's scrag the bastards!'

The crowd closed in.

Renzi faced them with a furious glare. '*¡Guerra al cuchillo! Mueran los Franceses traidores!*' he blazed.

Coming as it did from an unquestionable well-born, those nearest fell back, astonished, then delighted.

Standing defiantly with his arms folded, Renzi glared at them until, as quickly as it had come, the dangerous mood of the mob ebbed and was replaced by joyful rejoinders as each *caballero* strove to outdo another in violent and colourful curses on the French.

As they hurried on, Pedro sheathed his rapier and, with a suspicious glance at Renzi, thrust through to their residence.

Inside, he rounded on Renzi. 'So you know Spanish, Englishman. What are you, a spy?'

Renzi smiled and looked helplessly at Dolores.

'He wants to know if you are a spy. Are you?'

'A spy? I think not. "*¡Guerra al cuchillo!*" I heard day and night every damned hour from the crowds outside when locked indoors in Madrid. How can I not remember the words? Pray tell me, what does it mean?'

She looked at him, hesitating, thoughtful. Then said gaily, 'It means, "War to the knife – death to the French traitors!" so, you see, it was the right thing to say!'

The realisation of how close he'd come to being exposed shook Renzi. Until now he'd been safe: the crackling passport document he kept next to his breast his sure protection, proof of his innocence on a certified pilgrimage. It protected not just him but Dolores and others who were giving him shelter as a displaced pilgrim.

But it also specified rules of conduct and one was that he would leave Spain the way he'd come – in a cartel ship from the port of Cartagena.

To him it would be far preferable to take a British man-o'-war back to England but if it was thought he was communicating with the enemy offshore it could be for one purpose only: to spy for opportunities while Spain was suffering her present travails.

That left a journey through a dismembered corpse of a country across all southern Spain to Cartagena, with French troops ransacking it an abominable prospect.

Goaded by news arriving from Madrid of betrayals and

executions a visceral hatred was building for the French. There would be more scenes of barbarity, like those he'd seen in the capital, when Murat's forces had fanned out to the further provinces.

Chapter 29

Renzi ate his breakfast in his room, from one window able to take in a seaward view touched by a shy morning gilding the sails of the Inshore Squadron, catching the sunlight with stark clarity. From a smaller pane, he could see the anchored French battleships, illuminated on the other side, ominously darker.

Then, as he watched, he nearly dropped his spoon in surprise. From first one of the French battleships, then quickly the others, sail appeared, topsails with courses ready in their gear. They were putting to sea.

He held his breath. In a very short while action would be joined off Cádiz for the first time since Trafalgar – and again the British were outnumbered.

It was a shocking sight. Longing for a telescope, he stood and watched it unfold before him, heart in mouth for what was about to take place.

With the gentle north-easterly it was fair for the open sea directly, and once under way courses were set and they picked up speed, taking station on one of the big eighty-gun ships-of-the-line and making for the centre of the outer harbour.

Renzi turned his attention to the British fleet. There were two hoists up on the flagship and as he watched another soared. The admiral was in a taking – no scouting French frigate had warned of the sortie. Were the enemy trusting to a surprise lunge to sea?

But then came an even more extraordinary turn of events. In the precise centre of the wide bay, the lead French ship-of-the-line put over its helm, unbelievably making not for the open sea but the passage leading to the inner harbour, deeper into the enfolding defences of Cádiz.

Renzi couldn't sit down until he knew what was coming to pass – it made no sense, for the British could never enter the outer harbour against fire from the six massive fortresses.

The stately passage of the squadron took them within just a half-mile and he saw them in startling definition in the morning light. As they passed, he noted the straggling progress of some, gun-ports open, as if expecting an engagement, but also the dark streaks on their canvas that told of long stowage and little sea-time.

Then he understood. He was watching the last survivors of Trafalgar, still here after their fleeing those years before. And the admiral flying his flag in the largest had to be Rosily, whose dispatch by Bonaparte to replace Villeneuve for being too timid had precipitated the battle.

A shiver went through Renzi. This was the wreckage of history, left behind from a great event in the past. And a token of the ferocious effectiveness of the Royal Navy's blockade that never once, over those years, had these vessels been let loose on Britain's sea lanes.

They passed on, into the widening inner harbour. After reaching nearly to the opposite shore they shortened sail and all became clear: they were joining the small gaggle of masts and yards that was all he could see of the Spanish naval base.

But what did it mean?

Chapter 30

Pedro returned for the midday meal, by turns excited, apprehensive and boastful.

Word was that Murat had not delayed and at this hour near twenty-five thousand troops and guns were astride the road to Cádiz and expected in days only. This could only inflame a tense and angry situation, with the result that this afternoon the town council would go to Governor Solano, demanding he turn out the army of General Morla to defend the city, against a siege, if need be.

Sailors going ashore from the French squadron had been found murdered, the news and rumours from Madrid whipping up hatred in the local population that found release only in bloodshed. The ships had scuttled away for sanctuary in the well-defended naval base at Carracas until Murat's forces could relieve them.

Renzi heard it all with growing unease. He'd been hoping for a relatively peaceful transfer of power and calm in the countryside as he'd slipped away from Madrid, but with hotheads like Pedro it would be a savage process that would set the whole region into seething hostility.

He had a short time only to come up with a plan to get himself away from the tidal wave of barbarity about to fall on Cádiz.

Pedro pirouetted before the women in his hip-hugging pantaloons and elaborate high-heeled boots, set off by a lavishly ornamented frogged crimson and gold jacket. 'Ha! This is what I wear when we stand up for Spain's honour before *su excelencia* – what do you think, *mi corazón*?'

Benita looked at him adoringly, then hugged him tightly and burst into tears. 'You'll be careful, Pedro, please tell me you will.'

He smirked. 'There are times when sacrifice is demanded, *mi amor*, and know that I shall be always found there at the front.'

The streets were choked with even more excited, streaming crowds, for news of the deputation had got out. With bursting pride Pedro found he was recognised as a member of the town council and energetically cheered, lifted up and carried to the Plaza de los Pozos, before the stern nobility of the governor's residence and office.

It was the greatest day of his life.

The curtains at the rear of the balcony were firmly closed but above all, huge and majestic, floated the ornate colours of the Bourbon King of Spain. With a full heart, Don Pedro joined the others in the marble-floored reception area.

When the doors from the outside were finally closed, the tumult on the streets was cut off and a respectful hush descended. At the top of the sweeping staircase, to one side behind the balustrades where he could address the throng, Don Francisco Solano appeared.

'I know why you've come, gentlemen,' he began. 'There's

no need to tell me that the situation threatening us is singular and demanding.'

Fervid cries of agreement rang out. Solano frowned slightly. This was unbecoming behaviour in such distinguished surroundings. 'And you are here to ask counsel of your governor under His Majesty, as is right and proper in you.'

He chose to ignore the rumble of muttered discontent.

'I am, of course, privy to the King's desiring and my counsel to you is this: to be allied to the greatest and most powerful empire in this world is infinitely to be preferred to insulting it, and I do remind you all that we are in fact so united. That differences do arise from time to time—'

'We will not be dishonoured by these pigs! In Madrid they've—'

'Cádiz shall not fall beneath the boots of the cursed *francéses*!' Pedro blared. 'Never while I live!'

There was a roar from the council that turned Pedro pink with pleasure.

Solano, pained, waited for the bedlam to fade. 'Gentlemen. I can sympathise with your feelings but there are a number of good reasons why this cannot be. Apart from the impossibility of standing against the legions of French on their way here, might I point out that firing upon our ally will be seen as illegal, the act of murderers and pirates, and they will then be quite within their rights to hang every last one of you.'

Hostility was now radiating up from the massed councillors to Solano, and he shrank back.

Emboldened, Pedro roared, 'They'll have to get past me first! Arm every man who can carry a gun and let their blood run like water!'

A savage growl erupted into an angry howl.

Solano, pale-faced, waited long minutes to be heard. 'You don't know what you're saying!' he said loudly. 'This is an act of war and we're not at war. Emperor Bonaparte will take a fearful vengeance upon you if—'

Pedro snarled back, 'If we're not at war, we should be. All those of my comrades who vote to declare war on the *francéses* murderers, say aye!'

There was a storm of joyous shouting and Pedro smiled wickedly. 'So you see, Excelentísimo, we've declared war. What do you now counsel us?'

Solano tried to speak but had to wait for quiet. 'Gentlemen. Recollect yourselves. You're the Cádiz town council, and town councils do not declare war on nations. Only His Majesty the King may declare war and—'

'And he's guest of the French and can't speak for himself. So who does? You?'

By now the news that Cádiz had declared war on the French had spread, and yells of riotous approval came from outside. A muffled chanting – '*¡Muerte a los francéses! Muerte a los francéses!*' – grew in intensity.

Solano glanced around uncertainly for support but saw only the seething riot that was now the town council in session. A look of despair came over him. Abruptly he turned and left.

The council, offended, cast about in confusion but then a massive roar sounded from the plaza. 'It's the *cabrón* gone to the people. He thinks to ignore us, the elected town council!' Pedro spluttered. 'He's on the balcony.'

There was a general surge out into the plaza and the crowd looked up to see Solano standing under the huge flag motioning for quiet. Grudgingly, they fell silent.

'Citizens of Cádiz, I urge you with all my heart to pay no mind to those who'd drive you into the jaws of death. This is not the way to solve our differences. We shall find a means—'

'We have a way! We fight – for our soil, our people, our honour!' Pedro bawled, and was forced to his knees by the storm of acclamation. He staggered back to his feet and yelled hoarsely, 'We declare war on the butchers of Madrid! Long live Spain and all those who love their country!'

The crowd roared again. Pedro looked about – the army and militia were nowhere to be seen and the mood was furious and excited.

'Why doesn't Solano listen to us?' he dared. 'Is he bosom friends with the French? Does he pledge obedience to the *detestado* French puppet Joseph, instead of to the line of true Spanish kings?'

The crowd went wild, venom and hatred in their shouts.

'Declare war on the French, Solano, or we'll know what it means!'

'This is not something I can do, believe me! Only if—'

It was the end. Past reason, the huge crowd surged forward, knocking aside the ushers and flooding into the residence. Solano quickly disappeared from the balcony.

But as the mob invaded from below he came into view again, this time on the roof, where his appearance was met by a roar of triumph. Hesitating, he shot hunted glances about, then ran to the end, leaped across to the next building and vanished.

'Quick! To the back! Stop him getting away!'

There was an atmosphere of insane exhilaration in the crowd and Pedro revelled in it. 'Get him out, the bastard!' he shouted, smashing at the front door with his fists. It soon fell inwards to a swarm of enraged men.

Minutes passed, then confused faces appeared at the windows. 'He's not here! Gone!'

'He must be there – look again!' Pedro shouted angrily.

There was no result. Then a beefy man shouldered his way

through to Pedro. 'I'm Manuel El Albañil,' he puffed. 'Bricklayer. I know where he is, the pig. With my own hands I built a false fireplace in there – that's where he'll be.'

Pedro was exultant. 'Well, what are you waiting for? Go to it! Drag him out!'

Chapter 31

In the street the mob fell on Solano, tearing his ornaments of office from him, screaming hate and murder at the pitiable figure.

'Hang him!' a cry came anonymously from the crowd.

'You can't do that!' Pedro gasped, suddenly troubled.

'We can and we will, the French dog!'

'Where?' he demanded, playing for time.

'Ha! There's a gallows in the Plaza de San Juan de Dios.'

Solano was forced to a frog-march and the screaming throng made for the square in a frenzy of jubilation, Don Pedro caught up unwillingly in their wake. It had got out of hand, and someone would pay for it later, that much was certain.

The flood of humanity turned into the square – the small, grey-timbered gallows in shadows at the far end, its ropes tied neatly.

They jerked Solano's head back so he could see it but his bloodied face wore an unnerving serenity.

The press carried him forward until he was at its base. While some swarmed over it to prepare the noose, a young man in a gaudy uniform came close to him. 'You French traitor!' he screamed, drawing a blade. There was a flash of steel as it was plunged into Solano's back.

With a spasm of pain the governor jerked around. 'You fool! You couldn't even do that right!' he gasped. His head flopped to one side as his blood trickled into the ground.

Not knowing what to do next they held him as he lost consciousness. Then one called, in a peculiar off-key voice, 'We can't hang him now.'

'Why not?' came a rough reply. 'What law says you have to be in your senses when you're twitched off?'

After arguing they compromised by taking him to the church – the priest would know what to do.

The Marqués del Socorro, governor of Cádiz and captain general of Andalucía, died half an hour later.

The mob milled about, unsure, unsettled.

At the opposite side of the square a crash of muskets brought heads whipping round in fear. Soldiers were forming a line, and behind them, more. A volley was fired into the air and an officer rode into the square, the mob now cowering, frightened. The French already?

'It's General Morla!' breathed Pedro in relief, recognising the impressive figure on his fine charger. 'Sir, what should we do?' he called anxiously.

The soldier looked about in contempt. 'The town council to meet this instant!' he shouted.

Inside the familiar chamber, spirits returned. 'The French are coming. Only over the bodies of our slain shall they enter Cádiz!'

'Silence!' roared Morla, taking position at the head as though born to it. 'I am now the captain general of Andalucía and you'll take my orders.'

He waited until he had their complete attention. 'And you'll stand with me against the French as they do their worst.'

A storm of cheering erupted and went on and on. Don Pedro's heart swelled with pride. What it was to be a Spaniard and a Gaditano, a true son of Cádiz, at this time.

'They're ten days away to the north-east. Our defences had better be good and they will be. Now this is what we will contrive . . .'

A mild-featured gentleman in neat, conservative dress held up his hand. 'Ah, *mi capitán*.'

Morla gave way to the scholar and jurist of wide reputation, deciding to deal with whatever was troubling him at the outset. 'Señor Ezquerra?'

'Why are we fighting?'

That took Morla's breath away and stunned the rest of the chamber into silence.

'I mean, just what are we fighting for?' he went on.

A shout of disbelief echoed from one councillor, but the rest held silent to see what point the sharp-minded man was about to make.

'Should it be for the King – if so, which one? Or shall we simply say Fernando el Deseado, not the false French upstart?'

Uncertain cheers rang out but quickly faded.

'If so, we are paralysed. We cannot move without His Majesty's word on it.'

In the baffled quiet he went on, as though in a lecture hall, 'Perhaps we are fighting for Spain, our native land.'

This brought roars of agreement but he held up his hand. 'Her flag bears the royal arms, under which we cannot march in acts that do not bear the royal signature.'

'We fight for our honour, señor, as well you understand,' Morla said peevishly.

'This may be your intention, but any act under arms to

which you direct us may only be deemed treasonable, and must be seen as the actions of a warlord of no legitimacy whatsoever.'

'Then, sir, you are desiring us to lay down our weapons and allow the French hordes to enter Cádiz and trample us down with no resistance whatsoever?'

'I have not said that, *mi capitán*. My desire is as yours, to cast out the French, but within the bounds of legal practice. This demands that we find a way to empower our acts with the sanctity of the law.'

'Good God! I've several times ten thousand French on their way here and you prate of the law!'

'You ignore it at your peril, señor. Supposing you yearn to levy tax for your powder and shot, where is your warrant from the people? To conscript young men for your armies, to billet your battalions, to direct others to do your bidding? This is only the beginning, sir. Other provinces will rise up. Who then do you believe they will be speaking to when they desire to join us in our sacred task?'

Morla mopped his brow wearily. 'Then what is the answer? What piece of paper do we clap our names to? Tell us, good lawyer.'

'A form of assembly, of agreement. To which we bind ourselves each and severally. And swear due allegiance.'

'What shall it contain?'

'Ah. This is something only we may conjure for ourselves. It will not be a trivial matter. Shall we begin now?'

Chapter 32

At least the crowds had thinned and dispersed since the recent bloodshed and sacrifice, Renzi reflected, pulling back from the window. No longer were rowdy processions cramming the streets and alleys, and since the town council had taken to meeting for hours on end, some semblance of order had returned.

The market was in vigorous progress and the fishing boats had put out for the evening catch. It was probably safe to walk abroad, catch a breath of air in the early-summer afternoon warmth.

Dolores and Benita were deep in conversation, catching up on gossip, and didn't feel inclined to accompany him so, checking again that he was as similarly dressed as he could be to the locals, he stepped out.

In the aftermath of the confusion and drama of the day he was unnoticed and let his steps take him where they would. Soon he found he was threading his way directly west in the direction of the lowering sun – and the sight of the British fleet anchored offshore.

It wasn't far to the edge of the old city and a pleasant

beach that was the haunt of boats coming and going, some pulled up on the golden sand. And no more than a mile or so out the Inshore Squadron was at anchor.

He stopped and shaded his eyes, searching for one – and there she was, at the end of the regularly spaced line of ships: *Tyger*, and in her would be Captain Sir Thomas Kydd, his most particular friend, whose cool-headed and unruffled friendship he suddenly desired in this madness more than he could conceive.

Going to the railing along the top of the sea wall, he looked out at her longingly. In the mile or so that separated old Cádiz and the anchored ships, at least three or four boats were pulling out to them as though this were Portsmouth harbour itself.

Renzi guessed that this was a kind of informal and probably regular routine that he'd seen so often in harbours and roadsteads around the world – bumboats ferried by locals hoping to sell vegetables, fish and other fresh produce. It was a practice probably as old as the blockade itself, considerably helped by the fact that the customers were handily at anchor and it was of benefit to both sides to turn a blind eye.

Renzi smiled to himself. This was without doubt why the victuallers from England had seldom provided fresh foodstuffs.

And then he saw his chance. Casually, he went down the steps to the beach, joining the to-ing and fro-ing of the pedlars and porters until he found what he was looking for.

'*Hola, mi amigo!*' he called to a swarthy boat-owner, who was supervising the last loading of greens and potatoes.

The man squinted up but said nothing.

'You'll get the best price from that barky at the end,' Renzi said confidentially.

'Where you from?' The man frowned, his broad Andalucían a considerable contrast to Renzi's cool northern Castilian.

'Bilbao, but does it matter? I'm telling you I know that one, idiot captain who's always on at his crew to eat greens.'

'How do you know?'

'I'm in this line of business in Bilbao and Santander. Down here to see my poorly sister, wish I'd stayed. I tell you what – how much do you expect to get for this lot?'

'What's it to you? Naught beyond a hundred *reales* or eight English guineas.'

'So if I can help you get a better price, anything above a hundred, we split. Fair enough?'

The man grinned. 'Always up for a deal, Vasco. You're on!'

'Then, just to see fair play, I'll come out with you. Here, I'll give you a hand,' Renzi added, expertly taking one side of the bow for launching into deeper water.

It was like a dream. The easy trip out, the looming frigate and casual hail from the waist. When they hooked on at the fore-chains, the purser and his steward were summoned to deal with a gabble of pidgin English.

'I'll see how the old bastard is,' Renzi said casually, pulling his hat low over his face. In a practised swing he landed on the fore-deck.

''Ere, Manuelo, y' can't come aboard like that!' an astonished seaman said, and advanced on the figure.

Renzi flicked up the brim to impale the man with his eyes. 'Get me to Captain Kydd this instant, do you hear me?' he hissed.

Outside the door to the great cabin he heard a familiar voice: 'Come!'

'Some Spanish cove wants t' see yez, sir,' said the sailor, doubtfully, and ushered Renzi in.

Kydd looked up from his desk, Tysoe in the act of pouring an afternoon whisky.

'So?'

Renzi whipped off his hat and pirouetted, ending with a stamp, Spanish-style.

'Wha'?' Kydd blurted in amazement. 'Nicholas! You're . . . you're . . .'

'I'm here, if that is your meaning.'

'Good God! What on earth . . .?' He shot out of his chair, went to Renzi and clasped his hand in delight. 'Never mind, as you say, you're here, old trout!'

Tysoe was back with another glass, his celerity pleasing.

'I won't ask what the devil you're doing in Spain, you'll just pull me up with a round turn and serve me right.' He surveyed his friend with concern. 'But we've been hearing of some rum doings ashore, Nicholas.'

'Don't worry your kind self about me, dear fellow. I'm perfectly secure, just caught up in my, er, pilgrimage, as it were.'

'Well, you're now safely aboard but I can't say when we'll next be in England. However, we're off north, and then I can probably get you passage on a victualler.'

'That's kindly said, m' good friend, but I've Jago and some others I should take care of first. I mustn't stay long. Oh, I need this to be added to your payment for the fresh vegetables before I leave.' He passed some coins to Tysoe.

Kydd's forehead creased. 'What's going on ashore, can I ask it? We're hearing all kinds of rumours about the Dons taking against the Frogs or something.'

'Yes, there's just been a mort of unpleasantness against their own man, the governor of Cádiz. He was a moderate, reasonable kind of fellow but now they swear that, after Madrid, they'll stand against the French columns sent to subdue them. Bonaparte won't let it go, and all will end in nastiness, I fear.'

'But you'll be out of it.'

'Soon, I do hope. Yet I've a yen to see how it all ends.'

'Well, you can be sure *Tyger* will be here for you when you give me a hail. Er, can I beg you'll give me your address – in the case there's a need for, um . . .?'

Renzi scribbled it down and asked, 'And may I know what can worry the lords of the sea?'

'Ah. The main trouble is we haven't any idea what's afoot. We thought the Dons and the French were friends, even if they've got their differences, and now we've heard there's bad things happening in Madrid. Why?'

'Dear fellow, don't ask. What's plain is that Bonaparte has comprehensively fooled the Spanish and is now in the process of taking and pacifying the country, and anon we'll be seeing the tyrant Emperor with a brother on the throne of Spain. It's all but over, Tom.'

'Well, Whitehall's in a wretched moil. They know there's a fair-sized French squadron here and whoever ends up with it is going to be a right worry to us. They're saying to Collingwood that he's to deal with them as soon as they show themselves.'

'There's no chance of that, dear chap. I've seen them with my own eyes scuttle to the naval base at the inner harbour. You'll never get them there.'

A knock at the door interrupted them. 'Sir, the trader's asking where's his friend?'

Renzi got up. 'I have to go, Tom. You've no idea how soothing to a worry of spirits it is to know you're here. We'll see each other soon, I've no doubt.'

In the now-empty boat the vegetable-seller was exultant. 'You were right, Vasco. Here's your twenty *reales*.' The coins clinked into Renzi's hand. 'And I'm to wait on 'em again. Ha!'

As the sun was setting in a glorious golden blaze out to sea, Renzi made his way back and found that he hadn't been missed. Pedro was sprawled in the best chair, his feet on the table, eating an orange with coarse, tearing bites and regaling the women with his triumph.

'You're missing the fun, Inglés.'

Dolores explained that in their wisdom the good folk of the town council had come together in a quite different assembly. This was the Cádiz junta – and, by masterful command of words, they had created a form of sovereign assembly that was outside the direct rule of governance, releasing them to rise against the French in their own name. The inflammatory document would be rushed to wherever there were those who'd swear to stand together to throw off the yoke.

Most importantly, eventually there would be created a Grand Cortes, with representatives from all of Spain, which would convene to produce a constitution and government with comprehensive national legitimacy.

And they were declaring war in their own right on the greatest military power in the world.

Renzi listened politely. Was this the usual bombast of a warlord in rebellion, or something much more profound? 'How will your junta stand against Murat and his thousands?' he asked, hiding his doubts.

It seemed General Morla, now captain general of all Spanish forces in the south, had definite views on the defence of Cádiz and, by the simple device of requiring sworn allegiance to the junta, was raising a militia, a voluntary band that would eventually be numbered in their tens of thousands.

Renzi's attention grew. This was, in effect, a rebellion, but not of the usual kind. Not against the King, but in support of an ideal, whatever was laid out in their constitution, sovereignty apparently to reside in the nation, not in the person of the monarch. And, interestingly, this was not one man's work, no revolutionary figurehead leading it, and therefore it was free of the taint of personal ambition.

And, significantly, it promised to spread over all of Spain.

A general rising, no single head to be lopped off – the French would find the swallowing of their conquest far harder than the winning of it.

But by now all the fortresses, arsenals, military stores and highways would be firmly in Bonaparte's hands. How could they survive, let alone prevail?

Of course, if they found help, it might be another story.

He had to see Morla.

Chapter 33

It wasn't easy to gain audience with the captain general, and it was not until late evening that this was granted over a hasty meal in the chambers of the council, then among noisy debate and occasional flaring arguments.

'What is it you want, Englishman? I'm a busy man,' he asked, through an interpreter.

'General, I've been treated well by the Spanish and wish you well of your noble cause.'

'And?'

'Sir, this is an endeavour fraught with difficulties. How can you think to arm and train your citizenry, your militia, without the means to do so? If—'

'This is my business, Inglés, not yours. Is that all?' He broke off more bread, the toss of his head dismissive.

'You and I both know you haven't powder, shot or even pay for your army to make a good showing against the French, and if you don't, your glorious uprising will melt away in shame.'

'So? What do you suggest?'

'That England brings you help and sustaining. Not only ammunition and uniforms but—'

'No.'

Taken aback by Morla's blunt retort, Renzi asked quietly, 'May I know why not? You'll agree we have common cause against the French tyrant, surely.'

'I need to explain it to you?' Morla snarled. 'We've been at war for centuries past. Why should we trust you with our country now?'

'I can assure you that—'

'I'm a military man, Inglés, and I notice things different to your man of words only. Like Cádiz – an old city sticking out into the sea on an easily fortified peninsula. How you English would adore to possess a second Gibraltar!'

It took Renzi's breath away but the man was clearly sincere in his views. 'Sir, that's not at all in our conceiving.'

'No? Then you're going to pour in your arms and treasure and not take a price for it? You think me a fool? There's one prize you haven't wrung from us yet, Inglés. Our colonies in the Americas. You've forgotten your invasion of Buenos Aires already? We haven't.'

Renzi swallowed. He was losing the argument. And the infinitely precious chance to turn an enemy into an ally.

Morla finished his wine, drinking like a peasant from a skin. 'You'll act like a conquistador, see us weak and helpless, then trample over us. Ours is a proud country and never will allow this. Thank you for your preaching, now let me get on with my work.'

So that was it! The pride of a Spaniard that would never allow him to suffer the humiliation of begging, cap in hand, even for his own salvation. It was understandable and impossible to counter. Unless . . .

'This I do allow is nothing an honourable man can tolerate,' Renzi agreed. 'Yet it seems to me there is a way that at one stroke you can achieve a standing with the English that lets you look them in the eye as an equal. That enables you to accept anything they offer at the same degree as they offer it.'

Morla paused, his eyes speculative. 'Go on, Inglés.'

'The French are not just on the road from Madrid. They are here, now.'

The general narrowed his eyes but said nothing.

'With an artillery detachment of a hundred cannon and more, quite able to reduce Cádiz in hours.'

'What are you blathering about?' he barked.

'The French squadron, new shifted into the Carracas arsenal. If you move against them as they lie, set them to the torch or batter them to submission with your own pieces, you'll have the whole glory of finishing the battle of Trafalgar for the English, for these are the last survivors remaining. You'll do what Admiral Nelson did not and the world will hear about it, be assured of that, General. Will you not then be able to stand before any Englishman with this victory at your back and *demand* what you will?'

Morla's eyes gleamed. 'I hear you well. It will not be easy – the ground at the arsenal is well chosen by our fathers, marshes, soft going for guns of size. Yet I'll do it, I believe! It'll give much heart to our brave *soldados* as will lead them on to triumph later. Hey – wine for my friend! You'll drink with me, *mi amigo.*'

Chapter 34

Aboard Conqueror

Rowley put down the dispatch irritably. If there was one thing he disliked more than anything, it was another admiral telling him what to do. Here, Collingwood was claiming superior intelligence that Cádiz was in some state of anarchy in the face of the French advance from Madrid. Civil disorder, assassinations and similar.

He was being ordered to take advantage of this to make an approach to the authorities, offering assistance leading to some sort of entente, a manner of collaboration possible. It was all very vague.

He snorted. It was nonsense, of course. His entire professional career had been with Spaniards as foe, and there'd been nothing that indicated they'd made any kind of turncoat move. Indeed, the letter of his fighting instructions was that they were enemy and in consequence he should bend all possible efforts to their destruction. What if he were fool enough to fall for some knavish trick and took his fleet into an entrapment? He'd be blamed.

And the closing paragraph of the dispatch: it was of the first necessity to neutralise the French squadron while the situation was fluid – presumably before Murat's army reached Cádiz to put down the unrest. Well, that was now out of his hands. Reconnaissance had shown them moved from their usual anchorage, assumed to be taking refuge within the inner anchorage where they were essentially untouchable.

'Flags!' he called peevishly.

'Sir?'

'What's the form to parlay with the enemy?'

'T-to—'

'For God's sake! I want to talk to whoever's still in charge ashore. Encourage 'em to, well, come around to our way of thinking, that sort of thing.'

'Sir.'

'Well, get on with it. We haven't time to dither, man.'

He started pencilling notes, points at issue, a list of gun salutes and their number in case the heathen Spanish had no notion of honour due a flag. Absently, he tapped with his pencil, trying to bring things to some sort of order, but it was impossible. Just what was meant by assisting the enemy? Helping them haul down their flag?

He brightened at a thought: if they were willing to surrender to him, they would have no need to face the French and would thank him for it. Spain capitulating to Rear Admiral Rowley? It would be in the history books to the end of time.

The admiral's barge put off from *Conqueror* and, under a large white flag, boldly pressed on into the outer anchorage. From the castle of San Sebastián, at the end of its long causeway, a challenging shot thudded out.

The boat rounded to, its sails lowered, and waited, the huge flag wilting in the light breeze. Eventually an aviso under oars ventured out, Spanish colours vivid against the grey sea. Watchers from the flagship saw it go alongside the barge and a letter handed over before it turned about and returned, the barge remaining patiently where it was.

It was well over an hour before there was further movement: the aviso came out again and, with much bowing and ceremony, gave a letter to the flag-lieutenant. An impatient Rowley paced *Conqueror*'s quarterdeck until it was passed up and the contents disclosed, courtesy of Ransome, the thin-faced translator-cleric from *Leviathan*.

'A meeting! On a neutral ship that they'll provide from those in port. A military cove, Morla, and some junta or other. This afternoon at three.'

Shortly before the due time a homely barque of useful size beat its way out to the centre of the bay, which was the outer harbour, and cast anchor. Rowley boarded his barge, delayed only by discussion as to whether the Union Flag of Great Britain, as representing the national interest, should be at the single masthead or his own admiral's pennant. It was decided in favour of the latter: the Union Flag being flown as a pennant indicated a full admiral. A temporary staff was found for it at the transom.

Morla stood on one end of the main hatch, with equerries and attendants, a formidable figure in the magnificence of a captain general of Andalucía, stiff with gold lace, aiguillettes and an impossibly long rapier.

Mounting the other end of the hatch, Rowley took position, flanked by Ransome and the flag-lieutenant. His secretary stood ready to make record.

Bowing stiffly, Morla fired off some Spanish, his granite features alive with distaste.

'Says as what brings the English to seek parlay after twelve years of insults to their flag.'

Rowley smiled winningly. 'Tell him I'm here to offer the Spanish Crown any assistance they require to stand against the French.'

'He says he stands insulted. He is not the Spanish Crown: he is of the ruling Cádiz junta and reminds you that you are the sworn enemy of Spain.'

'Ah. We have a means to deal with that little problem.'

It took Morla by surprise and there was a sharp interchange before he threw back his reply.

'Er, sir. It is, that is to say, he wonders if you are here to offer terms . . . for your capitulation to, um, Spain.'

Rowley nearly choked. 'No, no! Tell the fellow it's the other way round. Does he wish to render up Cádiz and Spain to me in preference to the French, who are known to be merciless in their conquering?'

It brought an incredulous burst of savage laughter and Morla leaned forward to hiss his response.

'If this is why we're here, he declares it a contemptible waste of time.'

'Wait! There's another matter. The French squadron taking shelter in Cádiz. It is a powerful one, too great a weight of metal to consider engaging yourself. If it is not an inconvenience might I request the general to drive them out to us? We'll put them down in fine style, be assured of that.'

Morla's contempt was plain. 'If the French ships need assaulting, that is our business. Anything else?'

Thankful to be back in the sturdy refuge of his great cabin, Rowley smouldered. He'd done precisely what Collingwood had asked, offered help, tried to deal with the French squadron, and the cantankerous, ignorant Spaniard had gone out of his way to be obstructive. The trouble was, the navy didn't take kindly to excuses and he'd have to admit an achievement in the sum total of nothing.

It wasn't for some time that he came up with a solution. He would put it about that the reduction of the French squadron before the relieving force arrived was of prime importance to strategy at this stage of the war, which was not altogether an exaggeration. Every effort must be devoted to this end. Unhappily, the French had retired to the inner harbour but there was opportunity here for a brave and dedicated officer to press home a surprise attack in boats – fire craft, mortars, rockets, whatever was needed to bring ruin and destruction to the anchored ships.

This had a gratifying number of advantages. Even if it did not succeed, as was likely, it showed he was, in the most gallant manner, following Collingwood's orders in the teeth of Spanish opposition. And he knew who would take the bait, who would throw himself into the thick of the fighting. In failing, what a tragic loss to the service . . .

Chapter 35

Kydd entered *Conqueror*'s great cabin warily. He had no idea what the unusually polite summons to attend on the admiral was about. The flag-lieutenant sat to one side, industriously scribbling – there to act as witness?

Tyger was in the last day or so of preparation for another cruise south and, as far as Kydd knew, required no particular instructions, but a command from an admiral could not be disobeyed. A fence-mending move? Fearing his power to divulge, expose the past?

'Ah, Captain. Thank you for your prompt attendance – much appreciated.' The tone was light, almost jovial, and Kydd tensed.

'I won't waste your time any further, for the matter presses. You see, I have a difficulty that I'm sanguine you can help me with. Here, read this.' He handed over a letter.

It was hurriedly written but plain in its essentials. From Collingwood, it detailed expectations of his subordinate, quite improper for Kydd to see. He glanced up, but Rowley's expression remained impassive, composed.

'The last paragraph, if you please.'

It didn't take long to deduce that the Admiralty was being pressured by the government of the day and had passed this along to the reigning admiral of the station, Collingwood, who in turn was putting the matter to Rowley, the man on the spot.

'I've spoken to the Spanish commander, whose attitude has been both unsatisfactory and, might I say, disrespectful. They've shown no interest in driving out the French for us to deal with, and persist in treating us as the enemy.' He sniffed. 'Which leaves us in a hellish position.'

'Sir.'

'For the sake of the country, this squadron has to be destroyed. If it falls into the wrong hands we've a serious perplexity. And there is no other course than to mount an immediate operation against them where they lie, in the interior harbour.'

Rowley looked him full in the eye. 'Kydd, I've choice of a dozen captains, most senior to you, but despite our differences I'm obliged to recognise that you are best fitted of all to lead this daring assault.'

He continued to hold his gaze, and went on, 'It's to be a hard thing I'm asking – and I'd well understand it, should you refuse – but do you feel able to do your duty in this?'

A penetration into the unknown reaches of Cádiz, in the absence of a channel pilot having to be accomplished by boat – not even Nelson's famed hand-to-hand cutlass duels had achieved anything like this. Kydd could see the dire need to deal with the potent force before the French columns flooding in from the north reached them and knew in his heart he had to do it. What Rowley had said could not be denied: because of his past, he was the best suited to lead, and if it were any other, it could well turn into a bloodbath. It still might.

'I get full command. "Authority to decide" what comprises our force, timing, the rest?'

'You shall. Within the limits of what I can provide, that is.'

'Then, sir, I'll do it.'

Rowley hesitated, then his hand went out and he said silkily, 'I can only wish you well.'

Chapter 36

In a fury of activity Kydd turned over his cabin to be headquarters. First things first. It had to be a boat action as no one knew the bottom ground in the inner waters, where there was sufficient depth of water for a full-rigged ship, even what they'd be seeing there.

He set officers from various ships stepping out distances with dividers, determining cannon-shot range arcs from the forts and covering fire. Meanwhile he and the sailing master established what quadrants the wind could be in to allow them to close with the enemy. A foul wind would throw out all plans: miles under oars before a desperate action would be too much to ask of even the bravest.

The core of his attack was to be a murderous blaze. Nothing else would allow boats to take on ships. The only advantage they had was that the French would be securely anchored and unsuspecting. A mass attack by boats with fire-rafts in quantity on a dense, unmoving target would be a horrifying sight, and even if cables were cut, with the wind anywhere in the west they would drift on to the marshy ground beyond and still suffer the onslaught.

This would be but part of the attack. Each craft would have its share of boat mortars to fire carcasses, flaming infernals instead of shot, and he'd see if he could also find some of Colonel Congreve's rockets to mount in them.

He was going to demand boats from every ship in the fleet – twenty, thirty, forty – and all volunteers, for once action had been joined they'd have to fight their way out.

It was a desperate, wild venture, but there was much to be gained. If they destroyed the majority of the enemy they'd be achieving a victory in numbers and degree to set next to the action of the Glorious First of June!

The plan took shape. Boats were fitted out at a ferocious pace, rafts normally used for painting ships' sides loaded with powder and combustibles, and the evil-looking bronze boat mortars bedded in. In a surprisingly short time the assault flotilla was near ready, assembling out of sight to seaward. Kydd didn't want curious bumboats or others to catch sight of what was going on but on the other hand to forbid them their normal trade would arouse suspicion.

Remarkably, the breeze was with them, a mild west-south-westerly. There was an obliging moon that would not show its face before midnight and tides that, while not perfect, were on the flood for much of the time.

With no point in delay they would go in that night.

There would be no last-minute noble address to the warriors about to join battle for they'd be scattered in boats well out of earshot and, in any case, men like them did not need such. Instead they would be looking to their commander leading from the fore, in the first boat.

Left alone in *Tyger*'s great cabin, Kydd let his thoughts rush on in a chaotic stream as they usually did before a planned action.

But then, just as it did after a morning sight of sail turned to the certainty that this was the enemy, cold calculation came to the fore. Wind prevailing, currents, land proximity, all falling into their place in the larger reckoning and the result: a hot-blooded combat that required only intelligence, attention to detail and courage to result in victory.

It was the overlooking of detail in the rush and hurry that lost battles, not a want of courage. Had he done enough?

Then, with a start, Renzi came to mind. Kydd had no idea what the address meant in terms of proximity to the tempest of shot and shell that was to come, but there was a chance that his dear friend would be innocently caught up in the blaze of fighting.

However, it was within his power to warn him. Scribbling a message, he folded the paper tightly and looked around. There was nothing he could see that would serve so he rang for Tysoe. 'The largest jar of marmalade you can find in my cabin stores, if y' please.'

Tysoe hesitated only an eye-blink, then returned wordlessly with the article.

Carefully slipping the message under the lid, Kydd closed it with his personal seal. 'Find our grocer cove and tell him he may claim half-a-crown if it's delivered to this address before sunset.'

Chapter 37

La Viña

Renzi pondered. Morla had spurned the British offer of assistance. It was to be expected, for with a state of war still existing it would have to be an exceptional circumstance that could bring the proud Spaniards to accept. Their reduction of the French squadron would change things, certainly, but could they do it? Against three, four hundred pieces of artillery in the ships, three or four thousand men aboard them – these were fierce odds.

And time was against them. Who knew when the French would reach Cádiz? Unless they moved fast it would be too late to achieve their victory and claim British aid. Just like Madrid, the old city would fall into Bonaparte's hands and he would then have the finest harbour in Atlantic Iberia to mass his battleships to burst forth on the over-stretched British.

A tap on the door interrupted his thoughts and the maid entered, bobbing and proffering a jar of English marmalade. Taken aback Renzi accepted it, then looked it over with suspicion. To his great surprise, he recognised the unbroken seal.

It was incomprehensible that Kydd should think he needed such a gift at this time. He broke the seal, and under the lid was a folded piece of paper.

The message brought the worst conceivable news. There was going to be a move by the Inshore Squadron on the French ships in an attempt to neutralise them before the French troops reached Cádiz, to be led by Kydd himself.

Renzi screwed up the paper in despair and hurried to the door, heart pounding. It was a beautiful evening, but one imperative blotted out all else: Kydd must not be allowed to go through with it.

Apart from the hideous danger, such an act would comprehensively put paid to any chance of bringing the Spanish over. He had to get to him to stop the assault, whatever it took.

Couples stared at him curiously as he ran down to the beach. Where was the vegetable-seller? Not seeing him, he asked one of the idle boatmen, who said, as if to an idiot, 'They're all gone home, as any Christian gent does after they've sold up their fresh stock.'

Indeed no boats were plying out to the fleet, now darkening shadows against the sunset.

Catastrophe lay only small hours away – unless he could get credible word out to Kydd that would have him suspending a complex operation in its last stages before execution. He tried to think of something but, there being no communication with an 'enemy' fleet, there could be no pleading in the little time left. He must just watch helplessly as the drama played out to its end.

It was only as he reached the Los Carros alley that cold logic intervened. There was a way to prevent it happening – a sure and certain way.

He stopped and thought about it, but only for a moment. The stakes were too high.

Turning on his heel, he started to walk, quickly and purposefully.

Chapter 38

Darkness lay in every direction in the moonless night as the flotilla set off from their assembly point to seaward of the Inshore Squadron. Sail was shaken out in the light breeze – cutters and launches, barges and yawls all towing low rafts loaded with combustibles and men ready for the worst that the enemy could do.

The lights of the old town area were a fine seamark and, with the distant twinkle from Rota several miles on the other side of the bay, there was no mistaking their position. Almost invisible in the gloom they passed the outer San Sebastián fort without incident and shaped course for the next danger: the waters between Trocadero and the Cádiz peninsula, guarded by the Puntales and Matagorda fortresses.

Once past them, they were in the inner harbour and could make directly for their objective.

The blackness of the night was almost absolute, and it was difficult even to make out the nearer craft. They were maintaining fair speed, so transit between the two fortresses should be rapid; the half-mile or so in twenty minutes.

They were coming up to the narrowing, only just visible as a deeper blackness. If they could—

Then to larboard the unthinkable happened. A signal rocket soared skyward, exploding with a thud and spray of twinkling stars, followed almost immediately on the other side by another.

Suspended against the walls of both forts flares burst into flame, casting a deadly illumination over the scene, reflected in the calm night seas and bathing them in an unearthly light.

Then cannon opened up, heavy and concussive, gun-flash leaping from the casemates of the fortresses, sending shot slamming past in giant plumes all around them.

Ahead Kydd saw a line of fighting lanthorns. Gunboats.

With a sickening realisation he knew they'd been betrayed. Signal rockets had gone off as if waiting for a sign; the fortress guns had been loaded and primed; and the gunboats were already in the water, deployed in the right position. Hardly able to speak he gave the order to turn back, to give up. If ever he laid hands on the traitor he would choke the life out of him with his bare hands.

Chapter 39

From the shore Renzi had watched it all with a heavy expression. He knew what would be in his friend's thoughts and he was wrung with remorse. How could he look him in the face when next they met? And there was still the possibility that Morla would fail and the ships would fall to the French, their only chance to deal with them snatched away.

His explanation to Morla for his betrayal of his countrymen had been only half believed: that it was to prevent useless bloodshed, given that he knew Morla was man enough for the job but the British didn't, and there wasn't time to do other than warn of the attempt. Renzi wouldn't be pressed as to how he had come by this information.

He was now a 'guest' at the Spanish headquarters, watched all the time but free to follow Morla as he went about readying for the attack. He knew why. Confident of victory, the general wanted witnesses and, above all, someone who could take him to the English admiral afterwards to speak of his valour when he made his demands.

The general was energetic, imaginative and unforgiving.

The royal governor's residence was now his headquarters and a constant stream of military men hastened in and out. Horsed messengers, crashing to a stop outside, wasted no time in reporting to him.

The inner harbour, it seemed, was nothing much more than a depression in a marshy expanse of shallow islands, the naval base at its furthest interior. The French admiral had moored his ships not far from this, deliberately distant from the defending batteries and forts.

In the short term there was only one way to proceed.

The next day, without ceremony, the Cádiz junta showed its teeth. Across the bay a division of gunboats and mortar chaloupes set out in a broad phalanx, heading directly for the moored battleships. The French opened fire immediately, the light winds doing little to clear the mountainous roils of gun-smoke from the hundreds of guns at their command.

In a forest of splashes the courageous gunboats did their best, their single heavy guns thudding out as they closed to bring down the range but at the same time making themselves a bolder target. Within hours, pitiful floating wreckage marked the end of ten, then fifteen craft, with no visible effect on the French.

By nightfall it was clear that it was a hopeless cause and Morla called them off.

Renzi could see no way forward. The marshy shallows that the early defenders of Cádiz had taken advantage of to safeguard the naval base were working against Morla.

No ship of size could venture there, unless along the single deep channel that was now occupied by the French ships. More significant, the same treacherous tidal mud flats made any offensive by enemy artillery inconceivable. With no roads or tracks firm enough to support wheeled guns the area was safe from hostile operations. Morla was prevented from bringing up guns of anything like the same weight of metal as the French ships carried.

That night the crowds came out again, restless and dangerous. They knew they'd shown their hand and taken up arms against the French, who would now have every reason to exact swift and terrible vengeance. Only if General Morla could snatch a victory would they be in a position to make any kind of demands when it came to treating for terms.

Chapter 40

The following day the general took boat across the bay and landed on the desolate swamplands of the Isla de León. For hours he tramped and squelched over its length and breadth, frequently taking notes of sightings of the French ships across the flats.

On the third day he began a heroic operation with long twenty-four-pounders, naked, without tackle or carriage, eleven feet of iron lying in the mud. Hawsers were looped and scized around their trunnions and led out to traces a hundred feet long on each side. From the prisons and barracks, even the street, five hundred men, under the lash, began brute hauling their immense weight, breech first, through the impassable marshes. One by one, their gun-carriages and impedimenta following on makeshift mud-rafts, they were manoeuvred to the northern tip of the Isla de León – directly opposite the French.

Before long a white flag of parlay appeared from Admiral Rosily.

'No! I won't even hear the *cerdo francés*,' snarled Morla.

'Sir, he offers to disembark his guns, to lie quietly, knowing the English cannot touch him.'

'That's a falsehood. He waits for as long as it takes for Murat's battalions to reach here and rescue him. I'm no fool of his!'

The agony of hauling more guns went on.

On the fourth day before sunset another parlay was requested.

'The French admiral will haul down his colours, render his ships incapable of combat and—'

'He knows he's beat!' chuckled Morla, grimly. 'Let him stew. By morning I'll give him such a waking as will be heard in Madrid.'

Renzi, for the last three days sharing the general's field tent and rations in the mire and squalor, allowed a touch of hope. Morla was playing it well. One by one the big twenty-fours had been man-hauled through the mud along a broad front, placed on their gun-carriages and positioned atop a firm built-up ground behind a breastwork.

Renzi had been counting them as they'd been brought up at such cost. By this evening there would probably be thirty.

But six massive ships with near five hundred even bigger guns and four thousand seamen and marines outnumbered the Spanish ragtag militia and sailors by at least two to one. These were still terrifying odds.

Yet at the same time Rosily would be watching the steady and careful preparations, knowing that when Morla was ready, there would be more than a score of heavy guns blasting their shot into his ships, for which there could be no real reply to the protected emplacements. It would go on, night and day, until his ships were blood-soaked ruins – or he shifted his anchorage. And that would merely bring them into range of the main forts whose great guns with red-hot shot would make short work of them.

Or they could be driven out to face the British fleet.

What would the morning bring?

At break of day there was heightened tension in the Spanish encampment. Everyone knew that Morla was this day going to bring about the climax and they went about their duties with a wary watchfulness.

It was a wan, dreary morning, the dull sky a fit backdrop to what must come.

The order was issued: at eight, all guns would open fire and cease only by direct order of the captain general.

There was no change in the aspect of the French ships. Across the water they lay unmoving, their colours aloft, drooping in the still air. At this moment Admiral Rosily must be following every movement and would know what to expect. Did he have a trick ready to play at this point?

Anything could happen from this time forward.

The order rang out: 'Clear the guns!'

To hide preparations, fascines, bundles of brushwood, had been placed in front of each gun position. These were now removed, leaving muzzles bared in snarling menace.

It was a signal to the French captains: aboard every ship, ensigns dipped in rapid, angry jerks.

A boat put off under a white flag. Rosily's flag-captain had come to treat for a full surrender, his battle lost before it had begun.

Chapter 41

Aboard Tyger

'A message, sir,' the duty midshipman said dubiously, offering Kydd a folded piece of paper. 'From a vegetable-hawker. Says you're to read it at once.'

It could be from only one source and he opened it quickly.

It was indeed from Renzi, but it was formally phrased and he reread it in astonishment.

Be pleased to dispatch a boat to the Castle of San Sebastián at four, therewith to convey the person of the captain general of Andalucía and governor of Cádiz, chief deputy of the Provisional Cádiz Cortes and military governor of the junta, on board with a view to plenary discussion.

Who? Plenary discussion? Wasn't that something that was binding?

Reception in the nature of that accorded to a foreign admiral is advised, stand fast gun salutes. Entertainments will not be required.

So, no dinners and so forth, just talking.

Kydd read on.

Do signify acceptance in the usual way.

'Mr Maynard!' Kydd bellowed. 'Throw out "affirmative" at the main this instant!'

No mention of a white flag or the panoply of a cartel exchange.

Nevertheless, at the appointed time, when *Tyger*'s barge put off to perform the honours it bore on one mast stay the flag of Spain and on the other that of Great Britain. Halgren sat imperturbably at the tiller, Bray in full fig in the sternsheets, with Mr Midshipman Gilpin opposite him, trying to appear grave and noble, the boat's crew in their tiger-striped yellow and black bending effortlessly to their oars.

Side party assembled and the ship's company told off to their stations, Kydd waited in full dress-uniform for the august personage to appear.

General Morla, in a florid scarlet and gold-laced uniform, with prodigious bicorne, was a striking figure, his entourage only a little less so.

After all had been piped aboard and greeted, Kydd caught sight of Renzi, in plain dress, slipping over the bulwarks.

'What the devil's to do with this crew?' he hissed at him. 'Who—'

'Play it as you will, brother. I fancy you'll be well pleased by the news he brings.'

Accompanied by Renzi, Kydd returned to the Spaniards, ill at ease in a ship of war of such evident qualities as *Tyger*.

'Sir Thomas,' Renzi began, 'this is Captain General Tomás de Morla y Pacheco. He desires you to know that the French warships lately at large in Cádiz now lie under the guns of his fortresses and do so beneath the colours of Spain.'

A haughty interpreter rapidly conveyed this to the general, who nodded slowly.

Dumbfounded, Kydd stuttered a reply. That the victorious general thought to make immediate visit to the blockading fleet was significant – and the implications of this were incredible. Probably even more so than this worthy knew.

'General Morla has dispatched messengers to all of Spain telling of this victory, and wishes to explore the possibility of making common cause against the vile legions of Bonaparte, going forth equally together to effect his ruin and destruction.'

Kydd felt out of his depth. This was hardly a situation he could do much about. Recovering his composure, he declared, 'Tell him that there is a far greater commander than I who lies out to seaward who would be pleased to hear him.'

He hid a savage smile. By rights he should have passed the general and the decision up to his superior, Rowley, but after the boat assault, the man had gone away with half his squadron, no doubt for even more manoeuvres. Collingwood it would have to be.

'Hands to unmoor ship!'

At an urgent plea from Morla's interpreter Renzi hastily intervened: 'If this is a grand captain of the fleet, General Morla states that he requires opportunity to dress more appropriately. He wishes to send for his manservant and garb fit for an emissary of Spain.'

Kydd gave a nod of acknowledgement, and Renzi confided, 'And, to be truthful, it would be of some service to me to rescue Jago and my other loyal household hands from their plight.'

Chapter 42

Tyger rounded to in the lee of *Ocean* and hailed across the news that the distinguished visitor wished to confer with the commander-in-chief.

At the entry-port Collingwood personally handed aboard the Spanish grandee. 'You are most welcome to my ship,' he said, with the utmost courtesy. 'Whatever the occasion, sir.'

In *Ocean*'s spacious great cabin, room was made for the considerable number of the general's staff, and time allowed for their seating in the proper order.

Renzi retired to a chair in the corner, claiming only to be a gentleman of rank unwittingly drawn into events but an available witness.

It was left to Kydd to state the situation, having heard it from Renzi as they waited on Morla to complete his wardrobe.

'I wish to express my sensibility of the late actions of the general in defeating Rosily's fleet so roundly,' Collingwood declared. This brought a boyish smile of pleasure to Morla's face.

The translator, sitting next to Morla, replied, 'The general believes this victory allows him to beg assistance of a direct kind in order to withstand the French hordes even now marching on Cádiz.'

Collingwood pursed his lips, considering. 'Tell me, sir. To whom am I speaking?' he asked carefully.

In consternation the general snarled at the translator, who delicately replied, 'Captain General Morla is confused at your question, Excelentísimo, and desires you to be more . . . explicit.'

'Very well. Is it to the military commander of Cádiz city or to a member of the civil administration? Much depends on your answer, sir.'

'You speak, sir, to the head of the Cádiz junta. With the inability of the King to rule, sovereignty resides in this assembly of the people, the townsfolk of Cádiz.'

The commander-in-chief nodded slowly. 'Then I do regret there is nothing I can do to aid you. It would be classed by His Majesty's government as aid to a faction of the enemy and I would be made to answer for it before a court-martial.'

Morla's eyes glowed in anger.

Renzi intervened: 'Sir, General Morla is being less than just to his situation. True, he is at the head of the only junta that has thrown back the French in open battle, but his victory does inspire others. There is word that a similar junta is being brought together in Seville and more in other parts of Spain that cleave to the same constitution as that forged in Cádiz.'

He paused, letting the general be informed, and to his satisfaction saw the intelligence of the man rise to the challenge.

A barked declaration was translated as 'General Morla informs the distinguished admiral that this is to say, as time permits, there will be created a Supreme Junta of the people under whose banner the entire nation will turn upon the faithless French.'

'Then—'

'And as it has been in Cádiz that the flag of freedom has first been raised he dares to say that this body shall be located here in this city. And further, that naturally his own person will be to the fore when the Supreme Junta is constituted, and therefore when he is spoken to, properly, it is the people of Spain who are being addressed.'

It was outrageous – it was daring – and it had every chance of coming off.

Collingwood leaned back speculatively. 'The people of Spain.'

'Nothing less, Excelentísimo.'

'Then, sir, I can still do nothing.'

Before the affronted Morla could protest, he continued calmly, 'For this is a high matter, dealing as it does with weighty affairs of state. No longer am I dealing with a local military commander but all of Spain. Sir, this I do offer you: passage to Great Britain as your country's representative with the object of securing a species of peace between our two nations. My accompanying dispatch will also beg that aid and assistance be immediately given to the Spanish in their purpose to expel the invaders.'

'Sir, the captain general applauds your wisdom and wishes to take advantage of your generous offer. He does, however, desire me to point out that – merely as a technical oversight – we are still at war.'

'It has not escaped me, sir,' Collingwood said, with the ghost of a smile. 'Thusly it is my order as of this hour – to my entire fleet about the Iberian coasts – that no vessel bearing the Spanish flag shall be fired upon, save it fires first. There, sir. A peace by any other name. And of course you shall be given safe-conduct under my name for your mission in British waters.'

Kydd could only wonder at what he'd just witnessed. Was this a turning point in the war, or a dashing but foolhardy gesture by a local warlord against the hosts that had subjugated the entire Continent?

Chapter 43

The Inshore Squadron, off Cádiz

'Sir, it's a hard thing to lie at idleness these weeks,' Layton said, with barely hidden bitterness. As captain of *Jason* he was the most senior of the frigate commanders in Rowley's great cabin. Fast greying, his opportunities for prize money to cushion his retirement were receding by the day.

Mason of *Riposte* scowled, the powder burns on his face hinting, as they always did, of some diabolical encounter. 'I'm at a stand to think of anything more I can do to get those lazy scowbunkers up an' active. Always trouble when a barky isn't under way, I find.'

Rowley fiddled with a silver-chased letter opener, his features sulky. It was the regular weekly captains' meeting and as usual there was nothing to report, nothing to reveal, nothing to do.

Collingwood's order stood: active operations against the Spanish were suspended indefinitely pending the result of the mission to England. There was nothing else the Inshore Squadron could do except remain at anchor.

'You know my view, of course,' he rumbled. They did, but knew better than to say so.

'It's all a fizzle! A parcel of town-hall heroes think to drive out the French with our assistance. Pah! No administration worth its salt, not even Portland's, is going to listen to them. The navy stands ready to slap down any French sally but what we're talking about here is a full-blooded intervention by the army, like we did in Egypt, and we haven't got one. No, gentlemen, rest easy for a trifle longer and Bonaparte's marshals will put 'em to the finish and then it'll all be over – Spain is his, and it's business as usual.'

Kydd allowed the murmurs of dutiful agreement to die, then said, 'It's not just your general from Cádiz, it's everywhere. I heard tell of Asturias, Seville, all these other places rising up against the Frenchies. There'll come a time when the French won't have the numbers to hold 'em down. Then we'll be busy enough, getting arms and troops in to double their effort.'

Rowley made much of ignoring Kydd. His reaction to Kydd's failure with the boats had been a sullen reception of one who hadn't been able to provide him with a famous victory. At first Kydd had suspected that the betrayal had been his, an attempt to have him wiped out with his brave band, but the Spanish had shown their hand too early and he'd been able to win the open sea with few casualties. And then he reasoned that treachery would hardly have been part of the game if it was triumph that Rowley had wanted.

Hayward of *Vigilant* glanced at Kydd. 'He has a point, sir,' he said. 'It's highly in our interest to have our redcoats in Iberia – after all, over the border is France itself, never forget!'

'Ha! Keep your daydreams for those who'll believe pigs may fly, Hayward. We've got to find something to do, keep the swabs from getting stale.'

The captains of the Inshore Squadron looked at him wearily.

'I have it. Another admiral's inspection. Even more detail than the last. Right?'

The groans were loud and heartfelt.

Chapter 44

Kydd needed some fresh air after his hard morning's duel with the purser's paperwork and stumped up the ladder to the quarterdeck. To his surprise, nearly all the officers and not a few seamen were gazing down the line of ships, all pretence at work fled.

'How's this, nothing to do, you villains?' Kydd called, frowning. Hardly a face turned his way.

'Mr Bowden, what does this mean?' he demanded, irritated.

Reluctantly his second lieutenant lifted his gaze. 'An Admiralty aviso,' was his bald explanation. 'Attending on the flagship.'

These fast, secure packets were only used when their lordships had need of ready information from their far-flung squadrons – or had dispatches so urgent that justified the speed and expense of one.

'Us?' asked Brice.

'No, we're not to be noticed,' Bray said authoritatively. 'He's made his number with Collingwood, who thinks the matter so pressing he's sent him on to his rear admiral without delay.'

It was Kydd's conclusion too. And there could be only one

thing so important that it needed acting on with such speed. He joined them in their anticipation, all eyes now on the flagship.

When the signal came, it wasn't the summons Kydd had expected. Instead it was the peremptory three-flag hoist: 'All captains attend on commander-in-chief.'

This was cause for an instant hubbub: was it the rarely experienced call to a council-of-war on the eve of battle?

In minutes Kydd reappeared in full-dress uniform, the quarterdeck falling silent as he took boat for *Ocean*, trying to keep a countenance under the hundreds of eyes on him as he left to learn their fate.

The great cabin of Collingwood's flagship was crowded and Kydd had to join the other frigate captains in standing along the bulkhead. Already Collingwood was in his chair, as mute and unspeaking as a sphinx, his two admirals at either end of the table, both as clearly baffled as their humble captains.

The last officer squeezed in and the flag-captain announced, 'All present, sir.'

Nothing could be read from Collingwood's face, a granite rigidity.

Word from England it must be, but what? A refusal to be sucked into an Iberian war? A complete distrust of a clutch of rebels with no realistic prospects?

It would be disastrous for Britain's reputation to be associated with a wild revolt that was contemptuously defeated, even worse to be dragged into an endless land war in which she was outnumbered ten or a hundred to one far from her shores. Realistically it couldn't be—

'Gentlemen,' Collingwood said softly. The cabin fell suddenly still.

'It's peace.'

As this was digested there were sharply drawn breaths.

'I have received dispatches from my lords of the Admiralty and from the foreign secretary, both in the same tenor.'

He looked about him, then went on flatly, as though reciting, 'Hostilities against the kingdom of Spain are to cease with immediate effect, a state of amity now existing between us. Every practicable aid shall be furnished and Great Britain proceeds on the principle that any nation of Europe with a determination to oppose the common enemy becomes thereby our essential ally.'

In the stunned silence he beckoned over the flag-captain and whispered something. The officer nodded and left.

'What this means to us – to the world – is of immeasurable consequence. I would have you in no doubt of that.'

The flag-captain returned, ushering in stewards with trays of glasses. 'At this point I believe it meet and right we should raise a glass to our news.'

The usual toasts – 'Confusion to Boney', 'Damnation to the Tyrant' and the like – seemed in some way inadequate to the occasion and a strange pall descended on this group of veteran sea officers. Too much had happened, and now their traditional foe of centuries was that no longer.

'What's to become of us, sir?' Puget of *Goliath*, greatly daring, asked.

Collingwood looked up, suddenly weary, and Kydd was shocked at how drawn he appeared. A great man – but of another age.

'Ah, yes. I've given this some thought in the event it fell out as it has. The Inshore Squadron before Cádiz will be no more, of course. Portugal remains in French hands and will require our attentions still, as will occupied Spain, by which I mean the northern and Mediterranean coasts. Therefore I've a mind to create an Iberian command of three flags, the north, Lisbon and south. Ships-of-the-line will be redistributed among them but frigates will probably be on roving commissions a-twixt and a-tween as needs must.'

'And yourself, sir?'

'To Minorca, I believe, now the Dons are our friends. A fine dockyard, an even finer climate for my old bones – and within a day of Toulon.'

A babble of incredulous speculation arose, which Collingwood interrupted quietly: 'I would have you now return to your ships and inform your people. From this point forward all due marks of respect will be given and returned to Spanish officers and ships at sea. Detailed orders will follow as soon as I can manage it. Good day, gentlemen.'

Kydd left in an air of unreality. Almost his entire career had been pitted against Spaniards in one form or another, but from this day forward they were to be accounted comrades.

His boat surged along, his coxswain silent with the gravity of the occasion. When Kydd mounted the side of *Tyger*, nearly her entire ship's company was looking down at him.

Just as soon as he made the deck and answered his first lieutenant's polite enquiry, his brusque order was 'Clear lower deck! Hands to muster aft.'

Standing next to the wheel he waited while the sudden scramble for places subsided. Seamen were hanging from the rigging, cross-legged on hatch gratings, pressed together, agog for news. There were youngsters squatted on the deck in front, open-eyed with wonder, and the marines forgetting decorum in their need not to miss a thing. Behind him the officers and warrant officers shuffled their feet in their eagerness to hear.

'Tygers!' Kydd roared. Silence was instant. 'I'll tell you as I got it from the commander-in-chief. In one – it's peace. As of this moment we're to treat the Dons as friends, our allies, give 'em all the help they ask for in their struggle to throw out the Mongseers and get their country back. And we'll be doing our part like true British sailors. I haven't detailed orders yet but I believe we'll not be lacking entertainment. When we—'

Bray detached himself and came over, nudging him. He gave a significant glance over to the flagship, which had just hoisted a general signal.

Kydd recognised it instantly, but frowned in mock impatience, seeking out Maynard. 'Well, sir – important signal from Flag. What does it say, pray?'

The flustered signal master's mate found his book and, glancing again at the hoist, chanted, 'Brace, sir, and . . . main. Mainbrace. And—'

'Acknowledge, then, you looby. And it's "splice the mainbrace", I believe.'

No sooner had the order been obeyed than an even greater satisfaction was granted them. In the same aviso had been a precious cargo – mail, in stout canvas post-bags, with the ship's name stencilled prominently. The routine was always the same, the anticipation never less. And for the space of a few minutes Dillon was the most important man in His Majesty's Ship *Tyger*.

Taking the coach as his headquarters he upended the first bag and began his duty. To one side the seamen's growing pile of letters from home, the gunroom officers' in another, ship's official business to the purser and clerk and, finally, the captain's personal mail.

Kydd knew better than to hurry him but eventually it was presented. Rather more a fat package than a letter, on the outside was his name in an infinitely dear bold hand.

He was able to retire to the privacy of his cabin to savour

the moment but the common sailor must share his with his messmates. Kydd knew how it would be: each man would in that time be an island, unreachable, wrapped in his own warm thoughts as a loved one reached across the gulf of miles to touch him – and him alone – with sentiments that were private to them both.

The ship in an unnatural quiet, he made himself comfortable in his best armchair, reached for the package and opened it carefully and lovingly.

There was a letter, a long one, he noticed, with a warm thrill. But the bulk of the package was two newspapers, *The Times* and the *Exeter Flying Post*. As much to defer the pleasure of the letter he opened *The Times*.

It was alive with the ecstatic tidings from Iberia – the news from Cádiz had reached England well before and this was the response from an eager public. And it was as wholehearted and strident as any Kydd could remember seeing.

What a magnificent series of events is passing before us in Spain! I cannot describe to you the interest I feel in the Spanish cause. It exceeds anything except perhaps that which I felt in the first moments of the French Revolution. May the Spaniards obtain perfect liberty and raise the Goddess for the admiration of mankind from that abyss in which the French have left her!

He went on to read of the stirring and noble speeches from both benches in the Commons, Sheridan and Canning, the calls for immediate aid to the plucky Spaniards, the army vote increased.

Bemused, Kydd saw that nearly the entire newspaper was crowded with articles and opinions, all on the subject of Iberia and Bonaparte's probable coming fate. Turning to the *Post*, he saw much of the same but also some hard-headed

231

speculation. Barrelled pilchards and salted cod would be wanted in quantity in a newly opened trade, and Devon and Cornwall were well placed to supply them as of old. Spanish coast-wise trade, until now wiped from the seas by the navy, would require its multitude of brigs and barques replaced, a chance for the many tiny seaport slipyards in the south-west.

After a hurried perusal he had the papers sent to the gunroom and settled to his letter.

My very dear darling man! I'm before the fire, scratching away on this and you're somewhere off the land that everyone's talking about, having all the excitement. You'll write everything down, won't you, my love, just so we can curl up together and you can tell me?

In a daze of contentment he heard about progress on the herb garden, the bronze weather-cock, which she knew he'd be interested to learn had shown winds steady from the west all this last week, and the success of Farmer Davies at the county show in Widdecombe, notwithstanding the ill-fortune with his sheep earlier. Rufus the cat had taken to the chimney nook and was apparently adorable beyond words, while she herself was well advanced on a romantic portrayal of *Tyger* beset in a storm, and she prayed she had the ropes and sails all correct, this being her first cast at a sea piece.

A quiet knock intruded: it was Dillon. 'Ah, sir. Sorry to disturb but the gunroom is holding a dinner tonight to make notice of the peace and are wondering if . . .?'

'So kind in 'em. Of course I shall come. Delighted.'

The dreamlike air of unreality had not lifted when the officers came together in the hastily but splendidly decorated space. In an affected quiet they greeted one another, sat and toasted, and every so often could be seen staring into an unseeable distance, their minds and hearts somewhere out of this place, this time, to some personal encounter. An ordeal, a triumph, a loss, a tragedy.

Talk went on, but no one felt inclined to break into song or merriment. It didn't seem right.

The mess broke up before midnight, not a few officers feeling the need for a solitary turn about the upper deck in the whispering summer night, wrapped in their own thoughts.

In the morning Bray briskly asked, 'Sir – in the matter o' liberty?'

'Er, yes. Of course.' It was only right and proper that, in making a friendly port, shore leave would be granted. That the said port had turned overnight from an enemy to an ally was no reason for age-old customs to be ignored, as long as the port authorities permitted the sending ashore of floods of red-blooded sailors, something not always welcomed. But the opening of the port to trade from now on was going to do this anyway, and gleeful scenes would soon return to the Cádiz waterfront north of the Trocadero.

Something of the delight of the liberty men transmitted itself to Kydd, and when Dillon suggested they step ashore themselves to see the sights of the ancient Phoenician city he readily agreed.

It was a pity that Renzi had left with Morla for England but his confidential secretary was more than equal to both the language and the navigating and he found himself contemplating the sight of the old Cádiz of the Carthaginians, Rome, the Moors and Francis Drake.

There were quantities of churches, merchant miradors that enabled them to spy ships inward-bound leagues out to sea – and on the seawall, antique round sentinel closets with conical roofs and arrow slits that must have been manned continuously for half a thousand years.

Crossing from one side of the peninsula to the other in the maze of alleyways, Kydd became conscious of a regular beat, an undercurrent of excitement, swelling crowds.

'A procession!'

They hurried in its direction and saw a colourful, noisy parade marching along the sea-front road, raucously encouraged by spectators. The marchers were more military than religious and were being enthusiastically cheered on by a great crowd. 'I thought as this would be a papist procession, carrying a statue or some such,' Kydd remarked. 'Is it for our welcome?' he added, with a grin.

Dillon tugged the sleeve of one of the crowd, enquiring. The man pulled free irritably and snapped something, his eyes only for the procession.

'Not us, I fear. It seems there's just arrived news that the French lunge towards Cádiz to put down their rising has been defeated at a place called Bailén. No details, but this city is now safe – thanks to themselves only.'

Chapter 45

The stamp and go of seamen's feet sounded above Kydd's cabin as the larboard watch of the hands exercised at the main, the braces led aft. He knew the sequences and idly concluded that this must be Brice at exercise to furl the main topsail: the canny officer always waited to the last possible moment to lay the yard and allow the men out on it for hard work with gaskets and lines.

Kydd's thoughts turned to the broader picture. It had been somewhat of an anti-climax that had followed the capture of Rosily's ships and, more notably, the Spanish peace. Collingwood was now back in the Mediterranean and his orders had been received. Kydd had hoped that Admiral Rowley might have been sent away with the dissolution of his command, the Inshore Squadron, but it hadn't happened. True to Collingwood's word, there were now three separate flag commands and Rowley had retained the middle one, centred on Lisbon.

There was some talk of sending an army to join the struggle, presuming Britain could find one, but even if they could, it would be sent to Spain, not Portugal, which must wait.

This cruise was not going to be exciting. *Tyger* had been tasked to rove off the northern third of the country, intercepting coastal reinforcements for the French and enforcing the wider blockade. It was a necessary and important role but promised to be quiet, the prime location in Rowley's jurisdiction naturally being the capital, Lisbon, where Junot, the French military ruler of Portugal, held court. In effect, Kydd had been sent to a backwater, not part of Rowley's standing fleet.

There was an advantage nevertheless: detached for the task, he was his own master.

Not that there was much he could achieve. The only action they could hope to join was to intercept French transports and store-ships, attempting to resupply their armies. And this would mean having to share the prey with their smaller brethren, sloops and cutters more suited to inshore work.

Kydd decided to show himself on deck, take an interest in Brice's exercises – despite the nature of their mission, who knew when next a battle-winning move might be needed in a rush?

It was brisk and refreshing on deck and Kydd was pleased to see his third lieutenant taking advantage of the morning offshore breeze to keep in well with the land. This was close to Oporto, an important wine-exporting seaport now occupied by the French and therefore choked off from its trade by the blockade.

Nothing appeared to have changed: the low, sandy coast, the river mouth guarded by the fort São João da Foz, and a mile or so in, past the sandbar, the town itself, no more ships to see than the usual few at the docks.

He turned to watch a reef being put into the fore course, the movements of the topmen lithe and sure. There would be no hesitation in stress of battle with these men, probably the best he'd ever had the honour to command.

'Well done, Mr Brice,' he called unnecessarily. 'You've some good men there, I believe.'

But the officer was not listening. He had his telescope up, trained ashore. 'Sir, and here's a puzzle. The fort – those aren't your French colours at all. Portuguee, if I'm not pixy-led.'

Kydd borrowed his glass and concentrated on the old fortification. Without a doubt, the bunting was not French. Red, with a shield borne in the centre – this was the Portuguese national flag, he was sure of it, but what did it mean?

'I agree with you. Do you think . . .?'

Brice gave a sudden grin. 'Why not? If Spain is in revolt against the Mongseers, then why not the Portuguese?'

If they were, he should offer any help he could. The first thing was to confirm the situation without putting *Tyger* at risk.

'We pay our respects, Mr Brice.'

The frigate closed with the fort and, when within range, began a respectful gun salute to the standard of Portugal, firing safely out to sea, as was the custom. There was no response until they'd completed the salute. Then the fort thudded out its reply.

'So. They wouldn't dare if Boney's soldiers were about, and that means . . .'

'Ah, there's a boat putting off, sir.'

It was pulled by oars instead of sail, resembling a warship's pinnace, and an officer was in its sternsheets. It made its way out slowly while *Tyger* remained hove to.

'Side party,' Kydd growled. If this was who he thought it might be, he would see everything done the right way.

The boat came alongside, its rowers exhausted, but the officer sprang energetically up the ship's side and accepted Kydd's formal greeting with an easy grace.

He introduced himself. 'Capitão Manuel Meireles. Of the armed forces of the junta of Oporto.'

Kydd murmured a reply and asked politely, 'And of what service may we be to you, sir?'

'A half an hour to hear me would greatly oblige, sir.'

As *Tyger* got under way again, under easy sail, Kydd led his visitor to his great cabin.

'Your English is of the first order, Capitão.'

'As is why the bishop sends me to you.'

'Bishop?'

'Dom Antonio de Castro, leader of the Oporto junta.'

'I think you'd better tell me more,' Kydd said, eyeing Meireles with a degree of wariness.

It was a complex tale but delivered elegantly and succinctly.

Following the risings in Spain, the Portuguese had taken heart and risen against the French in isolated locations about the country. Junot's soldiery had responded in the usual brutal manner, triggering murderous attacks and assassinations in reprisal. This had set the French on the defensive, Junot ordering his garrisons and forts to draw in their lines to form a series of military concentrations in place of the previous thinly spread occupation force.

The most successful rising was in Oporto. It had been garrisoned by Spanish troops in accordance with the Treaty of Fontainebleau, but when they had heard of the outrages in Madrid their general had abruptly left, marching eastwards to join the Spanish risings in Galicia. This left a vacuum, quickly filled by insurgents, who had broken into barracks to seize arms and form a militia army.

In a fever of patriotism, officers of the disbanded royal army had been recalled to the colours, their mission to reconstruct the old battalions, but it was proving next to impossible. There was no lack of volunteers but they could be armed only with pitchforks, scythes and home-made pikes. These men, coming up with Junot's regulars, would be slaughtered in their thousands unless they were given arms, especially muskets and artillery.

As to the current situation in Oporto, the different juntas had vowed to stay together and allow themselves to be led by the trusted bishop, Dom Antonio de Castro.

At the moment the north shore of the Douro was in the hands of the insurgents while, in accordance with Junot's orders, the French were concentrated at an encampment in the south, poised to take back Oporto when ordered.

In dignified tones, Meireles concluded by asking that Kydd give thought to what he could do to bring hope to the Portuguese people in their peril.

Kydd was at a loss to see how he could do anything. A frigate was a sea beast, equipped for far ocean-ranging against ships of the foe. The Portuguese needed arms and something like an army to stand up to the French. All he had were the Royal Marines, only a couple of dozen at that, and no muskets or powder to spare. By rights, he should break off his cruise immediately and return to the fleet to alert them of the need, let them have the worry of putting together a relief force. But that would take too long, the French massing so close for a strike back. The people of Oporto needed something now, a tangible proof that they were not on their own in this brute struggle.

'Capitão, you will tell me of Oporto, where the French are, your own forces.'

'Certainly, Captain.' Meireles drew out a folded map, not detailed but quite sufficient to convey the gist of the matter.

Kydd gave him a glance of respect: the man was intelligent and resourceful, one he could work with. He studied the map: the French to the south around Vila Nova, at the narrowest point in the river Douro, the junta and its headquarters on the north shore. A bridge connected the two.

Kydd looked up. Yes! Without a doubt the French would be relying on the bridge. It took them from their cantonment directly into the heart of the town.

'Hmm. I believe, sir, we can do something for you. Shall we . . .?'

Chapter 46

Tyger anchored to seaward as Kydd took the pinnace in under sail, Meireles at his side in the sternsheets, pointing out the sights. Kydd had eyes only for terrain and fortifications. Besides the fort at the river entrance, there were others, those on the right manned by the French. As they sailed on, the river narrowed to a spectacular gorge, the town itself crowded on the left just before it, an imposing and beautiful sight.

The bridge ahead connecting the two sides was actually a bridge of boats stemming the current, its wooden roadway flat and open.

Yes, denying it to the French would be possible: a ship moored off the bank such that its broadside could be directed along the length of the bridge. Each gun loaded for canister or grape and firing in turn could render the bridge a killing ground for any column of troops attempting the crossing. The only other bridge of any kind for miles was up-river – no French general would hazard a crossing the long way around. Kydd's plan would effectively confine them to their side of the river, thus saving Oporto.

But he must find a ship of force to do it. This couldn't be *Tyger* – she had other work. He scanned the wharves and docks until he spotted an ocean-going ship, one of the Brazil traders in enforced idleness. 'Can you commandeer that ship?' he asked Meireles.

'It will be done if you require it, Comandante.'

There could be no question of wielding a warship's broadsides but shipping half a dozen of the fort's twelve-pounders would do the job, and the gunner, carpenter and willing hands made it so. The boatswain took charge of the mooring and, with tackles secured to shore bollards, the lofty trader could be made to train her lethal armament precisely.

They worked fast and hard for word had to be got out that Oporto was a city in successful insurrection, which needed aid badly.

Back aboard *Tyger*, Kydd gave serious thought to how things were turning out. If he was the only one locally in the knowledge of the opportunities thrown open by the Portuguese patriots, he should take every chance to gather intelligence and opinion with a view to the later role of English support. And, witness to the bravery and resource of the Portuguese, all his being urged him to find something else to do for them, instead of passively cruising offshore.

There was one possibility. Although talk had been of an army expedition in support of the Spanish, sooner or later there would be intervention in Portugal. Damn it, didn't his remit include finding a spot for a landing? They would need one quickly when the time came, and he would have it on hand.

He'd the experience – once at the Cape of Good Hope and again at Buenos Aires – and had no illusions about the dangers of landing an army in boats through the surf as well as the tactical need for open ground, free of enemy fire, for deploying prior to the push inland.

But Portugal was particularly difficult. For the entire Iberian coastline the North Atlantic, with its long fetch, made a fearful shore for boats.

The two most valuable objectives had to be Lisbon and Oporto. Not knowing which was more important, this implied a place reasonably equal in distance from both.

He called the master. 'Mr Joyce. You know this coast. Can you tell me of a sheltered place as would take a landing of some five thousand lobsterbacks? At around forty degrees o' latitude or so.'

The man pursed his lips. 'Can't say as I do, sir. No one's done it this age, they being our friends an' all.' He scratched his head thoughtfully, then offered, 'How about askin' your Portuguee? He'd have an idea, I'd wager.'

It was the obvious course and Kydd invited him aboard again.

'To land an army? This is not possible anywhere between Oporto and Lisbon. Close to these cities the French will have every beach and seaport defended, and in between, the terrain is hard country, no towns or harbours. Except one place,' he added, brightening. 'Figueira da Foz, an old village but at the mouth of the Mondego river, it has a good road to Coimbra.'

'And you say this is the only landing place possible before Lisbon?'

'The coast of Portugal is everywhere open to the roaring Atlantic, you must understand. Monstrous waves booming in all the time. At Figueira there are sandbars across the mouth. It protects the fishing boats putting to sea.'

'This sounds good, Capitão.'

'Ah, but it has a problem. The Santa Catarina fort. It overlooks the river mouth and the little town and will certainly cause trouble in a landing.'

'Be damned to it! We'll take a look at it all the same, my friend.'

'You're right to say "we", Comandante. I will come with you. You help us, we help you.'

With her men recovered from the floating battery, *Tyger* set off to the southward. They raised the rugged bluffs of Cabo Mondego in the early morning, a series of ridges extending inland, looking for all the world like an island, but torn from the headland was line upon line of white surf, the betraying sign of reef and shoal. Kydd made certain *Tyger* kept well to seaward as they fell away to the south-east into the bay of the river Mondego and Figueira da Foz.

'There, sir.' Meireles pointed to a light-coloured beach, which grew to a full quarter-mile width of pristine sand. At its end was a fort, its ancient brown weathered stone a dark contrast to the vast beach. Beyond it was the entrance to the Mondego, the town opening up further in.

'French,' Kydd said dully, seeing the tricolour floating high above the fortification and its guns, which dominated the broad, open beach, making it impassable. Any boat attempting the river must do so at point-blank range, foolhardy to attempt. And beyond, the opposite bank was a flat marshy wilderness.

Was there any point in going on?

Suddenly puffs of gun-smoke rose up from the sparse scrub and from along the parapets, soundless against the swash of ocean waves out to sea.

'This is interesting,' Kydd grunted, taking the officer-of-the-watch's telescope. It gave no better picture with the unknown assailants hidden by the vegetation but it told him that others besides themselves were in hostile action against the French.

He hesitated, listening. No heavy guns. The aggressors were

taking on a fortress with musketry only. They could only be the poorly equipped but fervent militia or insurgents.

They hadn't a prayer of success, but it sparked an idea. 'Capitão. You'd oblige me if you'd take boat ashore and speak to them. Find out if they're doing a strike-and-run, or whether the countryside is in general rebellion.'

Meireles was back quickly. 'They're in defiance of the French, who've retreated into the fort. They ask if you can batter down the walls. Can you, Comandante?'

'No. We're near to the five-fathom line already, and who knows what reefs and so forth stop us closing into range?'

The real reason was that *Tyger*'s eighteen-pounders could never be expected to smash through yards of thick stone. But it gave Kydd an idea.

'Ask Captain Clinton to attend on me.' The Royal Marines were going to earn their grog this day.

In something approaching consternation the marine officer heard Kydd's order: 'You will storm the fort, if you please.'

'Um, sir. Does this mean—'

Within an hour every boat *Tyger* possessed was in the water with a full complement of marines heading inshore. Not so very many, but it was enough.

Kydd saw them head in, as ordered, up the beach and out of range of the fort. Clinton was intelligent and had immediately seen Kydd's plan.

As soon as they landed, they headed inland in a wide circle around the citadel but before it was completed, to his intense satisfaction, he saw it had achieved what he'd wanted.

The gates of the fort were flung open and the French ran out, firing as they went, making for the road to the mountains, a streaming mass in fear of their lives.

It had worked. The fort commander had made the assumption that the Portuguese had the power to call on their allies to bring up a man-o'-war to pound the fort to dust and, to make sure of their destruction, had sent feared redcoats ashore to cut off their escape. They'd chosen to break for the hills instead of being left to the mercy of the insurgents.

Kydd knew he'd been lucky and would need to consolidate in some way. If this was going to be the landing spot he had to be sure the fort was theirs – that it had not been retaken. He knew he couldn't leave it in the hands of the Portuguese irregulars. Too much depended on it.

There was only one course: to keep Clinton and his men here in nominal command, visible red coats around the battlements token of the determination of the British to keep it. He would have no chance if the French sent a full-scale relieving column, but Kydd's plan was to clap on all sail for the fleet and tell of the situation – that they had sure possession of a landing place if they only sent reinforcements. If this was refused it would be easy enough to re-embark the marines when *Tyger* returned to her cruising station.

He'd tarry only as long as a quick precautionary peek at the terrain ashore took, then be away.

Chapter 47

Aboard Conqueror

'Sir.'

'What is it, Flags?' said Rowley, irritably, jerking awake in his armchair. 'You know I take my rest at this hour.' He'd been awakened after a very satisfactory midday meal, a Spanish claret of remarkable smoothness and depth rounding out the repast.

'Brig-sloop *Laertes* made her number, desires an army officer to board and speak with you.'

'Bloody cheek! Tell 'em to lay off until four bells like everyone else.'

'Er, the officer is one of rank as I saw, sir.' Unless he was mistaken the figure on the quarterdeck in dark green and gold epaulettes was a general at the least.

'Very well. Hoist him in, and I'll see whoever he is here.'

He reached for a cup of coffee, which had swiftly appeared, and waited sourly for the officer, sure to bring unwelcome demands for this or that army deficiency, or claim for ships.

'Sir, Lieutenant General Sir Arthur Wellesley.'

Rowley glanced up. 'Do sit, sir. I shan't be a moment.'

He made play of closely inspecting and shuffling his papers, the image of a busy admiral.

'While you are about your business, sir, I have a fleet of invasion about its own.'

The voice was distant but had an edge of restrained ferocity that had Rowley start with surprise.

'A fleet? What can you mean, sir?'

'Sufficient attention to your orders will tell you that lately the government of Great Britain has seen fit to set to sea an expedition of force intended for the relief and support of forces in opposition to the French in the Iberian peninsula. I am in command of that force.'

'Yes, yes, I'd heard of this – but it's going to Spain and therefore does not concern me.'

'It does. For various absurd reasons, I've been unable to make landing in northern Spain. My orders give me discretion to divert to Portugal, in particular Lisbon, if possible. At the moment my transports and escorts are floating about in a muddle, awaiting a destination.'

'A . . . destination? What is this to me, sir?'

'I require of you a suitable place of landing for my expedition on this shore, sufficiently sheltered to allow my boats to go in through the waves that bedevil this coast. Not too far from a road to Lisbon and, of course, sir, free of enemy interference as we land. Do you know of such?'

Rowley blinked in confusion. 'This has never been in contemplation, sir, and – and – no, sir, I do not.'

Wellesley's haughty, patrician manner carried an air of authority that perturbed Rowley, with its overtones of easy familiarity with Whitehall and politics.

'Then who does, if not you, pray?'

'Oh, well, our ships-of-the-line never venture so close and

the minor craft that do are commanded by officers of low rank. I rather fancy it's among my frigates that you'll find your answer.'

'So . . .'

'Which are all out on a cruise, sir.'

'Get one, if you please.'

'Er, that is not so easily done. It were better to wait for one to return – shall we say the first that reports?'

Wellesley rose abruptly. 'Then, sir, I shall be obliged should you let me know the very instant this happens. My ships have been at sea these several weeks and my men and horses are declining in condition with every day that passes. Good day to you.'

Chapter 48

Kydd brought *Tyger* into the anchorage north of the Tagus estuary between *Inferno* and *Mortal* where Rowley's squadron had their mooring. There were the usual minor vessels, no other frigates, but *Conqueror* bore her rear admiral's pennant – Rowley was aboard and Kydd was soon standing before him to report.

'What the devil are you doing, Kydd? To cut short your cruise – what is your explanation, sir?'

Why was Rowley so transparently annoyed?

'Oporto has risen and now lies free of the French.'

'So?'

'I rather thought it would interest you to know one part of this kingdom is standing proud for its liberty. A chance for intervention?'

'It's not yours to top it the high strategist, Kydd,' Rowley said cuttingly. 'Leave all that kind of thing to me.'

Kydd held his temper. 'You have my intelligence, sir. I'll return to station and—'

A hurried knock at the door and the flag-lieutenant was leaning into the cabin with an anxious expression. 'Sir, it's—'

Wellesley thrust in. 'This is your frigate captain?' he rapped, eyeing Kydd.

'It is a frigate captain, this is true. But a very junior one. I counsel we wait a little longer for—'

'I know you, sir,' Wellesley said crisply. 'The Copenhagen business, was it not?'

'Aye, Sir Arthur,' Kydd replied. He had recognised the tall figure immediately.

Ignoring Rowley, the general asked, 'You've had any experience in conjunct operations, Captain?'

'I have, sir. Minorca in the last war, with Abercrombie at the Nile, the Cape in the year six and Buenos Aires to follow—'

'Splendid!' Wellesley said. 'And you've been on this coast some little time since?'

'With respect, General,' Rowley said huffily, 'Captain Kydd is under my command and your questions should properly be directed to me.'

Kydd glanced at Rowley, then answered Wellesley, 'I believe I know this seaboard as well as any.'

'Then I trust you'll give as good advisement as I shall find from any in this vicinity. Now, sir, I have at sea this hour a fleet of force intended for the Spanish insurgency, which I find is not practicable in the particulars. My orders allow a diversion for the same purpose in Portugal, the final object being Lisbon.

'My question to you is, have you knowledge of any point on this territory that will furnish a suitable landing place for my army, bearing in mind that Lisbon be accessible by road yet the landing be not harassed by the enemy?'

'I do, sir.'

Kydd's instant answer goaded Rowley into snapping, 'Have a care, Kydd. How can you know this, for God's sake?'

'I took the precaution of looking out such a place after the Oporto affair was settled, thinking it to be a likely need.'

'Ha! A fine officer-like act, sir,' Wellesley exclaimed.

Rowley, taken aback, was not to be beaten. 'This is an operation of the utmost importance,' he growled. 'How can you know that your activities in discovering it did not attract attention and by now the French have drawn up defensive works against us?'

'There is a fort in full command of the beach and river both, out of which the French have been ejected. I took the liberty of making garrison in it with all the Royal Marines at my disposal. They stand in need of relief and reinforcement, I believe.'

'How dare you act in this way without orders?' Rowley spluttered. 'Your want of respect and—'

'Well done, Captain,' Wellesley said, with a frosty glare at the red-faced admiral. 'In virtue of the orders I bear, I require that you and your frigate be placed at my immediate disposal to make rendezvous with my fleet in preparation for a landing.'

'Sir.'

'In the meanwhile those marines will be reinforced, then, Admiral?'

'Sir, I must protest! I haven't troops of any kind to undertake such a service.'

'Then could I make suggestion that you strip your fat battleships of such marines as they have and send them?' Wellesley said, with a heavy patience.

He and Kydd left companionably together.

Chapter 49

Within an hour *Tyger* was under way for the north and the rendezvous line, the general's gear transferred from *Laertes* into her more spacious accommodation, the sloop following on. Wellesley and his staff had made *Tyger* their headquarters command ship during the operation.

It was an honour to ship the noted general aboard, but if her officers expected an affable guest with anecdotes of a distinguished military life, they were disappointed. Sir Arthur was cold, aloof and short with any he thought light in the article of intelligence.

He did, however, expand on the background for what was afoot. The eruption of feeling against the French had caught Parliament unprepared, even more so the patriotic roars of support from the English people, demanding direct military assistance for the brave Spanish hurling themselves at the tyrant's hordes.

It had happened all too quickly, and trained, equipped armies were not to be plucked out of mid-air. Very fortunately such an expedition was already in existence: assembled in Cork, tasked embarrassingly for a strike against the Spanish colony of Venezuela province, its commander none other than *Tyger*'s celebrated guest.

Orders quickly revised, the fleet had sailed to Spain and made contact with the junta of Corunna to begin disembarkation, but after Bailén the proud Spaniards had become arrogant and refused to allow Wellesley to land. It was in a way understandable, for the Spanish, with no help from the outside world, had confronted Dupont's army moving on Cádiz and had soundly defeated it in open battle, killing more than two thousand and taking nearly twenty thousand prisoners, including the French general and his entire staff.

Other juntas up and down the coast, exulting in this success, had similarly refused military co-operation, which had left Wellesley and his transports wallowing idly offshore in the Bay of Biscay. Fortunately his orders were wide and discretionary, and a descent on Portugal was put in consideration.

This was no easy matter: with the whole country in occupation by the French, any landing would attract an instant response, but with news of a rising in Oporto and resulting confusion, they had a chance – if there was a suitably discreet point for getting ashore.

With Britain's only army at risk of destruction on a continental shore, so much was riding on Kydd's selection, which was to say that if any were to be blamed for a botched landing it would not be General Wellesley, who was only asking the navy to bring about a safe disembarking.

Kydd slept badly that night. The blind rush into action was foreign to his cool mind, and in all his other conjunct enterprises there'd been extensive planning beforehand. He was being given the responsibility and he knew neither the extent of the forces he was being asked to place ashore nor where the individual support equipment was distributed in the transports. A disaster caused by either the elements or the enemy would put an end to his professional career in short order.

They raised the convoy, a mass of some seventy ships, in a cold dawn off Finisterre. It was escorted by an elderly 74, *Donegal*, and a frigate, *Resistance*. Kydd accompanied Wellesley to *Donegal* and a council-of-war was called immediately.

It was curious to be seated at one end of the table, Wellesley at the other while the captains of *Donegal* and *Resistance*, both senior to him, were given minor seating. The aristocratic general, though, made it abundantly clear that Kydd and his ship were to be the centre of operations for the actual landing and, without ceremony, turned the meeting over to him.

He was ready for it. Claiming Heron, a senior lieutenant, as his assistant, he spelled out his requirements: the numbers involved; a bill of lading of all transports by sunset the next day; a schedule of priorities from the army for landing men and equipment; and a comprehensive run-down of everything that floated, all the transports and naval craft, with the names of the commanders and their subordinates.

There was more but that could wait. He and Heron had the day to put it all together in the way he'd learned in other campaigns.

'Gentlemen, you'll have your orders before you as we land,' Kydd said firmly. 'It leaves us only to pray that the weather is not overmuch in the west or sou'-west.'

But there would be need for a lot more work before then. A comprehensive set of signals, from 'abandon the enterprise' to 'form up to repel an enemy advance'; tarpaulins to cover stores landed in rain; safe storage of powder; sketch maps of beach divided into regimental territory; corrals for the secure holding of horses terrified by their experiences . . . It went on and on.

Bray became temporary captain of *Tyger*, while Dillon acted as manager of the crowded team of clerks and functionaries that was to turn out the actual orders. The midshipmen were told off to be within hail at all times for messenger duties.

In three days Kydd had the plans complete. The landings would be on the morrow.

A total of 9,600 men would go ashore – infantry, artillery-men with their guns, four hundred cavalry and their horses. A respectable number, but a small fraction of what Bonaparte could throw against them.

The gunroom held a dinner in honour of the occasion, but Kydd was still working and could not attend.

A misty dawn broke – it was time to move in.

With the convoy hove to out of range of the shore, *Tyger* closed with the river. The correct code jerked up the fort's flagstaff, still in British hands and no enemy in sight.

So, it was not to be a bloody opposed assault. In huge relief the frigate came to anchor and threw out her hoist: 'commence landing'.

Tyger's launch was lowered to the water and boarded by the beach crew – Stirk, with his usual red kerchief, would have the honour of first ashore. But when Kydd scanned the beach and sand spit, he saw something at the entrance that made him pause. Along the line of the beach was the tell-tale creaming white of combers crashing in and at the entrance an even higher progression of rollers over the bar.

He watched anxiously. If the launch with a full naval crew couldn't make it, boats encumbered with soldiery and guns could not be expected to.

Poulden brought the launch in cautiously, the oarsmen giving short, rapid strokes as the waves beneath them felt the shelving bottom and rose higher and higher. At a well-judged point, Poulden gave an order. The men fought at their oars to catch the top of a wave and keep with it in a furious rush through the entrance of the Mondego to the less frenzied waters inside. There, the boat took the sandy bottom and slewed violently sideways.

The experienced seamen had known that would happen and threw themselves over the side before it came to rest, upside down.

If Stirk was first ashore Kydd didn't see it, but the doughty sailor soon had his piece of white bunting tied to an oar and hoisted high. 'Conditions acceptable'.

He felt a rush of nerves. Could he trust his judgement?

Then he saw the dozen men with Stirk take position waist deep in the sea. They were going to intercept the boats before they took ground and presumably heave out the occupants.

Kydd gave a twisted smile. He doubted the big man would be in any wise gentle.

Spread over what seemed like miles of sea, boats were steadily making their way in. And, in accordance with Kydd's instructions, they did so in regular order, the first lining up on the beach party and, after a hesitation, heading bravely in.

The boat was seized and steadied, the occupants turned out into the surf to stumble through the last tugging seethe of the sea to assemble on the higher beach.

Another came in, was held, and the previous passengers dragooned back to the task of hauling ashore stores as the first of their equipment was landed. Another *Tyger* boat came in to swell the beach party and the pace quickened.

As the afternoon wore on the weather grew boisterous and the seas increased in vigour, carrying real viciousness in their heave and roar. Inevitably one boat caught a broadside. In a flash it rolled over in a lethal tangle of oars and black shapes, men hammered under by the crumping waves, then reappearing as still shapes further up the beach.

Almost immediately another went in, its coxswain distracted, perhaps, by the fate of the other, and again there was the snarl of splintered wreckage, ropes – and corpses.

Kydd could do nothing except agonise: was it right to let them continue?

They had started out well – but only hundreds had reached the safety of dry land. Thousands were yet to make it, let alone the tons of stores. Should he—

A figure advanced into the surf and raised an oar with a swatch of red bunting tied to it. It was Stirk, signalling deteriorating conditions and relieving Kydd of a terrible decision.

Chapter 50

During the night there was a ragged rain squall, followed by a streaming westerly, setting the close-packed convoy to a miserable jibbing and snubbing at their anchors in the endless white-capped rollers coming in from seaward.

The morning brought little relief, the ragged scud of clouds above driving ceaselessly in and the combers continuing pitiless, relentless.

In the afternoon Wellesley asked for Kydd. 'I will not have this landing delayed further. They must go in, sir!'

'Man alone cannot command the seas, sir. I have men ashore who will signal the instant boats can be expected to land safely.'

'Have you any idea how important this assault is to the success of His Majesty's arms in this, the only active opposition the country is mounting against Emperor Bonaparte?'

Kydd felt resentment rising. The navy was hardly inactive – it had always been the Emperor's unrelenting foe with a success unmatched by any – but he could see the strain was telling on the general, who was in fact a junior field officer, however highly regarded.

But what did he expect Kydd to do in the face of the hostile elements?

Wellesley's face was rigid and hard; Kydd knew that the man was not above ordering him to send the boats into the cauldron again and take the inevitable casualties. He had to do something – and fast.

'I see, sir. Then there is a way forward, which I can't guarantee but will do my damnedest to try.'

'Do it.' There'd been no enquiry into what he proposed; as he'd suspected, only a cold determination to win by any means.

It was a long shot, and the only one he had left aboard *Tyger* he could trust with it was Brice.

Shortly, one of the boats manoeuvred to square off against the thundering surf, in it Brice at the tiller. Doud was in the foresheets, unblinkingly watching aft, a coiled line in his hand.

They came in with just four at the oars, two each side. Two more were along the centreline of the boat, crouched like a coiled spring. Brice was watching, judging, seeing the waves tumbling and noting the distance of the shore with its foaming line of breaking seas as it came closer.

His hand lifted – and chopped down.

In one fluid movement Doud had his line up and, swinging mightily, sailed it out on the beam, the black curl of the grapnel clearly visible. In the next moment the line was in turns around the samson post, a square vertical timber in the foresheets normally used for towing. The boat, still with forward way on, felt the grapnel's bite and at the same time, with oars pulling hard on one side and backing furiously on the other, the boat slewed about until it faced out to sea once more.

But this time there was a difference. Oars boated, Doud

eased the rope continually, the two men along the centre-line taking the strain and following his moves, Brice at the tiller with nothing to do but watch.

The next white creaming of a rising wave was met not with the squared-off transom at the stern of the boat but the stout bow, which shouldered aside the rampaging comber with a mighty rearing but not the slightest deflection to right or left, ready for the next. Doud eased more turns, and more – it was slow work but sure. Under the tension of the grapnel line the boat resolutely faced into the great seas as it was carried in.

The beach team were ready and took the boat each side on its gunwales with no need to rotate it in the shallows to seaward again.

Success! But it was slow. At this rate it would take weeks, and in that time the French, hearing of the landing, might well have brought up artillery and reinforcements to sweep the landing beaches clean.

Ironically the seas moderated in the next few hours and the following day saw innocently playful surging Atlantic rollers and the boats resuming streaming shoreward.

Capitão Meireles had suggested they make use of native craft. At Figuiera they could be seen drawn up on the sand. The barca serrana. Tall-prowed, double-ended boats, they nevertheless contrived a sturdy flat bottom for taking the beach at speed in the surf without toppling, well suited to these local conditions.

Ashore it was soon a scene of chaos and confusion. Dumps of stores were piling up on the foreshore. Gun mountings, monstrous casks of hard tack, barrels of salted meat, rum, officers' baggage, tenting for the soldiers and pyramids of shot, with cases of small-arms ammunition in endless rows. And without an encampment or any real task to keep them occupied, hundreds increased to thousands of soldiers – sitting or lying on the ground, or aimlessly milling about.

Wellesley and his staff went ashore when the disembarkation was two-thirds complete, and immediately blessed order radiated out from his field tent. By company, then by regiment, an army came into being. It prepared for the march in the age-old way Kydd had seen in earlier campaigns, and he accepted thankfully that his role was near complete. They'd been fortunate – there'd been no sign of the enemy in the five days it had taken and for the most part the elements had been kind to them.

Then, unexpectedly, a fleet was sighted from the south but this was soon resolved into a similar convoy of transports sent from Gibraltar as reinforcements, a much appreciated five thousand, who were efficiently brought ashore to join the others.

As Kydd watched the expedition spread out along the entire foreshore in a dense mass, forming up for their push inland, he pondered that this vast throng on the move, the size of an entire big city, would have to be fed and watered, shod, clothed and kept supplied with ammunition wherever it went. A daunting task – but not his.

Most of the transports had weighed and sailed off when Kydd took in the sight of the first column stepping off into the interior, faint sounds of drum and bagpipe carrying out on the water.

'Dip our colours, Mr Bray.' It was the least he could do as Britain's only army on the Continent of Europe moved off bravely to confront the colossus of Bonaparte and his legions.

Chapter 51

Brooks's, London

The minister for war, Lord Castlereagh, was not often to be found in his club: he was anything but gregarious in his socialising and lately much taken up with the rapid turn of events in Iberia.

A figure approached him. 'Well, hello, old stick. It's been quite some time, I believe.'

Castlereagh put down *The Times* and blinked. 'Oh, but all the better for the anticipating,' he murmured distantly, rising to his feet to greet the man. It never did to ignore the most influential merchant bankers, and Sir Philip Bentinck Lawder of the Baltic Exchange was as high as they came.

A club steward appeared and waited patiently.

'A little something against the cold, will it be?'

'A splash of brandy would answer, m' lord.'

'Do sit, Pip. What brings you here today?' Castlereagh asked politely.

'Curiosity is all, old fellow. You must know I did well out of your late Baltic expedition, damn well, and I'm duly thankful for it. Now all this upheaval in Spain – where's it going? That's what I'd like to know!'

'As would we all.' Castlereagh sighed.

'Yes, but I mean to say—'

'Pip. You have your money to hazard. I have the only army of size England possesses thrown promiscuously ashore in Iberia among a countless French horde to care about, put there at the howling of Parliament and the mob to aid the Dons. It seems they don't want our help, so it has to be the Portuguee, God help us.'

'They got ashore, didn't they?'

'They did. Thanks to the navy, as always, but it's not them I'm sore exercised about at the moment. It's what I'm being asked to do.'

'What's that, then, dear fellow?'

'Since the piping days of the elder Pitt it's been our golden rule never to tangle ourselves in a Continental quarrel. All our strategy and plans follow this dictum. It's worked to full satisfaction until now in so far as we've resisted the temptation to put troops ashore on some adventure or other.'

'Copenhagen?'

'In to do the job, out as soon as we may. No, Pip, this is different. There's no defined objective I can work to, no clear task I'm given that, being achieved, we can say we've won.'

'To help the Spanish, surely.'

'I can ship them arms and guineas, but as soon as it turns to troops on the ground, I have to ask some devilish hard questions. What are they to be used for? To fight the French in common cause. Until when? Presumably until they've been ejected from the country. How long will that take? At the very least years – mayhap many years. So there we are, moiled in a Continental land war for the indefinitely long term as we've always said we wouldn't be.'

'Don't be so cast down, m' friend. We've lost the Dons as an enemy and gained 'em as a friend. They're passionate about the thing, are they not?'

'I'm not at all sanguine they're an advantage. If you've heard what I have about the reign of chaos they call their government and the band of peasantry and bandits they call their army it would give you cause to weep.'

'Our own military is much to be esteemed, I fancy.'

'Such as we have,' Castlereagh muttered. 'And that only as good as the officers.'

'Why, how can you say that when it's the hero of the Mahrattas to their fore?'

'Wellesley? He may be the people's hero, but he's a politicking, fame-seeking popinjay who happened to be available at the time. He's an able general, I'll grant, but damned difficult to work with.' He paused, then said, 'In any event, he's not to be accounted anything more than a junior in the field. Horse Guards has realised that the only active military command is in Iberia, and now I have them loudly claiming the honour for themselves, so I've this day had to sign papers appointing three generals of seniority above Wellesley. No doubt they're already on their way to relieve him of his army.' He sighed extravagantly. 'With Junot's numbers being what they are, I can't imagine why. I wouldn't wish to be in the field against him. We'll see.'

'So what do you expect?'

'To be brutally honest, a gallant defeat. But we've obeyed the people's will, and as long as the military are prudent enough to keep within shouting distance of the sea, we'll be able to take them off again.'

'A damned cynical view, if I may say so. Surely there's a bright side.'

'Umm. Not as I'd term plausible, Pip. If by some miracle

we can prevail in Portugal, it would be the first time in Europe's recent history that the French are ejected from their own conquered territory. And if we could then back the monarchy, trade, their full liberty, we've near a thousand miles of the desert and mountains of Iberia to cross and restore before we can say the same about Spain. Do you think that credible, dear fellow?'

Lawder sipped his brandy, regarding Castlereagh steadily. 'I take your point, sir. And will await an outcome with some interest, this you may believe.'

Chapter 52

Aboard HMS Tyger

Kydd saw the last of the dusty columns march into the distance with mixed feelings. Any logical speculation would give weeks only before the French converged on them in an irresistible onslaught, resulting in misery and retreat. Yet he saw behind the aristocratic arrogance of the general who led them a will of tempered steel coupled with a razor-sharp mind and hardened battlefield ruthlessness. If they had any chance, Wellesley would be the one to give it to them.

The beachhead was by no means abandoned. For want of mules and carts, vast amounts of stores stood guarded in rows, growing by the day. Those tens of thousands would be kept supplied from the sea. Then, when sufficient horse and mule transport had been found, the stores would be carried inland to where the army marched on. Only when a port of size had been captured could any kind of regular commissariat be established.

Almost as soon as General Wellesley and his regiments had disappeared, Kydd was called to *Donegal.* This time there was no nonsense about who was in charge: the landing had been accomplished and Kydd's part completed. Brusquely he was told *Tyger*'s employment: to stay by the beachhead to regulate the landing of stores and their seaward defence until relieved. *Donegal* and all others would leave with the empty transports.

It was tedious work for a crack frigate, but the weather had moderated to a fine, warm cast and Kydd had the pleasure of seeing his midshipmen in the tops with the men, mast against mast in sail exercises, and occasionally out in a boat for a 'banyan' picnic ashore or in haughty challenge to one of the sloops that kept them company.

It was good, too, to see Brice developing, his social confidence building on his exemplary professional skills, maturing into a first-class naval officer Kydd was proud to have aboard.

In Bowden as well he had a reliable, top-quality officer, whose calm incisiveness under pressure and long-sighted decisions were models of reasoning. He was a little quiet, never one to push himself forward, but with his friends in high places he would in time get himself noticed in the service and find the preferment he deserved.

It was only his first lieutenant, Bray, who gave him cause for concern. One of the old school of sea officers, he led from the front in the thickest action. His courage in gale or battle brought out the sincerest admiration, his legendary short ways with skulkers and laziness precisely what were needed to forge a ship's company of matchless performance and dedication to duty.

What was becoming increasingly obvious, though, was his moodiness – nothing Kydd could put his finger on but worrying all the same. Was it to do with his future career path? Bray had performed impeccably in *Tyger* as her premier, taking on his appointment when she was at her lowest point, a mutiny ship, and seeing her through all her trials and triumphs since. However, for reasons most likely connected to Kydd's style of leadership, he had never had the opportunity to shine alone in some desperate engagement.

Bray was now approaching his forties and needed to make that crucial step to command, however lowly, when his ship's victories and successes would be in his own name and honour. Left too long, he would finally pace his own quarterdeck, his youthful vigour diminished, the vital drive to conquer no longer the foremost element of his character.

But Kydd could do nothing about it for the present.

Days passed into weeks.

It was odd to have positions reversed. For most of the war it had been the navy that had borne the brunt, keeping the seas in all weathers and at every dawn prepared to sight an enemy that would mean hours spent locked in bloody fighting. And, in the fearsome days of the threatened invasion, it had been in constant warfare off the French coast, keeping the flotillas at bay, while England trembled and the army waited behind their walls and battlements.

Years of this had passed, and the army for the most part had remained in Britain, in garrisons and barracks, never seeing a shot fired in anger.

Now the army was marching into danger, headed for a full-blooded confrontation with the enemy on the mainland of Europe while the navy stood by in support. How would Wellesley and his small army fare? Yet again Kydd had to learn patience and wait for what emerged from a situation that was no longer the navy's to direct or influence.

Chapter 53

One morning an army officer was spied approaching the makeshift landing stage in the river at the gallop. It caused much comment and the needless signal 'send boat' from the beach party was acted on with speed.

The launch made for *Tyger* and the officer came aboard. 'L'tenant Grieves, first battalion of the Thirty-eighth of Foot. I've dispatches, sir, as must be got to England.'

'A battle?' Kydd asked, trying not to let his eagerness show.

'Um, not as who's to say, sir. Its passage?'

'Of course. Mr Bowden, call in *Laertes* if you will. Now, Mr Grieves, while it readies for England, you will have time to tell us your news.'

It was no earth-shattering revelation but it was significant. General Wellesley had landed without opposition and had now boldly decided to march south immediately towards Lisbon. At Kydd's surprise that he was taking on the French headquarters in Portugal directly, Grieves confided that Wellesley was a man with little time. He'd received news that he was to be replaced as commander of the expedition by others senior to him and had barely days to make his mark before they arrived.

So far he'd made first contact with the enemy and had emerged victorious at the village of Roliça. The outnumbered enemy, surprised by the appearance of English soldiery, had grouped together and made good account of themselves, inflicting many casualties, but Wellesley had prevailed.

It was clear, though, that this was no more than a delaying tactic. Junot in Lisbon would have been informed and be on the march north with his thousands for a concluding engagement on quite another scale.

'General Wellesley hopes you will follow him south, sir. He cleaves to the coast in the trust you can shift your most admirable operations of supply to parallel his movements.'

The little packet addressed to Kydd would no doubt include these details. 'We shall, L'tenant.'

Charts and maps were consulted. Wellesley's soldiers had covered all of seventy-odd miles, close to the coast, through uplands and even mountains, all of which they had crossed on foot with pack and musket. Kydd would do his part. The only other point of land they could consider for a landing was the river leading inland to Maceira, only thirty miles from the outskirts of Lisbon; it must be taken to be in enemy hands until proved otherwise.

Until then, General Wellesley was on his own.

'I wish you well of the venture and God speed of your dispatch,' Kydd told Grieves, as he saw him off.

He sat down to think. If the English were routed by Junot and his forces before Lisbon they would need taking off. It was quite outside his capability – the transports had been taken back to England and the nearest ships of any kind were in the fleet off Cádiz, even now dispersing, and the few under Rowley off Lisbon. Both squadrons were forwarded intelligence by the sloops attached to their respective commands and presumably would know what to do in the event of a defeat and forced evacuation.

Therefore his job was as before: to ensure the army ashore was supplied and tracked day by day so he was on hand, God forbid, for any escape by sea.

Two days later a small squadron appeared out of the mists to the north – English. It was rapidly established that an important personage was aboard, Lieutenant General Sir Harry Burrard, with reinforcements and orders that placed him above Wellesley in command of the expedition, now elevated to the status of British Forces, Iberia.

Impatient and eager to assume his rightful place, the general had nevertheless to stand idle until his forces had been landed. His temper was not improved by the sudden appearance of Grieves with news of the departure from Lisbon of Junot's fighting columns. Not only that, but their pace was formidable and it was expected that a clash would occur within days, and at a place not so very far away.

The patient waiting was all too much for the red-faced general, who angrily took horse with his staff, then rode off to find Wellesley and take charge of the battle.

If there was going to be a sad ending to the expedition it would be now, and Kydd kept *Redwing*, a dispatch cutter, close by to send out the instant it became clear what had happened. Other than that there was nothing he could do.

A passing naval sloop had the courtesy to tell Kydd of a successful landing of reinforcements further south, at the Maceira river, under yet another senior general, Sir John Moore. It seemed Whitehall was doing all they could to support the enterprise.

Then news broke from three exhausted staff officers with urgent dispatches who'd put off in a boat together.

Moore had been too late on the scene, while Burrard had arrived when the battle was at its height and had to allow Wellesley to finish it, but it did not signify: the outcome was the same. A victory of gratifying proportions near the town of Vimeiro, the French even now falling back in disorder on Lisbon.

That evening Kydd joined the celebratory dinner in the gunroom when glasses were hoisted in toast to the prickly aristocrat who had put England's footprint so firmly on the Continent. Not only was it a victory but it must give heart to all who wished them well, especially the Portuguese people who still suffered under the French. And the word now was 'forward'.

The morning brought spreading sunshine, much speculation – and the arrival of a lone senior officer. He'd taken boat over calm seas to *Tyger*. Holding himself still and forbidding, he came aboard without demand of ceremony and asked to see the captain.

'I do thank you, sir,' he said gratefully, accepting a cordial. Tired and dusty, his faultlessly cut dark uniform showing signs of recent hard wear, he was obviously in need of respite. 'Colonel Hugh Packwood of the Thirty-sixth – or, more properly, the late colonel.'

'Captain Kydd and you're right welcome aboard my ship, Colonel,' Kydd replied, hiding his curiosity. 'You said "late", did you not?'

Packwood looked away, his expression unreadable.

'A hard-fought battle, then,' Kydd prompted.

'Not the worst I've encountered.' He drained the glass abruptly and gave Kydd a lop-sided grin.

He was of an age, and mature, lines in his face telling of long years in military service, but his humorous manner spoke of an irreverent spirit. 'This morning I resigned my post as colonel of the regiment and so therefore am no longer.'

At Kydd's uncomprehending look, he said, 'I see I must explain further. The resignation is nothing to do with the fighting, which was brisk enough. Rather it was as a result of the actions of my commanding general, to which I took grave exception.' He smiled sadly. 'You're not of the military tribe so I may feel free to be frank. Well, the action was fine done and we saw the French off in noble fashion. Yet the first order of General Burrard on taking command was to General Wellesley – to halt the pursuit of the fleeing French. Yes! Just so – to leave off an action that would result in something approaching annihilation and the road wide open for Lisbon.'

'I see,' Kydd said. 'And your general agreed?'

'No, sir, but he was with strenuous protest overruled by Lieutenant General Dalrymple, one sent to rule over them both. The reason? That it was too risky to chance our only army in a pursuit and we should pause to consolidate. Just forty miles from the capital, as the crow doth fly, and we sit on our hands!'

Packwood slumped, dejected, in his chair. 'I'm getting too old for the tolerating of idiocy – I swear I cannot find it in me to serve under such.'

Kydd was not sure how he should respond and kept his silence until Packwood looked up hopefully. 'I understand you're the officer in charge of transports and shipping. I'd be infinitely obliged for passage back to England, sir.'

'Ah. All dispatch cutters are absent on service at this time, I fear.' He sympathised with the man but what he was saying was nothing but the truth. 'Returning transports will be going to Gibraltar, and anything of a naval stripe will be standing by until matters become clearer.'

'Oh.'

On impulse he offered, 'You may consider staying aboard

Tyger until a ship is found for you, our deploying remaining the same, of course.'

'This is handsome in you, sir.'

'Purely as a guest with no official status, you'll understand. I'd let you have my cabin but at the moment it must act as a species of headquarters and—'

'Not at all, my dear fellow. I'll keep well out of your way.'

'We'll rig something for you in the gunroom, then. They're always ready to welcome a new face.'

The gunroom found him amiable and courteous and quite able to tell them everything they wanted to know of the decisive victory, a raconteur who would be missed when things settled.

Just two days later, however, a galloper from Dalrymple's headquarters brought a blunt summons: in view of certain developments, the services of Colonel Packwood were required forthwith.

The ensign was interrogated on just what developments had occurred that demanded the presence of their obliging guest.

'Why, gentlemen – you haven't heard?' the young man teased. What he said shattered the calm of the morning. 'The Frog chief, Dupont, has given it away. He's asked for terms!'

The commander of all French forces in Portugal, the trusted instrument of Napoleon Bonaparte, asking for surrender terms before the campaign had been under way more than a dog-watch?

The ensign concluded, 'So, Colonel, sir, you're asked to return and be part of a council-of-war as will try to fathom what's to do. They're all to be in on it, the navy as well.'

Packwood took horse immediately, with a solemn promise to let them know what was happening, and *Tyger* was left to digest the extraordinary news.

'It's a trick, of course,' Bray rumbled dismissively. 'Can't understand why they're not hot-foot on the road to lay siege to Lisbon instead o' wasting time, the sluggards.'

Kydd shook his head in confusion. That the whole of Portugal was to be relinquished as a consequence of a single battle made no sense, but then again, a capitulation was a definitive act that could not be reversed.

'Simple,' offered Brice. 'They're playing for time. Spin it out over weeks, gives them the chance to whistle for help and they're ready for a return fight.'

'So we're to swing about our anchor until things get hot again,' Bowden said glumly. 'Shocking waste of a fine ship and prime crew.'

Astonishingly Packwood was back within two days. 'Gentlemen. I shall tell you my tidings, but only on the back of a muzzler as shall steady me.'

This was more extraordinary than before. An armistice was now in force. Not only was Dupont going to follow through without delay on his seeking of terms but these were to cover the yielding up of the country as a whole: the two sides would meet in conclave at a national convention in the magnificent medieval city of Cintra to determine the fate of Portugal and its French occupiers.

Appreciative of a gunroom dinner after army field victuals, the colonel tried to answer the obvious question: why was Dupont conceding so much for so little?

'The best kind of general does not spy out the field and look for his advantage,' he explained. 'Instead he gets inside the head of his opponent and sees it through his eyes.'

'So this is what the generals are doing?'

'I didn't say that. No, sir, this is my reckoning of Dupont's motives.' He took another grateful sip of his claret. 'When the risings began in Spain they fanned out quickly to Portugal and he found himself spread all too thinly about the country. The natives rose up in general, not at one place, which made it impossible for him to put it down. This threw him on the defensive and he did what he could – told his field commanders to contract their boundaries around strongholds into local concentrations of force.'

The naval officers tried to nod wisely.

'A reasonable thing, you'd say. But not in this instance. The French in Portugal have been brutal and forceful in their occupation and the people have learned to hate them. As a result the areas between these force concentrations are impassable to Dupont's military communications on account of assassinations and similar. And you know what that means.'

'Er, do elaborate for us unlearned sailor-men, please.'

'Why, first, he has no knowledge of what is going on in his field of operations. This is insupportable for him, as he no longer knows which of his concentrations is in trouble, and which ones he can call on to help the other. Next, he has no intelligence of the enemy – the insurgent armies springing into life around him that threaten to overwhelm these concentrations. Worse, he's not in a position to supply them with victuals, let alone powder and shot. They are therefore inevitably lost to him. To these woes add the final: that, thanks to their ownership of the sea, the British are landing in strength at unknown points in his domain and might be expected at any moment to seize the capital. What should he do?'

He had complete attention as he went on, 'He can have no hope of succour from Spain – after Bailén their forces there are under the same adversities and therefore he can entertain no prospect of relief. Good sirs, his only course now is to lay down his arms on the best terms he can get at this time.'

'So that's why . . . And what do you conceive these will be?' Kydd asked.

'With our forces swelling daily, undoubtedly he'll be held to an unconditional surrender. Nothing less.'

As it sank in, there was a collective sigh of incredulity.

'It's high tide, then, for Mr Bonaparte,' Kydd said slowly. 'And then it's Spain and . . .'

'Yes.'

'Can I ask it – the cause removed, will you return to your regiment, Colonel?'

'The circumstances being as they are, I feel I must. Shortly there'll be motions made towards Spain, as you've fancied. I have desire to be at the head of my men when that happens. And may I ask it of you to keep the fortunes of war of the Thirty-sixth of Foot, the Herefords, which is to say the "Saucy Greens" always to the fore in your gatherings?'

Kydd stood immediately. 'Gentlemen, do raise your glasses! To His Majesty's Thirty-sixth Regiment, the Saucy Greens, and all who serve in it.'

The colonel coloured with pleasure. 'And might I be allowed to propose a toast to the health and prosperity of the captain and crew of HMS *Tyger*, as being her success at arms is patently assured?'

They saw off their colonel in fine style and, in accordance with orders, followed the army south to lay off the coast, Cintra not more than five miles inland on the heights overlooking Lisbon.

Impressively, most of the fleet was present, *Conqueror* prominent with her rear admiral's pennant. Kydd remembered Packwood mentioning that the navy would be represented and this would include Rowley. Not that he would have much to do, the initiatives lying with the army.

In thrall to the moment, *Tyger* awaited events.

Chapter 54

Gunter's Tea Shop, London

'Disgraceful! I'd never have believed it – even of a Dalrymple, my dear!' Lady Leveson-Gower sniffed in mortification, other patrons of the fashionable establishment pausing in their conversations at the words so strongly expressed by the formidably attired woman. 'A convention, no less, with Bonaparte's horrid functionaries, and so demeaning it makes my blood run cold.

'Here we have the French, in defeat for the first time at our arms, and before the gaze of the world, they are allowed to keep their colours, their honours of war – even their arms. But what is worse in my eyes, which will stir even the most lost to honour in this land, is that fully at the expense of England the whole French Army is to be conveyed back to their homeland, with all their baggage and foul plunder, ready to take up arms against us once more!'

'Yes, Harriet,' Millicent Nugent replied patiently, for with her friend's husband high in the Foreign Office she could be trusted to know more of the suddenly notorious convention than most.

Lady Leveson-Gower glared at her, as though it were all her doing. 'Spencer is quite beside himself with vexation, the poor dear. The military principals forgot themselves even to the omitting of sending word of their negotiating until after it was signed and all too late to change.

'Dishonourable is not too strong a term for such behaviour!' she went on. 'If this is how we are to conduct our wars on the land in future, I despair of our ever succeeding to laurels.'

A delicately built gentleman in fashionable frock coat made his way through the noisy throng to them. 'M' lady.' He acknowledged Millicent with a civil bow, then turned distracted to his wife.

'I do apologise for the tardiness, my dear. It's all in a moil at the office, I can tell you. The newspapers got hold of the terms before we did and we're sadly at a loss as to how we should counter the dissatisfaction, even less the outrage.'

'Then you shall disavow this ridiculous convention, Spencer, do you hear me?' Lady Leveson-Gower pronounced imperiously. 'For the sake of common honour and decency!'

'That will be hardly possible, madam. The signatories are victorious on the field of battle and thus entitled to demand any terms of the defeated as they think proper.'

'Oh, do sit down, Spencer.'

'Unhappily, Harriet, I have now to make visit to Number Ten. I rather fear I shall be late home tonight, the matter being so pressing. Send the servants to bed, my dear. I will have no need of them.'

He bowed again and left.

The streets seemed even noisier and more rancorous than before and Leveson-Gower hurried on, noticing the print-shops filling with vulgar cartoons capitalising on the topical interest – one, of the entire Convention of Cintra wearing white feathers, another of them all swinging at the gibbet.

Turning into Whitehall, he hesitated at the crowds gathering but persevered, passing close enough to learn they were forcefully demanding that His Majesty be advised without delay how it could be that such a shameful convention had been allowed to come into existence.

Chapter 55

'Your Grace?' Leveson-Gower ventured softly. The prime minister remained at the window, looking down on the angry crowd, his aide supporting him in his infirmity.

'Sir?' he persisted.

'Oh, yes, Spencer,' he muttered, in a thin, whispery voice. He turned away from the window, shuffled over to the empty cabinet table and sat painfully. 'What does all this agitation and perplexity mean, pray?'

The man's age was now a crippling burden, his lifetime of service barely remembered in the weak, confused figure of William Cavendish, the Duke of Portland, as world-shaking changes were taking place. It was said he had only a short time left in this mortal world – but who could replace him without shaking the fragile political balance that kept the administration in power?

'It is the convention lately signed, Your Grace. The people do consider the terms shameful, our part in its conjuring despicable.'

'Convention? I've not heard of this. Go to Canning and find out what's to do, there's a good fellow. He's sure to know.'

*   *   *

Canning was not in a good temper. 'Convention? Convention? I'm only secretary of state for the foreign affairs of this benighted kingdom, how should I know anything about what's happening outside our gates? Hmm?'

In answer Leveson-Gower passed across a newspaper. 'The mobility are restless, George. They want heads for what they see as a besmirching of our honour with all this about—'

'I know, I know – I've just read the foolish twaddle. Well, I'm not the one who can answer – let the military out on their own and this is what results. They didn't consult this office so I've no idea what possessed them. See Castlereagh. He's minister for war and supposed to be in charge of those tin soldiers, the useless fool.'

Leveson-Gower knew better than to go immediately to Canning's deadly enemy and let it lie until the afternoon.

'There's going to be a question in the House, nothing surer,' he advised the minister quietly.

'God forbid,' Castlereagh muttered. 'And blood at the end of it,' he added, with a sigh.

'There's one answer for it all,' Leveson-Gower offered.

'Yes?'

'Come what may, we have Portugal and the French do not.'

'You mean well, old fellow, but it won't do. Not at all.'

'Why not?'

'The terms. The generals got what they wanted, and without fighting for it. They should have asked themselves why they were being handed the entire country.'

'Why?'

'Neither Dupont nor any other could have held Portugal in the face of a general uprising and no aid possible from a Spain in retreat. They had to leave, and on the best terms they could get. And our generals fell right into it in their eagerness to show victorious.'

'So . . .'

'This explains why the terms are so disgraceful. In fact, could they be worse?' Castlereagh groaned, holding his head in his hands.

'The foreign minister implies that he will defend this by telling it as a military blunder.'

'I'm sure the villain will. So I'm to answer the question, I believe. Thank you, Spencer, m' friend.'

The cabinet met later that evening. The prime minister took his seat and, as was his wont, some minutes to marshal his wits before opening the meeting.

As all present were well aware, the Convention of Cintra was the foremost matter in hand and a business-like summary was quickly delivered by Camden, lord president.

At its conclusion the prime minister quavered, 'This is . . . disgraceful. And – and not to be borne.'

The lord chancellor stirred uncomfortably. 'I rather fear it must be, Your Grace. An act duly signed under the articles in the presence of—'

'This is none of my doing, that is to say, neither is it my department,' Canning snarled. 'The Foreign Office stands absolved of blame in the matter of this shameful act done without its knowledge. I call on the secretary of state for war to make explanation of this farrago – if he can.'

Castlereagh looked up wearily. 'As well the minister knows, I'm not privy to the full circumstances of all the deliberations leading up to their, er, act of state.'

'Then what possible use are you, then, sir?'

Ignoring Canning's venomous gibe, he went on calmly, 'There is, however, a course open to me that serves not only to enlighten us but give answer to the carping wretches in the streets below us.'

'Pray tell,' the foreign minister said sarcastically. 'We'd like to know.'

'Why, the simple measure of shipping back the principals of the convention to answer for their conduct before a committee of inquiry.'

'A full recall, all of 'em?'

'All three – Dalrymple, Burrard and Wellesley.'

'Who is a public hero and has friends.'

'Who will no doubt protect him in the event it goes badly for them.'

'The chief object will be achieved, sir.'

'That the public will be mollified. This I can see well enough. But what of the army left in Iberia? Who will—'

Castlereagh's pale face was growing steadily pallid at the interrogation and he snapped back, 'There's one senior general still in the field, Sir John Moore, who I'd think well able to take the war to the enemy.' He drew a sharp breath. 'Sir, this is naught to do with foreign affairs and I will not have your stepping into areas of competence that do not concern you. I've outlined a course of action—'

'Gentlemen, gentlemen.' The weary voice of the prime minister intervened. 'Let it be so. Recall the signatories and have your inquiry but let it be privy, not for public spectacle. And directly – the sooner this distasteful business is behind us the better.'

Chapter 56

At anchor, Lisbon

Nobody dared approach the figure that stalked the quarterdeck of HMS *Tyger*. The appalling news from Cintra had broken over the anchorage in a surge of disgust and anger, but what had made Kydd seethe was the brief orders he had received soon afterwards.

In accordance with the terms of the convention, the entire French Army, from commander-in-chief to meanest private, was to be repatriated to France by the British and the vessel selected to be flagship and escort was HMS *Tyger*. Her captain being a knight of the realm she was considered most appropriate to the solemnity of the occasion.

Kydd was under no illusion: this was Rowley cynically hoping the shame and disrepute of the whole thing would rub off on him. His blood boiled at the certain knowledge that the admiral had been aware of how it would wound his sense of rightness, and he tried in vain to think of a way out – but duty laid down was duty to be done.

There was one bright light in all the gloom: the military

liaison officer he was directed to work with was none other than Major General Beresford, the upright but sorely tested commander of the failed British attempt on Buenos Aires in which Kydd had played his part. They would understand each other.

Tyger sailed into the Tagus, past Forte de São Laurenço at the entrance that Kydd had last seen on his attack only some weeks before, now with an enormous Portuguese flag lazily floating atop its stout tower, then by the centuries-old carved-stone Belém tower before the mile or so of wharves, alive with newly liberated shipping.

Beresford's courteous note had indicated that the French would be assigned the Belém Square for their embarkation point, and he would meet Kydd there for details of the departure, timed to begin the next day.

Tyger lay off, well clear of the docks and moored to two anchors. Ashore it was difficult to make out what was going on as it was crowded with masses of moving figures, most in the vivid colours of the military, and the transports were even now jockeying to be warped in alongside.

'My barge – Mr Dillon to accompany, Mr Clayton in the launch to provide a dozen marines issued with ball to land with bayonets fixed.'

Beresford would have suitable military but Kydd meant to take personal charge in the boarding of the transports. Who knew what would blow up, with the Portuguese rumoured to be in an ugly mood?

The barge found the steps and Kydd mounted them with a dignified air. Beresford was waiting for him at the top with a few of his staff and gave a comradely smile, advancing to shake his hand.

'I'm bound to say it's most gratifying to meet you again,

sir,' Kydd said, with all sincerity, 'since last I saw you in such provoking circumstances.'

'Buenos Aires? Yes, a trying state of affairs.' They had both escaped, but at different times, then gone on to more illustrious futures. 'Yet perhaps not as provoking as what we face here, my friend,' Beresford added.

He briefly gestured. The square was crowded but remarkably neat. Dominating all was a headquarters tent with a tasselled regimental flag above it and, in no less than four other places, a French national standard in arrogant defiance. A stream of carts and soldiers bearing packs and bundles was adding to mountains of baggage near filling the area. With a start Kydd took in the sight of field guns at the sides and rear of the square, ranged for firing outward, complete with limber and smoking portfire – manned entirely by Frenchmen.

'Yes. They've every reason to fear the vengeance of the Portuguese people, and the convention allowing 'em to keep their military equipment, I can't well deny them.'

Officers of Junot's army sauntered about in full dress uniform, their swords conspicuously by their sides, with expressions ranging from lordly disdain to sullen animosity. To Kydd, it resembled more a gathering of triumphant veterans than a defeated army being ejected after just one battle.

'You have plans for the transports, Sir Thomas?' asked Beresford.

'I have. In all we are allowed by the Board of Transport thirty of the full-rigged breed and sixty-two of the lesser. As were used by General Wellesley in his descent on the Mondego river. These will—'

'This will be barely enough. The wording of the convention is so loose as to allow your coach and horses through. "The honours of war" – all pennons, eagles, baubles and similar to be paraded whenever they see fit, with bands and horses. "Military equipment" – every gun they possess with its impedimenta and munitions, all bladed weapons, of any kind, and stores thereto. And "personal property" by which we are to understand not merely their clothing and accoutrements but as well their full share of plunder from this ravaged country.'

'I cannot ask for more transports! They'll have to leave it behind.'

'Not so, old chap,' Beresford said sadly. 'The terms of the convention are not to be breached. If their personal property must be returned it is not their concern how it's to be done, merely that it is. How – this is your affair, I'm sorry to say.'

'Be damned to the knaves!' Kydd blurted hotly. 'I won't have it!'

'Dear fellow. Should you refuse them, it will be my own good self that will be held accountable and I know you wouldn't want that.'

Smouldering, Kydd glared at the gathering horde. Here was the enemy, his duty to fall upon and destroy, and they were dictating to him. 'Very well. Each of the transports alongside the quay will have two brows – that's gang-planks. The forward one will be for rank and file, the after one for the officers, who will board last. Those with heavy gear will load separately. I want to get away as soon as I may. The vessels will be warped out and lie at anchor until all are ready for sea at which we'll proceed, without touching anywhere, to Rochefort.'

'You'll want guards?'

'Not on the ships. They cause trouble, they don't get home. I've a notion they'll more need guards here in the square.'

'We've a battalion of foot in barracks, if needed. British bayonets saving a French army for another day,' he muttered sourly.

Kydd sensed the bitterness that lay under his words but moved on. 'I'll need 'em mustered here by ship. I'll let you know numbers when each is ready to load.'

A rectangle was quickly laid out, using ropes. 'Men here, their baggage there for ticketing.'

The first transport: *Lord McAllan*, a substantial full-rigged vessel being worked in up to the quay. 'Mr Clayton. Guard of honour, bayonets fixed.'

Clayton grinned mirthlessly. He knew what Kydd meant: a double line of marines facing inwards at each brow just as the Botany Bay convicts were duly honoured at their transportation.

Several French officers strolled forward, their servants standing by their baggage.

Kydd went to the first, a tall, supercilious staff officer. 'Your papers?' he demanded.

The man looked astonished, then reluctantly extracted a well-thumbed military notecase and took out a document that meant little to Kydd.

'Baggage?'

Wearily the man gestured to a considerable pile of well-secured pieces of kit.

'Open it.'

Two seamen went to the mound and began unlacing the first bag.

The officer started with horror and, with a snarl, tried to intervene but was held back. It contained jewellery and plate, carefully wrapped and very obviously of ecclesiastical origin.

Red-faced, the officer bellowed in outrage. It brought others running but Kydd snapped an order and the marines took position.

Beresford hurried forward. 'What's the problem?' he puffed.

Kydd pointed to the gold and silver. 'Personal property?' he asked sarcastically.

The officer spat out his answer. It seemed Kydd had no right whatsoever to make search of his baggage, as if he were a common criminal. As an officer and gentleman, if he declared it as his personal property who was Kydd to interfere?

'If he swears it's his, there's little we can do to argue otherwise,' Beresford muttered.

'Look at it! I'm not allowing the results of this thievery aboard my ships,' Kydd barked, folding his arms with a pointed finality.

It provoked a bedlam of protest but he remained unmoving. More Frenchmen arrived, drawn by the shouting.

'We're not going anywhere at this rate,' Beresford snapped. 'Wait here. I'm seeing Kellermann, their chief.'

Kydd made sure nothing moved until Beresford returned with a haughty, dusky-featured cavalryman in impossibly ornate uniform who, with a bored expression, resolutely ignored Kydd.

'We've agreed to form a commission as will decide whether disputed items may be considered legitimate under the terms of the convention or no. Carry on, please.'

A table was brought up and they sat stiffly together.

'This officer swears he bought these paltry baubles at a country church, there being no question of receipt from those ignorant peasants.'

'Passed,' snapped Kellermann. 'Or do you propose to challenge the word of a gentleman?' he sneered.

Kydd ground his teeth, then held up his hand. 'Hold! Sergeant, double away and bring before me the priest who mans that cathedral.'

The black-frocked cleric appeared promptly. 'Ask him if he's ever seen these "baubles" before.'

At the dawning joy and happy babble, there was no need to go further. The French officer was stripped of his loot and sent aboard.

Others were harder to crack. And the higher the rank of officer, the worse the peculation. In one, gold bars worth a million francs were claimed to be the official reparation of the Portuguese government to the French Empire, a perfectly genuine and verifiable levy. Kydd disposed of this with savage pleasure: if it was indeed properly certified official, how could it possibly be personal property?

Beresford intervened when a regimental chest of some weight of specie was produced as 'military equipment'. He allowed it, but cunningly enquired where the accounting was that proved in the usual form all shore debts had been cleared when the regiment sailed?

They were less successful with others, whose more anonymous thefts were untraceable, but it wasn't until the baggage of Junot, the commander-in-chief, was searched under furious protest from his aide that the outrageous scale of the ransacking was revealed.

Fifty-three large chests of Brazilian indigo worth a fortune, fourteen volumes of a priceless Florentine Renaissance Bible, and many other works stolen from the Royal Library. And the general had even ordered the bare-faced breaking into the Depósito Público and seizure of all coin as private booty. Nothing was too shameful or despicable for one of Napoleon's heroes.

'When will you want to clap eyes on your guest?' Beresford murmured at one point.

'Guest?'

'Junot himself, in course.' There was nothing but sympathy in his expression. 'Demands royal treatment in the flagship by right of equality, old man. Has a point, too.'

'When I'm ready for the damned thief and not before.' If he had to give passage to a self-appointed potentate, the Tygers would be hard to handle. He'd have to give it thought or end up with crew and passengers at each other's throats.

By this point the boundary of French 'territory' was beginning to contract. Outlying forts and encampments were marching in, dumping their equipment and demanding ships. As numbers crowding onto the transports increased, so did pressure on Kydd's stores of victuals and water. And the inhabitants of Lisbon, sensing their freedom and the humiliation of their previous occupiers, were now screaming threats and defiance.

A report came in from the suburbs that a detachment of Frenchmen had been set upon and battered to death by enraged townsfolk before they could reach the safety of the British bayonet squares. From now on, any finding themselves isolated could expect a rapid and squalid end.

Beresford approached Kydd. 'His Nibs is getting restless, old fellow. Can't you get him away from this deadly mess? I'll do the introductions for you.'

The headquarters tent turned out to be a Persian sybarite's den, with Oriental carpet, hangings, fragrant candles smoking and, in a curved Romanesque chair the image of Napoleon's, a sullen Junot. Thin-faced and slight his voice was high and demanding. 'I shall go aboard my flagship now, I believe. Are you its master?'

'No, I'm not,' Kydd snapped coldly.

Confused, Junot looked quizzically at Beresford, who, equally at a loss, could not answer.

As though to a child, Kydd explained in French: 'Your *maître* is demeaning to me. A *maître pilote*, the only *maître* we have aboard, ranks below a lieutenant in the Royal Navy and is responsible to me, a *capitaine de vaisseau.*'

A distant squealing in a street beyond made the general wince.

'I rather think it time to go, don't you, *mon brave*?'

Kydd stood silent and unblinking.

'What the devil's the matter with this dolt?' spat Junot, peevishly. 'He doesn't seem to—'

'I rather think "*capitaine*" would answer, *mon général*.'

'So, Capitaine. We go, *hein*?'

This was someone who'd risen through the ranks in the lethal feverishness of the Directorate and later furthered his ambitions in slavish devotion to the Bonaparte empire, not a man to cross. Further humiliation would not be in anyone's interest.

'A boat will be sent in one hour.' Kydd doffed his bicorne and left.

Chapter 57

Tyger was seething with speculation, which Kydd put down at once.

'The chief Frog takes my cabin, his staffers in the first two lieutenants' cabins, I will take the third's. I dare to say he'll bring his own cook and there'll be servants and stewards by the dozen. They'll all doss down at the after end of the mess-deck, hammocks or nothing. Baggage in roped off area of the orlop. Clear?'

Clayton delicately asked, 'Just as an observation, sir – security? I wouldn't think it impossible that once off Rochefort they could try something foolish and . . .'

'Relieve 'em of all weapons as we'll be looking after 'em. They're a scurvy crew of land-lubbers and can't stand up to a jack tar in anything of a mill.'

'And if'n the Crapauds make mock of our men, who's to blame 'em for getting back at the shicers?' Bray's fierce rumble intervened.

'Hear me well, Mr Bray. Any who lays a fist on a Frenchman will get a striped back at the gangway in front of the same party. Compree?' Even the slightest incident could flare into a wholesale affray, which would inevitably end with *Tyger* being blamed for it.

Junot's boat arrived alongside promptly, at the tiller Halgren's features a study in blankness.

Helped up by the boat's crew Junot stood on *Tyger*'s deck while the boatswain's call pealed out, smoothing his tunic and looking about scornfully. 'You've forgotten something, Capitaine.'

'You shall be introduced to my officers in—'

'Where is the *tricolore* of France, sir?'

'This is a ship of His Britannic Majesty,' Kydd ground out thickly, 'and a French flag has no business—'

'The convention, Capitaine. "The honours of war to be afforded in full" is the specification. As on the march, so are we on the sea. I shall not be suffered to proceed except under our glorious colours. Kindly hoist them.' He folded his arms and turned his back.

With *Tyger* at anchor, the blue ensign of the Lisbon squadron floated at the taffrail; Kydd would be rather seen in hell than lower his ship's colours to a Frenchman but he had an idea. 'Mr Bray – the French standard. At the fore masthead.'

One was found and mounted slowly up the signal halliards. 'There, sir. Right at the fore and higher than our own, you see.'

Junot squinted up then gave a lazy smile. 'That will do very well, Capitaine.'

The remainder of his entourage awkwardly made their way up the side, looking about apprehensively.

Brice scratched his head with a twisted grin. 'What about that dunnage, sir?' Over the side in two barges was the astonishing sight of tons' weight of impedimenta.

'Strike it below as you may,' Kydd said shortly. 'As long as it clears the guns.'

He turned to Junot. 'If you'll accompany me to your quarters, General, you shall hear the rules of the ship.'

Affronted, but unable to find reply, the officer followed Kydd down to his cabin and stared about in distaste. 'This is hardly worthy of one of rank, Capitaine. Have you no better?'

'The first rule,' Kydd snarled inexorably. 'At sea the captain's word is law. The second, that under all and every instance your men keep clear of the sailors while they're working ship, on risk of being swept overboard.'

It hurt unbearably to see the man standing so pompous and conceited beneath the portrait of Persephone in all her vivacity and decency, and he turned away to bring forward Tysoe. 'Should you require something your own men cannot provide, they may consult my man, Tysoe, here.'

'There will be no need . . .' But Kydd had left.

He resumed the deck, breathing deeply of the good clean sea air. 'What's this damned bobbery?' he barked, finding himself part of a milling crowd of lost-looking individuals on his quarterdeck.

Bowden had more sense than to answer.

'Find a senior one who speaks English, make him your Frenchy bo'sun and responsible to you for getting 'em all below, out of my sight,' Kydd growled at him.

He went to leave the deck while his orders were carried out, then realised he had no cabin to go to. Fuming, he cursed under his breath and paced up and down, knowing Brice was having to perform his watch-on-deck duties, then find time to clear his cabin for Kydd's use.

It was an age before there was any kind of order, but Kydd took the opportunity of warning off the first division of the convoy that it would put to sea with *Tyger* on the tide the following morning. Not more than a week or so to Rochefort and they'd be rid of the insanity.

No sooner had the decks been cleared than French officers and idlers in ones and twos appeared, strolling about as though it was all a spectacle in a park. Bowden caught Kydd's eye helplessly. About to give orders to pack them off below again, Kydd realised it was asking too much. But with his men trying to get about their duties, sooner or later there might be an interaction that would spark open conflict.

Kydd hid a smile as he saw the Tygers in their own way had found a solution, one that was apt and preserved their respect.

They turned their backs. If any seaman was approached by a Frenchman they would contemptuously face away. When the officers objected to this blatant disrespect, Kydd would have none of it – what else could they do? They didn't have the Mongseers' lingo, did they?

Junot came up and was immediately surrounded by his followers and began his evening peregrinations: how amazing it was that so many of Kydd's officers did not have the French . . .

'*Haands* to stations to unmoor ship!'

The call was as early as Kydd could contrive, knowing that the more Frenchmen still at their cots the better. It didn't deter Junot, who stalked up the ladder to the quarterdeck, well swathed against the morning chill in a cashmere wrap, haughtily critical.

The first thing the general checked was that the *tricolore* was still in place at the foremast head, with *Tyger*'s ensign in its lowly place well to the rear. Satisfied, he went to the wheel and waited, legs abrace, looking forward in imperious fashion.

The age-old routine of winning the anchor began, but it was beneath the general to stay. A pity, for behind him, in accordance with routine, he could have seen *Tyger*'s ensign taken in as she got under weigh and the Union Flag of Great Britain bent to the main-mast halliards. As they left the forts at the entrance abeam, it soared up and took position at the truck, the highest point in the ship. And this was a battle flag, nearly twice the size of the standard colour.

On spying it after resuming the quarterdeck, Junot spluttered with outrage but Kydd pointed out politely that the *tricolore* still flew unchanged in exactly the same position as he'd approved earlier, that nothing in the convention required a British ship to strike its own colours and, finally, that he could always take it up at the next port of call, which just happened to be Rochefort.

After the Tagus bar had been crossed, and the first heaving swells came in from the Atlantic, Kydd sniffed appreciatively. This was a portent of a blow coming on, a west-north-westerly to be expected on the beam for their passage north to Finisterre and, if the gods were kind, veering more northerly and therefore still on the beam as they rounded the cape into Biscay for the run into Rochefort. A deep and screwing roll that would extract the maximum discomfort.

Cheered, he went below to his – to Brice's cabin. It was neat and domestic but so diminutive, pocket-sized! He'd long forgotten what it was to sleep below where there was no opening to let through a refreshing breeze.

It was something over a week of this, little to see of the land except once a distant, furious tumbling of white against the louring heights of Finisterre, then further endless nothingness as the thirty-odd ships swept on in thanks for the fair winds.

Kydd ate in the gunroom with the rest – in a tense stillness: conversation in the presence of the four Frenchmen with sca-lcgs and a littlc English was not feasible, and he always left as soon as he decently could.

At last they raised the French coast: two remarkably flat islands with a broad channel between. This was the Pertuis d'Antioche strait, between Île de Ré and Île d'Oléron. And their rendezvous for the final act.

On deck came crowding those to whom this was blessed home, a few with tears streaming, others on their knees and some with a faraway stare.

Kydd had seen much of France from seaward, from blockade duty to his ill-fated descent in the last war on Brittany with his shipmates of the old *Duke William*. And to him it was the land that had turned the world on its head.

He brought the convoy to a stop, spying vessels on their way out to them.

The first brought an officer in a resplendent uniform who sought out Junot. They embraced formally, salutes were given and, after a quick interchange, Junot marched over to Kydd, as contemptuous and arrogant as ever. 'You will raise a white flag, then follow the boat with a yellow flag. Any attempt to divert from its directing will result in your instant destruction.'

Kydd hid a smile, but replied coldly that on the contrary it was his avowed intention to be away just as soon as he was able.

Nonetheless, in the bay ahead were two of the largest French ports, La Rochelle to the left and Rochefort to the right. As far as he knew, his was the only one of His Majesty's ships ever to penetrate unhindered deep into this focus of France's seapower, the legendary ports from which countless battle squadrons had sailed to fall on far parts of Britain's empire, and it still commanded respect and a squadron of British men-o'-war to sustain its blockade.

As they got under way for the inner regions Kydd told Bowden to find all the midshipmen and send them into the tops with sketching gear, a compass, a small telescope and the strictest instructions to hunker down and make good views of all they could see.

They passed within the lee of Île d'Oléron and ahead was the tiny Île d'Aix – before it lay, in full view, what the blockade cruisers would give a barrel of gold to see. Buoyed together were overlapping rows of ships-of-the-line. At least four separate divisions and others of frigates, more of sloops.

They were at the heart of a great naval concentration. This must therefore be the fabled Rade des Basques, the Basque Roads, where the French Navy lay in all its puissance. Rochefort would be somewhere beyond the little island, with its dockyards, slips and all that was necessary to maintain an ocean-going navy. Kydd fought down an impulse to climb the mast to take a lingering look – he knew it would provoke fury – but trusted his midshipmen were hard at work.

The boat they were following dropped its yellow flag and a red one took its place. Anchor.

This was at a place well away from the ranks of men-o'-war and it soon became clear why. Scores of rafts, punts, barges and lighters were mustering to transfer the passengers and their chattels. They were going no further and Kydd's attempts at espionage must end at this point.

Junot and his entourage were rapidly removed from *Tyger* in a great show of splendour and formality, the returning hero with his spoils of war, a 74-gun battleship sent out to receive him and overawe the single-decker that had conveyed him. To head off any show of mocking or ridicule, Kydd had all but a handful of the men confined to the lower deck while this was proceeding but he couldn't hold back a tidal wave of shouts and jeers afterwards.

The mountain of baggage swayed down into the lighters and quite suddenly *Tyger* was clear of the interlopers.

And time to be quit of the scene of their debasement.

'Sir. A word.' A grim-faced Bray took him to one side and told him about the appalling mess their guests had left, after days of seasickness, carelessness with food and the discarding of refuse straight into *Tyger's* previously pristine scuppers.

As the once-proud frigate turned her bowsprit for the open sea Kydd's heart wept at what she'd become. And on the faces of her officers and crew he saw that he was not alone.

There was only one thing that could give them back pride in themselves and their ship – and lay the unfortunate episode behind.

Far out to sea, where the ocean breezes blew clean and free, Kydd gave orders that saw *Tyger* strike every sail safely down to bare poles.

He didn't have to explain, and joined the others at the boatswain's table where he collected his rag and, with Bray as his matey carrying the soogee bucket, marched forward and began the arduous process of 'clean ship' – as it had never been done before.

From the trailboards of the beakhead to the balusters of the stern-lights, relays of men scrubbed and swabbed, sluiced and soaked hour after hour until *Tyger* emerged cleansed and bright, the seamen's souls and spirits renewed and restored.

Sail set and course laid, the ship settled down to splice the mainbrace and toast their future in a bumper.

Chapter 58

'A sight to warm the cockles!' Brice said, with feeling, as they felt their way to an anchorage with the fleet off Lisbon.

The docks and quays were near hidden in the press of shipping that lay there. Trade was now well and truly astir, all ocean-going and all British, testament to the failure of Bonaparte's economic blockade, the Continental System.

There was no need for Kydd to make his number with Rowley, for his interrupted cruising off the Portuguese coast would resume after he'd watered and stored. There was opportunity for liberty for both watches, though, and lazily he reviewed possibilities for a jaunt of sorts ashore. Possibly with Bowden, or Dillon who was keen to sharpen up his Portuguese, with its apparently beguiling Celtic expression of Vulgar Latin.

The decision was made moot by the pleasant young lieutenant in command of the aviso greeting them. 'Much has changed you'll find, Sir Thomas. If you've a yen to linger ashore might I recommend the Captain's Club? Much cried up as a rendezvous for the heaven-blessed of the sea.'

The absence of the French from anywhere that could be termed close by, along with the great increase of shipping in the Tagus, had revitalised the ancient city. Well supplied with exotic provisions from over the seas it had an air of gaiety and busyness that made a stroll through the old streets a distinct pleasure.

And the lieutenant was right: in the immemorial way of it, the English had not wasted any time in founding an establishment where they might relax in comfort, and the esteemed Captain's Club was in a leafy side-street off the Praça do Comércio on the waterfront. The membership was delighted to welcome their distinguished visitor, and Captain Sir Thomas Kydd was installed without delay.

It was a fine building, the interior of a pre-war style of opulence, on all sides cool marble and balustraded galleries.

'So good to see you again, Sir T,' greeted Hayward of *Vigilant*, lifting a glass in the handsome dining room. 'Always entertaining when your good self is tops'ls over.'

'Just right glad to be rid of those Crapauds,' Kydd said gustily, making much of his ruby-shot Dão. 'As were a scurvy thieving crew.' He watched Hayward surreptitiously. Would he be mocked or disdained for his degrading voyage?

'Oh, yes, as I heard,' Hayward returned. 'Bad luck to land the job, old fellow. But I do envy you. Is it true that, before you scuttled back, you got a grand view of the French Navy in its lair?'

Kydd relaxed. Rowley was not going to get his satisfaction of casting him as the poor wight remembered as the one who had played deliveryman to the French.

'What's the news?' he asked. 'Lisbon's looking so dimber these days.'

'Why, better by the day. We've Ilis Nibs, Sir John Moore, now landed with a respectable army and in barracks in town somewhere. He's to march on Spain fairly soon, chasing the French back – but there's a bit of a pother in this, as far as the Dons are concerned.'

'Oh?'

'The French are falling back fast – it's a treat to see. Only a day or two ago, we had news that they've abandoned Madrid, would you credit it?'

'Damned good to hear. The Dons?'

'Well, the junta they started in Cádiz is not good enough. They want a Grand Supreme Junta. That's well and good, but the beggars can't seem to decide things.'

'Their constitution, laws and similar?'

'Not at all. They're at a stand as to what to call each other, the colour of their pantaloons, who's to bow to whom, do they need a new palace and such, before ever they'll get on with the war.'

Kydd chuckled. 'Your Don is always looking to his dignity, very proud. I'd say leave 'em to it, if they—'

'We can't. Think on it – if there's no one in charge, who does Moore talk to about strategicals, co-operation? And when our Foreign Affairs wants to send arms and coin to support, who do they give it to? No, m' friend, this is a fair way to lunacy.'

'A hard thing for us.'

'Harder still for the French. Ha! They don't know whether we're going to land more troops and, worse, where. After Bailén they're fearful of the Spanish and are on the run everywhere. Some say as they won't stop until they're safe behind the Ebro.'

'What's that?'

'A river, runs parallel with the Pyrenees on the Spanish side, about eighty miles off the French border.'

'So close!'

'Quite.' Hayward laughed. 'Boney'll be sore vexed, it all happening so quick. But there's problems for us, too. Nobody has any real idea where the French are this hour. And without a doubt the Frogs at the Ebro don't know where their forces are either, the roads being so wretched and impassable. Moore will have to tread carefully – he could well trip over a lost army.'

'Don't jest,' Kydd said. 'If that's the story inland, will it be any different on the coast? Some ports are still held by the French, who won't know everyone else is falling back, and ready to give us a hot time if we think to land.'

'I'll agree – but if we're on the Portuguee coast we've none of that to worry on. They're all our friends, my philosophy to take relish on this station while the Dons sort 'emselves out betimes. There's compensations – shall I tempt you to some of these local victuals? Right tasty, your chilli sardines.'

Even before the larboard watch could taste the sweets of the shore, *Tyger* received her orders.

Curt, with nothing in the way of explanation, they were on a single paper. That she was, in accordance with instructions received direct from London, simply to cruise in the north of Spain and take any opportunity to harry the enemy, subject to local conditions.

No intelligence included, or helpful pointers to what 'harry' meant – a frigate was not intended to confront an army beyond the intercepting of its coastal supply shipping. And local conditions? This couldn't mean weather, as this was a given in any naval service. It must imply the likelihood or no of Spanish co-operation, which, after Cádiz, Kydd knew was anything but probable.

It was lazy staff work and even worse tactical planning: without co-ordination with shore authorities they were blundering about, casting around for things to do. It was in keeping with Rowley's character – as was his disinclination to see Kydd face to face in handing over the orders.

'Edward,' Kydd said, to Dillon at breakfast, 'you may do me a service, old chap. Go to the military barracks and ask them for what intelligence they have of the north part of Spain, as our business is there.'

He sent Joyce, the master, to the ship chandlers, with a mission of securing charts of northern Spain – not standard navigation works but those used by Iberian masters for coastal passage showing porths, watering places, shelter coves, anchorages and the like. If Kydd was going to be chasing vermin, like privateers, this was the kind of detail he wanted.

Two masters' mates were set to a minute inspection of every water cask and provision barrel before storing ship, while the carpenter and boatswain mustered their gear and stores in readiness. This was going to be operations in a friendless and harsh land five hundred miles from Lisbon, the nearest dockyard; they would have to rely on themselves and what they had on board.

Dillon was back before midday with a doleful expression. The adjutant had given him a fair grasp of the situation: while the Supreme Junta in Seville still argued, there were no reliable lines of communication set up and no one seemed to have any idea of the circumstances and conditions anywhere. In a general sense the Spanish didn't want any interference by the British and saw no reason to co-operate – in fact, according to many, the two countries were still at war.

In despair it had been pointed out that the country was fragmented, the allegiance of whole districts doubtful and unknown, not so much siding with the French but whichever faction was in favour: the witless King Carlos or his young and feckless son, helpless prisoners of France. Or, in the absence of a strong central junta, a vague patriotism and loyalty that could only be termed local.

There were as yet no British bayonets on the soil of Spain, and until such time as there were, no intelligence worth speaking of would be available.

Chapter 59

Two days later, *Tyger* put to sea, sailing north out of Portuguese waters and to the extreme north-west tip of Iberia, her captain little the wiser for what they would do after they put over the helm for the run along the straight length of the rocky spine that was northern Spain.

For all this distance tortured rocks faced the Bay of Biscay, more often than not half glimpsed through the drifting mist of rain and squall, mile after mile the same blustery wretchedness and almost always as a deadly lee shore. What possible duty were they performing? There would be few privateers, and coastal shipping in support of French garrisons must have ceased. True, the French naval bases lay across the Bay but until it was evident what the British were doing – which was not clear to themselves – there would be no sorties from there to menace any landings.

The autumn gales were on them and there were few worse conditions for sailoring than Biscay in season.

Not long after rounding the furthest tip of Spain, Cape Ortegal, a ship was sighted. Full-rigged, much the same as themselves – a frigate!

This couldn't be an enemy, not in this part of the world. Kydd gave orders to close and the other did the same, at the right time a challenge being thrown out, which *Tyger* correctly answered. The two fell into company under easy sail a hundred yards apart.

The frigate was *Menander* 38, Captain Mowlam. As junior to him, Kydd took boat to visit.

'All hail an' well met, Sir Thomas,' he greeted, as Kydd hauled himself over the bulwark. 'And what brings you to these infernal regions?'

His cabin out of the raw breeze was grateful to the senses and Kydd was appreciative of the warmth.

It didn't take long to give the essence, and Mowlam groaned. 'I'm of the Channel Fleet, the Rochefort squadron. Why the devil your Lisbon Flag sees fit to send you here poaching into our little empire I've no idea.'

'I've the feeling the shabs just don't talk to each other,' Kydd replied, with a grim smile. 'I've a duty to do, and would be much obliged for a steer in the matter.'

'In fine, naught to do. We've no idea where the Frenchies are, or what the Spanish are doing, and we don't step ashore on account of some of Boney's finest on the loose. I'd advise the same. That leaves us watching the only ports of size on the coast, all up against the French border and all well held by 'em.'

'Putting down coastal support and similar.'

'Yes. Well, if you want to hear more, should you venture as far as Bayonne you'll find two more of we frigates, *Seine* and *Iris*, who're doing just that. I'm more this end o' Iberia.'

Kydd shortly took his leave, resolved on at least seeking them out to get the best picture he could. How like Rowley carelessly to waste the services of a valuable frigate in overlapping operations!

Tyger took up again, heading eastward, day after day, lookouts primed for anything including the two English frigates. There were no signs of these, coastwise shipping was nowhere to be seen, and while the north-westerly was fair for their track there was indication of a blow coming on.

'If this is Santander we'll look in, I believe,' Kydd announced, with a glance at the log. The chill grey day with its occasional driving white rain squalls was not favourable but they had a duty.

'Sir. If'n we lie off an' take a line o' bearing west-sou'-west we can see right in without we need to hazard ourselves.'

'Well noted, Mr Joyce,' Kydd said to the master.

'Not as if I wouldn't know,' the grey-haired man said happily, puffing out his cheeks. 'Was in *Seagull* sloop in the last war, chasin' down a privateersman who thought to go a-hiding in Santander.'

'Thank you, Mr Joyce. We'll do as you suggest.'

'Didn't do the villain any good, as we had a Don aboard taken out of a coaster and he tips me the wink as we'd cut him the wheedle on anything we gets.'

'Quite.'

'Got our sightin' and saw the chase alongside. Kept on past, but that night sends in our boat, wakens the whole town, ye've no idea the noise, but our tars took no notice an' bent their oars in a-laying hold on it.'

'A fine action,' Kydd told him. Why begrudge him his yarn, if the core of it was to their own advantage?

'Aye, sir. That I'll agree. But then just as they's a cable off, someone sees they've set the barky afire. Well vexed, they claps on speed and tumbles ashore on the wharf and goes f'r the beggar. Half on 'em hold off the townsfolk, the other goes to board but it's too late, she's well gone, flames up right t' the masthead.'

'Bad luck, Mr Joyce.'

'Not luck, sir. She's loaded wi' coffins and these made a clinking great bonfire in a brace o' shakes. Even set off some laid on the quay nearby, in case that was what we were after, like.'

'Coffins?'

'Ah, well, the weather's blashy that day, we muddled up our sightings an' found too late we was after the wrong 'un.' He sniffed, then added, 'Still an' all, we got the right 'un the next day, scampering off to the east'd. But it seems we got a bad name, torchin' their supply o' coffins for the whole year.'

Joyce duly directed them around a headland, and beyond was a river mouth less than a mile wide, which they crossed, leaving a stumpy light at one side and heading for an island the other.

Kydd sighed for the simpler days of Joyce's time: if a ship was sighted it would be an enemy and lawful prey. These days it could be anything – a merchantman taking advantage of the change in conditions, a Spanish trader now upon its lawful occasions and even a British vessel trying for new markets.

What he was after was evidence of a huddle of ships that pointed to support vessels for a French garrison, or even a man-o'-war or several, able to make sortie against them.

In the event, Joyce was proved right. Just three or four miles ahead, the docks of Santander were in full view and, apart from what looked like a fishing boat, empty. He could venture into the port, but what if it was in French hands, as it most likely was? He'd seen that there was naught of interest, so he'd move on.

'Our nor'-westerly, sir.'

Scud was beginning to race overhead, sure portent of an increase to a gale – and this made it a dangerously lee shore.

'Mr Joyce. Do you know—'

'Santoña. Less'n ten miles ahead.'

The master conned *Tyger* around the broad, rock-infested coastline, not deigning to make to seaward. The same hard wind gave them a rapid passage past, seamen glancing ashore with sombre faces at the ceaseless thunder and explosions of white Atlantic combers with a fetch of thousands of miles breaking at last against the land.

A dismal evening clamped in, the flat, hard blast of the gale wearying and tedious, and Kydd's instincts were all for putting down the helm and going for the open sea before darkness set in.

'Five miles more of this and we head out,' he warned, but Joyce was confident, and shortly they sighted a long, flat beach and, beyond, a massive, rearing hill a mile or more across. They rounded it and, to Kydd's grateful surprise, it went further, exposing a river mouth a bare couple of hundred yards wide, giving a snug lee of a good mile and a half.

The gale abruptly cut off as they felt the blocking effect of the four-hundred-odd-foot hill, and Kydd eased. A fine place to see out the gale. Both bowers went down and *Tyger* settled to her rest.

Shaking his oilskins, Kydd glanced round. There was little sign of habitation, what looked like an ancient town on the inner side of the island-like hill and marshes inland. Nothing to worry about, and he went below.

It was typical Biscay meanness but the gale blew itself out over two days.

Kydd gave orders to sail on the following morning. The crew would appreciate another all night in and, in any case, things could change back just as rapidly.

He took a light dinner and decided to continue his letter to Persephone.

This night he felt a special bond, a golden thread that connected them over the miles of sea. From their position he knew they were precisely at the longitude of Knowle Manor. If by some magic he could faithfully follow true north he would eventually end up in her garden, she tending the roses then suddenly looking up in surprise, running to him and . . .

Full of tender thoughts he pulled out the sheet of paper that he'd already begun writing on. Like those of all sailors, it was in the form of an endless missive that only concluded when a mail boat was about to sail for England. To put pen to paper so privately, just to her, was a warm and touching experience, the next best thing to being with one's love. And, as he'd discovered, there was an ease to saying things in a letter that he was diffident to say face to face.

Suddenly weary, he turned in and the ship went to routine for the silent hours.

When urgent shouts pierced his sleep he was on deck before he was fully awake. More shouts, the thump of running feet. His mind scrambled to make sense of it – they were at anchor, and if it were any sudden sail it would have the officer-of-the-watch beating the ship to quarters.

He pushed past to the after hatchway, jostled by men recklessly bolting for the upper deck. The ship sinking? His heart started to pound at the ominous rushing for the open air and when he finally reached the quarterdeck he hurried over to the group around the wheel and Brice, the officer on watch.

'What's to do, sir?' he blurted, breathless. 'Why is the ship in such a confounding?'

There were now dozens, scores of seamen on deck, what they were doing unclear in the dark.

'Didn't know whether to call you or no,' Brice said, the whites of his eyes showing in the dimness.

'Well, quickly, man, I'm here now! What's it all about?'

More seamen were racing up from below, a rising babble of confusion spreading fast.

'I – I— Well, the fore larboard lookout, he, umm . . .'

'For God's sake! Get on with it!'

'Well, sir,' Brice gulped, 'He thought it proper to inform me that he'd sighted an, er . . . mermaid.'

'A what?' Kydd gasped in disbelief.

'A mermaid. That's what he said, sir.'

'And you—'

'I went forrard and . . . and saw that he was, um, right in the particulars. I myself saw a mermaid out to leeward a half pistol shot, swimming as who'd believe it. I sent for a lanthorn and when the mermaid came close, the looby who held it took fright and dropped it, seeing it close up like.'

'Have you called for another?' Kydd snapped, although internally he felt the creeping chill of the supernatural invade his vitals.

'Yes, sir. And sent for the doctor, he being in the physiological line and all.'

'Where's it now?'

'Um, last seen close to the hull, making slow way aft, then out o' sight under the counter. She – that is, it must be thereabouts at this moment.'

Kydd hesitated as all the sailors' superstitions of his past came back to him. A mermaid – if it was – posed no threat other than luring the common sailor to his doom. Should he give orders not to let the creature come aboard, no one to talk to it?

Another lanthorn arrived. 'Clear the after end of the upper deck and keep silent,' he ordered.

When the noise had died, he went to the taffrail and looked nervously over the side into the inky depths, letting the light play down where the upper edge of the massive rudder could be seen . . . There was something down there!

Then, shocking in its unexpectedness, the form of a mermaid flicked into view, half clothed with pale arms and a pallid face with long dark hair, staring up at him with a piercing look of entreaty.

Kydd froze. She rolled on her back and called up at him in a thin, haunting voice, 'Capitán! Do let me come on board your ship, I beg you!'

He jerked back – into his mind came a frightful thought: the mermaid was trying to lure *him*!

She shoved off effortlessly into full view, her face still on his, the voice calling, her legs a shimmer of—

Legs? Mermaid?

'Mr Brice! Away seaboat's crew. Get your *mermaid* inboard this minute, sir!'

The Tygers crowded round, goggling in fascination as a girl was brought in, her clothing plastered to her body, shivering uncontrollably in the blustering night wind. On the deck there were small wet female footprints. The practical Tysoe quickly appeared with one of Kydd's dressing-gowns, which he fussed on before shepherding her below. Kydd followed, knowing every single eye was on him. 'Get turned in, you blaggards! We sail at daybreak!' he roared over his shoulder.

With the girl tidying herself in his bedplace, he snapped, 'Get Mr Dillon.'

His secretary appeared with suspicious alacrity.

'I didn't see you to the fore when I went to find out what we'd snagged.'

'Ah. I was . . . asleep,' he answered, shamefaced.

'Well, wake yourself up. I need some answers.'

The girl appeared shyly, so petite in Kydd's gown. 'I – I'm so sorry, Capitán,' she said in delightfully accented English, clutching the robe, her tiny feet peeping out beneath.

'Ah, yes. Now, we can't have a young lady swimming about in the dark like a . . . like a mermaid,' he harrumphed.

'My name is Lucila Ochoa,' she said, ignoring his clumsy fatherly tone. 'I risk my life because I trust the English and swim to you from the land. For a very important reason.' She could only be sixteen or so but her air was that of someone much older.

'I am Captain Sir Thomas Kydd. This is His Majesty's Ship *Tyger*. What reason have you for swimming out to us?' Very few sailors could swim a stroke, he himself only barely.

She bit her lip. 'Sir, I ask you to pity Spain at this time. The French are barbarians. They steal and destroy without mercy. It is a torment for the people. And so they have risen up. I am of a band of patriots, that of Koldo Uribe, and we have sworn to stay in arms until they are cast out entirely.'

It was odd, even disturbing, to hear such words from so young a girl.

'Lucila, you've swum nearly a mile to my ship. What does this mean?' It was not only the sheer distance, but when she'd reached *Tyger* she'd had to scrabble along the side of the hull to find some means of getting aboard.

'Sir, I will be open with you. The French have Santander in their grip and they hold Bilbao as well. The people are frightened but they cannot act against them. Sir, if you help us we will strike against the French, give them hurt that they'll pursue us into the mountains where there are many who lie in wait to slay them. Capitán Kydd, I beg you will help us!'

Help them? In the regular order of things a man-o'-war wasn't fitted to join in an open-ended war, unless it was well planned and equipped. Now he was being asked in some way to be part of a force of irregulars on an ill-defined uprising that had no clear objective.

'Miss Ochoa. I greatly sympathise with your cause but I'm

at a loss to know how I can help. A man-o'-war is not fitted for army operations. I have very few men I can land to help you.' All he had on board was Clinton and some two dozen or so marines, intended as a quickly deployable landing force, not to set before a French army of thousands.

'Oh, no, sir! We do not ask for your soldiers but only to give us the means to do the work ourselves. Guns – muskets, powder, flints, shot! These we will use to bring vengeance down on the heads of the foe, to drive them back over the mountains until they're entirely gone.' Tears glistened. 'If you could see what we've suffered, you'd understand, sir!'

Kydd softened, but it didn't alter the fact that he had no spare muskets and therefore could do nothing for her. But what if he returned to Lisbon and arranged for a vessel to deliver arms from the depot there? It could certainly be justified, for here was a small band with the potential to tie down whole battalions of the French.

Before he put this before the army quartermaster or whoever, though, he would need numbers. He would look a prize looby if thcy turned out to be a dozen or two wretched peasants – or, on the other hand, if he seriously underestimated what turned out to be a great band's military needs.

'I do understand, please believe me,' he told her. 'But first I wish to see for myself your forces, meet your commander. Would this be possible?'

'Of course! Of course!' she said, clapping her hands in excitement. 'General Uribe will adore to see you, Capitán.'

Chapter 60

It was arranged: in the morning he would go ashore and she would take him to their stronghold in the hills. He was assured that the nearest French were in Santoña, over the water, and long since had given up troubling them in their mountain fastness.

Just he and Dillon would be all that were needed: if there was trouble the handful in a landing party would make no difference and, in any case, that would suggest their hosts could not be trusted to look after them.

'Should be aboard by nightfall,' Kydd told a distrustful Bray, and set off ashore.

At the end of a long beach there was a twist of rock and in its lee a stone jetty where they disembarked.

'Stand down the boat's crew – remain within hail,' he ordered. The men, blank-faced, complied. For them it would be a lazy day under the sunshine away from ship's discipline, a valued perquisite of being captain's boat's crew. Kydd smiled to himself, remembering with a pang that when he had been a seaman he'd never been fortunate enough to claim a place in the captain's boat.

They walked down the jetty until they reached the two pillars at its landward end. Noiselessly two men appeared from behind them and stood arrogantly in their path.

Swarthy, moustachioed and with glittering dark eyes, they snapped at Lucila, who shot back a rejoinder that had them tamely standing aside.

These were no soldiers that Kydd could recognise. They were not in uniform, simply a rough coatee, russet breeches and homespun cloak. A shapeless cap proudly bore a red riband and they carried their carbines with a lithe familiarity.

'We go to the camp,' Lucila said firmly. After a quick exchange, horses were found and they picked their way up a stony track into the mountains. Before the woods closed in, Kydd kept his bearings of the sea, comforted by knowing this.

Lucila smiled encouragingly at him but Kydd was unused to the strange saddle so, stiff and sore, he was glad to smell wood-smoke on the air and sight the rock-strewn clearing in the forest, men and women moving about the huts and tents that must be their destination.

Shouts of welcome sounded and a giant of a man strode forward to greet them.

Kydd swung down and straightened painfully.

'This is Supreme General Koldo Uribe, Capitán,' Lucila said shyly, and explained something to the man. 'I tell him why you are here and he's very pleased you come.'

The big man beamed.

'I say that you've come from the English frigate, which he saw sail in three days ago.' She pointed at the edge of the clearing, and Kydd detected a small building at the top of a ridge, presumably with a view of the sea.

'He said how he swore I couldn't swim to you, but I love to swim. It was not so hard,' she said, with a toss of her head.

Uribe gave a friendly bellow, slapping Kydd on the back and sending his cocked hat askew, then moved off to the yellow-stone building on the ridge. As they followed, Dillon whispered nervously, 'They're all speaking a species of Vizcaya, the Basque, and I can't understand a word they're saying.'

'Then we'd better hope that Miss Lucila keeps station on us,' Kydd muttered. It was the last thing he wanted, to lose communication, but as they stepped into the building he was comforted by seeing *Tyger* at anchor far below, as neat and beautiful as an elaborate model.

Inside it was small, nothing much more than a habitation for hermits set into the rock. They went inside the largest room, its only window a high slit, and sat down at a plain table on a beaten-earth floor.

Refreshments were brought, sheep's cheese and sausage, cider; rough but satisfying.

'Please ask the general how many soldiers he has.'

'He begs to say he has more than five hundred under arms.' This was extraordinary – Kydd had seen a few score about the camp but surely not that many.

Lucila explained that this naturally included the outriders on guard, those out on forage duty, more in the adjacent valley and, counted among their fiercest warriors, the women.

'Including you?'

'Of course,' she said, affronted.

'I would like to address them all, to convey His Majesty's sincere admiration at your remarkable bravery in standing up to the invaders.' This, of course, would have them in one place at the same time, proof of numbers.

'The general would rather you give them muskets.'

'We'll discuss that afterwards,' Kydd said firmly, and arrangements were put in place.

Kydd could see that Uribe had not lied. Close to twice the number of *Tyger*'s entire ship's company were packed into the area, a mass of individually dressed figures with sashes, embroidered jackets and pouches. Only a few had fire-locks; most carried pikes, long knives and other blades.

'The general says to behold his magnificent *guerrilleros*, those he calls the Corso Terrestre – the Corsairs of the Land!'

Kydd was satisfied. This band, living up here in their ever-shifting camp, leaving their homes to eke out a dangerous and hard life for a cause to which they had dedicated their lives – the least he could do was acknowledge it without wild promises.

'Fighters for the motherland!' he began; if it was a father-land Lucila would have the sense to change it. 'We two peoples, so long in misunderstanding, now march forward together, arm in arm against the foe!'

Her girlish voice rang with passion as she threw the words at the thronged *guerrilleros*, each with his eyes fixed on Kydd.

He went on, feeling the words rousing them, for here was the outside world, at last acknowledging their existence.

As he finished he bowed low, left and right, answering their cries with a wave of his hat but in his heart he felt guilt: just what could he do to help them?

In the heightened atmosphere, Uribe roared out a command, which was answered from five hundred throats. 'It is a *euskal jaiak*, in your honour, Capitán.' She laughed proudly. 'A feast!'

'Tell the general I'd be greatly honoured to attend.'

'After he's talked with you.'

They returned to the little room.

'You want the help of the British.'

'I want muskets. And ammunition.'

'If – and I cannot promise it – you receive these, what is your intention?'

The guerrilla commander's eyes glowed with satisfaction. 'To use them against the enemy, to turn the tables so we change from a stinging wasp to a charging bull!'

'If this can be arranged, and it is far from certain, what are your needs?'

'One thousand muskets, a hundred thousand cartridges, flints, patches, tools,' Uribe said instantly. 'Clothing, boots, haversacks, kitchen pots . . .'

'Thank you. You've made yourself clear.'

Uribe looked at him intently. 'What price do you ask?' he asked.

Kydd stiffened. 'No price, General. Only that you put them to good use.'

'That I can promise,' the general said, with a rapacious gleam in his eyes. 'When shall we—'

'My ship sails this night to make report to my superiors. I shall return when I have your requirements – a slight delay might be expected only.' If Lisbon couldn't see that a force of five hundred well armed and motivated *guerrilleros* causing havoc in the French rear wasn't a good use for their stock of weapons, he'd couldn't conceive of a better. It might take a while to prise the shipment from the depot bureaucracy but it would come.

The evening was drawing in. A happy bustle was under way as he and Lucila wandered through the camp, and Kydd saw for himself how they'd adapted to their nomadic exile, clearly doing so for the long term. It was touching and deadly, domestic and war-like, whole families living here together.

At the same time he was aware of what a strange and romantic figure he must look to them. In his splendid full-dress uniform and imposing bicorne, its gold lace glittering in the firelight, he caught many darted glances his way as he strolled through their mountain existence, a being from the same outside world that had sent the French.

Darkness fell, and rough-hewn chairs were brought. Lucila sat between Kydd and Dillon and, to the sound of drum and tambourine, there was a stirring display of dancing. The women wore colourful long skirts and shawls, with kerchiefs covering their heads.

Uribe and his henchmen joined them with more Basque cider and, of a glow, Kydd sat back as a large dish of lamb and peppers was brought in.

In the flickering gold flame of the fires, the outlandish forest fragrance and alien babble reached out to Kydd. Naval service had taken him to strange and exotic places – and what wouldn't Persephone give to be here with him?

Another sip of cider.

He'd be late back on board but he'd have plenty to remember of the day. Next to him Dillon was quiet and reflective and he knew it would be the same for him.

Without warning, distant shouts echoed up from the track followed by more from deeper into the forest. The gaiety fell away and Uribe leaped to his feet.

Then a shot, more – a tearing shriek and more shots.

It caused pandemonium. Uribe roared orders and men snatched up weapons and raced down the track, fanning out into the woodland.

A savage fusillade met them and Lucila screamed, then collected herself. 'We've been betrayed,' she sobbed and, snatching Kydd's hand, she ran back with him to the little building, wrenching open the door.

'Get in!' she said savagely, pushing him hard.

Kydd didn't argue and pulled Dillon in with him before the door slammed shut and there was the scrabbling of a key in the lock. They were left in the darkness but, for the moment, safe.

Outside the noise of battle swelled – demented screams and furious shrieks, death cries and the clash of weapons. This was a full-scale attack and the outcome couldn't be known. They felt around in the dimness for anything that could be a weapon but there was nothing except the debris of feasting.

The tide of struggle ebbed and flowed around them. Kydd knew that with bloodlust up the attackers would not stop to consider who they were so he waited for the sudden bursting in of the door and their sordid end at the hands of some peasant *guerrillero*. Once or twice, heart in mouth, they heard the door handle roughly tried but both times the would-be killer moved off to find easier victims.

Eventually they heard the confusion and strife fade into the distance.

Shouts rang out nearby. It sounded like the crack of command but Dillon could only shrug helplessly, and from other parts shouted reports came. The door handle rattled uselessly. An angry hail was distantly answered and, at the approaching voices, Kydd fell back from the door.

There was the crash of a pistol and the lock hung down. In the smoke the door pushed aside.

In the doorway were three figures, more behind. They carried lanterns that illuminated them and, with a sickening surge, Kydd saw French uniforms on the soldiers who held their bayonets at the ready.

He knew better than to move and rapped, 'Capitaine de vaisseau Thomas Kydd, *officier de la marine royale de sa majesté.*'

The officer pushed forward and sneered something in Basque. Kydd gave a tight smile and shook his head.

'Tell them that in Spanish,' he murmured to Dillon.

It brought a start of incomprehension, then a leer of disbelief. Dillon translated: 'You're French! I heard you myself.'

Kydd blinked in bewilderment. What was going on?

'I'm an English officer – from that vessel to seaward.' Too late, he realised that in the darkness of night *Tyger* would not be visible from the shore.

'A ship, out there? What are you doing here, then? Answer me that!'

'I came to see what help I could give these people,' Kydd admitted stoutly.

There was a gasp of surprise and incredulity. 'You confess freely before me, now, you want to give aid to these vermin?'

'Any who are enemies of France are our friends,' Kydd snapped.

The officer shook his head wordlessly. 'You are making no sense, sir. We are the sworn enemies of Bonaparte and all he stands for. Why then do you throw in your lot with these?'

They stared at each other for a long moment. Then Kydd demanded, 'Who then are you, sir?'

'Coronel García Noriega, of the Bilbao Freedom Junta of Patriots.'

'You wear French uniforms.'

'We have none of our own so we strip the dead. We are on our own, sir, and must make shift.'

'Then . . . then who are these people, that you attack them as they feast?'

The sneer returned. 'These are not true patriots, if that is your question. They take advantage of our fight with the French invader to rebel against our rightful king and set up their own state following the old Basque ways. We have spies in their camp. They told of some plot to seize weapons and we thought to act first.'

With a flash of white teeth, he went on, 'And we were right to do so. I dare to say you were going to give them guns, powder, shot to go against the French? A most gratifying gift for them.'

Kydd winced. The girl had been a master-stroke by Koldo Uribe and he had fallen for it.

'Is not Bilbao under the French? Santander also?'

'No, it is not. It still stands firm for Regent Fernando, *El Deseado*, sir!'

He had been lied to. Kydd snapped upright and bowed deeply. 'I do apologise if there has been any misunderstanding, Coronel. It seems we are of the same mind and loyalty. I would wish I could make amends.'

Suspicion, hope, pride and satisfaction chased each other across Noriega's face before he answered, 'Capitán. Perhaps there is something you can do for us.'

'Oh?'

'The arms you were going to give the—'

'Certainly. You will understand that my superiors must be satisfied that they are for good purpose. Shall we go to Bilbao at all?'

'To see the junta? Of course, if you desire it, sir.'

If Bilbao was still in the hands of the Spanish, it proved the duplicity of the Basque rebels, and if this faction were actively fighting the French, he had a definite duty to them.

'I have a boat—'

'We know. The crew will be released immediately, sir.'

In a wash of relief he stepped outside. Moonlight now delicately touched the scene with silver and shadows. It lay as well on a still form among others near to the door: Lucila, her body grotesquely skewed but still with a heavy pistol in one hand, blood showing black against her girlish dress, her face mercifully shadowed.

It caught him off guard and, seized by a swell of pity, he felt the prick of tears at the extinction of a young and ardent life, now silent for ever.

Chapter 61

Bilbao

The city was in a ferment of excitement and fear. A well-known trading port, it was set up the Nervión river behind a considerable bar. Dillon was delighted to discover that the old naval term for the shackles of malefactors in the bowels of a ship, the bilboes, had its origin there.

Kydd learned the French had occupied the city soon after Murat had moved on Madrid but, hearing of the revolt there, it had risen and now stood alone, no contact with the outside world except Santander, which was containing the French for now. Their loyalty was to king and country, but having three kings with claims to the throne – the old King Carlos, his son and regent, Fernando, and the French puppet Joseph – which was he?

The leader of the Bilbao junta, Iñaki Haro, had been effusive in his greetings to Kydd but the situation was grave.

The withdrawing French had moved only a small way inland to prepared positions and seemed to be awaiting further orders, no doubt the retaking of Bilbao. They had to be stopped, but while there were plenty of volunteers there were few weapons. Without guns it was a hopeless cause.

Kydd listened politely to the pleas but knew there was nothing he could do for them. Those guns were weeks away at best when they were needed in days.

He returned to *Tyger*, anchored offshore. A city that lay more than a dozen miles up a river, between lofty hills and inside a considerable bar, was no place for a frigate.

In his cabin he let his thoughts run free. Logic meant giving up any pretence at help and sailing away, regretfully but by necessity. This would, though, have the inevitable result of turning the inhabitants against the faithless British who, it would be felt, could never be relied on, even in better circumstances later. Was there nothing, even a token, he could do? A few boat-loads of muskets would be sufficient to keep faith and support the cause – but to sail back to the Lisbon depot would leave it far too late.

And then he had it. Why not ransack *Tyger*'s own armoury of muskets, powder and shot? It wouldn't be much, but it would be something. That would leave the Royal Marines unarmed, naked of weapons, and his ship unable to mount any offensive action on land – and what would the authorities say about his freely giving away articles of His Majesty's ordnance?

Yet why leave it at that? Somewhere out there, this side of Bayonne, were another two frigates. Adding their armouries to his would make quite a respectable showing – albeit at the cost of rendering three frigates incapable of shore operations.

In his opinion it was worth the sacrifice: the border with France was not so far away, and to supply their isolated Spanish garrisons, the French would have to pass Bilbao. If this was not in their hands they would be prevented from doing so.

* * *

Less than a day's sail further east he found *Seine* and *Iris* cruising to seaward of Bayonne.

Kydd lost no time in calling them aboard, he being senior officer on the coast.

Both were surprised that Bilbao was in Spanish hands. They'd sailed off a lee shore in the recent blow, but with the city inland they'd seen nothing out of the ordinary as they'd cruised to prevent French resupply.

And 'To harry the enemy' was a usual phrase within written orders but why was it as loose as that? No other specific instructions?

Kydd's response was that, while the enemy might be on land and out of reach, it didn't mean they couldn't be harried. And in this instance there was a very good reason why they should be – if Bilbao could stand unconquered it would be a strategic blow of the first rank to the French.

But when he outlined how this could be done, there were long faces from the veteran frigate captains. Thinking nothing of plunging into the thick of battle against terrible odds, they shrank at the spectre of a stern accounting for the handing over to rebels of a significant portion of their ship's armament.

Only after long and earnest pleading by Kydd, with the bookkeeping stratagem that they were in fact making loan of their muskets only to him, a King's ship, never to a parcel of foreigners, did they relent.

As *Tyger* hove to off Bilbao, waiting for a pilot, it was evident from the sight of fleeing humanity streaming along the coast roads that the French were on the move.

Kydd needed to act fast, but the pilot informed him that at this state of tide the bar was too dangerous to attempt a crossing. He cursed under his breath. If they were going to have any effect on events, they had to get the guns in quickly.

It could only be boats, his barge to take the lead, the launch and pinnace behind loaded with muskets under a doubled tarpaulin.

As if in discouragement, first one then another wind-driven rain squall whipped across their little flotilla as they entered the Bilbao *ría*, canvas flapping irritably, and the mizzle soaking Kydd with a biting autumnal chill. Ahead there was a white confusion of leaping seas – the bar. This was where three rivers met the open sea together, and on a making tide the contending flows were fierce.

They nevertheless headed into its bucking wild currents and unruly waters until they made it into an inner calm, the long river Nervión leading to Bilbao.

Haro came down the steps of his town hall in the rain to receive them, his praise for his British friends and benefactor loud and heartfelt. 'The *Frantziako* are advancing each side of the Nervión valley,' he told Kydd. 'With these we'll give them true greeting.'

The soldiers who came up to claim their weapons were in the same motley uniforms as before but their eyes glittered with feeling as they snatched at the muskets and loaded them, leaving at the trot for their posts. In the face of things, the several hundred muskets they'd been able to get together was a pitiful amount and, despite stopping the French at a choke point, they surely had little chance against a flood of trained troops.

'Launch and pinnace to return now,' Kydd ordered. 'I'm staying a while longer.' He hoped his presence might give moral support and proof to the citizens that their plight was not unknown in the outside world.

He strolled about, as if enjoying a promenade through the

old town, aware from the stares and warm cheers that he was doing much to raise the standing of Britain, Spain's new friend in whatever lay ahead.

Deciding to return to *Tyger* the following morning, he found beds for the night for himself, Dillon and the boat's crew in a near-deserted dockside tavern. At dinner he heard from the few other guests rumour and gossip that left him no wiser as to the full story.

On the one hand those who'd been travelling in the interior were gleefully telling of the French falling back in dismay at the now nationwide rising by the Spanish people, some said nearly to the border. On the other, the French returning to seize the valuable port, while they could, would be a bitter blow to Bilbao.

It all depended on whether a desperate assault could be staved off until the local French commander decided to join the others behind the Ebro.

Kydd went to bed with more than a few misgivings.

Some time after midnight he was awoken. Shouts, running feet, and what were probably distant shots. He began to struggle into his uniform and suddenly Dillon burst in. 'Sir Thomas, we must go now! The French have made a surprise night attack and are in the city. We must fly, sir!'

'Muster the boat's crew down on the quay. We quit the place this minute.' As soon as he was dressed he ran out into the darkness. There was a spattering of rain but he didn't care, bolting for the lower quay where his boat lay. There were figures there, one with a lantern who appeared to be in an altercation.

'Thank the Lord you're here, sir!' said Halgren, standing with the tiller bar, menacing a growing crowd. Others of the boat's crew stood behind him and, from the flash of white eyes in the gathering, he saw that they were near panic.

'Get aboard,' Kydd ordered evenly, pushing through and standing with him.

The painter to his barge was shortened. The crew tumbled aboard and took position. Growls and angry cries came from the onlookers but Kydd could do nothing for them. 'Into the boat,' he snapped at Dillon, then pulled himself over the bows and looked back to where the big figure of Halgren still stood, his stolid presence keeping the mob at bay.

Singling up the painter through the ring-bolt, he waited for the right moment then ordered Halgren in. For such a big man he turned nimbly, dropped into the bows and, at the same time, Kydd shoved off, leaving the crowd to curse and shout as they put out around a mole and into the inky blackness towards the harbour entrance.

They were safe.

He settled in the sternsheets with Dillon, looking forward to the sanity and comforts of his cabin.

Five men were at the oars and two were attending to the rolled-up sails along the centreline, rigging the boat by feel alone. Kydd felt a stab of unease at the unfolding realisation that their return would not be easy. The wind had shifted, backing into the north-west, and with the tide well on the ebb, it didn't take much imagination to see that with the seas heaping up under the driving winds to meet the ebbing tide over the shallows of the bar, their relatively slim-waisted and petite craft would be at a perilous disadvantage.

As soon as they emerged beyond the shelter of the mole he saw that he was right. The dimness of the overcast night was pierced by white combers driven by a flat blast out of the north-west. It was dead foul for the open sea, but in his fore-and-aft rigged craft this should not have been cause for concern. What was of such danger was the erratic lumping and surging of the foreshortened waves as the two forces disputed, wave peaks shooting up, some as high as six feet, others meeting in a confused sliding against each other, an unnavigable welter of angry seas.

Their barge would not live long in that.

'Sir, we're not going t' make it through,' Halgren said calmly, feeling the unruly cross currents slam at his rudder.

'We put back.'

Into a city about to fall – from blessed safety back into the inferno. What else could they do?

Inside the mole it was immediately quieter, giving him time to think.

The French were coming in down the valley and in a general sense from the east. Therefore he would head in the opposite direction and find some kind of haven, a boat and the open sea. And the nearest had to be Santander, some forty sea miles away or an uncountable distance through the forested Cantabrian mountains.

'Put into this wharf to starb'd,' Kydd told Halgren. He eyed the shoreline. There were a number of sinister moving figures in the darkness but he prayed there was a road over the mountains they could take.

As the boat glided in, there were sudden shouts from the shore – the shapes stopped and wheeled about.

'Take us in.' They'd have to get through them: there was no other choice.

The bowman hooked on and forms appeared along the wharf edge, first several and then many. Kydd braced himself but there was a single hoarse shout he thought he recognised. Soon there were happy calls and hands extended.

Dillon translated. These were the patriot fighters who had received their weapons and were now on their way into the mountains to continue the fight. With pride they displayed their muskets – they would now be put to very good use in the hard struggle to come.

And, yes, they knew of the bar and agreed that Santander would offer the best place to get out to his ship. It would be their honour to find a means of transport and be both escort and guide.

Chapter 62

Lisbon

The capacious harbour was alive with seaborne traffic: victuallers and powder hoys, transports of every kind, all in a purposeful criss-crossing.

Something was afoot.

Conqueror was at the naval anchorage, her admiral's pennant drooping in the light breeze. Kydd made sure *Tyger* went to the most inconspicuous mooring and prepared to make his report. It would not be pleasant and he braced himself as he came aboard.

'What in Hades . . .?'

'Sir Thomas Kydd, *Tyger* frigate,' Campbell, the long-suffering flag-captain, said quietly, ushering Kydd in.

'I know that!' Rowley spluttered. 'What I don't know is why he's here. Tired of cruising in the north, is it, Kydd?'

'Pursuant to your orders, sir, I proceeded to the north coast of Spain on patrol, seeking to harry the enemy wherever he might be found.'

'And?'

'There was no sign of the enemy – except at Bilbao.' He'd leave the piece about Santoña and the Basque rebels to the written report. 'There, the city had risen and driven the French out. They desired that I render assistance in their defence, which, we now being their friends, I endeavoured to do.'

'Boats, with your usual fireworks, then.'

'No, sir. Their request was for weapons – muskets and equipment. They have men enough to do the fighting.'

'Be brief, Kydd. I've a lot to do.'

'Sir, knowing the value of a strong port held by the Spanish so close to the French border, I conceived it as a vital objective. For the price of a few muskets the city would be held for us without we send a man ashore.'

'You're not making much sense, sir.'

'This is to say I landed such muskets as were carried by *Tyger* and passed them over to the junta, which is the—'

'You what?' roared Rowley, slapping his palms down on his desk.

'I fell in with *Seine* and *Iris* frigates and added their muskets to mine to increase the effectiveness. They were well received.'

Rowley rose slowly, his eyes blazing. 'Do I understand you to mean you cleaned out three frigates of their arms and handed the lot over to some ragabash parcel of Spaniards?'

'In the interests of prosecuting the war against Bonaparte in the conditions obtaining, yes, I did.'

'You – you expect me to excuse the reckless disposing of His Majesty's ordnance in such a manner? It's monstrous! Damn it – tell me why I shouldn't put you under open arrest, Kydd.'

He burned. 'There's many who'd agree that their use by others to achieve the same object as if used by ourselves, but without the hazard, begs some measure of approval.'

'Approval? Why, it's nothing but—'

'Sir,' Campbell intervened smoothly, 'I'm bound to observe that Admiral Collingwood may well consider that Captain Kydd's action does in fact conform to the recent desires of their lordships to afford aid and assistance to the Spanish wherever practical in their rising against the French.'

'I know that!' Rowley snapped venomously. 'Why wasn't I informed? Hey? And tell me this, Kydd – did it achieve anything? I'd wager it was a rank waste!'

'Bilbao unfortunately fell soon after —'

'Ha! I knew it! You've now some explaining to do, Kydd, and—'

'— but the arms are preserved and in the hands of the *guerrilleros* in the mountains from where they're preparing to descend invisibly to, er, harry the enemy.'

He caught a fleeting glance of respect from Campbell, who advanced on Rowley with papers. 'You've a busy day, sir. We should—'

'Hold, Flags, I've not finished with this officer.'

Rowley sat down petulantly, shuffled his papers and looked up at Kydd with a dark arrogance. 'You try a harum-scarum scheme like this again without my explicit permission and I'll have you broke! Do you hear me, Kydd?'

Before he could reply Rowley leaned forward, took a pen and began scribbling. Kydd was dismissed.

Chapter 63

The Captain's Club, Lisbon

'I pay no mind to that strut-noddy,' Broadwood of *Lynx* said loftily, helping himself to a sherry from a steward after Kydd had bitterly given his opinion of Rear Admiral Rowley. 'Never can remember what the codshead said two minutes after I walk out.'

Kydd gave a wintry smile. Was Rowley's malice just a reflection of a weak character or was he indeed out to get rid of him? But the man was an admiral – and his superior.

He forced his mind to another track. 'Where is everybody?' he asked, puzzled by the few men-o'-war in harbour when he'd arrived.

'Because it's happened, is all.'

'What?'

'We've made our move. General Moore has upped anchor so to speak and marched off into Spain, lad. Lots of ceremony and such, quantities of the beauty and fashion of Lisbon to see 'em off but they've done it.'

'Do we know how he's succeeding?'

'Main well, is most people's reckoning. Set off eastwards, straight into the Dons' territory on a compass course for Paris and disappeared from view. Next thing we hear, Madrid is relieved, the French are running like rabbits back to the frontier and all of Spain looks to be free before Christmas, b'God.'

'A right good crack on the nose for Boney,' another chimed in, 'and a gnashing of teeth I wouldn't wonder, as this puts France itself before a row of cannon mouths and lines of redcoats, which I doubt they'll relish.'

It was a stunning prospect: could this be a royal road into Bonaparte's France through which Britain could at last pour men and guns, possibly bring Bonaparte to the peace table and end the war?

'He's still got a monstrous navy,' Kydd mused, finding it difficult to picture Napoleon Bonaparte on the defensive.

'Which in course he pulls in to defend the homeland,' Broadwood said.

'And we're not talking navy here, we're talking about soldiery, marching in to finish him. He can't stop that – his men are all on the run!'

'So we're every one out as escorts bringing in more?'

'Well, not as who's to say. There's not so many under arms in England as we can call on, I've heard. Never had much to do with big armies, we. My understanding is that Moore's is the only army of consequence we can muster. Good thing we're doing so well.'

It seemed the future would be one of supporting the army as it finished the job. Kydd had never really thought about it – the final chapters of the war and how it would all end, for until now Bonaparte's evil genius had seen them lurch in reaction from one desperate crisis to another, which in truth only the navy had been able to pull the nation through.

At the same time he was uneasy. It was all too quick – but he could see that a vain emperor with conquered territories to hold down, ranging from the distant outposts of Russia nearly to the Atlantic, would have few and thinly spread troops available to deal with an uprising on a nation-wide scale. If Moore was swift he might soon be storming across the frontier. After all, the Spanish must be seeing what he'd achieved and be ready at last to join with him in the driving out of the hated enemy.

The depot had readily replaced *Tyger*'s small arms so in a day or so Kydd would be back on the north coast ready for who knew what? All that could be said was that he should be prepared for anything.

'Another one here, steward. As I think we must raise a glass to General Moore's health and success, bless him!'

Chapter 64

The town of Vitoria on the Ebro river

Major FitzOwen Inglis eased up the roof tile a little further and, wedging his back against a rafter, trained his telescope carefully on the knot of officers waiting respectfully. He'd been told the identity of the personage who would be arriving by two reliable sources but needed to have it confirmed, for if true it would be a development of catastrophic proportions.

He was hard by the medieval square, and the news that it had been filling with French troops all week had drawn the major from his hideaway in Saragossa.

Inglis was fluent in Spanish through his Galician mother. A careful and intelligent individual, as newly appointed English envoy to the Spanish general José de Palafox y Melci, he'd lost a leg in the chaos of the uprising. While recovering he'd lain low behind the lines and relayed such information as he could garner to the coast for passing on to Wellesley.

He'd seen much, but nothing more pleasing than the streaming thousands of French occupation forces retreating from all parts of Spain. After Bailén they'd abandoned their positions to fall back here, behind the Ebro.

Rumours had been heady and many as to what it meant for Spain, but the British command needed solid facts. Inglis had done his best, but without a network of spies he had to make do with what he could glean from the flow of gossip and his own small but valuable observations.

Shortly, though, he would have in his hands a piece of information that threatened to turn everything on its head.

The French officers were in a tight group, watching the road into town, an array of soldiery in lines to one side of the square, their regimental colours aloft.

Then on the air came the near visceral sound of massed cavalry, and a trumpet baying distantly. It drew nearer, and Inglis focused on the highway where it became visible past the wall of a baker's shop. Suddenly the first horsemen came into view – and he caught his breath. Yes! An escort detachment of the Imperial Mounted Chasseurs, identified by the golden eagle on their ornate saddlecloths, the shabraques, and their bushy cockades in distinctive bearskins. Their horses steamed in the autumn air from hard riding.

It had to be!

He reached for his crutches and made his way down to the alley, pausing only to check his disguise. He was unshaven, with his still-bandaged leg stump, remnants of a shabby uniform and a battered shako that could have come from any one of the many armies at war in Spain. A bedraggled, wounded soldier, one of so many to be seen these days.

Swinging along as fast as he could, he reached the back of the gawping crowd and made ill-tempered jabs with his crutch until, seeing his condition, they let him through to the front.

The cavalry passed close, with an almost deafening jingle of harness, the faces of the riders hard and ruthless, the gold frogging glinting in the wan autumn sunshine, the stink of their horses rich and heavy on the air.

They proceeded out of sight, only to be displaced by troopers of the Gendarmerie d'élite, tall, perfectly matched, each on a black horse and resplendent with a lofty busby and heavy sabre. Their task was to establish an impenetrable security cordon – for a most important person was increasingly likely to descend from the carriage not far behind.

No less than Napoleon Bonaparte, Emperor of France.

Inglis had heard the legends, the stories of this man who had laid low nearly the entire civilised world single-handed, and he knew, too, all details of how he progressed in military cavalcade with his army about his fiefdom. If this was an impostor sent to awe the Spanish he would be detected, but for now the impressive panoply was convincing.

At last a hush fell on the crowd. The gleaming coach was approaching at a brisk trot, a species of four-in-hand landau with the arms of the Emperor emblazoned on its side.

Inglis squinted. At the reins the driver was wearing a fat turban and flowing silk trousers. That must be Roustam, a Mameluke from Egypt, one of two that went everywhere with the Emperor. And under his seat a capacious box was built into the bodywork, which held Bonaparte's campaign documents.

The carriage swept around in a half-circle and came to a stop before the group of officers.

Inglis could see them clearly in their finery now, marshals of France all. There was the much admired Soult, boyish and round-faced, confident and erect. Next to him, Ney was ruddy-faced and intense and, hanging back slightly, Lefebvre, a thin, nervous figure, his uniform nearly hidden by decorations. Others, he didn't recognise.

There was an electric tension in the air. Then the carriage

door opened and none other than the Emperor himself was stepping down. Tired, pale and drawn, he stood for a moment in an imperial pose, gravely acknowledging the bows of the marshals, some of whom went to their knees. Then he raised his gaze to the crowd that began an awe-struck chanting, '*Vive l'Empereur!*'

Bonaparte turned and went to the officers, chatting amiably, the slapping of his gloves against his thigh the only sign of impatience. Inglis watched like a hawk: the Emperor spent most time with Soult, exchanged a jest or two with Ney but ignored Lefebvre.

It was difficult to throw off the thrall of the scene, the almost mystical reverence that held them all in a compelling embrace. Inglis pulled himself together, his thoughts racing as the Emperor walked across to chat amiably with individuals in the rigid lines of the Imperial Guard.

It was one thing that Bonaparte had visited Spain, presumably to stiffen spines, but another to know just how far this went. Rumour had it that he was being followed by an army on the march but what did that mean? Reinforcements, or the usual host around an emperor?

Whatever it was, Inglis was at its epicentre and he couldn't waste time speculating. As soon as he decently could, he returned to his eyrie and continued his discreet observations.

By the time the parade had dispersed he had compiled a list of notables he'd seen. At least half of the top military talent of the empire had been present. The overriding question was, were they accompanied by troops? He knew that corps commanders didn't leave their men leaderless while they paraded themselves on the other side of the country, so this could be much more than a defiant show.

That night he laid his plans to discover the true situation. He hobbled down the main street of the town, ignored by the excited, milling crowds. He sought out a tapas parlour and found the proprietor, who regarded him distastefully. He made his play: he was an old soldier down on his luck and all he wanted was a few silver *reales* to tide him over for which he'd industriously sweep the floors of the olive stones, cheese rind and other litter customarily discarded there by diners. The patron grudgingly handed him a scraggy broom.

Inglis started at the back, eyeing the customers. French, almost to a man. In full flow of bonhomie, and with copious draughts of Spanish wine, they were loud and uninhibited.

They joked and laughed at him, one tripping him as he balanced on his crutch to get into a corner and he fell, near blinded by pain. They taunted him in French but, being an ignorant Spaniard, he couldn't possibly understand them. He shouted back, 'Species of a goat!' in coarse Galician, which brought puzzled looks and ensured his unhindered access to the rest of the diners – and the riches of revelation they provided.

Soon he had established the main elements and it chilled him to the core. The marshals of France were not there by coincidence or for show. There were at this hour no fewer than five armies marching to the Ebro at the legendary speed for which Bonaparte's veterans were known. Adding together the strength of each division and corps mentioned, he came up with an appalling figure, which at first his stunned mind could not accept.

Against Moore's twenty thousand the truly horrifying total of a quarter of a million were now massing behind the Ebro, ready for their lunge into the vitals of Spain.

As he mechanically continued sweeping, he heard what lay behind the careless euphoria he'd seen. None other than Emperor Bonaparte himself would lead this gigantic punishing crusade. He would personally take charge and set about the vengeful reoccupation and subjugation of Spain.

In a lightning dash across Europe from a last-minute humbling of the Austrians, he'd reached the Ebro to take up his command. A full imperial headquarters was being prepared; a field-train with all the appurtenances of a campaign in depth was on its way, and each divisional headquarters laboured under his eye to have their artillery, baggage and communications assembled, their men in readiness to take the road at a moment's notice.

Just as he'd done all across the Continent, the Emperor would bring his ragged and mismatched foes to battle and, with his overwhelming numbers, wipe them from the face of the earth.

Somewhere on the other side of Spain, Moore was marching blindly towards him, his last information that the French were scrambling to get away. Was he, and the only army of size England possessed, headed for annihilation?

Sick at heart Inglis returned to his wretched hiding place, while raucous noise spilled out from the streets all around him. Without delay, he pulled out pen and paper and began to write.

Chapter 65

Aboard HMS Tyger

It was tedious beyond the usual, this pointless cruise about the north. *Tyger* was hardly going to send ashore at every port and ask politely if anyone needed help, muskets or other – it was up to those on land to ask. In any case, with the French on the run for the frontier it was unlikely they'd need the small cargo of arms they carried now for such an eventuality.

Bray was becoming tetchy, finding fault with the men's work and given to moods of silence. It was not hard to see why: the war was seemingly in its last stages and the chance of a brilliant action worthy of promotion was on the point of vanishing in those dismal seas. It had seemed a certain thing, first lieutenant in a crack frigate under a famous captain, but in these waters? He could look forward only to half-pay as a lieutenant in the peace, like thousands of others, instead of retiring in the dignity of a sea-captain.

Kydd knew the other officers would be weighing up their own prospects. There would be a merciless decimation of their ranks, their only chance being that *Tyger* was kept on in commission, not one of those endless lines of deserted hulks lying in ordinary at any British naval port. And then only to serve in some distant sea, with not even the chance of prize money once peace had been declared.

For himself, all depended on *Tyger* keeping the seas. In a way it was what would please Persephone most – regular, predictable home leave and freedom from the anxieties of war with a slow but certain path to his flag. Little ones to come, growing roots in the lovely countryside of Devon and trips to London for the season, while—

'Sir? Mr Brice's respects and we've sighted a frigate,' reported Rowan, duty midshipman-of-the-watch, crisp and assured. What did the future hold for the lad? Midshipmen on the beach received no half-pay. 'The lookout thinks it's *Menander*.'

'I'll be up presently,' Kydd said, coming out of his reverie. At least this would be a break, a distraction from the endless round.

The pattern of *Menander*'s masts and sails changed their alignment as she altered towards, and, *Tyger* doing likewise, they were soon up with one another, heaving together slightly on the grey Biscay swell.

'Captain Kydd!' came Mowlam's blaring hail from the speaking trumpet.

'Aye aye, sir!' Kydd responded.

'I've news for you, old fellow.'

'Shall I come aboard?'

'No. I've to find the rest of my brood and tell 'em. It's this, and stand by to be well flummoxed.'

Mowlam's tone was charged with a curious excitement, or was that nervousness? Kydd's interest quickened. 'Sir?'

'Things ashore have changed very suddenly arsy-versy, as it were. We've word that the French have stopped running. They're now readying a strike back into Spain.'

The light breeze and small slop of waters allowed every word to cross very clearly and Mowlam went on quickly, 'Not your ordinary sortie but a vast one.'

'Sir?'

'At the Ebro – a quarter-million in arms against us.'

Kydd could hardly believe his ears. Where at this stage of the war were the French finding the men?

'Led by Boney himself.'

Napoleon Bonaparte, who, the previous year on the battle-field of Eylau, had looked upon some twenty thousand corpses in the bloodstained snow where he'd beaten the combined armies of Prussia and Russia. Now he'd come to wreak the same in Spain.

It was the worst news conceivable.

'Um, what about General Moore?'

'Somewhere well into the centre of Spain – no one has any idea. Well, now you know, old chap.'

'Ah, yes. So what do you believe we can do?'

'Carry on until we receive orders to the contrary,' Mowlam said decisively. 'And if the Dons want help, give 'em all you have. By God, they'll need it.'

The speaking trumpet fell and, with a dismissive wave from Mowlam, *Menander* got under way.

There was no need to tell *Tyger*'s company: they'd all heard the exchange and, for most, the ship had been off Prussia while that terrible carnage was taking place and needed no explanation.

Among all the grave and drawn expressions about the deck, there was one that had brightened considerably. 'Be damned to ye all as a parcel o' useless pickerooning lubbers! Get that fore tack inboard this instant or I'll ask the bo'sun to tickle your backs until you do!'

Bray's happy roaring was the best possible medicine for

the long faces and Kydd went below. He realised there was nothing he could do, not without knowledge of what was happening in the interior, or without the real means to make a difference. It added up to continuing until, as Mowlam had suggested, he received further orders from one who was in a position to know.

When he emerged on deck, all eyes were on him. Without a word he paced over to the conn, peered approvingly at the binnacle and looked up. 'Very good, Mr Brice. Carry on.' There would be lively talk in the gunroom that evening but, without proven intelligence, there was no point in supposition and he wouldn't be drawn into it.

Tyger lay over to the mild north-westerly with the swell on her quarter and sailed on serenely into the night.

Chapter 66

Eight days later, as the skies were darkening for yet another autumn storm, a lookout spotted one of the fisher-craft often seen close inshore, sheeted hard and straining seawards, obviously in a despairing reach to the frigate.

'Heave to,' Kydd ordered, his pulse quickening.

Coming alongside, the boat hooked on. A piratical-looking crew peered up, their red bandannas and colourful sashes not the attire of fishermen.

A figure, sitting apart from the others, cupped his hands and yelled, 'L'tenant Wishart of the Ninety-third o' Foot. My purpose is urgent, I do declare, so beg to come aboard, sir!'

Below, after sipping appreciatively at a toddy, the young man asked Kydd, 'Have you knowledge of what's happening on the land, sir?' He was unshaven in an ill-matched garb of military uniform and peasant's clothing but spoke an easy English with an undoubted north-country accent.

'Not as who can say,' Kydd said guardedly. 'We know Boney's on the march with a sizeable horde, but where he is and so forth we've no news to give you.'

'Sir, it's not information I'm asking. In fact, I can tell you more, even if I've only a tolerably cloudy idea of where things stand. Bonaparte is moving with great speed, punching through the Spanish as though they're not there, for he's Madrid in his sights. He's leaving his marshals to broaden the advance, some over to his left and the Med, and others in a wide hook on his right, which concerns me.'

'Ah, would it be impertinent of me to ask who you are to be so concerned, sir?' Kydd asked drily.

'I'm liaison officer to the Spanish Army. In fine, I'm an English officer sent to put backbone into our new allies – and find them something to fight with.'

Kydd ignored the last for now. 'So they're not reluctant to accept British soldiery on their soil?'

'Captain, you must know that until lately we were their sworn enemies from the time of Francis Drake. How can you ask them to trust us at the first shot?'

'You said "something to fight with", Lieutenant. Does this mean . . .'

The young man put down his cup and leaned forward earnestly. 'Let me tell you a little of what it is to be in Asturias. If any country can claim an excess of mountains then it is Spain, and of its lands the northern region is the most infested. A very puckled and crumpled land it is too, sir. And greatly unsuited to the movement of armies, you may believe. The only roads worth the name run through the interior, to Madrid. The coastal and peripheral tracts are left with craggy tracks that oblige an armed company to proceed forward often in the file singular, a most hazardous formation, while the transit of field guns is not to be contemplated.

'Sir, Bonaparte stays with the Royal Roads and punches through at a pace but the unfortunate generals on his flank are not so well served. It is here that my rag-tag band has a chance. Strike and run, sir! Hammer the ungodly and retire at discretion! My men are courageous to a fault. They know their mountains and have a score to settle with the defiler of their homeland.

'Captain, I have a plan, one as will embarrass the enemy, give cause for much rejoicing in our ranks – and, not least, strengthen my position against certain parties desirous of casting out the English infidel. Do you care to hear it, sir?'

'Tell me and I shall be the judge of it.'

He gave a boyish grin. 'The French are advancing as fast as they may from Bilbao along the coast road. Not so far from here it skirts the fearfully precipitous Cantabrian mountains along not much more than a track. Sir, if the road is exploded behind them, it will leave 'em exposed to much sport from your ship guns. They will break and run ahead, where we will lie in wait. I can promise them a warm welcome.'

Kydd rubbed his chin thoughtfully. It was simple enough and promised an easy success. 'How many French do you expect?'

'A cohort or so, dragoons, infantry, some light field guns. Less than half a thousand men.'

'And how many of you, pray?'

'As many as I can find arms for, is the short of it, sir.'

'Meaning if I can supply you with such, this will be sufficient?'

'I can promise that. The French so far have not encountered any resistance worth the name and will not be prepared for any.'

'Very well. You shall have your muskets. Anything other?'

'To destroy the road with gunpowder. There are none skilled in this – have you one of that kind with the necessaries?'

Kydd nodded. 'Captain Clinton of the Royal Marines, as will be going ashore to command the blast and to regulate the distribution of your muskets. Shall we now look to the details, Lieutenant?'

The unkempt youngster had clearly given it some thought and a plan was soon agreed.

'So, Captain Clinton to prepare ashore, lying concealed until they have passed, then destroy the road. *Tyger* plays its great guns on the enemy, who will flee ahead into your ambuscade. On completion of the engagement, boats will be sent ashore to relieve you of the prisoners. Yes?'

Chapter 67

The seas, glittering pleasantly under a pale sky, were a marked contrast to the stark grimness of the Spanish coast. Most of the work was to be done ashore by others but none of it would be possible without *Tyger*.

Cruising offshore, waiting for the signal that the enemy were approaching, Kydd had the launch hoisted out and towed astern after being loaded with Clinton's necessaries; he was taking an escort of only five and they waited stolidly in the waist, their sergeant loudly insistent they form rank.

'Signal, sir,' the officer-of-the-watch reported quietly, seeing a dash of colour at the crest of a bluff.

'Very well. Carry on, the marines.' A launch under sail, even if seen, would not be in the least threatening to the marching column.

It left quickly and *Tyger* made out to sea on a triangular course that would see her angle inshore at the right place for her cataclysm of fire.

Telescopes followed the launch until it disappeared into the sprawl of beach and crag.

Within a short time they were focusing on the emerging

caterpillar of marching troops with their glint of steel bayonets, the splash of colour of their uniforms against the drab rocky face of the bulking mountain, the series of horse-drawn guns and, here and there, officers on their mounts.

Too far off to take in details, Kydd wondered what they made of *Tyger*. Probably she would not be seen with any great concern – the army was on land, the navy at sea and it was said that the twain never met in battle. This day there would be a rapid changing of opinions.

There was no slackening of pace, only the occasional face turned towards the exotic sight of a graceful man-o'-war so near. The mountainside was as steep and abrupt as Wishart had described and Kydd felt the first stirrings of pity.

His attention was taken over to the left by a soundless angry flash and rising pall of smoke and dust. Seconds later the dull thud of the explosion reached him. Clinton had set off his charge and now the road was cut in the rear of the marching column.

At first there was confused movement in the ranks, mainly the rearmost ones closest, but then it steadied and the march resumed, no doubt scornful that an attack by Spanish irregulars had missed its mark.

'At two cables offing,' Kydd decided. The chart showed a bold coast, steep to, and he didn't have to worry about shoal water.

Tyger shaped course in. At less than a quarter-mile away the tramping soldiers were now in full detail, faces looking out curiously at the diverting sight of the frigate. It seemed an endless procession but Kydd realised they were probably proceeding in pairs along the confining cart-track.

'As you bear,' he ordered levelly. Many men unknown to him would die at his command in the next few minutes.

A slight pause, the poignant chuckle at the waterline and

the usual comfortable squeaking of rigging loud in the antici-
patory hush – then the heart-stopping, shattering roar of the
first gun, and a rippling slam as the others took it up.

As the smoke drifted clear Kydd saw the result: ragged
holes torn in the column, rising dust from shot-strike, still
bodies – the marching progress brought to a sudden stop.
The shock must have been complete: that the graceful craft
with swan-like wings had in a split second delivered death
and destruction to them was inconceivable.

Tyger could sustain about three aimed shots every five
minutes – a minute and a half to reload.

It gave the French time to come to their senses. Some tried
to flee back whence they'd come but quickly came up against
the chasm of fallen rock; a few tried instinctively to scramble
up the impossible raw heights above them, but eventually the
officers realised their best chance was to go forward and
urged the men on at double pace.

With a sudden crash *Tyger*'s guns resumed their lethal work.

Between the gouts of gun-smoke Kydd took in the effect.
The same tearing of the line and the sight of an officer and
his horse falling together down the precipice below, bouncing
several times, glittering blood-smear from the horse's disin-
tegrating corpse visible even at this range. Disorder was now
general and more plunged to their death as the rest scrambled
to escape the lethal avalanche from the sea.

The first cheers from the gun-crews died back as they saw
what their shots were doing. Kydd felt his gorge rising at
the helpless slaughter, and guilty relief when they reached
the twist in the road that took them behind a projecting
headland, even as he knew what waited ahead for the routed
soldiery.

'Heave to,' Kydd said hoarsely. 'Send the launch and recover
Mr Clinton.'

The Royal Marines captain returned and made his report. 'We're away soon, sir?' A slight quaver in his voice showed that even the fiery Bray had been touched by the carnage.

Beyond the headland gun-smoke rose, in awful witness to what was taking place, then died away until there was no more.

'Take away the pinnace, Mr Brice, and find out how many prisoners to prepare for,' Kydd told his third lieutenant.

For some reason Kydd needed to go ashore too, to see at first-hand the results of *Tyger*'s guns.

The boat came in to a small beach the other side of the headland, away from the scene. Several of Wishart's men came down to greet them, guffawing and hooting exultantly. Kydd recoiled in distaste – they were wearing bloodstained items of despoiled French uniforms, along with swords, bright ribands and cockades.

He signed to them that he wanted to find Wishart. They gleefully led the way up and around a debris-strewn road to an open slope. It was the slaughter-place, corpses scattered everywhere, each with its human vulture robbing it, no sign anywhere of corralled prisoners.

Hurrying through, Kydd suddenly stopped, held speechless by a hideous sight that had him gagging for sanity.

On the old wooden door of a mountain hut was the half-stripped body of a French officer who had been nailed upside-down, the corpse hanging lifeless and pallid, its hair dripping blood.

Reeling away, he felt his arm gripped hard.

'Hold hard, old man. This is a different war – a hellishly different war.'

Kydd turned to stare at Wishart.

'These men have seen their families shot and bayonetted, their friends hounded to death, villages burned – you've no idea. Now they've a chance to get back at 'em. Judge not, old fellow . . .'

'N-no prisoners, then?'

'No prisoners.'

Brice was retching to one side. Hauling him to his feet, Kydd led him away from the charnel field to another world.

Tyger shortly set all sail for the open cleansing sea, Kydd's wordless going below, and the shock on Brice's face, enough to still any questions before they were uttered.

Chapter 68

Two days later, an aviso hove into view through a spiteful rain squall. Kydd stood at the ship's side as the little vessel bucketed in to leeward and brailed up to make hail.

There were no dispatches for *Tyger* but a verbal requirement was passed to quit his station and with best speed make for Lisbon in the face of a grave and important development that he would learn about on arrival.

The lieutenant was clearly under orders for the utmost haste and respectfully asked Kydd if he knew of the likely locations of the other three frigates. After a hasty farewell the cutter plunged off into the murk while *Tyger* wore about for Lisbon and the fleet.

Under grey skies and a thin rain they raised the roadstead. To Kydd's surprise and wonder he saw a major fleet there – not only the legendary *Victory* but the great 110-gun *Ville de Paris*, both in the centre of half-a-dozen line-of-battle ships and a crowd of frigates and sloops. What was it all about?

As was usual in harbour, gun salutes to the flag were held

over – at least three admirals' pennants were in plain sight as Kydd picked his way past to the inner anchorage.

Rowley's pennant in *Conqueror* was absent: he was therefore not on board and Kydd was relieved from reporting until it reappeared – but at the price of not knowing what the devil was afoot.

To assemble a powerful force like this must have stretched the Admiralty considerably. What was behind it? He paced up and down, hearing the heated discussions among those on deck as they regarded the armada.

'My barge, Mr Brice. I'm going ashore to sort this out.'

He could step off, but none of *Tyger*'s ship's company could until he'd reported and the frigate was released for liberty.

The Captain's Club was packed with naval officers. 'Oh, hello, Kydd. They hauled you in too, then.' Hayward of *Vigilant* laid down his newspaper and saw Kydd's wet footprints. 'Here, old chap. Let me get you an *aguardiente*. Sovereign cure for the winter's chill.'

Kydd stood near his friend, all chairs long since occupied, and spared a thought for his boat's crew, sheltering as best they could from the rain, believing him to be on some kind of important ship's business. Well, damn it, in a way he was.

'Hayward, dear fellow, do tell, what in Hades are we all doing here?'

The brandy came and did its duty but Kydd was consumed with the need to find out why the roadstead was packed with so many ships.

'You've been at sea, you're not to know.'

'No,' Kydd said pointedly.

'Boney has joined the party.'

'I know that.'

'What you don't know is he's doing right well. Slashing down direct for Madrid which we can't expect other than it

362

should fall. Another gang to his right is carving up Galicia—'

'I know that too.'

'— and in the centre his legions massing for the big coup.'

'Being?'

'Bonaparte doesn't want to beat Spaniards, he wants Englishmen for breakfast.'

'He wants Moore?'

'Quite. He's all the numbers, the resources, the men, and he's after the general. Kydd, m' friend, it has to be admitted, however brave and taut a hand at soldiering our man is, he hasn't a prayer against the tyrant.'

'And?' Kydd prompted.

'Well, it doesn't take much working out – he has to retreat, get out. And by that I mean to say, be taken off.'

'Not abandoning Iberia – no!'

'We're overborne, old chap. He stays and offers battle, and England loses its only army fit for a serious expeditionary war. That's a price too far to pay for keeping a foot in the door of the Continent.'

'We lose all we've done in Spain – even Portugal. We can't just—'

'We must and we will. This fleet and the hangers-on are all for the purpose of evacuating our army.'

'Good God!' Kydd breathed. When he'd last been here the talk was all of the imminent defeat and ejecting of the French. That it had come to this so rapidly?

'Sadly, it is so.'

'But the fleet – *Victory*, *Ville*, all those—'

'There only to keep the Crapauds at Brest, and similar off our backs, as we pull them out.'

Kydd struggled to keep up with the implications. 'Where do we, um, go to take 'em away?'

'All in good time, dear chap. We've yet to have our council

o' war – mainly because we don't know for sure where our sainted Moore is. Or what *he* wants to do.'

The gathering was held under armed guard in a customs hall and with minimum ceremony.

It was chaired not by the navy but by the army, in the person of General Wellesley, stiff and formal, taking his place at a table with three admirals and two generals next to them.

Rowley was one, and Kydd felt contempt rising that the man was being given any role at all in what was to follow and hoped that he would not have to take orders directly from him.

Almost a hundred naval and military officers faced them, grave and still.

The preliminaries over, Wellesley got down to the heart of the matter. 'Events have turned out not necessarily in our favour, gentlemen,' he said crisply. 'So much so that we have no alternative than to withdraw our military presence in Spain.'

The underlying assumption was that this had been accepted or even ordered by Whitehall.

'To evacuate,' intoned one of the admirals, who, Kydd remembered, had been introduced as De Courcy.

Without a glance at him, Wellesley agreed. 'The object of this meeting is to establish the point of embarkation and the necessary operations precedent to the uptake of General Moore's expeditionary force.'

'This contingent on his expected movements in the next days.' De Courcy was careful, courteous but firm. 'Have we word yet, pray?'

'He's advanced well into Spain and now must be close to Madrid. He will have heard of Bonaparte's advance on the capital and must make decision based on the readiness of the Spanish Army to make a stand before it. He will not be in possession of the intelligence we have of the complete picture but we've sent several riders with dispatches to this end.'

'What alternatives has he, in the event he must withdraw?'

'The first, a retreat back here along the road he took from Lisbon. The second, a rapid march across Estremadura to the Mediterranean. The third, an equally rapid overland march to Spain's northern ports.'

'Should we recommend, what do you suggest?'

'The north. The mountains will impede pursuit and it is nearer,' Wellesley said instantly. 'Depending on what the navy says, to Vigo, Ferrol or similar.'

De Courcy came back positively. 'The navy would like to see it Vigo. Direct sailing, big port, easily defensible. And, if I'm not mistaken, a road direct from the interior.'

Cynically, Kydd heard Rowley harrumphing lofty agreement.

'Very well. We shall say Vigo. What does this mean for the navy?'

'We've a powerful enough force to keep at bay any interference from the French Brest squadron or other, this I'm convinced of, sir. Transports of a number sufficient have already been taken up by the Board and are as of this hour on the high seas, and now will be directed to Vigo.'

'Who shall be the commander?'

'I shall be in overall command, my flag in *Tonnant* with the strategic defence. Cruisers and sloops in the vicinity of Vigo will be the responsibility of Rear Admiral Rowley, who will appoint an inshore authority responsible for managing the actual embarking.'

'Admiral Rowley?'

'A post-captain of repute – Captain Kydd, in whom I have the greatest confidence.'

Kydd tensed. He could almost hear it coming. All responsibility, no honour, for a protracted and thankless task – served with an oily smile and pudgy hands.

'Quite. For the army there are dispositions to be made that need not trouble this gathering. In essence these are defensive, centred around Lisbon. Well, shall we to other details?'

For the navy there were signals and contingencies, storing for twenty thousand or more, frigate dispositions, escort designations and lengthy details conditional on circumstances.

Refreshments were brought for a midday repast but there was no slackening of pace.

'Captain Kydd,' Rowley called across haughtily, at one point. 'You'll have a detailed scheme pending my approval for your operation within twenty-four hours. Clear?'

It would take more than wild horses for Rowley to address Kydd with recognition of his knighthood – but his naval rank always took precedence.

Kydd bit off an acknowledgement. It meant a ruined night and early morning, without a doubt with malice intended.

Unexpectedly, at four a halt was called.

'Gentlemen.' Wellesley's air of unbending severity had eased a degree or two. 'We go our ways shortly. I'd think it not amiss should we this night dine together in amity and good countenance, if only to display to the people of Lisbon our tranquil confidence at the outcome.'

Kydd brightened. This would mean that Rowley couldn't demand his papers for another day.

In the event it promised to be a jolly, defiant occasion, well suited to show that, in the febrile atmosphere, the British were showing no sign of panic or even nervousness.

As Kydd processed with the others, a splendid vision of a crack frigate captain in his star and sash, he saw that the seating was promiscuous, the few ladies well spread out and no attention paid to rank or standing. He was ushered to a seat at the extravagantly ornamented table, between a colonel and a post-captain he didn't recognise, and opposite a plainly dressed, stern-faced and venerable man displaying the riband and star of the rare and prestigious Order of the Garter, in precedent well above Kydd's knightly place . . . and then Rowley, with his flag-lieutenant alongside.

Frowning, Rowley gave the barest of nods to Kydd and turned to the plain-dressed man, engaging him in deep conversation.

It couldn't have suited Kydd better and, after discovering his naval companion was Ambrose, captain of *Implacable* 74 and a genial fellow, he then did his duty by the army officer, a distracted and morose staff colonel.

The dinner progressed agreeably, Kydd learning that the distinguished gentleman of the Garter opposite was Lord Haig, an Admiralty secretary of long standing, who clearly preferred listening to talking.

Ambrose had a fine line in dits, and the flag-lieutenant joined in the gusts of laughter at the right places, bringing a savage glare from Rowley to return him to his duty.

'Mind you, Kydd, there's one saucy frigate I can bring to remembrance as can put your *Tyger* to the blush.'

'I'd be entertained to hear it, old fellow,' Kydd said, with feeling.

'Ah. Going back a mite, before the last war. Wonderful creature, I was first luff in her for a year or so, sorry indeed to leave. You probably heard of her – *Artemis*, the flying *Artemis* as was. In the time just before Black Jack Powlett was owner and took her around the world.'

Kydd froze, his fork stopped in mid-air. And, opposite, Rowley stared, then looked away quickly.

'Yes. Lovely thing, would beat anything afloat on a bowline.

Heard that she came to a sad end on a reef somewhere Godforsaken. Crying shame – a ship to love, bless her. Bahamas, was it?'

'Azores,' Kydd answered quietly, watching Rowley.

'Oh? Could have sworn it was the Bahamas.' Puzzled, he saw who Kydd was looking at and added his own polite glance of interrogation.

Rowley gave a start. 'What? Don't know what you're talking about,' he stuttered.

'Sir, you did have service in *Artemis*, did you not?' the flag-lieutenant said silkily. 'And wasn't that when she took the rocks?'

Giving him a venomous look, Rowley muttered, 'Oh, yes. I do recall now.'

Haig trailed off his conversation abruptly while he listened keenly, leaving his brigadier dinner companion mystified.

'Wouldn't you say, then, a barky of the finest sort?' prompted Ambrose.

'Perhaps, but a scurvy crew of the worst kind,' Rowley threw back. 'Could do nothing with 'em, the scrubs. Their fault, of course. Let's leave it at that, shall we?'

Kydd felt a dull burn but tried to clamp a fierce hold on the volcano of feeling building. 'Many would take issue with that,' he said thickly. 'The fault doesn't lie there, does it?'

Haig sat absolutely still, his eyes unblinking.

'You wouldn't know, Kydd, you were just a miserable fore-mast jack then!'

Kydd choked back his anger but under the tablecloth bunched his fists.

Rowley spat, 'How can press-gang meat have a clue of what's going on, in a filthy night when—'

'I saw everything. Everything! Quartermaster-o'-the-watch – *your* watch!' Kydd's face was pale, rigid and accusing.

Rowley didn't say a word but gave Kydd a look of such appalling hatred that it had others at the table falter and stare back.

With a curious look Haig glanced from one to the other. 'Interesting, indeed. Nothing of this was mentioned at the inquiry. I remember it well – I sat on it. *Artemis* frigate lost in mysterious circumstances in the Atlantic, no on-deck witnesses surviving – perhaps we should look into it a whit further.'

Chapter 69

The encampment of General Moore, forty miles from Madrid

Rain drummed on the canvas of the tent and made noisy waterfalls where it descended to the ground.

'It's true, then,' Moore muttered dully, holding a grubby piece of paper before a candle.

'Sir?' Packwood said, suddenly alert.

'The Spanish right has broken, fallen back – they're routed. And here we are, not two days' march from Madrid and nothing between us and Bonaparte. He has the capital now. He's to put brother Joseph back on the throne and then he'll be after us.'

'The men are in good heart, sir. As are your generals. If you choose to stand against Napoleon they'll be there with you in good spirit.'

'No, Packwood, I'm not going to ask that. This is the only army England has at this time and it's as much my duty to preserve it as win battles.'

It had been Moore who, at the Shorncliffe military ranges, had forged the professionalism and dedication that had transformed the army from its stolid eighteenth-century lines of tramping redcoats to an active and aggressive modern force.

The wood and canvas chair creaked as he shifted position. 'We'll have to move quickly. This dispatch directs us to Vigo where the transports will mass to take us off. The question is how to get there.'

'While the French are descending on us all from the same direction, surely we're talking about retracing our route in the opposite direction back to the coast, to Lisbon?'

'No,' Moore said decisively. 'Our Spanish allies are a broken reed but we owe it to them not to scuttle away without a show of spirit. It's to be Galicia, across the mountains.'

Packwood chose his words carefully. 'Sir, if we make Lisbon we've no need to go to Vigo and—'

'We go overland to the north. Bonaparte at our heels I don't worry on. He's a huge army and massive field train to move and the mountains will check even him.'

'The weather is—'

'Be damned to the weather. My men know what's at stake. They'll do their duty and, once at Vigo, they'll be able to get on board and take their rest. The navy will never let us down, Packwood, trust me.'

Chapter 70

The islands across the entrance of Vigo loomed up through the sea-fret, misty and dull, the only dash of brightness the continuous band of white at their base. The rain was now a torment, bitterly cold, driving and appearing out of nowhere without warning.

After the rapid but uncomfortable rolling passage north, *Tyger* took the southern channel, grateful for the shelter, yet another seasonal gale was lashing the coast from the south-west. But where were the hundreds of transports, clawed from every port in the south of England and fitted out for the evacuation of a whole army? As far as Kydd could see, only a scattered handful of the smaller sort was tucked away in the lee of the islands.

These were strange waters for Kydd. In all the years of blockade it had been an enemy port, heavily defended, and he was entering it now for the first time and without the comfort of a decent chart. Vigo itself lay seven miles further in; *Tyger* pressed on and made her way to Vigo roads, hoping to see more transports, but none were there.

The carefully laid plans he'd drawn up were useless without the transports – he couldn't even begin to allot berthing and stores, if the ships and their capacities were unknown.

But at least he was away from the toxic atmosphere in Lisbon. He'd left without tendering the detailed plans demanded by Rowley. His orders were brusque, pointed and demanding: at his peril, to render services at Vigo that would see the British expeditionary force safely embarked in the transports provided.

Kydd had been in more than a few conjunct operations with the army and knew what to ask for from the transport agent, the victualler, the shore authorities. But the key to it all was a good understanding between the navy and the transport masters: unless he could get them to co-operate fully, the first ones to board could consume all their stores before the last ship was fully laden – and there were so many other hindrances and impediments to achieving an orderly retreat.

Some of the shore people were in attendance: the army quartermasters were setting out to establish makeshift barracks for the evacuees, others preparing vast temporary field kitchens, still more making a start on peripheral defences. All of these were needed but, as a priority, Kydd had to find boats and lighters in their hundreds and just where would the transports moor for loading?

Vigo was spacious enough, a triangle of water with its base at the entrance seven miles across, and two sides the same length meeting at Vigo town. Depth of water was generous and the islands across the entrance were fending off the worst of the gale, but as Kydd finished a quick reconnaissance, he felt a growing sense of unease.

Instead of the welcoming refuge from Atlantic storms that it had been for centuries, the situation was reversed: the danger was coming from the land, not the sea. An exhausted army was on its way, pursued by the French battalions, led by Napoleon Bonaparte. There would be a narrow bracket of time to get Moore's army aboard, then make a hasty exit for the open sea.

Putting aside all other considerations, the operation of some hundreds of unhandy, thinly manned but heavily loaded sail putting to sea at the same time was a daunting prospect – but what if the elements conspired against them?

The south-westerly that had brought *Tyger* to Vigo was fair for her and she'd sailed in under storm clouds without drama. It was, however, foul for the empty transports flailing across Biscay from England, delaying them.

With a sinking heart, Kydd could foresee unmitigated disaster if the transports arrived, Moore's army embarked – and the wind veered just a few points. The islands that protected Vigo had two channels a mile or less wide past them and he'd found that for half a tide or more their safe depth width would contract as extensive sandbanks rose from the seabed. Yet it would be no problem with the winds in anything but the west. Then it would be foul for leaving and, worse, there would be insufficient channel width to tack into it, a condition exaggerated by spring tides, as there were at present.

The entire armada of transports would be trapped within, and Bonaparte would have leisure to bring his artillery up and reduce them all to burning wrecks.

And he, Kydd, would be seen as presiding over the destruction of Moore's army and the hopes of the nation.

In a tide of despair he kept to his cabin, trying desperately to come up with a solution but always there was the same result: if Neptune chose to let the winds veer there was nothing that man or beast could do about it.

Two days passed, then an idea came – a desperate remedy, but it deserved consideration. There were few other ports of refuge on the Costa da Morte, the Coast of Death, but there was one he knew about from a brief visit in the past with a convoy on the way to the north: Corunna.

He recalled a bluff north-south promontory with a neat harbour tucked in its lee – and heights above it, which, if held by the British, could prevent Bonaparte's artillery from putting the evacuation fleet under fire. And, above all, a fair run to seaward whatever the wind's direction.

Peering over the small-scale chart, he located Vigo. It was around two hundred miles further to Corunna – but if Moore was vaguely in the centre of Spain, then the radial distance to either was about the same.

Was it lunatic to think of taking it upon himself to change the port of embarkation from Vigo to Corunna?

There was no time to go back and forth to Lisbon for conferring, not in this south-westerly gale. Any decision, and therefore responsibility, was his alone and time was critical. If it didn't succeed, what he was contemplating could result in arrest and court-martial, with a sentence extreme enough to placate an outraged public. But he'd never shied before from a hard decision and wouldn't start now. If the facts and reasoning held water, he would stand by them and be damned to the consequences.

A course decided on, he gave it his best concentration.

If he went ahead, apart from defying orders, there were two major difficulties either of which, if not met, would bring down the whole scheme.

One was the elementary task of telling Moore in time to change the course of his army away from Vigo to Corunna. The other was how to intercept the transports still on the high seas to divert to the new port.

Could he do it, and in time?

He bent to the map again. By now Moore would have had word from Lisbon to make for Vigo. Therefore if Kydd sent a runner out from Vigo he would eventually meet up with Moore coming in the opposite direction – there was only the one good road connecting with the interior.

The other question had a straightforward solution. He would stay in Vigo until the transports arrived, then take them in convoy to Corunna. The diversion should take less time than for an army to cross the mountains so it was safe to say he'd be there ready for them.

A runner? Who? Obviously he couldn't go himself, and neither could any of his officers, whom he couldn't spare in case of sudden action against an enemy. The man would have to be naval and credible in the sea arts, and for a commander-in-chief the reasons would have to be well argued.

Dillon? Needed.

A non-executive officer, such as the purser or doctor? No credibility.

A warrant officer, petty officer or other skilled seaman? Hardly likely to make an impression on a commander-in-chief.

In despair he cast around for one he could trust but at the same time could be spared – who was in the last essence expendable.

Rowan. His mind rebelled instantly. Barely sixteen, a boy. Was it fair?

But he was sufficiently intelligent, reliable and credibly seamanlike – and could be spared.

The mission was vital – he would need support: who in the last instance could be relied on to deliver the message? Clinton's mature and steady sergeant, Dodd, came to mind.

He would know army ways, advise on fieldcraft, stand by his young charge.

He felt a rush of hope. It could work!

'Pass the word for Mr Midshipman Rowan.'

Eyes wide, the lad stood before him, still with jam on his face from feasting on duff with his messmates in the midshipmen's berth.

'I've a mission that's vital and I can't but think that there's none other in *Tyger* more suitable for it than yourself, younker.'

'S-sir?' Rowan stuttered.

Kydd invited him to sit and unfolded the plan.

'You'll go assisted by Sergeant Dodd, but you'll be in charge. Clear?'

'Aye aye, sir,' the lad replied manfully, eyes even wider.

'After I speak with Dodd, we'll go over what you'll say to General Moore. Then hold yourself ready to leave first thing tomorrow.'

The cheerless morning saw the two muster at the gangway, their small bundles by their sides.

'A lot depends on you, men,' Kydd began, as the entire ship turned out to see them off. 'So I shall fare you well and desire you don't overstay your liberty ashore as shall see you back on board before long.'

Chapter 71

Moore's army on the march

Out of a Continental heart came a frigid blast, the herald of winter. Gathering force it blustered over the high Spanish central plateau, turning thin rain into icy snowflakes, driven almost horizontal and draining the life-force from the exposed skin of every man.

The regiments tramped on, mile after mile, the stony road treacherous and painful as the thin snow carpeted it. Mule carts creaked and slowed as the beasts bent under the onslaught, their bodies twitching in the bone-chilling cold.

Soldiers bore their lot as they had to, their uniforms now streaked with white, the metal of their muskets burning cold to the touch, their knapsacks almost comical lumps of white, their feet trudging on, one in front of the other, their only hope and dream the hot meal and grog at day's end.

Officers at the front rode their horses, heads down with shapeless mufflers over their faces in a vain attempt to ease the bite of the weather. The more canny soldiers marched in the lee of the beasts and snatched shelter.

The snow got thicker and then the most unexpected of weather phenomena: silent stabs of light to the east spread across the sky in a paroxysm of harsh strokes against lurid sheet lightning, all near hidden in the increasingly dense snow.

Packwood rode with Moore. Neither spoke.

Mile after mile they progressed, the familiar massed crunch and jingle of men on the march now muffled by the whirling snowflakes – and then from ahead a random series of shots, in the smothering snowfall sounding more like harmless *plops* than gunshots.

Moore instantly halted the column. 'See what that was, Packwood.'

He urged his horse forward past the halted column to the empty road ahead and intercepted a dragoon officer on his way back to report. In the fearful conditions they'd surprised a French forward post whose picquets had been dealt with immediately while a squadron of Hussars had ridden off to locate the main force.

Packwood waited patiently in the driving snow for the reconnaissance team to return – it was far more important for Moore to be in receipt of this intelligence than the mere knowledge that the French were abroad.

Within the hour a galloper reined in. 'Sir. From prisoners – General Debelle and eight hundred horse and guns lie across the road three miles ahead, heading south.'

Towards them.

Packwood cantered back with the news and Moore moved at once. Giving his orders in decisive sequence he resumed the march, his van now a spearhead for punching through the French, relying on the confusion in their ranks at confronting the British here, of all places, in this hell on earth.

* * *

When they made contact with the enemy the fighting was brutal and swift, close quarters and bloody. At first the usual French skirmishers, thrown out ahead, had not been able to make out the vague shapes in the snow flurries and kept calling an anxious '*Qui vive?*' to the British forward sections, who kept their silence as they moved unflinchingly forward.

The skirmishers hesitated, holding their fire, and in the dim light and freezing cold of the snowstorm the British were through and fell on the main French positions, roaring their regimental battle-cries and laying about them until the terrified French, not knowing where the feared Highlanders had come from, retreated in disorder, allowing Moore's main column to follow. His cavalry fanned out to fall on the confused formations. The clash and impact on the running foe brought terror-shrieks, hopeless bravery and dying screams as the action faded into the distance.

They were through, but Packwood was only too aware that the French would regroup and follow, whatever the conditions. Their location was now known and Bonaparte would stop at nothing to bring about an overwhelming and conclusive engagement. Their only chance was to stay ahead of the military genius whose capability for rapid marches to discomfit his enemies was well known – the terrible battle of Eylau had been fought not so long ago in weather worse than this.

Moore did not need reminding. The fighting retreat continued but now the best and most powerful battalions would be concentrated as a rearguard – and any who fell out of the line of march would be left by the roadside for the French.

Grim and sparing in humour, the general whipped the column back into marching order and set off to the north and the Vigo road, to put some miles between themselves and the gathering foe before they halted for the night.

Mercifully the snow stopped, but as the men tried to bivouac it was, if anything, worse. Liquid mud, a few degrees above freezing, was everywhere in pools and mires and the few miserable fires that could be started did little to ease their spirits. As darkness fell on the lonely desert moor, Packwood could think of no more bleak existence.

They started out before dawn, unspeaking and sullen. It had got around that Vigo was their destination, but the more knowing let out that to reach it there was no longer the easy going of this high plateau but range after range of mountains, effectively doubling the distance, with steep tracks up their flanks and dangerous precipices waiting for them going down.

They trudged on.

At the midday halt, a cold easterly wind blustering and freezing, a rider brought dispatches – and a prize worth more than gold.

Somewhere to the south an arrogant French officer had demanded rooms in a *pousada* and had been murdered by peasants. He'd been comprehensively plundered but a plain sabretache had been left, found by a curious Spanish militia officer. In it were papers of some kind that he couldn't read, but would it be of interest to the *inglés* courier passing through?

Packwood's eyes glowed – for this was nothing less than a dispatch from Bonaparte's headquarters to Marshal Soult in the north.

It was detailed and exhaustive, an operational directive to Soult that would enable Bonaparte to spring a lethal trap on the Englishman Moore and his contemptible army.

While Bonaparte closed in from the south, Soult was to spare neither himself nor his brigades in lunging across the north in a pincer movement to bring Moore at last to bay in a converging annihilation, an engulfing tide that nothing could withstand. Even the Imperial Guard had been called out of Madrid in merciless pursuit of the single-minded objective to extirpate the British intruders.

It was a masterful plan – the directive spelled out in full how it was to be done, even going so far as to include a helpful map showing all French positions, their character and commander.

Moore now had possession of what amounted to Bonaparte's actual plan of campaign.

How to proceed was another matter.

Into the night Moore and his generals gave careful consideration to what must be done.

One thing was paramount: it had now turned into a race against time, a desperate march to escape the jaws of the trap. Any battle, however necessary, any delay of any kind, would play into the enemy's hands. This had to be a forced march like no other: hundreds of miles across rivers and mountains, with the penalty for lagging being the snapping shut of the trap and another slaughtering triumph for Napoleon Bonaparte.

Before dawn all had been decided.

'Packwood. I rely on you, sir. Do see that my orders are obeyed no matter how distressing the case. We have no other recourse and we march at midday.'

It was mind-numbing. The baggage train, the impedimenta and kit of an army of some twenty thousand was to be abandoned. Men would be permitted only that which they could carry on their person, the march made in quick time with no allowance made for stragglers.

Camp followers? There were many women, useful if not vital to the domestics of the march, most standing by their menfolk in the ranks, some whose men had been lost to disease or the enemy and knew no other life. These in mercy could not be left to the French, and if they could keep with the march, they would stay on rations.

Released draught animals would be put to the hauling of guns and the few vehicles carrying the bare minimum of provisions; essentially lines of communication and supply would now no longer exist.

Moore's army stepped off at noon precisely, making good speed, each man with his inner thoughts knowing the alternative. That night they made bivouac in old sheep fields, the ordure mixed into the mud a trial. No heavy tents or carts to sleep under – the hours passed in a misery of wet and cold.

The next day was a punishing march over a stony track, which tore at boots and shoes until they were in ribbons. Redcoat uniforms were now ragged and hidden under peasant cloaks, tarpaulin, anything to give warmth from the cutting winds. Only their weapons were gleaming and ready.

That night there was reprieve: unbelievably a village, with houses, barns, sheds and huts where a soldier might lie down and be fed.

With hot food in their bellies, spirits rose and men at the ragged end of endurance burst their bonds of discipline and found coarse wine and fierce brandy, then rampaged unstoppably through the streets and alleys, roaring and shouting their cares away.

No bellowed commands, dire threats or pleading made any difference: crowds of soldiers continued their drunken frenzy until in the early hours they collapsed in exhaustion, bodies in the street still clutching bottles, some frozen to death where they fell, a chaos of wild disorder and indiscipline.

The morning brought news of the French hard on their heels. It was imperative to get back on the road or be taken.

Moore threw out his rearguard and, by heroic efforts, prepared his troops for the march.

Then, from the direction of Vigo, an apparition from another world appeared: an absurdly young naval officer, his face pale and pinched, with what resembled a well-seasoned marine.

'Um, would you kindly take me to General Moore?' the lad enquired of an outrider, struck dumb by the sight.

'Sah, let me,' the marine said firmly. 'You, m' man. Tell us where's the headquarters company, smartly now!'

Moore was ready on his mount, his eyes roving over the slowly assembling line of march.

'Er, sir. I've news for you.'

Unbelieving, Moore looked down at the little party on their domestic ponies. 'Who the devil are you, sir?' he managed at last. 'Explain yourself!'

'Sir, I'm sent by Captain Sir Thomas Kydd in charge of your embarkation,' he stammered. 'He begs to inform you that the port of Vigo is not to be used and you should go to Corunna instead.'

'Why the . . . Who is this insolent scoundrel who dares tell me my orders? I shall do no such thing and am appalled at such impudence. Packwood, what's going on? I demand to know!'

Packwood took them aside. In a few minutes he had the essentials and returned to the impatient commander-in-chief.

'Sir, it appears that these are genuine envoys of the authority concerned with our taking off, and—'

'How do you know?' Moore barked.

Packwood gave a tiny smile. 'Because, sir, I once took passage in their vessel, the good ship *Tyger*, and do recognise them.'

'Go on.'

'For mysterious sea reasons, it seems Vigo at this time has a fatal flaw in the embarking exercise in that we might well find ourselves trapped while Bonaparte surrounds us and puts us under punishment with his artillery. I believe we should listen to them, sir.'

'Confound it!' Moore exploded. 'I refuse to change the line of march of a whole army on the say-so of any sailor boy who comes along, Packwood. Give me reasons why I should, quickly, man!'

'I doubt that Captain Kydd would put these men to hazard unless he had very good reason and—'

'If it was so critical to our survival, why did he send damned juniors like this and not his best officer to speak with me? Hey? Answer me that!'

'Sir, I can tell you, there's never a superfluity of officers on board a frigate, but I suspect his main trust is that, through this young man, his reasons will be sufficiently compelling in themselves not to require a high officer to absent himself from his place of duty.'

Moore simmered, considering. 'Corunna straight ahead, through God's own purgatory of the Cantabrian mountains. Vigo, ahead a handful of miles and turn left for the sea – into the Montes de León, as bad.'

He frowned for a long moment, then snapped, 'We've no time for debate, the French press us sorely. We march – now. Packwood, you've until the crossroads to Vigo to persuade me, else we ignore this lunacy.'

The column stepped out, the weather cold and driven but without the sapping snow or rain.

Packwood and the sailors fell back, conferring.

The colonel was quick and astute, and soon caught on to the nightmare of a fleet trapped by a contrary wind under the relentless pounding of Bonaparte's guns.

He cantered back to the commander-in-chief. 'Sir, I have the elements and they are truly unanswerable.' Going over the points he could evoke only an ill-tempered grunt.

'Sir. There is a final consideration that makes all other considerations moot.'

'What?'

'Captain Kydd allows that the transports have already sailed for Corunna, sir. If none are at Vigo we stand to be invested and destroyed. We therefore have no alternative but Corunna.'

Moore glanced at him once and unexpectedly smiled. 'As I always wanted, Colonel.'

'Sir?' Packwood said. Then he understood: Moore was now taking the idea as his own.

'Corunna. A far better place to defend as we board. Have you ever given thought to what it must be to suffer under fire as our ships are loaded? Here we can keep 'em at bay while we safely embark our troops, guns and stores. The nabobs in Lisbon haven't the wits to see this and you've given me all the reasons I need to go to Corunna.'

'So . . .'

'Let Staff know, there's a good chap. It'll be hard going very shortly.'

Chapter 72

The foothills were bleak and rugged, but the mountains were savage and cruel. Only the certain knowledge that Napoleon Bonaparté himself was on their heels kept the toiling soldiers on the crumbling stone tracks, the desolate passes, the edge of precipices for hours on end.

Rowan, bowed down under the winter blast, trudged along manfully ahead of Dodd: they'd been relieved of their ponies and, with the French so close behind, there was no other option. Packwood had given orders that saw them on the ration list but there was little else he could do for them.

The adventure of the mission had turned by degrees into a trial of endurance. They'd found their objective, they'd succeeded in what Captain Kydd had asked of them, but they'd strayed into a species of hell. This was now a nightmare.

Days of trudging, endless miles always the same, a ragged column wending its way up into the mountains, little sound except the stolid tramp of so many thousands, spread out for miles on the march.

The soldiers were in fearful condition, shabby, frayed,

tattered – by now also filthy and unshaven and, as Rowan had quickly found at the campfire, alive with lice and other vermin. They said little, staring into the embers and chewing dried beef strips and biscuit, slurping their grog and occasionally cursing in a low monotone.

The pain of muscles relaxing at the end of the day was only exceeded by the agony of driving them into motion the next day, and shoulders wrung with the day-long weight of a haversack. Rowan didn't realise until he had to go to Sergeant Dodd's pack that he'd been quietly extracting some of his gear and adding it to his own to carry.

Dodd said little on the march, but at the end of a long day he cracked jokes and spun yarns from the seven seas that kept Rowan for a little while out of that purgatory on earth.

Then it was the struggle between exhaustion and the sapping cold from rain, snow and hail for a precious few hours of sleep . . . and in the pre-dawn misery it was a start all over again.

Unbelievably there were women on the march, some with children, babies in their arms even, keeping with their men, no matter the cold and wet, yet at the end of the day caring for them and their brood in a pitiable bid for normality in the fiendish conditions.

As they reached higher altitudes the bitter cold seeped through any attempt at clothing and Rowan's increasing distress brought on a hopeless homesickness: childish tears formed and his head bent in an extremity of enduring.

He became aware of a figure looming next to him and then the kindly, patient voice of Dodd was telling him he knew for a certainty that the sea and the end of the march were just over a few more ridges. It steadied him, an old soldier trying to reach out to one who, on shipboard, would never have had anything to do with him, and gave him the strength to go on – he could never tell the man what he'd done for him but would never forget as long as he lived.

The narrow track with death in wait on either hand had more afflictions to lay on the suffering army. Draft animals slipped and plunged down ravines, Spanish muleteers deserted at the frightful path they were taking into the north, and rations failed to make their way up the interminable winding length of stumbling soldiers.

Starving men snarled and fought each other for bread, and many left the march under cover of dark to forage in the wilderness. Perspectives altered; things took on a different value. Once, when the shortage of pack animals began to tell, a heavy chest of regimental coin was upended down a steep ravine, the silver tinkling and bouncing in a gay frenzy until all was quiet. In this utterly desolate landscape of scree and crag, a king's ransom couldn't buy a loaf of bread, a pair of boots, a warm cloak.

At one point a snowstorm bullied them as they reached a ridge and Rowan's heart went out when he saw the ground he was trudging forward on was a mass of bloody footprints where suffering men had passed. The welts on his own ship-board boots had given way and now his naked feet showed through, too.

A village firmed out of the mists – the same pillage for wine and debauching, the same ferocious scenes in the morning, and the same mindless tramp on into the bleakness.

Somehow Rowan found the strength and endurance to survive, his young muscles tightening and building, moving on oblivious to the agony of the bitter cold in his feet. On one side of him was the silent, bowed form of Dodd. He managed a smile: they would win through whatever it took.

They descended into a valley with a single bridge. Far ahead Rowan saw a caterpillar of men begin to cross, others behind them in a long, winding file occasionally broken by a cart or two officers riding together.

The scene was a break in the monotony, but then the opposite bank erupted in musket fire.

Some went down under the murderous volley but the effect was miraculous. Men who'd been shambling wrecks now straightened, threw off their packs and charged out to meet the enemy with savage roars. Officers bellowed their orders and, taking their positions like a military exercise at Shorncliffe, they returned fire with a ferocious concentration.

It was electrifying: if the French thought that their harassment would dismay the British they were sadly mistaken, for they'd turned these wretched stumblers into a maddened host and were paying for it.

It finished as quickly as it had started; the enemy faded away and the march resumed in a wary trudge, Moore not allowing a moment's delay in the resumption of their calvary.

Messengers from the rearguard had told of a swirling mass of Bonaparte's legions – 'they were close now but suffering themselves. That they were not falling on Moore's rear was part of the Emperor's campaign strategy, to allow the other jaw of the trap to snap shut and bring about a sure victory over the British. That their rear consisted of Moore's finest – the Foot Guards – was a reason not to try too early.

To a man, Moore's army knew that only by reaching Corunna and the sea before Soult had they any chance for life.

They marched on.

Quite unexpectedly a pale sun broke through.

And there, not so very far away, was a sight that seized every man with a joy that surged out in a great shout that went on and on.

The glitter of sea.

The pace quickened; other tracks converged and their path broadened to a road – within only a few miles lay Corunna and the navy.

In a delirium of emotion Rowan paced on, and then, between the sombre mountainsides, he saw where a bay spread out. To the right it swept tidily around to a headland but to the left a substantial promontory stretched out seaward, forming a snug and enfolding lee. The promontory itself in the distance was girded by a wall, and within, it was tightly packed with houses. From Kydd's description this indeed was Corunna.

They'd succeeded.

On the heights above the town and harbour Moore halted their progress.

Scouts were sent out and reported back that there was no sign of Soult's forward troops. They had won! They were in possession of Corunna before the French and, by defending it and these heights, could safely embark.

Yet hundreds of ships should have been waiting for them at anchor below but only two or three small vessels rode to their moorings, well out.

'Get that navy courier, Packwood. Now!' Moore snapped.

Rowan was deposited at the general's feet, bewildered and not a little frightened.

'You'll explain to me now why I don't see our transports, sir.'

He gulped, mind whirling in contradictions. 'This is Corunna, sir?' he asked feebly.

'Of course it is, you fool!'

It was, as Kydd had said, a perfect place to moor and take off the army. In fact, if he looked out to sea, he could make out white horses and all the signs of a Biscay blow, while within the harbour it was wonderfully calm and placid yet with a broad access to the open sea.

'Well?' snapped Moore, his expression ferocious. If he'd been duped into going to Corunna instead of Vigo, both he and his entire army stood to be destroyed in a very short while as Bonaparte took his opportunity and closed in.

Rowan's mind froze. His captain was the most trusted and true person he'd ever known and would never have let them down.

Miserably he stared out to sea as if it could give an answer.

Around Moore, the command and staff group came together, some curious, others hard-faced, even more with unreadable hostility.

Rowan couldn't think of an answer. Tears pricked.

Chapter 73

Vigo, earlier

A twinge of guilt touched Kydd as he saw off the two into the duty cutter. It should have been Bray at the least going to brace a commander-in-chief but almost anything could happen in this absurd Iberian war and he didn't want to lose his first lieutenant at this time. Rowan was really the only one he could spare and just had to present the facts. General Moore would see the problem of foul winds in Vigo and fall in with his altered destination.

It was a straightforward enough assignment, with no real hardship – after all, he would be safely in the middle of an army of some twenty thousand, with its massive and elaborate field train. Rowan would return with valuable experience of military life.

For the twentieth time he sniffed the wind. Damn! Still from the south-west and brisk with it, foul for the transports from England. It was worrying and frustrating but he knew that at this time of the year the very intensity of the weather would ensure a change before long.

He went below to find something to do while he waited for their arrival and decided to make a start on the inevitable paper war that would begin when Rowley received his dispatch that told of his decision to vary the port of embarkation. Anyone with a smattering of sea sense would see the trap immediately it was pointed out to them, but he had a fool for a superior and would need to spell it out at length.

After all, he had not only seen the potential pitfall but had provided and executed a workmanlike solution. There should be no difficulty, even with Rowley.

A faint cry from the deck above made him pause, and almost at the same time a breathless messenger announced that their transports were coming through the northern entrance into Vigo Bay.

Kydd was out and on the upper deck in moments. And there they were: under reduced sail and shepherded in by two sloops; plain, unlovely, but a most welcome sight.

Five, seven then twelve . . . fifteen. Was that all?

The senior officer escort presented himself. It had been a hard sail from Plymouth and Portland and on two occasions gales had scattered his charges, requiring a long and tedious wait for the convoy to come together again. Fifteen? This was only one of five joiner convoys that would bring the number up to seventy-three sail. At least two consisted solely of the specialist vessels that had flat-built lighters with sweeps to bring out field guns and horses. There was nothing Kydd could do but find the patience to await them.

He was unable to move on Corunna until he had the majority in hand and time was not on his side.

Two convoys came in together, and after a fourth it left only the last.

And then Kydd finally received Rowley's response to his initiative via a brig-sloop, with an order by hand-of-officer.

It was dire and final – both a condemnation and ultimate professional ruin. For disregarding orders lawfully given by a superior, in flagrant breach of the Articles of War, Kydd was forthwith to consider himself under open arrest. He was to remain in Vigo until relieved by another before handing over his task and returning to Lisbon to face charges.

Rowley had found a way to achieve his object: Kydd's disgrace and ruination.

He sat back, appalled. There were really only two alternatives: to obey – or to continue on to Corunna.

If he obeyed, there would be a confrontation with Rowley that could go either way. If he disobeyed, it was most certainly a court-martial, without any doubt about the end result.

The first would give him a fighting chance, but would leave General Moore in a perilous situation – and his word to him broken.

He gave a twisted smile. There really wasn't any choice. He'd go on to Corunna.

That left the brig-sloop, whose commander needed his signature on receipt before returning to Lisbon.

But, as his superior still, he'd require the man first to be employed in escort for the convoy to Corunna, after which it didn't really matter anyway.

The officer was surprised but obeyed, clearly not knowing the contents of the orders he'd brought.

And late that afternoon the last of the transports sailed through the northern channel in an untidy gaggle. Without a moment to lose, Kydd had them watering and storing for the evacuation voyage while he got to work with the masters of the ships. Having had plenty of time to prepare the sailing order folder and similar beforehand, it did not take long and, with much relief, he set daybreak as departure time for Corunna.

He slept fitfully, refusing to dwell on the future past the embarkation, but awoke to *Tyger*'s uneasy jibbing at her anchor.

As soon as he glanced out of the stern windows he knew something was wrong.

Wind-rode, instead of a fine view upstream he was now looking into Vigo itself on the southern shore and the dense mass of shipping waiting to leave.

There was only one explanation and in his worry and concern he hadn't paid as much attention to this possibility as he should have.

The gods had thrown their dice and it had come out against him – during the night the south-westerly had veered, just as he had initially feared it might. Now from the west-south-west, it effectively stoppered the exits to the open sea for any square-rigged vessel in Vigo Bay.

They were trapped until the wind shifted again.

And if Napoleon Bonaparte arrived with his great guns, just as he'd warned, they'd be pounded to splinters, as helpless as a sucking shrimp.

It couldn't be worse – or could it? That instead Bonaparte had gone to Corunna and, surrounding the stranded British Army, was in the process of exterminating it.

Chapter 74

Corunna

General Moore waited for his answer with a terrible patience.

Rowan reached out for strength. *Tyger*'s jolly sailing master, Joyce, who'd been his instructor in the sea arts, always leavening learning with yarns from a colourful past, would explain what was happening to the ship by imagining a seagull soaring way up, then looking down, seeing one by one the elements come into play – winds, currents, the mass of tide in its channel sliding the ship to one side apparently against the breeze. It all made sense when taken at that perspective.

And he realised what had happened to *Tyger*. Sniffing the wind, like the deep-sea mariner he was turning into, he saw that it was in the west-south-west, the very quarter Kydd had feared would trap his transports.

'Sir, I can explain.'

'Do so, sir!'

Rowan sketched in the dust the aspect of Vigo open to one direction only, the wind now foul for leaving.

'Sir, I counsel that you wait but a short time, for just as soon as the wind shifts, so shall you see your transports within a day, two days. Captain Kydd will then be here, this I promise you.'

Moore considered this. 'And when will this wind shift?'

'Sir, I cannot say. The ways of the winds are hidden from us. I can only say that at this time of the year it may be hours or days but, sir, they will shift.'

'Very well. And thank you for your lucid explanation. When this shift occurs let me know, Mr, er . . .'

'Mr Midshipman Rowan, sir.'

Later in the afternoon the scouts came back. Their heroic march had gained for them a priceless advantage of several days' distance from the pursuing French and Moore didn't waste it. Quickly he identified the central heights as crucial – if left to the enemy, artillery could be brought to rain fire down on the embarkation. Therefore it would be held at all costs, preserving the coastal plain, the town of Corunna and its harbour from the enemy.

'The village atop Monte Mero – Elviña. This is where we shall stand,' he pronounced.

Set among walled olive gardens and fields of prickly aloes, the French could never deploy cavalry there, and it provided excellent cover for the light infantry Moore had trained. And while those troops took up position, the remainder of his army collapsed to their rest of exhaustion on the slopes below, knowing that very soon the French would come.

Chapter 75

Two days later, patrolling vedettes warned of the first enemy – from the direction of Soult's advance. For the moment Bonaparte's horde was not in sight.

The defenders on the heights were stood to and the first shock of contact was made.

Marshal Soult took his time in reconnoitre and seemed to come to the same conclusion as Moore – that Elviña was the key to Corunna.

Quickly he took position on the heights opposite and brought up his guns, which began ranging out towards Elviña. They had little effect, only six-pounder field guns against solid walls and rocky bastions, but for the French it was as much a question of time as for their opponents. Soult threw in his forward troops in a massive attack up the slopes towards the little village.

So close did they press the assault that the British could hear the shouts of officers and sergeants: *'En avant! Tue! Tue!'* But they were met at the crest by riflemen and grenadiers in a furious hand-to-hand fight that ended only with a withdrawal to enable the French artillery to open fire again.

If these were only Soult's forward troops, it needed little imagination to realise what would be their fate if the entire advancing army went against them.

But in a single hour the situation was transformed.

From around the promontory came a shining vision – first a graceful frigate, then dozens, scores, hundreds of transports in glorious array, one by one taking their place in the harbour off the old town.

In a delirium of cheering, Moore's men hailed the navy that had come as their salvation.

Kydd felt a wash of release course through him when Corunna Bay opened up and he saw on the foreshore, the quays, even the flanks of hills, an uncountable number of men. General Moore had taken his word and made for Corunna instead.

Giddy with relief, he ordered away his boat. He was met by the army and on horseback taken up Monte Mero to the commander-in-chief.

'Well met, sir!' were Moore's first words. 'As now we may get on with the business.' His handshake was crisp and sincere.

'My apologies, sir, for the lateness as due to contrary winds—'

'I do understand, Sir Thomas, being as I have my naval adviser,' he said sharply. 'Shall we?'

It didn't take long. Moore's known order of battle had been translated by Kydd and his staff to individual and specific berths in a ship, both men and guns. As directed by the army, when each was released they would muster on the quayside and be taken out to their assigned transport by a vast flotilla of ship's boats, lighters and anything that floated.

Back aboard *Tyger* Rowan reported to Kydd. 'Sir. My party safe. No casualties.'

The lad was changed almost beyond recognition, thin, rangy and, in some way, nobler in his bearing.

'Well done, Rowan,' managed Kydd, touched by the transformation. 'And I'll wager you've seen enough to keep the midshipmen's berth tolerably entertained for a year or more to come.'

'Enough to know the meaning of duty, Sir Thomas,' he said quietly.

Chapter 76

The evacuation got under way.

With sailors' muscles burning after pulling at the oars for hours on end, men were taken off in their hundreds, watched by an enemy helpless to intervene. This was what it was to have mastery of the seas.

On flat lighters, field guns made their way out to the specialist ships with heavy lifting gear, while at one point the whole anchorage was shaken by a massive concussion as powder and munitions were detonated to deny them to the enemy.

Doggedly it went on, now thousands safe in the ships and ready to leave, her precious army preserved for England. Would it continue so?

Kydd could see the drifting dun-coloured clouds of gun-smoke around the heights of Monte Mero and knew that he owed his uninterrupted rescue mission to the heroes locked in close-quarter battle on those heights. If they faltered, Soult would be upon them and the ordered retreat would turn into a murderous rout.

Hour after hour the ships loaded with more exhausted,

filthy, worn and stare-eyed soldiers, too dazed to make much of their deliverance. But this was a gallant and successful undertaking that would be talked of for ever – if the final act was carried through successfully.

On Monte Mero some thousands were holding back Soult. How could they safely disengage and extricate themselves with the French poised to occupy their positions as soon as they'd left, ready to rain down fire as they boarded their ships?

That afternoon General Beresford was given the post of honour: his brigade to remain to the last as rearguard for the evacuation. Carefully selecting his ground while he could, he laid down a last line across the neck of the promontory in front of Corunna's walls.

It didn't go unnoticed by the French, who threw themselves at the defenders of Elviña in a fury of frustration. The crescendo of fighting swelled in the afternoon and on into the night, when it petered out in anticipation of an even harder-fought clash in the morning.

But in the darkness another scene was unfolding: the British were stealthily pulling out of their hard-fought positions.

Cunningly keeping their forward picquets in place, camp fires burning bright and all the apparatus of defence alive, the soldiers in their thousands scrabbled down the hill in the darkness, heading for the quays and their embarking.

It was essential to keep up the pace – at daybreak Soult's men would uncover the ruse. But as first light began stealing in there were still many huddled on the quayside waiting for a boat.

Guns appeared along the skyline and opened up on the anchored fleet. At the same time French troops poured down the foothills and towards the city walls; but Beresford was ready for them and brought them to a standstill in a fierce engagement.

Chapter 77

As the last of the troops were embarked Kydd gave the signal to prepare for sea.

However, he had no intention of leaving Beresford, and as the ships began slipping out to sea *Tyger* remained, firing up at the gun positions in Elviña. All attention was on her – and Beresford's brigade, under cover of fire from the city walls, vanished inside. They lost no time in racing to the opposite side of the promontory to the harbour, to a curving, rock-strewn beach – where boats were waiting to take them to their transport out of sight of the Elviña position.

'Cease fire,' Kydd ordered. 'The straggler patrol is in?'

'Aye, sir,' Brice reported. This had been a last rounding up of the quayside and town, to be sure none remained on enemy soil.

'And I'm to say we have a guest, Sir Thomas.'

It was Packwood.

'I needed to satisfy myself there's none of our brave fellows left,' he croaked. 'And beg that I might take passage back to England with you, sir.'

He was in a shocking condition, sunken eyes, weariness to a near-mortal degree and in threadbare uniform.

'My dear fellow, and so you shall!' Kydd answered immediately. 'You know my cabin. If you bear with me, I shall be with you presently.'

He gave orders that saw *Tyger* under weigh and making out to sea, out of Corunna, the last sail of all – to join with the homeward-bound armada of shipping. After a final lingering glance at the receding shore, overhung with smoke and now in the possession of Napoleon Bonaparte, he went below, waves of fatigue after a night without rest threatening to unman him.

Packwood was slumped in a chair, an untouched whisky by his side. He pulled himself upright when Kydd entered and gave a rueful smile. 'The peace, the order, indeed a haven of tranquillity,' he allowed softly, then, playing with his glass, murmured, 'I do confess I have my reasons for desiring passage in *Tyger.*'

'Oh?'

'As it gives me chance to make certain you're aware of just what you achieved, my friend.'

'My duty only, old fellow. Yet I stand to face court-martial on my return in the matter of having disobeyed the orders of my admiral to take station on Vigo, never Corunna.'

'Ha! He's to now explain why he failed to see the trap of Vigo. Have no fear of this – is that the sound of papers being torn up I hear?'

Kydd gave an awkward smile, and Packwood went on, 'Duty? Never in life, sir. Some twenty-seven thousand all told taken up in four days, their guns and equipment. Preserved for the nation, their sweethearts and their wives. You'll get no thanks in Parliament for it, but accept from me, it's as strategical as a mighty battle. There'll be some who'll bless you every day of their lives and others who won't even think on it, but you'll value above all the opinions of those who know what it is to struggle and fight to reach Corunna in the firm, sure trust that the navy will be there for them.'

Touched, Kydd mumbled something.

'My only sorrow is that our great leader – our dauntless pilot and commander – is no longer here to laud the achievement.'

'General Moore?' Kydd said in astonishment. 'You mean . . .'

'He fell on the field of Elviña, mortally wounded by a round-shot on the eve of his victory – for victory it most assuredly was. Soult beaten back, never to prevail, and thereby permitting us to conclude our miracle.'

Shocked, Kydd could think of nothing he could say that was adequate to the moment.

'The last night we carried him down in a blanket, he still issuing his orders. Just before dawn he gave up the ghost and is no more.'

Packwood paused, then picked up again in a softer tone: 'We buried him immediately, the blankets his shroud, willing the French to hold off their counter-attack while the padre said his words. As magnificent a farewell as a soldier can deserve.'

Moore. Gone. It didn't seem possible that such a figure should be removed from the world of men.

'I . . . I grieve with you, m' friend,' Kydd said softly.

They sat together in silence.

'So, we gained a species of triumph,' Kydd said at length, 'but have we lost our purpose? Bonaparte has cast us out entirely and now rules Spain. We've forfeited our chance to face him on the battlefield and are back where we started, all Europe under his heel.'

Packwood eased into a wry smile. 'Ah, you don't know our sepoy general. Wellesley is a tough nut. We may have been thrown out of Spain but not Iberia. The flame of resistance will not go out and Wellesley will stick by Lisbon like a limpet. When the tide turns he'll lead us back into Spain – and a victory that will be all the sweeter!'

Author's Note

The origins of the Peninsular War are an extraordinary mix of greed, betrayal, patriotism, lust for glory and conquest – and more than a few gross miscalculations, which in the end brought impoverishment and despair to an ancient and illustrious nation. It's a complex and myth-laden story and if, in the process of teasing out the elements, I've not included all events or have adjusted times slightly it is only to smooth the way for the reader of this latest Kydd tale rather than provide a footnoted history of this profoundly interesting period.

When Kydd encounters his notable prisoner-of-war in Tavistock this is indeed based on the history of the times, as I found researching newspapers and other archives. Extraordinarily, enemy officers, having given their parole, could live the life of a gentleman, means being found to transfer money to them from home. This was regularly abused with Napoleonic approval, officers breaking their parole in order to return to France, helped in no small way by British smugglers, who found it a lucrative sideline for the outward voyage, receiving their customers from elaborate networks operating for cash-in-hand.

The French officers cynically obeyed the letter of their parole agreement by formally informing the authorities of the withdrawal of their pledge – in a note left on a pillow in their lodgings. As far as I've been able to discover, there was never a case of a British officer breaking his parole, the surprisingly numerous escapees from France doing it the hard way from close confinement. As for the attempt on the ship, if the reader cares to take a stroll around the further reaches of Plymouth Hoe they will find a mysterious stone set in the ground with the single incised numeral '3'. This marks the spot where, somewhat earlier in the war, a firing squad put an end to three Irish soldiers convicted of an uprising in the Mill Bay prison with a view to making off with a ship in the same way.

A breakout of the French fleet from Brest was still a nightmare. With numerous invasion barges in northern ports and ships-of-the-line building fast – some hundred or more at Bonaparte's immediate disposal in Europe – all the elements that threatened before Trafalgar only a handful of years previously were still there, and any sortie in strength from the French Atlantic or Mediterranean ports was a feared prospect. It would be a recurring theme of sea warfare foreseeably.

The individuals encountered outside *Tyger*'s doughty crew are mostly taken from history, and I've gone to some lengths to portray their qualities as they have been recorded for, above all, events in this period are character-led. Godoy, for instance: a genius of guile and effrontery, from humble beginnings to entering service in the royal palace at seventeen, he quickly made colonel and became a royal favourite and lover of the Queen. By his early twenties he'd become adjutant general, then field marshal, and in the same year minister for foreign affairs, close counsellor to the autocratic King and then prime minister. It was his bad luck to be at the helm when Napoleon Bonaparte banged on the door of Spain, and, totally out of his depth, was in turn right royally deceived. Most Spanish blame him for the disastrous decision to go to war against Great Britain that ruined Spain's finances and set her colonies at defiance. Yet he lived on into his eighties in comfortable exile in France, bedecked with honours.

And his master, the King: completely in thrall to Godoy, he abdicated in favour of his son Fernando, hailed by his people as *El Deseado*, the Desired. Goya's fearsome portrait of the new King at his accession after liberation gives a clue to his destiny: from the hope of the country and its new liberal constitution, he turned viciously reactionary and absolutist, called by some the basest, most cowardly and selfish king Spain has ever been cursed with. He well earned his new sobriquet of *el rey felón*, the criminal majesty.

As for Bonaparte, his cupidity over Spain's imagined wealth from the New World led him into the disastrous endeavour to betray and conquer his ally and crown his brother King of Spain. It would turn into his 'Spanish Ulcer' and, jointly with disasters in Eastern Europe, would lead to his downfall. Given his revolutionary hatred of the Bourbon dynasty, he would no doubt be appalled if he knew that, in Spain, the Bourbons in the twenty-first century are very much in evidence in the person of King Felipe VI, through his father Juan Carlos I.

Cádiz is fiercely proud of its heritage, especially so of its role in the creation of the nation's constitution. The visitor can see many of the locations mentioned in this book for it was never despoiled by the French. A fine maritime museum took my interest, particularly the Trafalgar exhibits, which were very fairly shown, and through many portraits, I came face to face with our main players. The city itself has a veneer of tourism but, particularly in the old city, Moorish relics can be found, and the ancient Gaditano dialect still fills the market air. The naval base occupies to this day its traditional position deep within the marshy inner harbour, and in its library I was thrilled to set eyes on charts of the time and find explanation for many of the questions I came with.

The precise point at which it can be said with certainty that the long Peninsular War had its beginning I do believe can be defined, depending on your point of view. It is either the moment at which Bonaparte decided to turn an ally into a victim and thereby brought upon himself the tribulations that followed, or the point at which the British first landed in support of the Iberians, never to leave until their work was done. I tend to the latter – and not only because it was the Royal Navy that did the deed. The landing by Royal Marines at Figueira da Foz until relieved by Wellesley's landings, depicted here, was indeed Britain's first permanent foothold on the peninsula, and the navy, guarding the sea-lanes as efficiently as it did, was able to keep it so until victory was gained.

The terms of the highly questionable Convention of Cintra, so reviled in England, were actually brought about by Kellermann, the astute French negotiator at the talks. Keeping his knowledge of English hidden from Burrard, he learned of the general's pressing need for a tangible victory and held out for outrageous conditions, including the transport of his entire army, with its flags, honours and loot intact, back to France to continue his war.

It is not so well known that Bonaparte himself came to confront the British intervention, and it is piquant to think that, but for Wellesley's junior status, it would have been him, not Moore, who would have faced him and his juggernaut army. As it was, Bonaparte noted the headlong retreat with much satisfaction but fatally left the final destruction details to his marshals, abandoning the Spanish winter and mountains for Paris. Soult was no match for Moore, and history took its course with Britain's only effective army preserved for another day.

The passage back to England for the army through the winter storms of Biscay was a hard one, officers with drawn swords posted to stop the mass of men in the over-packed transports moving about in the savage gales. When the exhausted, dirty, ragged soldiers staggered ashore, people ran from them in horror but at last, after their inhuman march, they had got their rest.

Some would deride Corunna as another Dunkirk, a defeat touted as a triumph. Yet in both cases it was only territory that was lost, the precious trained men saved for another day, and at Corunna their cannon as well, both owing all to Britannia's mastery of the seas. What followed the death of this hero, Moore, like Wolfe before Québec, was a full-hearted demand by the British people for support of any kind to the Iberians, resulting in a confused alliance with the Spanish patriots. In token, Portland's government thought to make the magnanimous gesture of returning to Spain their arms from the Tower of London captured from the Spanish Armada. Wellesley doggedly remained in Iberia, erecting the impregnable defences of the Lines of Torres Vedras at Lisbon to become the bridgehead for his later advances. Eventually he admitted reluctantly that without the navy his victories would have been impossible.

To the many who assisted me in the research for this book I am deeply grateful. My appreciation also goes to my agent Isobel Dixon, my editor at Hodder & Stoughton Oliver Johnson, designer Larry Rostant for another stunning cover, and copy editor Hazel Orme. And, as always, my heartfelt thanks to my wife and literary partner, Kathy.

And to those interested in what the future holds for Thomas Kydd, rest assured there are more adventures to come . . .

Glossary

aviso	small craft employed for fleet communications, not combat
binnacle	wooden case protecting the compass with a light at night
blashy	blustery, rainy weather
bobbery	high jinks
bonne bouche	sweetmeat
braxy	an inflammatory disease of sheep
bumboat	a boat carrying provisions or small merchandise out to ships on speculation
cabal	a clandestine association for purposes not always benign
carcass	a shell of iron containing incendiary materials
cartel	an official agreement covering, for instance, the exchange of prisoners
catching crabs	an oar plied clumsily that catches the water instead of a smooth in and out pull
conjunct	term used in Kydd's day for amphibious operations
Cortes	a form of legislative assembly in Iberia
Crapaud	French for toad; pejorative term by an Englishman for a Frenchman
dimber	handsome-looking
El Escorial	the historical residence of the King of Spain; also a monastery, basilica, pantheon, etc.
fascines	bundles of twigs and branches bound together to form a quick blocking of a breach
Fencibles	a body of men raised for local maritime defence of the realm
foul-weather jack	sailor who relishes bad weather for its grandeur and spectacle
gibbous moon	when more than half but less than full

Gunter's scale	a general-purpose ruler in navigation with one side in natural, the other logarithmic lines
hard tack	'bread' that is long-lasting, a form of biscuit as opposed to 'soft-tommy' soft baked bread
hulks	vessels condemned from sea employment, used for housing convicts and others
in a bumper	a toast with glasses filled to brimming
Indiaman	a ship employed by the East India Company for trade; usually with rich cargoes
kilderkin	a small cask containing eighteen gallons
larboard	to the left (later 'port') as opposed to starboard, to the right
league	three sea miles
lee	to the side downwind
lee shore	if the coast is downwind from a vessel, a dangerous situation if the ship is disabled
Mamelukes	a military body consisting of Circassian slaves employed by various Muslim countries
mandrel	a metal bar or fitment around which a material may be shaped
mirador	a decorated observation tower
missal	a Roman Catholic book containing all the prayers and responses needed to celebrate Mass
mizzen halliards	those lines responsible for raising and lowering sails on the mizzen mast
nob	a person of wealth and social standing
noggin	a unit of liquid measure equal to one quarter of a pint
objets de bizarrerie	a curiosity
offing	to seaward; keeping clear of tricky inshore waters
ostler	one employed to take care of horses at an inn or other establishment
pannier market	country stall market where sale goods are limited to what can be carried on an animal pannier
parole	freedom granted an officer for his word of honour he will not abscond
pavillon	French flag
pelf	riches, lucre
pillion	riding behind
pistol-shot	a distance of twenty-five yards
poltroon	base or cowardly character
poop	the smaller deck raised above the quarterdeck in vessels larger than a frigate
porth	a sheltered, sandy cove where a coasting vessel might informally land or take on cargo
raise the wind	have such an energetic and full-on celebration to be the centre of a vortex of wind
reales	Spanish: twenty *reales* to the peso, about a hundred to a pound sterling

roadstead	offshore anchorage outside a harbour where dues need not be paid
roil	to be in a state of turbulence or agitation
rope-hooky	an affected curl to the fingers about the palm to flaunt one's deep-sea mariner's credentials
rummer	a type of glass for drinking rum or whisky
scowbunker	pejorative term for a seaman fit to serve only in a lowly scow
sea cant	jargon of the sea not understandable to the common folk
shabraque	ornamental saddle-cloth distinguishing first-line cavalry
shicer	a shady character bound to trick you
soogee bucket	a receptacle to carry the strong soda-based cleaner for paint or wood aboard ship
sorrel	brownish-orange to light-brown-coloured horse
sottish	inclined to bibulousness, sunk in one's cups
spout lanthorn	smugglers guide light; a long tube allows the light to be seen only from one precise direction
stingo	strong beer
strut-noddy	a poseur who doesn't realise what a ridiculous figure he is
surcoat	outer coat or gown over valuable inner garb
tingle	soft copper rectangle still used to apply a temporary patch to a hole in a wooden boat
van	the leading position in a fleet progressing in line ahead
waist	that part of the main-deck between the fore and main hatchways, part-of-ship for new or worn seamen